Queechy – Part II

Elizabeth Wetherell

"I hope I may speak of woman without offence to ladies."

THE GUARDIAN

CONTENTS.

CHAPTER XXX.

Ant. He misses not much.
Seb. No; he doth but mistake the truth totally.

Tempest.

It was the very next morning that several ladies and gentlemen were gathered on the piazza of the hotel at Montepoole, to brace minds or appetites with the sweet mountain air while waiting for breakfast. As they stood there a young countryman came by bearing on his hip a large basket of fruit and vegetables.

"O look at those lovely strawberries!" exclaimed Constance Evelyn running down the steps. — "Stop if you please — where are you going with these?"

"Marm!" responded the somewhat startled carrier.

"What are you going to do with them?"

"I ain't going to do nothin' with 'em."

"Whose are they? Are they for sale?"

"Well, 'twon't deu no harm, as I know," said the young man making a virtue of necessity, for the fingers of Constance were already hovering over the dainty little leaf-strewn baskets and her eyes complacently searching for the most promising; — "I ha'n't got nothin' to deu with 'em."

"Constance!" said Mrs. Evelyn from the piazza, — "don't take that! I dare say they are for Mr. Sweet."

"Well, mamma! — " said Constance with great equanimity, — "Mr. Sweet gets them for me, and I only save him the trouble of spoiling

1

them. My taste leads me to prefer the simplicity of primitive arrangements this morning."

"Young man!" called out the landlady's reproving voice, "won't you never recollect to bring that basket round the back way?"

"'Tain't no handier than this way," said Philetus, with so much belligerent demonstration that the landlady thought best in presence of her guests to give over the question.

"Where do you get them?" said Mrs. Evelyn.

"How?—" said Philetus.

"Where do they come from? Are they fresh picked?"

"Just afore I started."

"Started from where?" said a gentleman standing by Mrs. Evelyn.

"From Mr. Rossitur's down to Queechy."

"Mr. Rossitur's!" said Mrs. Evelyn;—"does he send them here?"

"He doos not," said Philetus;—"he doosn't keep to hum for a long spell."

"Who does send them then?" said Constance.

"Who doos? It's Miss Fliddy Ringgan."

"Mamma!" exclaimed Constance looking up.

"What does she have to do with it?" said Mrs. Evelyn.

"There don't nobody else have nothin' to deu with it—I guess she's pretty much the hull," said her coadjutor. "Her and me was a picking 'em afore sunrise."

"All that basketful!"

"'Tain't all strawberries—there's garden sass up to the top."

"And does she send that too?"

"She sends that teu," said Philetus succinctly.

"But hasn't she any help in taking care of the garden?" said Constance.

"Yes marm—I calculate to help considerable in the back garden—she won't let no one into the front where she grows her posies."

"But where is Mr. Hugh?"

"He's to hum."

"But has he nothing to do with all this? does he leave it all to his cousin?"

"He's to the mill."

"And Miss Ringgan manages farm and garden and all?" said Mrs. Evelyn.

"She doos," said Philetus.

And receiving a gratuity which he accepted without demonstration of any kind whatever, the basket-bearer at length released moved off.

"Poor Fleda!" said Miss Evelyn as he disappeared with his load.

"She's a very clever girl," said Mrs. Evelyn dismissing the subject.

"She's too lovely for anything!" said Constance. "Mr. Carleton,—if you will just imagine we are in China, and introduce a pair of familiar chop-sticks into this basket, I shall be repaid for the loss of a strawberry by the expression of ecstasy which will immediately spread itself over your features. I intend to patronize the natural mode of eating in future. I find the ends of my fingers decidedly odoriferous."

He smiled a little as he complied with the young lady's invitation, but the expression of ecstasy did not come.

"Are Mr. Rossitur's circumstances so much reduced?" he said, drawing nearer to Mrs. Evelyn.

"Do you know them!" exclaimed both the daughters at once.

"I knew Mrs. Rossitur very well some years ago, when she was in Paris."

"They are all broken to pieces," said Mrs. Evelyn, as Mr. Carleton's eye went back to her for his answer;—"Mr. Rossitur failed and lost everything—bankrupt—a year or two after they came home."

"And what has he been doing since?'

"I don't know!—trying to farm it here; but I am afraid he has not succeeded well—I am afraid not. They don't look like it. Mrs. Rossitur will not see anybody, and I don't believe they have done any more than struggle for a living since they came here."

"Where is Mr. Rossitur now?"

"He is at the West somewhere—Fleda tells me he is engaged in some agencies there; but I doubt," said Mrs. Evelyn shaking her head compassionately,—"there is more in the name of it than anything else. He has gone down hill sadly since his misfortunes. I am very sorry for them."

"And his niece takes care of his farm in the meantime?"

"Do you know her?" asked both the Miss Evelyns again.

"I can hardly say that," he replied. "I had such a pleasure formerly. Do I understand that *she* is the person to fill Mr. Rossitur's place when he is away?"

"So she says."

"And so she acts," said Constance. "I wish you had heard her yesterday. It was beyond everything. We were conversing very amicably, regarding each other through a friendly vista formed by the sugar-bowl and tea-pot, when a horrid man, that looked as if he had slept all his life in a hay-cock and only waked up to turn it over, stuck his head in and immediately introduced a clover-field; and Fleda and he went to tumbling about the cocks till I do assure you I was deluded into a momentary belief that hay-making was the principal end of human nature, and looked upon myself as a burden to society; and after I had recovered my locality and ventured upon a sentence of gentle commiseration for her sufferings, Fleda went off into a eulogium upon the intelligence of hay-makers in general and the strength of mind barbarians are universally known to possess."

The manner still more than the matter of this speech was beyond the withstanding of any good-natured muscles, though the gentleman's smile was a grave one and quickly lost in gravity. Mrs. Evelyn laughed and reproved in a breath; but the laugh was admiring and the reproof was stimulative. The bright eye of Constance danced in return with the mischievous delight of a horse that has slipped his bridle and knows you can't catch him.

"And this has been her life ever since Mr. Rossitur lost his property?"

"Entirely,—sacrificed!—" said Mrs. Evelyn, with a compassionately resigned air;—"education, advantages and everything given up; and set down here where she has seen nobody from year's end to year's end but the country people about—very good people—but not the kind of people she ought to have been brought up among."

5

"Oh mamma!" said the eldest Miss Evelyn in a deprecatory tone,—
"you shouldn't talk so—it isn't right—I am sure she is very nice—
nicer now than anybody else I know; and clever too."

"Nice!" said Edith. "I wish *I* had such a sister!"

"She is a good girl—a very good girl," said Mrs. Evelyn, in a tone
which would have deterred any one from wishing to make her
acquaintance.

"And happy, mamma—Fleda don't look miserable—she seems
perfectly happy and contented!"

"Yes," said Mrs. Evelyn,—"she has got accustomed to this state of
things—it's her life—she makes delicious bread and puddings for
her aunt, and raises vegetables for market, and oversees her uncle's
farmers, and it isn't a hardship to her; she finds her happiness in it.
She is a very good girl! but she might have been made something
much better than a farmer's wife."

"You may set your mind at rest on that subject, mamma," said
Constance, still using her chop-sticks with great complacency;—"it's
my opinion that the farmer is not in existence who is blessed with
such a conjugal futurity. I think Fleda's strong pastoral tastes are
likely to develope themselves in a new direction."

Mrs. Evelyn looked with a partial smile at the pretty features which
the business of eating the strawberries displayed in sundry novel
and picturesque points of view; and asked what she meant?

"I don't know,—" said Constance, intent upon her basket,—"I feel a
friend's distress for Mr. Thorn—it's all your doing, mamma,—you
won't be able to look him in the face when we have Fleda next fall—I
am sure I shall not want to look at his! He'll be too savage for
anything."

"Mr. Thorn!" said Mr. Carleton.

"Yes," said Mrs. Evelyn in an indulgent tone,—"he was very attentive to her last winter when she was with us, but she went away before anything was decided. I don't think he has forgotten her."

"I shouldn't think anybody could forget her," said Edith.

"I am confident he would be here at this moment," said Constance, "if he wasn't in London."

"But what is 'all mamma's doing,' Constance?" inquired her sister.

"The destruction of the peace of the whole family of Thorns— shouldn't sleep sound in my bed if I were she with such a reflection. I look forward to heart-rending scenes,—with a very disturbed state of mind."

"But what have I done, my child?" said Mrs. Evelyn.

"Didn't you introduce your favourite Mr. Olmney to Miss Ringgan last summer? I don't know!—her native delicacy shrunk from making any disclosures, and of course the tongue of friendship is silent,—but they were out ages yesterday while I was waiting for her, and their parting at the gate was—I feel myself unequal to the task of describing it!" said Constance ecstatically;—"and she was in the most elevated tone of mind during our whole interview afterwards, and took all my brilliant remarks with as much coolness as if they had been drops of rain—more, I presume, considering that it was hay-time."

"Did you see him?" said Mrs. Evelyn.

"Only at that impracticable distance, mamma; but I introduced his name afterwards in my usual happy manner and I found that Miss Ringgan's cheeks were by no means indifferent to it. I didn't dare go any further."

"I am very glad of it! I hope it is so!" said Mrs. Evelyn energetically. "It would be a most excellent match. He is a charming young man and would make her very happy."

"You are exciting gloomy feelings in Mr. Carleton's mind, mamma, by your felicitous suggestions. Mr. Carleton, did your ears receive a faint announcement of ham and eggs which went quite through and through mine just now?"

He bowed and handed the young lady in; but Constance declared that though he sat beside her and took care of her at breakfast he had on one of his intangible fits which drove her to the last extreme of impatience, and captivation.

The sun was not much more than two hours high the next morning when a rider was slowly approaching Mr. Rossitur's house from the bridge, walking his horse like a man who wished to look well at all he was passing. He paused behind a clump of locusts and rose-acacias in the corner of the courtyard as a figure bonneted and gloved came out of the house and began to be busy among the rose-bushes. Another figure presently appeared at the hall-door and called out,

"Fleda!—"

"Well, Barby—"

This second voice was hardly raised, but it came from so much nearer that the words could be distinctly heard.

"Mr. Skillcorn wants to know if you're going to fix the flowers for him to carry?"

"They're not ready, and it won't do for him to vait—Mr. Sweet must send for them if he wants them. Philetus must make haste back, for you know Mr. Douglass wants him to help in the barn meadow. Lucas won't be here and now the weather is so fine I want to make haste with the hay."

"Well, will you have the samp for breakfast?"

"No—we'll keep that for dinner. I'll come in and poach some eggs, Barby,—if you'll make me some thin pieces of toast—and call me when it's time. Thin, Barby."

The gentleman turned his horse and galloped back to Montepoole.

Some disappointment was created among a portion of Mr. Sweet's guests that afternoon by the intelligence that Mr. Carleton purposed setting off the next morning to join his English friends at Saratoga on their way to the falls and Canada. Which purpose was duly carried into effect.

CHAPTER XXXI.

With your leave, sir, an' there were no more men living
upon the face of the earth, I should not fancy him, by St.
George.—Every Man Out of His Humour.

October had come; and a fair season and a fine harvest had enabled
Fleda to ease her mind by sending a good remittance to Dr. Gregory.
The family were still living upon her and Hugh's energies. Mr.
Rossitur talked of coming home, that was all.

It sometimes happened that a pause in the urgency of business
permitted Hugh to take a day's holiday. One of these falling soon
after the frosts had opened the burrs of the chestnut trees and the
shells of the hickories, Fleda seized upon it for a nutting frolic. They
took Philetus and went up to the fine group of trees on the
mountain, the most difficult to reach and the best worth reaching of
all their nut wood. The sport was very fine; and after spoiling the
trees Philetus was left to "shuck" and bring home a load of the fruit;
while Fleda and Hugh took their way slowly down the mountain.
She stopped him, as usual, on the old lookout place. The leaves were
just then in their richest colouring; and the October sky in its strong
vitality seemed to fill all inanimate nature with the breath of lile. If
ever, then on that day, to the fancy, "the little hills rejoiced on every
side." The woods stood thick with honours, and earth lay smiling
under the tokens of the summer's harvest and the promise for the
coming year; and the wind came in gusts over the lower country and
up the hill-side with a hearty good-will that blew away all vapours,
physical and mental, from its path, bidding everything follow its
example and be up and doing. Fleda drew a long breath or two that
seemed to recognize its freshening power.

"How long it seems," she said,—"how very long—since I was here
with Mr. Carleton;—just nine years ago. How changed everything is!
I was a little child then. It seems such an age ago!—"

"It is very odd he didn't come to see us," said Hugh.

"He did—don't you know?—the very next day after we heard he was here—when most unluckily I was up at aunt Miriam's."

"I should think he might have come again, considering what friends you used to be."

"I dare say he would if he had not left Montepoole so soon. But dear Hugh! I was a mere child—how could he remember me much."

"You remember him," said Hugh.

"Ah but I have good reason. Besides I never forget anything. I would have given a great deal to see him—if I had it."

"I wish the Evelyns had staid longer," said Hugh. "I think you have wanted something to brighten you up. They did you a great deal of good last year. I am afraid all this taking care of Philetus and Earl Douglass is too much for you."

Fleda gave him a very bright smile, half affection, half fun.

"Don't you admire my management?" said she. "Because I do. Philetus is firmly persuaded that he is an invaluable assistant to me in the mystery of gardening; and the origin of Earl Douglass's new ideas is so enveloped in mist that he does not himself know where they come from. It was rich to hear him the other day descanting to Lucas upon the evil effects of earthing up corn and the advantages of curing hay in cocks, as to both which matters Lucas is a thorough unbeliever, and Earl was a year ago."

"But that doesn't hinder your looking pale and thin, and a great deal soberer than I like to see you," said Hugh. "You want a change, I know. I don't know how you are to get it. I wish they would send for you to New York again."

"I don't know that I should want to go if they did," said Fleda. "They don't raise my spirits, Hugh. I am amused sometimes,—I can't help that,—but such excessive gayety rather makes me shrink within myself; I am too out of tone with it. I never feel more absolutely quiet than sometimes when I am laughing at Constance Evelyn's mad sallies—and sometimes I cannot laugh at them. I do not know what they must think of me; it is what they can have no means of understanding."

"I wish you didn't understand it either, Fleda."

"But you shouldn't say that. I am happier than they are, now, Hugh,—now that you are better,—with all their means of happiness. They know nothing of our quiet enjoyments, they must live in a whirl or they would think they are not living at all, and I do not believe that all New York can give them the real pleasure that I have in such a day as this. They would see almost nothing in all this beauty that my eyes 'drink in,' as Cowper says; and they would be certain to quarrel with the wind, that to me is like the shake of an old friend's hand. Delicious!—" said Fleda, at the wind rewarded this eulogium with a very hearty shake indeed.

"I believe you would make friends with everything, Fleda," said Hugh laughing.

"The wind is always that to me," said Fleda,—"not always in such a cheerful mood as to-day, though. It talks to me often of a thousand old-time things and sighs over them with me—a most sympathizing friend!—but to day he invites me to a waltz—Come!——"

And pulling Hugh after her away she went down the rocky path, with a step too light to care for the stones; the little feet capering down the mountain with a disdain of the ground that made Hugh smile to see her; and eyes dancing for company; till they reached the lower woodland.

"A most, spirited waltz!" said Hugh.

"And a most slack partner. Why didn't you keep me company?"

"I never was made for waltzing," said Hugh shaking his head.

"Not to the tune of the North wind? That has done me good, Hugh."

"So I should judge, by your cheeks."

"Poverty need not always make people poor," said Fleda taking breath and his arm together. "You and I are rich, Hugh."

"And our riches cannot take to themselves wings and flyaway," said Hugh.

"No, but besides those riches—there are the pleasures of the eye and the mind that one may enjoy everywhere—everywhere in the country at least—unless poverty bear one down very hard; and they are some of the purest and most satisfying of any. O the blessing of a good education! how it makes one independent of circumstances."

"And circumstances are education too," said Hugh smiling. "I dare say we should not appreciate our mountains and woods so well if we had had our old plenty of everything else."

"I always loved them," said Fleda. "But what good company they have been to us for years past, Hugh;—to me especially; I have more reason to love them."

They walked on quietly and soberly to the brow of the tableland, where they parted; Hugh being obliged to go home, and Fleda wishing to pay a visit to her aunt Miriam.

She turned off alone to take the way to the high road and went softly on, no longer certainly in the momentary spirits with which she had shaken hands with the wind and skipped down the mountain; but feeling, and thankful that she felt, a cheerful patience to tread the dusty highway of life.

The old lady had been rather ailing, and from one or two expressions she had let fall Fleda could not help thinking that she looked upon her ailments with a much more serious eye than anybody else thought was called for. It did not, however, appear to-day. She was not worse, and Fleda's slight anxious feeling could find nothing to justify it, if it were not the very calm and quietly happy face and manner of the old lady; and that if it had something to alarm, did much more to sooth. Fleda had sat with her a long time, patience and cheerfulness all the while unconsciously growing in her company; when catching up her bonnet with a sudden haste very unlike her usual collectedness of manner Fleda kissed her aunt and was rushing away.

"But stop!—where are you going, Fleda?"

"Home, aunt Miriam—I must—don't keep me!"

"But what are you going that way for? you can't go home that way?"

"Yes I can."

"How?"

"I can cross the blackberry hill behind the barn and then over the east hill, and then there's nothing but the water-cress meadow."

"I sha'n't let you go that way alone—sit down and tell me what you mean,—what is this desperate hurry?"

But with equal precipitation Fleda had cast her bonnet out of sight behind the table, and the next moment turned with the utmost possible quietness to shake hands with Mr. Olmney. Aunt Miriam had presence of mind enough to make no remark and receive the young gentleman with her usual dignity and kindness.

He staid some time, but Fleda's hurry seemed to have forsaken her. She had seized upon an interminable long grey stocking her aunt was knitting, and sat in the corner working at it most diligently, without raising her eyes unless spoken to.

"Do you give yourself no rest at home or abroad, Miss Fleda?" said the gentleman.

"Put that stocking down, Fleda," said her aunt, "it is in no hurry."

"I like to do it, aunt Miriam."

But she felt with warming cheeks that she did not like to do it with two people sitting still and looking at her. The gentleman presently rose.

"Don't go till we have had tea, Mr. Olmney," said Mrs. Plumfield.

"Thank you, ma'am,—I cannot stay, I believe,—unless Miss Fleda will let me take care of her down the hill by and by."

"Thank you, Mr. Olmney," said Fleda, "but I am not going home before night, unless they send for me."

"I am afraid," said he looking at her, "that the agricultural turn has proved an over-match for your energies."

"The farm don't complain of me, does it?" said Fleda, looking up at him with a comic grave expression of countenance.

"No," said he laughing,—"certainly not; but—if you will forgive me for saying so—I think you complain of it,—tacitly,—and that will raise a good many complaints in other quarters—if you do not take care of yourself."

He shook hands and left them; and Mrs. Plumfield sat silently looking at Fleda, who on her part looked at nothing but the grey stocking.

"What is all this, Fleda?"

"What is what, aunt Miriam?" said Fleda, picking up a stitch with desperate diligence.

"Why did you want to run away from Mr. Olmney?"

"I didn't wish to be delayed—I wanted to get home."

"Then why wouldn't you let him go home with you?"

"I liked better to go alone, aunt Miriam."

"Don't you like him, Fleda?"

"Certainly, aunt Miriam—very much.'

"I think he likes you, Fleda," said her aunt smiling.

"I am very sorry for it," said Fleda with great gravity.

Mrs. Plumfield looked at her for a few minutes in silence and then said,

"Fleda, love, come over here and sit by me and tell me what you mean. Why are you sorry? It has given me a great deal of pleasure to think of it."

But Fleda did not budge from her seat or her stocking and seemed tongue-tied. Mrs. Plumfield pressed for an answer.

"Because, aunt Miriam," said Fleda, with the prettiest red cheeks in the world but speaking very clearly and steadily,—"my liking only goes to a point which I am afraid will not satisfy either him or you."

"But why?—it will go further."

"No ma'am."

"Why not? why do you say so?"

"Because I must if you ask me."

"But what can be more excellent and estimable, Fleda?—who could be more worth liking? I should have thought he would just please you. He is one of the most lovely young men I have ever seen."

"Dear aunt Miriam!" said Fleda looking up beseechingly,—"why should we talk about it?"

"Because I want to understand you, Fleda, and to be sure that you understand yourself."

"I do," said Fleda, quietly and with a quivering lip.

"What is there that you dislike about Mr. Olmney?"

"Nothing in the world, aunt Miriam."

"Then what is the reason you cannot like him enough?"

"Because, aunt Miriam," said Fleda speaking in desperation,—"there isn't enough of him. He is *very* good and excellent in every way—nobody feels that more than I do—I don't want to say a word against him—but I do not think he has a very strong mind; and he isn't cultivated enough."

"But you cannot have everything, Fleda."

"No ma'am—I don't expect it."

"I am afraid you have set up too high a standard for yourself," said Mrs. Plumfield, looking rather troubled.

"I don't think that is possible, aunt Miriam."

"But I am afraid it will prevent your ever liking anybody?"

"It will not prevent my liking the friends I have already—it may prevent my leaving them for somebody else," said Fleda, with a gravity that was touching in its expression.

"But Mr. Olmney is sensible,—and well educated."

"Yes, but his tastes are not. He could not at all enter into a great many things that give me the most pleasure. I do not think he quite understands above half of what I say to him."

"Are you sure? I know he admires you, Fleda."

"Ah, but that is only half enough, you see, aunt Miriam, unless I could admire him too."

Mrs. Plumfield looked at her in some difficulty;—Mr. Olmney was not the only one, clearly, whose powers of comprehension were not equal to the subject.

"Fleda," said her aunt inquiringly,—"is there anybody else that has put Mr. Olmney out of your head?"

"Nobody in the world!" exclaimed Fleda with a frank look and tone of astonishment at the question, and cheeks colouring as promptly. "How could you ask?—But he never was in my head, aunt Miriam."

"Mr. Thorn?" said Mrs. Plumfield.

"Mr. Thorn!" said Fleda indignantly. "Don't you know me better than that, aunt Miriam? But you do not know him."

"I believe I know you, dear Fleda, but I heard he had paid you a great deal of attention last year; and you would not have been the first unsuspecting nature that has been mistaken."

Fleda was silent, flushed and disturbed; and Mrs. Plumfield was silent and meditating; when Hugh came in. He came to fetch Fleda home. Dr. Gregory had arrived. In haste again Fleda sought her bonnet, and exchanging a more than usually wistful and affectionate kiss and embrace with her aunt, set off with Hugh down the hill.

Hugh had a great deal to say to her all the way home, of which Fleda's ears alone took the benefit, for her understanding received none of it; and when she at last came into the breakfast room where the doctor was sitting, the fact of his being there was the only one which had entered her mind.

"Here she is!—I declare!" said the doctor, holding her back to look at her after the first greetings had passed,—"I'll be hanged if you ain't handsome!—Now what's the use of pinking your cheeks any more at that, as if you didn't know it before?—eh?"

"I will always do my best to deserve your good opinion, sir," said Fleda laughing.

"Well sit down now," said he shaking his head, "and pour me out a cup of tea—your mother can't make it right."

And sipping his tea, for some time the old doctor sat listening to Mrs. Rossitur and eating bread and butter; saying little, but casting a very frequent glance at the figure opposite him behind the tea-board.

"I am afraid," said he after a while, "that your care for my good opinion won't outlast an occasion. Is *that* the way you look for every day?"

The colour came with the smile; but the old doctor looked at her in a way that made the tears come too. He turned his eyes to Mrs. Rossitur for an explanation.

"She is well," said Mrs. Rossitur fondly,—"she has been very well—except her old headaches now and then;—I think she has grown rather thin lately."

"Thin!" said the old doctor,—"etherealized to a mere abstract of herself; only that is a very bad figure, for an abstract should have all the bone and muscle of the subject; and I should say you had little left but pure spirit. You are the best proof I ever saw of the principle of the homoeopaths—I see now that though a little corn may fatten a man, a great deal may be the death of him."

"But I have tried it both ways, uncle Orrin," said Fleda laughing. "I ought to be a happy medium between plethora and starvation. I am pretty substantial, what there is of me."

"Substantial!" said the doctor; "you look as substantial a personage as your old friend the 'faire Una,' just about. Well prepare yourself, gentle Saxon, to ride home with me the day after to-morrow. I'll try a little humanizing regimen with you."

"I don't think that is possible, uncle Orrin," said Fleda gently.

"We'll talk about the possibility afterwards—at present all you have to do is to get ready. If you raise difficulties you will find me a very Hercules to clear them away—I'm substantial enough I can tell you—so it's just as well to spare yourself and me the trouble."

"There are no difficulties," Mrs. Rossitur and Hugh said both at once.

"I knew there weren't. Put a pair or two of clean stockings in your trunk—that's all you want—Mrs. Pritchard and I will find the rest. There's the people in Fourteenth street wants you the first of November and I want you all the time till then, and longer too.— Stop—I've got a missive of some sort here for you—"

He foisted out of his breast-pocket a little package of notes; one from Mrs. Evelyn and one from Florence begging Fleda to come to them at the time the doctor had named; the third from Constance.

"My darling little Fleda,

"I am dying to see you—so pack up and come down with Dr. Gregory if the least spark of regard for me is slumbering in your breast—Mamma and Florence are writing to beg you,—but though an insignificant member of the family, considering that instead of being 'next to head' only little Edith prevents my being at the less dignified end of this branch of the social system, — I could not prevail upon myself to let the representations of my respected elders go unsupported by mine — especially as I felt persuaded of the superior efficacy of the motives I had it in my power to present to your truly philanthropical mind.

"I am in a state of mind that baffles description — Mr. Carleton is going home!! — —

"I have not worn earrings in my ears for a fortnight — my personal appearance is become a matter of indifference to me — any description of mental exertion is excruciating — I sit constantly listening for the ringing of the door-bell, and when it sounds I rush frantically to the head of the staircase and look over to see who it is — the mere sight of pen and ink excites delirious ideas — judge what I suffer in writing to you —

"To make the matter worse (if it could be) I have been informed privately that he is going home to crown at the altar of Hymen an old attachment to one of the loveliest of all England's daughters. Conceive the complication of my feelings! — —

"Nothing is left me but the resources of friendship — so come darling Fleda, before a barrier of ice interposes itself between my chilled heart and your sympathy.

"Mr. Thorn's state would move my pity if I were capable of being moved by anything — by this you will comprehend he is returned. He has been informed by somebody that there is a wolf in sheep's clothing prowling about Queechy, and his head is filled with the idea that you have fallen a victim, of which in my calmer moments I have in vain endeavoured to dispossess him — Every morning we are wakened up at an unseasonable hour by a furious ringing at the door-bell — Joe Manton pulls off his nightcap and slowly descending the stairs opens the door and finds Mr. Thorn, who enquires distractedly whether Miss Ringgan has arrived; and being answered in the negative gloomily walks off towards the East river — The state of anxiety in which his mother is thereby kept is rapidly depriving her of all her flesh—but we have directed Joe lately to reply 'no sir, but she is expected,'—upon which Mr. Thorn regularly smiles faintly and rewards the 'fowling piece' with a quarter dollar—

"So make haste, dear Fleda, or I shall feel that we are acting the part of innocent swindlers.

"C.E."

There was but one voice at home on the point whether Fleda should go. So she went.

Chapter XXXII.

Host. Now, my young guest! methinks you're allycholy; I
pray you, why is it?
Jul. Marry, mine host, because I cannot be merry.

Two Gentlemen of Verona.

Some nights after their arrival the doctor and Fleda were seated at
tea in the little snug old-fashioned back parlour, where the doctor's
nicest of housekeepers, Mrs. Pritchard, had made it ready for them.
In general Mrs. Pritchard herself poured it out for the doctor, but she
descended most cheerfully from her post of elevation whenever
Fleda was there to fill it.

The doctor and Fleda sat cosily looking at each other across the toast
and chipped beef, their glances grazing the tea-urn which was just
on one side of their range of vision. A comfortable Liverpool-coal fire
in a state of repletion burned away indolently and gave everything
else in the room somewhat of its own look of sousy independence.
Except perhaps the delicate creature at whom the doctor between
sips of his tea took rather wistful observations.

"When are you going to Mrs. Evelyn?" he said breaking the silence.

"They say next week, sir."

"I shall be glad of it!" said the doctor.

"Glad of it?" said Fleda smiling. "Do you want to get rid of me,
uncle Orrin?"

"Yes!" said he. "This isn't the right place for you. You are too much
alone."

"No indeed, sir. I have been reading voraciously, and enjoying myself as much as possible. I would quite as lieve be here as there, putting you out of the question."

"I wouldn't as lieve have you," said he shaking his head. "What were you musing about before tea? your face gave me the heartache."

"My face!" said Fleda, smiling, while an instant flush of the eyes answered him, —"what was the matter with my face?"

"That is the very thing I want to know."

"Before tea?—I was only thinking, —" said Fleda, her look going back to the fire from association, —"thinking of different things—not disagreeably—taking a kind of bird's-eye view of things, as one does sometimes."

"I don't believe you ever take other than a bird's-eye view of anything," said her uncle. "But what were you viewing just then, my little Saxon?"

"I was thinking of them at home," said Fleda smiling thoughtfully, —"and I somehow had perched myself on a point of observation and was taking one of those wider views which are always rather sobering."

"Views of what?"

"Of life, sir."

"As how?" said the doctor.

"How near the end is to the beginning, and how short the space between, and how little the ups and downs of it will matter if we take the right road and get home."

"Pshaw!" said the doctor.

But Fleda knew him too well to take his interjection otherwise than most kindly. And indeed though he whirled round and eat his toast at the fire discontentedly, his look came back to her after a little with even more than its usual gentle appreciation.

"What do you suppose you have come to New York for?" said he.

"To see you, sir, in the first place, and the Evelyns in the second."

"And who in the third?"

"I am afraid the third place is vacant," said Fleda smiling.

"You are, eh? Well—I don't know—but I know that I have been inquired of by two several and distinct people as to your coming. Ah, you needn't open your bright eyes at me, because I shall not tell you. Only let me ask,—you have no notion of fencing off my Queechy rose with a hedge of blackthorn,—or anything of that kind, have you?"

"I have no notion of any fences at all, except invisible ones, sir," said Fleda, laughing and colouring very prettily.

"Well those are not American fences," said the doctor, "so I suppose I am safe enough. Whom did I see you out riding with yesterday?"

"I was with Mrs. Evelyn," said Fleda,—"I didn't want to go, but I couldn't very well help myself."

"Mrs. Evelyn.—Mrs. Evelyn wasn't driving, was she?"

"No sir; Mr. Thorn was driving."

"I thought so. Have you seen your old friend Mr. Carleton yet?"

"Do you know him uncle Orrin?"

"Why shouldn't I? What's the difficulty of knowing people? Have you seen him?"

"But how did you know that he was an old friend of mine?"

"Question?—" said the doctor. "Hum—well, I won't tell you—so there's the answer. Now will you answer me?"

"I have not seen him, sir."

"Haven't met him in all the times you have been to Mrs. Evelyn's?"

"No sir. I have been there but once in the evening, uncle Orrin. He is just about sailing for England."

"Well, you're going there to-night, aren't you? Run and bundle yourself up and I'll take you there before I begin my work."

There was a small party that evening at Mrs. Evelyn's. Fleda was very early. She ran up to the first floor,—rooms lighted and open, but nobody there.

"Fleda Ringgan," called out the voice of Constance from over the stairs,—"is that you?"

"Yes," said Fleda.

"Well just wait till I come down to you.—My darling little Fleda, it's delicious of you to come so early. Now just tell me,—am I captivating?"

"Well,—I retain self-possession," said Fleda. "I cannot tell about the strength of head of other people."

"You wretched little creature!—Fleda, don't you admire my hair?— it's new style, my dear,—just come out,—the Delancys brought it out with them—Eloise Delancy taught it us—isn't it graceful? Nobody in New York has it yet, except the Delancys and we."

26

"How do you know but they have taught somebody else?" said Fleda.

"I won't talk to you!—Don't you like it?"

"I am not sure that I do not like you in your ordinary way better."

Constance made a gesture of impatience, and then pulled Fleda after her into the drawing-rooms.

"Come in here—I won't waste the elegancies of my toilet upon your dull perceptions—come here and let me shew you some flowers— aren't those lovely? This bunch came to-day, 'for Miss Evelyn,' so Florence will have it it is hers, and it's very mean of her, for I am perfectly certain it is mine—it's come from somebody who wasn't enlightened on the subject of my family circle and has innocently imagined that *two* Miss Evelyns could not belong to the same one! I know the floral representatives of all Florence's dear friends and admirers, and this isn't from any of them— I have been distractedly endeavouring all day to find who it came from, for if I don't I can't take the least comfort in it."

"But you might enjoy the flowers for their own sake, I should think," said Fleda, breathing the sweetness of myrtle and heliotrope.

"No I can't, for I have all the time the association of some horrid creature they might have come from, you know; but it will do just as well to humbug people—I shall make Cornelia Schenck believe that this came from my dear Mr. Carleton!"

"No you won't, Constance," said Fleda gently.

"My dear little Fleda, I shock you, don't I? but I sha'n't tell any lies— I shall merely expressively indicate a particular specimen and say, 'My dear Cornelia, do you perceive that this is an English rose?'— and then it's none of my business, you know, what she believes— and she will be dying with curiosity and despair all the rest of the evening."

"I shouldn't think there would be much pleasure in that, I confess," said Fleda gravely. "How very ungracefully and stiffly those are made up!"

"My dear little Queechy rose?" said Constance impatiently, "you are, pardon me, as fresh as possible. They can't cut the flowers with long stems, you know,—the gardeners would be ruined. That is perfectly elegant—it must have cost at least ten dollars. My dear little Fleda!" said Constance capering off before the long pier-glass,—"I am afraid I am not captivating!—Do you think it would be an improvement if I put drops in my ears?—or one curl behind them? I don't know which Mr. Carleton likes best!—"

And with her head first on one side and then on the other she stood before the glass looking at herself and Fleda by turns with such a comic expression of mock doubt and anxiety that no gravity but her own could stand it.

"She is a silly girl, Fleda, isn't she?" said Mrs. Evelyn coming up behind them.

"Mamma!—am I captivating?" cried Constance wheeling round.

The mother's smile said "Very!"

"Fleda is wishing she were out of the sphere of my influence, mamma.—Wasn't Mr. Olmney afraid of my corrupting you?" she said with a sudden pull-up in front of Fleda.—"My blessed stars!— there's somebody's voice I know.—Well I believe it is true that a rose without thorns is a desideratum.—Mamma, is Mrs. Thorn's turban to be an invariable *pendant* to your coiffure all the while Miss Ringgan is here?"

"Hush!—"

With the entrance of company came Constance's return from extravaganzas to a sufficiently graceful every-day manner, only enough touched with high spirits and lawlessness to free it from the charge of commonplace. But the contrast of these high spirits with her own rather made Fleda's mood more quiet, and it needed no quieting. Of the sundry people that she knew among those presently assembled there were none that she wanted to talk to; the rooms were hot and she felt nervous and fluttered, partly from encounters already sustained and partly from a little anxious expecting of Mr. Carleton's appearance. The Evelyns had not said he was to be there but she had rather gathered it; and the remembrance of old times was strong enough to make her very earnestly wish to see him and dread to be disappointed. She swung clear of Mr. Thorn, with some difficulty, and ensconced herself under the shadow of a large cabinet, between that and a young lady who was very good society for she wanted no help in carrying on the business of it. All Fleda had to do was to sit still and listen, or not listen, which she generally preferred. Miss Tomlinson discoursed upon varieties, with great sociableness and satisfaction; while poor Fleda's mind, letting all her sense and nonsense go, was again taking a somewhat bird's-eye view of things, and from the little centre of her post in Mrs. Evelyn's drawing-room casting curious glances over the panorama of her life—England, France, New York, and Queechy!—half coming to the conclusion that her place henceforth was only at the last and that the world and she had nothing to do with each other. The tide of life and gayety seemed to have thrown her on one side, as something that could not swim with it; and to be rushing past too strongly and swiftly for her slight bark ever to launch upon it again. Perhaps the shore might be the safest and happiest place; but it was sober in the comparison; and as a stranded bark might look upon the white sails flying by, Fleda saw the gay faces and heard the light tones with which her own could so little keep company. But as little they with her. Their enjoyment was not more foreign to her than the causes which moved it were strange. Merry?—she might like to be merry; but she could sooner laugh with the North wind than with one of those vapid faces, or with any face that she could not trust. Conversation might be pleasant,—but it must be something different from the noisy cross-fire of nonsense that was going on in one quarter, or the profitless barter of nothings that was kept up on the other side of her. Rather Queechy and silence, by far, than New York and *this!*

And through it all Miss Tomlinson talked on and was happy.

"My dear Fleda!—what are you back here for?" said Florence coming up to her.

"I was glad to be at a safe distance from the fire."

"Take a screen—here! Miss Tomlinson, your conversation is too exciting for Miss Ringgan—look at her cheeks—I must carry you off—I want to shew you a delightful contrivance for transparencies, that I learned the other day—"

The seat beside her was vacated, and not casting so much as a look towards any quarter whence a possible successor to Miss Tomlinson might be arriving, Fleda sprang up and took a place in the far corner of the room by Mrs. Thorn, happily not another vacant chair in the neighbourhood. Mrs. Thorn had shewn a very great fancy for her and was almost as good company as Miss Tomlinson; not quite, for it was necessary sometimes to answer and therefore necessary always to hear. But Fleda liked her; she was thoroughly amiable, sensible, and good-hearted. And Mrs. Thorn, very much gratified at Fleda's choice of a seat, talked to her with a benignity which Fleda could not help answering with grateful pleasure.

"Little Queechy, what has driven you into the corner?" said Constance pausing a moment before her.

"It must have been a retiring spirit," said Fleda.

"Mrs. Thorn, isn't she lovely?"

Mrs. Thorn's smile at Fleda might almost have been called that, it was so full of benevolent pleasure. But she spoiled it by her answer.

"I don't believe I am the first one to find it out."

"But what are you looking so sober for?" Constance went on, taking Fleda's screen from her hand and fanning her diligently with it,—

"you don't talk! The gravity of Miss Ringgan's face casts a gloom over the brightness of the evening. I couldn't conceive what made me feel chilly in the other room, till I looked about and found that the shade came from this corner; and Mr. Thorn's teeth, I saw, were chattering."

"Constance!" said Fleda laughing and vexed, and making the reproof more strongly with her eyes,—"how can you talk so!"

"Mrs. Thorn, isn't it true?"

Mrs. Thorn's look at Fleda was the essence of good-humour.

"Will you let Lewis come and take you a good long ride to-morrow?"

"No, Mrs. Thorn, I believe not—I intend to stay perseveringly at home to-morrow and see if it is possible to be quiet a day in New York."

"But you will go with me to the concert to-morrow night?—both of you—and hear Truffi;—come to my house and take tea and go from there? will you, Constance?"

"My dear Mrs. Thorn!" said Constance,—"I shall be in ecstacies, and Miss Ringgan was privately imploring me last night to find some way of getting her to it. We regard such material pleasures as tea and muffins with great indifference, but when you look up after swallowing your last cup you will see Miss Ringgan and Miss Evelyn, cloaked and hooded, anxiously awaiting your next movement. My dear Fleda!—there is a ring!—"

And giving her the benefit of a most comic and expressive arching of her eyebrows, Constance flung back the screen into Fleda's lap and skimmed away.

Fleda was too vexed for a few minutes to understand more of Mrs. Thorn's talk than that she was first enlarging upon the concert, and afterwards detailing to her a long shopping expedition in search of something which had been a morning's annoyance. She almost thought Constance was unkind, because she wanted to go to the concert herself to lug her in so unceremoniously; and wished herself back in her uncle's snug little quiet parlour,—unless Mr. Carleton would come.

And there he is!—said a quick beat of her heart, as his entrance explained Constance's "ring."

Such a rush of associations came over Fleda that she was in imminent danger of losing Mrs. Thorn altogether. She managed however by some sort of instinct to disprove the assertion that the mind cannot attend to two things at once, and carried on a double conversation, with herself and with Mrs. Thorn, for some time very vigorously.

"Just the same!—he has not altered a jot," she said to herself as he came forward to Mrs. Evelyn;—"it is himself!—his very self—he doesn't look a day older—I'm very glad!—(Yes, ma'am—it's extremely tiresome—) How exactly as when he left me in Paris,—and how much pleasanter than anybody else!—more pleasant than ever, it seems to me, but that is because I have not seen him in so long; he only wanted one thing. That same grave eye— but quieter, isn't it,—than it used to be?—I think so—(It's the best store in town, I think, Mrs. Thorn, by far,—yes, ma'am—) Those eyes are certainly the finest I ever saw—How I have seen him stand and look just so when he was talking to his workmen—without that air of consciousness that all these people have, comparatively—what a difference! (I know very little about it, ma'am;—I am not learned in laces—I never bought any—) I wish he would look this way—I wonder if Mrs. Evelyn does not mean to bring him to see me—she must remember;—now there is that curious old smile and looking down! how much better I know what it means than Mrs. Evelyn does—(Yes, ma'am, I understand—I mean!—it is very convenient—I never go anywhere else to get anything,—at least I should not if I lived here—) She does not know whom she is talking to.—She is going to walk him off into the other room! How very much more gracefully he does everything than anybody else—it comes from that entire high-mindedness and frankness, I think,—not altogether, a fine person must aid the effect, and that complete independence of other people.——I wonder if Mrs. Evelyn has forgotten my existence!—he has not, I am sure—I think she is a little odd—(Yes, ma'am, my face is flushed—the room is very warm—)"

"But the fire has gone down—it will be cooler now," said Mrs. Thorn.

Which were the first words that fairly entered Fleda's understanding. She was glad to use the screen to hide her face now, not the fire.

Apparently the gentleman and lady found nothing to detain them in the other room, for after sauntering off to it they sauntered back again and placed themselves to talk just opposite her. Fleda had an additional screen now in the person of Miss Tomlinson, who had sought her corner and was earnestly talking across her to Mrs. Thorn; so that she was sure even if Mr. Carleton's eyes should chance to wander that way they would see nothing but the unremarkable skirt of her green silk dress, most unlikely to detain them. The trade in nothings going on over the said green silk was very brisk indeed; but disregarding the buzz of tongues near at hand Fleda's quick ears were able to free the barrier and catch every one of the quiet tones beyond.

"And you leave us the day after to-morrow?" said Mrs. Evelyn.

"No, Mrs. Evelyn,—I shall wait another steamer."

The lady's brow instantly revealed to Fleda a trap setting beneath to catch his reason.

"I'm very glad!" exclaimed little Edith who in defiance of conventionalities and proprieties made good her claim to be in the drawing room on all occasions;—"then you will take me another ride, won't you, Mr. Carleton?"

"You do not flatter us with a very long stay," pursued Mrs. Evelyn.

"Quite as long as I expected—longer than I meant it to be," he answered rather thoughtfully.

"Mr. Carleton," said Constance sidling up in front of him,—"I have been in distress to ask you a question, and I am afraid——"

"Of what are you afraid, Miss Constance?"

"That you would reward me with one of your severe looks,—which would petrify me,—and then I am afraid I should feel uncomfortable—"

"I hope he will!" said Mrs. Evelyn, settling herself back in the corner of the sofa, and with a look at her daughter which was complacency itself,—"I hope Mr. Carleton will, if you are guilty of any impertinence."

"What is the question, Miss Constance?"

"I want to know what brought you out here?"

"Fie, Constance!" said her mother. "I am ashamed of you. Do not answer her, Mr. Carleton."

"Mr. Carleton will answer me, mamma,—he looks benevolently upon my faults, which are entirely those of education! What was it, Mr. Carleton?"

"I suppose," said he smiling, "it might be traced more or less remotely to the restlessness incident to human nature."

"But *you* are not restless, Mr. Carleton," said Florence, with a glance which might be taken as complimentary.

"And knowing that I am," said Constance in comic impatience,—
"you are maliciously prolonging my agonies. It is not what I
expected of you, Mr. Carleton."

"My dear," said her father, "Mr. Carleton, I am sure, will fulfil all
reasonable expectations. What is the matter?"

"I asked him where a certain tribe of Indians was to be found, papa,
and he told me they were supposed originally to have come across
Behring's Straits one cold winter!"

Mr. Evelyn looked a little doubtfully and Constance with so
unhesitating gravity that the gravity of nobody else was worth
talking about.

"But it is so uncommon," said Mrs. Evelyn when they had done
laughing, "to see an Englishman of your class here at all, that when
he comes a second time we may be forgiven for wondering what has
procured us such an honour."

"Women may always be forgiven for wondering, my dear," said Mr.
Evelyn,—"or the rest of mankind must live at odds with them."

"Your principal object was to visit our western prairies, wasn't it,
Mr. Carleton?" said Florence.

"No," he replied quietly,—"I cannot say that. I should choose to give
a less romantic explanation of my movements. From some
knowledge growing out of my former visit to this country I thought
there were certain negotiations I might enter into here with
advantage; and it was for the purpose of attending to these, Miss
Constance, that I came."

"And have you succeeded?" said Mrs. Evelyn with an expression of
benevolent interest.

"No, ma'am—my information had not been sufficient."

"Very likely!" said Mr. Evelyn. "There isn't one man in a hundred whose representations on such a matter are to be trusted at a distance."

"'On such a matter'!" repeated his wife funnily,—"you don't know what the matter was, Mr. Evelyn—you don't know what you are talking about."

"Business, my dear,—business—I take only what Mr. Carleton said;—it doesn't signify a straw what business. A man must always see with his own eyes."

Whether Mr. Carleton had seen or had not seen, or whether even he had his faculty of hearing in present exercise, a glance at his face was incompetent to discover.

"I never should have imagined," said Constance eying him keenly, "that Mr. Carleton's errand to this country was one of business and not of romance, I believe it's a humbug!"

For an instant this was answered by one of those looks of absolute composure in every muscle and feature which put an effectual bar to all further attempts from without or revelations from within; a look Fleda remembered well, and felt even in her corner. But it presently relaxed, and he said with his usual manner,

"You cannot understand then, Miss Constance, that there should be any romance about business?"

"I cannot understand," said Mrs. Evelyn, "why romance should not come after business. Mr. Carleton, sir, you have seen American scenery this summer—isn't American beauty worth staying a little while longer for?"

"My dear," said Mr. Evelyn, "Mr. Carleton is too much of a philosopher to care about beauty—every man of sense is."

"I am sure he is not," said Mrs. Evelyn smoothly. "Mr. Carleton,—you are an admirer of beauty, are you not, sir?"

"I hope so, Mrs. Evelyn," he said smiling,—"but perhaps I shall shock you by adding,—not of *beauties*."

"That sounds very odd," said Florence.

"But let us understand," said Mrs. Evelyn with the air of a person solving a problem,—"I suppose we are to infer that your taste in beauty is of a peculiar kind?"

"That may be a fair inference," he said.

"What is it then?" said Constance eagerly.

"Yes—what is it you look for in a face?" said Mrs. Evelyn.

"Let us hear whether America has any chance," said Mr. Thorn, who had joined the group and placed himself precisely so as to hinder Fleda's view.

"My fancy has no stamp of nationality, in this, at least," he said pleasantly.

"Now for instance, the Miss Delancys—don't you call them handsome, Mr. Carleton?" said Florence.

"Yes," he said, half smiling.

"But not beautiful?—Now what is it they want?"

"I do not wish, if I could, to make the want visible to other eyes than my own."

"Well, Cornelia Schenck,—how do you like her face?"

"It is very pretty-featured."

"Pretty-featured!—Why she is called beautiful. She has a beautiful smile, Mr. Carleton?"

"She has only one."

"Only one! and how many smiles ought the same person to have?" cried Florence impatiently. But that which instantly answered her said forcibly that a plurality of them was possible.

"I have seen one face," he said gravely, and his eye seeking the floor,—"that had I think a thousand."

"Different smiles?" said Mrs. Evelyn in a constrained voice.

"If they were not all absolutely that, they had so much of freshness and variety that they all seemed new."

"Was the mouth so beautiful?" said Florence.

"Perhaps it would not have been remarked for beauty when it was perfectly at rest; but it could not move with the least play of feeling, grave or gay, that it did not become so in a very high degree. I think there was no touch or shade of sentiment in the mind that the lips did not give with singular nicety; and the mind was one of the most finely wrought I have ever known."

"And what other features went with this mouth?" said Florence.

"The usual complement, I suppose," said Thorn. "'Item, two lips indifferent red; item, two grey eyes with lids to them; item, one neck, one chin, and so forth.'"

"Mr. Carleton, sir," said Mrs. Evelyn blandly—"as Mr. Evelyn says women may be forgiven for wondering, won't you answer Florence's question?"

"Mr. Thorn has done it, Mrs. Evelyn, for me."

"But I have great doubts of the correctness of Mr. Thorn's description, sir—won't you indulge us with yours?"

"Word-painting is a difficult matter, Mrs. Evelyn, in some instances;—if I must do it I will borrow my colours. In general, 'that which made her fairness much the fairer was that it was but an ambassador of a most fair mind.'"

"A most exquisite picture!" said Thorn, "and the original don't stand so thick that one is in any danger of mistaking them. Is the painter Shakspeare?—I don't recollect—"

"I think Sidney, sir—I am not sure."

"But still, Mr. Carleton," said Mrs Evelyn, "this is only in general—I want very much to know the particulars;—what style of features belonged to this face?"

"The fairest, I think, I have ever known," said Mr. Carleton. "You asked me, Miss Evelyn, what was my notion of beauty;—this face was a good illustration of it. Not perfection of outline, though it had that too in very uncommon degree;—but the loveliness of mind and character to which these features were only an index; the thoughts were invariably telegraphed through eye and mouth more faithfully than words could give them."

"What kind of eyes?" said Florence.

His own grew dark as he answered,—

"Clear and pure as one might imagine an angel's—through which I am sure my good angel many a time looked at me."

Good angels were at a premium among the eyes that were exchanging glances just then.

"And Mr. Carleton," said Mrs. Evelyn,—"is it fair to ask—this paragon—is she living still?"

"I hope so," he answered, with his old light smile, dismissing the subject.

"You spoke so much in the past tense," said Mrs. Evelyn apologetically.

"Yes, I have not seen it since it was a child's."

"A child's face!—Oh," said Florence, "I think you see a great many children's faces with that kind of look."

"I never saw but the one," said Mr. Carleton dryly.

So far Fleda listened, with cheeks that would certainly have excited Mrs. Thorn's alarm if she had not been happily engrossed with Miss Tomlinson's affairs; though up to the last two minutes the idea of herself had not entered Fleda's head in connection with the subject of conversation. But then feeling it impossible to make her appearance in public that evening, she quietly slipped out of the open window close by, which led into a little greenhouse on the piazza, and by another door gained the hall and the dressing-room.

When Dr. Gregory came to Mrs. Evelyn's an hour or two after, a figure all cloaked and hooded ran down the stairs and met him in the hall.

"Ready!" said the doctor in surprise.

"I have been ready some time, sir," said Fleda.

"Well," said he, "then we'll go straight home, for I've not done my work yet."

"Dear uncle Orrin!" said Fleda, "if I had known you had work to do I wouldn't have come."

"Yes you would!" said he decidedly.

She clasped her uncle's arm and walked with him briskly home through the frosty air, looking at the silent lights and shadows on the walls of the street and feeling a great desire to cry.

"Did you have a pleasant evening?" said the doctor when they were about half way.

"Not particularly, sir," said Fleda hesitating.

He said not another word till they got home and Fleda went up to her room. But the habit of patience overcame the wish to cry; and though the outside of her little gold-clasped Bible awoke it again, a few words of the inside were enough to lay it quietly to sleep.

"Well," said the doctor as they sat at breakfast the next morning,— "where are you going next?"

"To the concert, I must, to-night," said Fleda. "I couldn't help myself."

"Why should you want to help yourself?" said the doctor. "And to Mrs. Thorn's to-morrow night?"

"No sir, I believe not."

"I believe you will," said he looking at her.

"I am sure I should enjoy myself more at home, uncle Orrin. There is very little rational pleasure to be had in these assemblages."

"Rational pleasure!" said he. "Didn't you have any rational pleasure last night?"

"I didn't hear a single word spoken, sir, that was worth listening to,—at least that was spoken to me; and the hollow kind of rattle that one hears from every tongue makes me more tired than anything else, I believe;—I am out of tune with it, somehow."

"Out of tune!" said the old doctor, giving her a look made up of humourous vexation and real sadness,—"I wish I knew the right tuning-key to take hold of you!"

"I become harmonious rapidly, uncle Orrin, when I am in this pleasant little room alone with you."

"That won't do!" said he, shaking his head at the smile with which this was said,—"there is too much tension upon the strings. So that was the reason you were all ready waiting for me last night?—Well, you must tune up, my little piece of discordance, and go with me to Mrs. Thorn's to-morrow night—I won't let you off."

"With you, sir!" said Fleda.

"Yes," he said. "I'll go along and take care of you lest you get drawn into something else you don't like."

"But, dear uncle Orrin, there is another difficulty—it is to be a large party and I have not a dress exactly fit."

"What have you got?" said he with a comic kind of fierceness.

"I have silks, but they are none of them proper for this occasion— they are ever so little old-fashioned."

"What do you want?"

"Nothing, sir," said Fleda; "for I don't want to go."

"You mend a pair of stockings to put on," said he nodding at her, "and I'll see to the rest."

"Apparently you place great importance in stockings," said Fleda laughing, "for you always mention them first. But please don't get anything for me, uncle Orrin—please don't! I have plenty for common occasions, and I don't care to go to Mrs. Thorn's."

"I don't care either," said the doctor, working himself into his great coat. "By the by, do you want to invoke the aid of St. Crispin?"

He went off, and Fleda did not know whether to cry or to laugh at the vigorous way in which he trod through the hall and slammed the front door after him. Her spirits just kept the medium and did neither. But they were in the same doubtful mood still an hour after when he came back with a paper parcel he had brought home under his arm, and unrolled a fine embroidered muslin; her eyes were very unsteady in carrying their brief messages of thankfulness, as if they feared saying too much. The doctor, however, was in the mood for doing, not talking, by looks or otherwise. Mrs. Pritchard was called into consultation, and with great pride and delight engaged to have the dress and all things else in due order by the following night; *her* eyes saying all manner of gratulatory things as they went from the muslin to Fleda and from Fleda to Dr. Gregory.

The rest of the day was, not books, but needlefuls of thread; and from the confusion of laces and draperies Fleda was almost glad to escape and go to the concert,—but for one item; that spoiled it.

They were in their seats early. Fleda managed successfully to place the two Evelyns between her and Mr. Thorn, and then prepared herself to wear out the evening with patience.

"My dear Fleda!" whispered Constance, after some time spent in restless reconnoitring of everybody and everything,—"I don't see my English rose anywhere!"

"Hush!" said Fleda smiling. "That happened not to be an English rose, Constance."

"What was it?"

"American, unfortunately; it was a Noisette; the variety I think that they call 'Conque de Venus.'"

"My dear little Fleda, you're too wise for anything!" said Constance with a rather significant arching of her eyebrows. "You mustn't expect other people to be as rural in their acquirements as yourself. I don't pretend to know any rose by sight but the Queechy," she said, with a change of expression meant to cover the former one.

Fleda's face, however, did not call for any apology. It was perfectly quiet.

"But what has become of him?" said Constance with her comic impatience.—"My dear Fleda! if my eyes cannot rest upon that development of elegance the parterre is become a wilderness to me!"

"Hush, Constance!" Fleda whispered earnestly,—"you are not safe—he may be near you."

"Safe!—" ejaculated Constance; but a half backward hasty glance of her eye brought home so strong an impression that the person in question was seated a little behind her that she dared not venture another look, and became straightway extremely well-behaved.

He was there; and being presently convinced that he was in the neighbourhood of his little friend of former days he resolved with his own excellent eyes to test the truth of the opinion he had formed as to the natural and inevitable effect of circumstances upon her character; whether it could by possibility have retained its great delicacy and refinement under the rough handling and unkindly bearing of things seemingly foreign to both. He had thought not.

Truffi did not sing, and the entertainment was of a very secondary quality. This seemed to give no uneasiness to the Miss Evelyns, for if they pouted they laughed and talked in the same breath, and that incessantly. It was nothing to Mr. Carleton, for his mind was bent on something else. And with a little surprise he saw that it was nothing to the subject of his thoughts,—either because her own were elsewhere too, or because they were in league with a nice taste that permitted them to take no interest in what was going on. Even her eyes, trained as they had been to recluse habits, were far less busy than those of her companions; indeed they were not busy at all; for the greater part of the time one hand was upon the brow, shielding them from the glare of the gas-lights. Ostensibly,—but the very quiet air of the face led him to guess that the mind was glad of a shield too. It relaxed sometimes. Constance and Florence and Mr. Thorn and Mr. Thorn's mother were every now and then making demands upon her, and they were met always with an intelligent well-bred eye, and often with a smile of equal gentleness and character; but her observer noticed that though the smile came readily, it went as readily, and the lines of the face quickly settled again into what seemed to be an habitual composure. There were the same outlines, the same characters, he remembered very well; yet there was a difference; not grief had changed them, but life had. The brow had all its fine chiselling and high purity of expression; but now there sat there a hopelessness, or rather a want of hopefulness, that a child's face never knows. The mouth was sweet and pliable as ever, but now often patience and endurance did not quit their seat upon the lip even when it smiled. The eye with all its old clearness and truthfulness had a shade upon it that nine years ago only fell at the bidding of sorrow; and in every line of the face there was a quiet gravity that went to the heart of the person who was studying it. Whatever causes had been at work he was very sure had done no harm to the character; its old simplicity had suffered no change, as every look and movement proved; the very unstudied careless position of the fingers over the eyes shewed that the thoughts had nothing to do there.

On one half of his doubt Mr. Carleton's mind was entirely made up;—but education? the training and storing of the mind?—how had that fared? He would know!—

Perhaps he would have made some attempt that very evening towards satisfying himself; but noticing that in coming out Thorn permitted the Evelyns to pass him and attached himself determinately to Fleda, he drew back, and resolved to make his observations indirectly and on more than one point before he should seem to make them at all.

CHAPTER XXXIII

Hark! I hear the sound of coaches,
The hour of attack approaches.

Gay.

Mrs. Pritchard had arrayed Fleda in the white muslin, with an amount of satisfaction and admiration that all the lines of her face were insufficient to express.

"Now," she said, "you must just run down and let the doctor see you—afore you take the shine off—or he won't be able to look at anything else when you get to the place."

"That would be unfortunate!" said Fleda, and she ran down laughing into the room where the doctor was waiting for her; but her astonished eyes encountering the figure of Dr. Quackenboss she stopped short, with an air that no woman of the world could have bettered. The physician of Queechy on his part was at least equally taken aback.

"Dr. Quackenboss!" said Fleda.

"I—I was going to say, Miss Ringgan!" said the doctor with a most unaffected obeisance,—"but—a—I am afraid, sir, it is a deceptive influence!"

"I hope not," said Dr. Gregory smiling, one corner of his mouth for his guest and the other for his niece. "Real enough to do real execution, or I am mistaken, sir."

"Upon my word, sir," said Dr. Quackenboss bowing again,—"I hope—a—Miss Ringgan!—will remember the acts of her executive power at home, and return in time to prevent an unfortunate termination!"

Dr. Gregory laughed heartily now, while Fleda's cheeks relieved her dress to admiration.

"Who will complain of her if she don't?" said the doctor. "Who will complain of her if she don't?"

But Fleda put in her question.

"How are you all at home, Dr. Quackenboss?"

"All Queechy, sir," answered the doctor politely, on the principle of 'first come, first served,'—"and individuals,—I shouldn't like to specify—"

"How are you all in Queechy, Dr. Quackenboss!" said Fleda.

"I—have the pleasure to say—we are coming along as usual," replied the doctor, who seemed to have lost his power of standing up straight;—"My sister Flora enjoys but poor health lately,—they are all holding their heads up at your house. Mr. Rossitur has come home."

"Uncle Rolf! Has he!" exclaimed Fleda, the colour of joy quite supplanting the other. "O I'm very glad!"

"Yes," said the doctor,—"he's been home now,—I guess, going on four days."

"I am very glad!" repeated Fleda. "But won't you come and see me another time, Dr. Quackenboss?—I am obliged to go out."

The doctor professed his great willingness, adding that he had only come down to the city to do two or three chores and thought she might perhaps like to take the opportunity—which would afford him such very great gratification.

"No indeed, faire Una," said Dr. Gregory, when they were on their way to Mrs. Thorn's,—"they've got your uncle at home now and we've got you; and I mean to keep you till I'm satisfied. So you may bring home that eye that has been squinting at Queechy ever since you have been here and make up your mind to enjoy yourself; I sha'n't let you go till you do."

"I ought to enjoy myself, uncle Orrin," said Fleda, squeezing his arm gratefully.

"See you do," said he.

The pleasant news from home had given Fleda's spirits the needed spur which the quick walk to Mrs. Thorn's did not take off.

"Did you ever see Fleda look so well, mamma?" said Florence, as the former entered the drawing-room.

"That is the loveliest and best face in the room," said Mr. Evelyn; "and she looks like herself to-night."

"There is a matchless simplicity about her," said a gentleman standing by.

"Her dress is becoming," said Mrs. Evelyn.

"Why where did you ever see her, Mr. Stackpole, except at our house?" said Constance.

"At Mrs. Decatur's—I have had that pleasure—and once at her uncle's."

"I didn't know you ever noticed ladies' faces, Mr. Stackpole," said Florence.

"How Mrs. Thorn does look at her!" said Constance, under her breath. "It is too much!"

It was almost too much for Fleda's equanimity, for the colour began to come.

"And there goes Mr. Carleton!" said Constance. "I expect momentarily to hear the company strike up 'Sparkling and Bright.'"

"They should have done that some time ago, Miss Constance," said the gentleman.

Which compliment, however, Constance received with hardly disguised scorn, and turned her attention again to Mr. Carleton.

"I trust I do not need presentation," said his voice and his smile at once, as he presented himself to Fleda.

How little he needed it the flash of feeling which met his eyes said sufficiently well. But apparently the feeling was a little too deep, for the colour mounted and the eyes fell, and the smile suddenly died on the lips. Mr. Thorn came up to them, and releasing her hand Mr. Carleton stepped back and permitted him to lead her away.

"What do think of *that* face?" said Constance finding herself a few minutes after at his side.

"'That' must define itself," said he, "or I can hardly give a safe answer."

"What face? Why I mean of course the one Mr. Thorn carried off just now."

"You are her friend, Miss Constance," he said coolly. "May I ask for your judgment upon it before I give mine?"

"Mine? why I expected every minute that Mr. Thorn would make the musicians play 'Sparkling and Bright,' and tell Miss Ringgan that to save trouble he had directed them to express what he was sure were the sentiments of the whole company in one burst."

He smiled a little, but in a way that Constance could not understand and did not like.

"Those are common epithets," he said.

"Must I use uncommon?" said Constance significantly.

"No—but these may say one thing or another."

"I have said one thing," said Constance; "and now you may say the other."

"Pardon me—you have said nothing. These epithets are deserved by a great many faces, but on very different grounds; and the praise is a different thing accordingly."

"Well what is the difference?" said Constance.

"On what do you think this lady's title to it rests?"

"On what?—why on that bewitching little air of the eyes and mouth, I suppose."

"Bewitching is a very vague term," said he smiling again more quietly. "But you have had an opportunity of knowing it much better of late than I—to which class of bright faces would you refer this one? Where does the light come from?"

"I never studied faces in a class," said Constance a little scornfully. "Come from?—a region of mist and clouds I should say, for it is sometimes pretty well covered up."

"There are some eyes whose sparkling is nothing more than the play of light upon a bright bead of glass."

"It is not that," said Constance, answering in spite of herself after delaying as long as she dared.

"There is the brightness that is only the reflection of outward circumstances, and passes away with them."

"It isn't that in Fleda Ringgan," said Constance, "for her outward circumstances have no brightness, I should think, that reflection would not utterly absorb."

She would fain have turned the conversation, but the questions were put so lightly and quietly that it could not be gracefully done. She longed to cut it short, but her hand was upon Mr. Carleton's arm and they were slowly sauntering down the rooms, — too pleasant a state of things to be relinquished for a trifle.

"There is the broad day-light of mere animal spirits," he went on, seeming rather to be suggesting these things for her consideration than eager to set forth any opinions of his own; — "there is the sparkling of mischief, and the fire of hidden passions, — there is the passing brilliance of wit, as satisfactory and resting as these gas-lights, — and there is now and then the light of refined affections out of a heart unspotted from the world, as pure and abiding as the stars, and like them throwing its soft ray especially upon the shadows of life."

"I have always understood," said Constance, "that cats' eyes are brightest in the dark."

"They do not love the light, I believe," said Mr. Carleton calmly.

"Well," said Constance, not relishing the expression of her companion's eye, which from glowing had suddenly become cool and bright, — "where would you put me, Mr. Carleton, among all these illuminators of the social system?"

"You may put yourself—where you please, Miss Constance," he said, again turning upon her an eye so deep and full in its meaning that her own and her humour fell before it; for a moment she looked most unlike the gay scene around her.

"Is not that the best brightness," he said speaking low, "that will last forever? — and is not that lightness of heart best worth having which does not depend on circumstances, and will find its perfection just when all other kinds of happiness fail utterly?"

"I can't conceive," said Constance presently, rallying or trying to rally herself, — "what you and I have to do in a place where people are enjoying themselves at this moment, Mr. Carleton!"

He smiled at that and led her out of it into the conservatory, close to which they found themselves. It was a large and fine one, terminating the suite of rooms in this direction. Few people were there; but at the far end stood a group among whom Fleda and Mr. Thorn were conspicuous. He was busying himself in putting together a quantity of flowers for her; and Mrs. Evelyn and old Mr. Thorn stood looking on; with Mr. Stackpole. Mr. Stackpole was an Englishman, of certainly not very prepossessing exterior but somewhat noted as an author and a good deal sought after in consequence. At present he was engaged by Mrs. Evelyn. Mr. Carleton and Constance sauntered up towards them and paused at a little distance to look at some curious plants.

"Don't try for that, Mr. Thorn," said Fleda, as the gentleman was making rather ticklish efforts to reach a superb Fuchsia that hung high, — "You are endangering sundry things besides yourself."

"I have learned, Miss Fleda," said Thorn as with much ado he grasped the beautiful cluster, — "that what we take the most pains for is apt to be reckoned the best prize, — a truth I should never think of putting into a lady's head if I believed it possible that a single one of them was ignorant of its practical value."

"I have this same rose in my garden at home," said Fleda.

"You are a great gardener, Miss Fleda, I hear," said the old gentleman. "My son says you are an adept in it."

"I am very fond of it, sir," said Fleda, answering *him* with an entirely different face.

"I thought the delicacy of American ladies was beyond such a masculine employment as gardening," said Mr. Stackpole, edging away from Mrs. Evelyn.

"I guess this young lady is an exception to the rule," said old Mr. Thorn.

"I guess she is an exception to most rules that you have got in your note-book, Mr. Stackpole," said the younger man. "But there is no guessing about the garden, for I have with my own eyes seen these gentle hands at one end of a spade and her foot at the other;—a sight that—I declare I don't know whether I was most filled with astonishment or admiration!"

"Yes," said Fleda half laughing and colouring,—"and he ingenuously confessed in his surprise that he didn't know whether politeness ought to oblige him to stop and shake hands or to pass by without seeing me; evidently shewing that he thought I was about something equivocal."

The laugh was now turned against Mr. Thorn, but he went on cutting his geraniums with a grave face.

"Well," said he at length, "I think it *is* something of very equivocal utility. Why should such gentle hands and feet spend their strength in clod-breaking, when rough ones are at command?"

There was nothing equivocal about Fleda's merriment this time.

"I have learned, Mr. Thorn, by sad experience, that the rough hands break more than the clods. One day I set Philetus to work among my flowers; and the first thing I knew he had pulled up a fine passion-flower which didn't make much shew above ground and was displaying it to me with the grave commentary, 'Well! that root did grow to a great haigth!'"

"Some mental clod-breaking to be done up there, isn't there?" said Thorn in a kind of aside. "I cannot express my admiration at the idea of your dealing with those boors, as it has been described to me."

"They do not deserve the name, Mr. Thorn," said Fleda. "They are many of them most sensible and excellent people, and friends that I value very highly."

"Ah, your goodness would made friends of everything."

"Not of boors, I hope," said Fleda coolly. "Besides, what do you mean by the name?"

"Anybody incapable of appreciating that of which you alone should be unconscious," he said softly.

Fleda stood impatiently tapping her flowers against her left hand.

"I doubt their power of appreciation reaches a point that would surprise you, sir."

"It does indeed—if I am mistaken in my supposition," he said with a glance which Fleda refused to acknowledge.

"What proportion do you suppose," she went on, "of all these roomfuls of people behind us,—without saying anything uncharitable,—what proportion of them, if compelled to amuse themselves for two hours at a bookcase, would pitch upon Macaulay's Essays, or anything like them, to spend the time?"

"Hum—really, Miss Fleda," said Thorn, "I should want to brush up my Algebra considerably before I could hope to find x, y, and z in such a confusion of the alphabet."

"Or extract the small sensible root of such a quantity of light matter," said Mr. Stackpole.

"Will you bear with my vindication of my country friends?—Hugh and I sent for a carpenter to make some new arrangement of shelves in a cupboard where we kept our books; he was one of these boors, Mr. Thorn, in no respect above the rest. The right stuff for his work was wanting, and while it was sent for he took up one of the volumes that were lying about and read perseveringly until the messenger returned. It was a volume of Macaulay's Miscellanies; and afterwards he borrowed the book of me."

"And you lent it to him?" said Constance.

"Most assuredly! and with a great deal of pleasure."

"And is this no more than a common instance, Miss Ringgan?" said Mr. Carleton.

"No, I think not," said Fleda; the quick blood in her cheeks again answering the familiar voice and old associations;—"I know several of the farmers' daughters around us that have studied Latin and Greek; and philosophy is a common thing; and I am sure there is more sense"—

She suddenly checked herself, and her eye which had been sparkling grew quiet.

"It is very absurd!" said Mr. Stackpole

"Why, sir?"

"O—these people have nothing to do with such things—do them nothing but harm!"

"May I ask again, what harm?" said Fleda gently.

"Unfit them for the duties of their station and make them discontented with it."

"By making it pleasanter?"

"No, no—not by making it pleasanter."

"By what then, Mr. Stackpole?" said Thorn, to draw him on and to draw her out, Fleda was sure.

"By lifting them out of it."

"And what objection to lifting them out of it?" said Thorn.

"You can't lift everybody out of it," said the gentleman with a little irritation in his manner,—"that station must be filled—there must always be poor people."

"And what degree of poverty ought to debar a man from the pleasures of education and a cultivated taste? such as he can attain?

"No, no, not that," said Mr. Stackpole;—"but it all goes to fill them with absurd notions about their place in society, inconsistent with proper subordination."

Fleda looked at him, but shook her head slightly and was silent.

"Things are in very different order on our side the water," said Mr. Stackpole hugging himself.

"Are they?" said Fleda.

"Yes—we understand how to keep things in their places a little better."

"I did not know," said Fleda quietly, "that it was by *design* of the rulers of England that so many of her lower class are in the intellectual condition of our slaves."

"Mr. Carleton," said Mrs. Evelyn laughing,—"what do you say to that, sir?"

Fleda's face turned suddenly to him with a quick look of apology, which she immediately knew was not needed.

"But this kind of thing don't make the people any happier," pursued Mr. Stackpole;—"only serves to give them uppish and dissatisfied longings that cannot be gratified."

"Somebody says," observed Thorn, "that 'under a despotism all are contented because none can get on, and in a republic none are contented because all can get on.'"

"Precisely," said Mr. Stackpole.

"That might do very well if the world were in a state of perfection," said Fleda. "As it is, commend me to discontent and getting on. And the uppishness I am afraid is a national fault, sir; you know our state motto is 'Excelsior.'"

"We are at liberty to suppose," said Thorn, "that Miss Ringgan has followed the example of her friends the farmers' daughters?—or led them in it?—"

"It is dangerous to make surmises," said Fleda colouring.

"It is a pleasant way of running into danger," said Mr. Thorn, who was leisurely pruning the prickles from the stem of a rose.

"I was talking to a gentleman once," said Fleda, "about the birds and flowers we find in our wilds; and he told me afterwards gravely that he was afraid I was studying too many things at once!—when I was innocent of all ornithology but what my eyes and ears had picked up in the woods; except some childish reminiscences of Audubon."

"That is just the right sort of learning for a lady," said Mr. Stackpole, smiling at her, however;—"women have nothing to do with books."

"What do you say to that, Miss Fleda?" said Thorn.

"Nothing, sir; it is one of those positions that are unanswerable."

"But Mr. Stackpole," said Mrs. Evelyn, "I don't like that doctrine, sir. I do not believe in it at all."

"That is unfortunate—for my doctrine," said the gentleman.

"But I do not believe it is yours. Why must women have nothing to do with books? what harm do they do, Mr. Stackpole?"

"Not needed, ma'am,—a woman, as somebody says, knows intuitively all that is really worth knowing."

"Of what use is a mine that is never worked?" said Mr. Carleton.

"It *is* worked," said Mr. Stackpole. "Domestic life is the true training for the female mind. One woman will learn more wisdom from the child on her breast than another will learn from ten thousand volumes."

"It is very doubtful how much wisdom the child will ever learn from her," said Mr. Carleton smiling.

"A woman who never saw a book," pursued Mr. Stackpole, unconsciously quoting his author, "may be infinitely superior, even in all those matters of which books treat, to the woman who has read, and read intelligently, a whole library."

"Unquestionably—and it is likewise beyond question that a silver sixpence may be worth more than a washed guinea."

"But a woman's true sphere is in her family—in her home duties, which furnish the best and most appropriate training for her faculties—pointed out by nature itself."

"Yes!" said Mr. Carleton,—"and for those duties, some of the very highest and noblest that are entrusted to human agency, the fine machinery that is to perform them should be wrought to its last point of perfectness. The wealth of a woman's mind, instead of lying in the rough, should be richly brought out and fashioned for its various ends, while yet those ends are in the future, or it will never meet the demand. And for her own happiness, all the more because her sphere is at home, her home stores should be exhaustless—the stores she cannot go abroad to seek. I would add to strength beauty, and to beauty grace, in the intellectual proportions, so far as possible. It were ungenerous, in man to condemn the *best* half of human intellect to insignificance merely because it is not his own."

Mrs. Evelyn wore a smile of admiration that nobody saw, but Fleda's face was a study while Mr. Carleton was saying this. Her look was fixed upon him with such intent satisfaction and eagerness that it was not till he had finished that she became aware that those dark eyes were going very deep into hers, and suddenly put a stop to the inquisition.

"Very pleasant doctrine to the ears that have an interest in it!" said Mr. Stackpole rather discontentedly.

"The man knows little of his own interest," said Mr. Carleton, "who would leave that ground waste, or would cultivate it only in the narrow spirit of a utilitarian. He needs an influence in his family not more refreshing than rectifying; and no man will seek that in one greatly his inferior. He is to be pitied who cannot fall back upon his home with the assurance that he has there something better than himself."

"Why, Mr. Carleton, sir—" said Mrs. Evelyn, with every line of her mouth saying funny things,—"I am afraid you have sadly neglected your own interest—have you anything at Carleton better than yourself?"

Suddenly cool again, he laughed and said, "You were there, Mrs. Evelyn."

"But Mr. Carleton,—" pursued the lady with a mixture of insinuation and fun,—"why were you never married?"

"Circumstances have always forbade it," he answered with a smile which Constance declared was the most fascinating thing she ever saw in her life.

Fleda was arranging her flowers, with the help of some very unnecessary suggestions from the donor.

"Mr. Lewis," said Constance with a kind of insinuation very different from her mother's, made up of fun and daring,—"Mr. Carleton has been giving me a long lecture on botany; while my attention was distracted by listening to your *spirituel* conversation."

"Well, Miss Constance?"

"And I am morally certain I sha'n't recollect a word of it if I don't carry away some specimens to refresh my memory—and in that case he would never give me another!"

It was impossible to help laughing at the distressful position of the young lady's eyebrows, and with at least some measure of outward grace Mr. Thorn set about complying with her request. Fleda again stood tapping her left hand with her flowers, wondering a little that somebody else did not come and speak to her; but he was talking to Mrs. Evelyn and Mr. Stackpole. Fleda did not wish to join them, and nothing better occurred to her than to arrange her flowers over again; so throwing them all down before her on a marble slab, she began to pick them up one by one and put them together, with it must be confessed a very indistinct realization of the difference between myrtle and lemon blossoms, and as she seemed to be laying acacia to rose, and disposing some sprigs of beautiful heath behind them, in reality she was laying kindness alongside of kindness and looking at the years beyond years where their place had been. It was with a little start that she suddenly found the person of her thoughts standing at her elbow and talking to her in bodily presence. But while he spoke with all the ease and simplicity of old times, almost making Fleda think it was but last week they had been strolling through the Place de la Concorde together, there was a constraint upon her that she could not get rid of and that bound eye and tongue. It might have worn off, but his attention was presently claimed again by Mrs. Evelyn; and Fleda thought best while yet Constance's bouquet was unfinished, to join another party and make her escape into the drawing-rooms.

Chapter XXXIV.

Have you observed a sitting hare,
List'ning, and fearful of the storm
Of horns and hounds, clap back her ear,
Afraid to keep or leave her form?

Prior.

By the Evelyns' own desire Fleda's going to them was delayed for a week, because, they said, a furnace was to be brought into the house and they would be all topsy-turvy till that fuss was over. Fleda kept herself very quiet in the mean time, seeing almost nobody but the person whom it was her especial object to shun. Do her best she could not quite escape him, and was even drawn into two or three walks and rides; in spite of denying herself utterly to gentlemen at home, and losing in consequence a visit from her old friend. She was glad at last to go to the Evelyns and see company again, hoping that Mr. Thorn would be merged in a crowd.

But she could not merge him; and sometimes was almost inclined to suspect that his constant prominence in the picture must be owing to some mysterious and wilful conjuration going on in the background. She was at a loss to conceive how else it happened that despite her utmost endeavours to the contrary she was so often thrown upon his care and obliged to take up with his company. It was very disagreeable. Mr. Carleton she saw almost as constantly, but though frequently near she had never much to do with him. There seemed to be a dividing atmosphere always in the way; and whenever he did speak to her she felt miserably constrained and unable to appear like herself. Why was it?—she asked herself in a very vexed state of mind. No doubt partly from the remembrance of that overheard conversation which she could not help applying, but much more from an indefinable sense that at these times there were always eyes upon her. She tried to charge the feeling upon her consciousness of their having heard that same talk, but it would not the more go off. And it had no chance to wear off, for somehow the occasions never lasted long; something was sure to break them up; while an unfortunate combination of circumstances, or of connivers, seemed to give Mr. Thorn unlimited facilities in the same kind. Fleda was quick witted and skilful enough to work herself out of them once in a while; more often the combination was too much for her simplicity and straight-forwardness.

She was a little disappointed and a little surprised at Mr. Carleton's coolness. He was quite equal to withstand or out-general the schemes of any set of manoeuvrers; therefore it was plain he did not care for the society of his little friend and companion of old time. Fleda felt it, especially as she now and then heard him in delightful talk with somebody else; making himself so interesting that when Fleda could get a chance to listen she was quite ready to forgive his not talking to her for the pleasure of hearing him talk at all. But at other times she said sorrowfully to herself, "He will be going home presently, and I shall not have seen him!"

One day she had successfully defended herself against taking a drive which Mr. Thorn came to propose, though the proposition had been laughingly backed by Mrs. Evelyn. Raillery was much harder to withstand than persuasion; but Fleda's quiet resolution had proved a match for both. The better to cover her ground, she declined to go out at all, and remained at home the only one of the family that fine day.

In the afternoon Mr. Carleton was there. Fleda sat a little apart from the rest, industriously bending over a complicated piece of embroidery belonging to Constance and in which that young lady had made a great blunder which she declared her patience unequal to the task of rectifying. The conversation went gayly forward among the others; Fleda taking no part in it beyond an involuntary one. Mr. Carleton's part was rather reserved and grave; according to his manner in ordinary society.

"What do you keep bothering yourself with that for?" said Edith coming to Fleda's side.

"One must be doing something, you know," said Fleda lightly.

"No you mustn't—not when you're tired—and I know you are. I'd let Constance pick out her own work."

"I promised her I would do it," said Fleda.

"Well, you didn't promise her when. Come!—everybody's been out but you, and you have sat here over this the whole day. Why don't you come over there and talk with the rest?—I know you want to, for I've watched your mouth going."

"Going!—how?"

"Going—off at the corners. I've seen it! Come."

But Fleda said she could listen and work at once, and would not budge. Edith stood looking at her a little while in a kind of admiring sympathy, and then went back to the group.

"Mr. Carleton," said the young lady, who was treading with laudable success in the steps of her sister Constance,—"what has become of that ride you promised to give me?"

"I do not know, Miss Edith," said Mr. Carleton smiling, "for my conscience never had the keeping of it."

"Hush, Edith!" said her mother; "do you think Mr. Carleton has nothing to do but to take you riding?"

"I don't believe he has much to do," said Edith securely. "But Mr. Carleton, you did promise, for I asked you and you said nothing; and I always have been told that silence gives consent; so what is to become of it?"

"Will you go now, Miss Edith?"

"Now?—O yes! And will you go out to Manhattanville, Mr. Carleton!—along by the river?"

"If you like. But Miss Edith, the carriage will hold another—cannot you persuade one of these ladies to go with us?"

"Fleda!" said Edith, springing off to her with extravagant capers of joy,—"Fleda, you shall go! you haven't been out to-day."

"And I cannot go out to-day," said Fleda gently.

"The air is very fine," said Mr. Carleton approaching her table, with no want of alacrity in step or tone, her ears knew;—"and this weather makes everything beautiful—has that piece of canvas any claims upon you that cannot be put aside for a little?"

"No sir," said Fleda,—"but—I am sorry I have a stronger reason that must keep me at home."

"She knows how the weather looks," said Edith,—"Mr. Thorn takes her out every other day. It's no use to talk to her, Mr. Carleton,—when she says she won't, she won't."

"Every other day!" said Fleda.

"No, no," said Mrs. Evelyn coming up, and with that smile which Fleda had never liked so little as at that minute,—"not *every other day*, Edith, what are you talking of? Go and don't keep Mr. Carleton waiting."

Fleda worked on, feeling a little aggrieved. Mr. Carleton stood still by her table, watching her, while his companions were getting themselves ready; but he said no more, and Fleda did not raise her head till the party were off. Florence had taken her resigned place.

"I dare say the weather will be quite as fine to-morrow, dear Fleda," said Mrs. Evelyn softly.

"I hope it will," said Fleda in a tone of resolute simplicity.

"I only hope it will not bring too great a throng of carriages to the door," Mrs. Evelyn went on in a tone of great internal amusement; — "I never used to mind it, but I have lately a nervous fear of collisions."

"To-morrow is not your reception-day," said Fleda.

"No, not mine," said Mrs. Evelyn softly, — "but that doesn't signify — it may be one of my neighbours'."

Fleda pulled away at her threads of worsted and wouldn't know anything else.

"I have read of the servants of Lot and the servants of Abraham quarrelling," Mrs. Evelyn went on in the same undertone of delight, — "because the land was too strait for them — I should be very sorry to have anything of the sort happen again, for I cannot imagine where Lot would go to find a plain that would suit him."

"Lot and Abraham, mamma!" said Constance from the sofa, — "what on earth are you talking about?"

"None of your business," said Mrs. Evelyn; — "I was talking of some country friends of mine that you don't know."

Constance knew her mother's laugh very well; but Mrs. Evelyn was impenetrable.

The next day Fleda ran away and spent a good part of the morning with her uncle in the library, looking over new books; among which she found herself quite a stranger, so many had made their appearance since the time when she had much to do with libraries or bookstores. Living friends, male and female, were happily forgotten in the delighted acquaintance-making with those quiet companions which, whatever their deficiencies in other respects, are at least never importunate nor unfaithful. Fleda had come home rather late and was dressing for dinner with Constance's company and help, when Mrs. Evelyn came into her room.

"My dear Fleda," said the lady, her face and voice as full as possible of fun,—"Mr. Carleton wants to know if you will ride with him this afternoon.—I told him I believed you were in general shy of gentlemen that drove their own horses—that I thought I had noticed you were,—but I would come up and see."

"Mrs. Evelyn!—you did not tell him that?"

"He said he was sorry to see you looked pale yesterday when he was asking you; and he was afraid that embroidery is not good for you. He thinks you are a very charming girl!—"

And Mrs. Evelyn went off into little fits of laughter which unstrung all Fleda's nerves. She stood absolutely trembling.

"Mamma!—don't plague her!" said Constance. "He didn't say so."

"He did!—upon my word!—" said Mrs. Evelyn, speaking with great difficulty;—"he said she was very charming, and it might be dangerous to see too much of her."

"You made him say that, Mrs. Evelyn!" said Fleda, reproachfully.

"Well I did ask him if you were not very charming, but he answered—without hesitation—" said the lady,—"I am only so afraid that Lot will make his appearance!—"

Fleda turned round to the glass, and went on arranging her hair, with a quivering lip.

"Lot, mamma!" said Constance somewhat indignantly.

"Yes," said Mrs. Evelyn in ecstacies,—"because the land will not bear both of them.—But Mr. Carleton is very much in earnest for his answer, Fleda my dear—what shall I tell him?—You need be under no apprehensions about going—he will perhaps tell you that you are charming, but I don't think he will say anything more. You know he is a kind of patriarch!—And when I asked him if he didn't think it might be dangerous to see too much of you, he said he thought it might to some people—so you see you are safe."

"Mrs. Evelyn, how could you use my name so!" said Fleda with a voice that carried a good deal of reproach.

"My dear Fleda, shall I tell him you will go?—You need not be afraid to go riding, only you must not let yourself be seen walking with him."

"I shall not go, ma'am," said Fleda quietly.

"I wanted to send Edith with you, thinking it would be pleasanter; but I knew Mr. Carleton's carriage would hold but two to-day. So what shall I tell him?"

"I am not going, ma'am," repeated Fleda.

"But what shall I tell him? I must give him some reason. Shall I say that you think a sea-breeze is blowing, and you don't like it?—or shall I say that prospects are a matter of indifference to you?"

Fleda was quite silent, and went on dressing herself with trembling fingers.

"My dear Fleda," said the lady bringing her face a little into order,— "won't you go?—I am very sorry—"

"So am I sorry," said Fleda. "I can't go, Mrs. Evelyn."

"I will tell Mr. Carleton you are very sorry," said Mrs. Evelyn, every line of her face drawing again,—"that will console him; and let him hope that you will not mind sea-breezes by and by, after you have been a little longer in the neighbourhood of them. I will tell him you are a good republican, and have an objection at present to an English equipage, but I have no doubt that it is a prejudice which will wear off."

She stopped to laugh, while Fleda had the greatest difficulty not to cry. The lady did not seem to see her disturbed brow; but recovering herself after a little, though not readily, she bent forward and touched her lips to it in kind fashion. Fleda did not look up; and saying again, "I will tell him, dear Fleda!"—Mrs. Evelyn left the room.

Constance after a little laughing and condoling, neither of which Fleda attempted to answer, ran off too, to dress herself; and Fleda after finishing her own toilette locked her door, sat down and cried heartily. She thought Mrs. Evelyn had been, perhaps unconsciously, very unkind; and to say that unkindness has not been meant is but to shift the charge from one to another vital point in the character of a friend, and one perhaps sometimes not less grave. A moment's passionate wrong may consist with the endurance of a friendship worth having, better than the thoughtlessness of obtuse wits that can never know how to be kind. Fleda's whole frame was still in a tremor from disagreeable excitement; and she had serious causes of sorrow to cry for. She was sorry she had lost what would have been a great pleasure in the ride,—and her great pleasures were not often,—but nothing would have been more impossible than for her to go after what Mrs. Evelyn had said;—she was sorry Mr. Carleton should have asked her twice in vain; what must he think?—she was exceeding sorry that a thought should have been put into her head that never before had visited the most distant dreams of her imagination,—so needlessly, so gratuitously;—she was very sorry, for she could not be free of it again, and she felt it would make her miserably hampered and constrained in mind and manner both, in any future intercourse with the person in question. And then again what would he think of that? Poor Fleda came to the conclusion that her best place was at home; and made up her mind to take the first good opportunity of getting there.

She went down to dinner with no traces of either tears or unkindness on her sweet face, but her nerves were quivering all the afternoon;

she could not tell whether Mrs. Evelyn and her daughters found it out. And it was impossible for her to get back even her old degree of freedom of manner before either Mr. Carleton or Mr Thorn. All the more because Mrs. Evelyn was every now and then bringing out some sly allusion which afforded herself intense delight and wrought Fleda to the last degree of quietness. Unkind.—Fleda thought now it was but half from ignorance of the mischief she was doing, and the other half from the mere desire of selfish gratification. The times and ways in which Lot and Abraham were walked into the conversation were incalculable,—and unintelligible except to the person who understood it only too well. On one occasion Mrs. Evelyn went on with a long rigmarole to Mr. Thorn about sea-breezes, with a face of most exquisite delight at his mystification and her own hidden fun; till Fleda was absolutely trembling. Fleda shunned both the gentlemen at length with a kind of nervous horror.

One steamer had left New York, and another, and still Mr. Carleton did not leave it. Why he staid, Constance was as much in a puzzle as ever, for no mortal could guess. Clearly, she said, he did not delight in New York society, for he honoured it as slightly and partially as might be, and it was equally clear if he had a particular reason for staying he didn't mean anybody should know it.

"If he don't mean it, you won't find it out, Constance," said Fleda.

"But it is that very consideration, you see, which inflames my impatience to a most dreadful degree. I think our house is distinguished with his regards, though I am sure I can't imagine why, for he never condescends to anything beyond general benevolence when he is here, and not always to that. He has no taste for embroidery, or Miss Ringgan's crewels would receive more of his notice—he listens to my spirited conversation with a self-possession which invariably deprives me of mine!—and his ear is evidently dull to musical sensibilities, or Florence's harp would have greater charms. I hope there is a web weaving somewhere that will catch him—at present he stands in an attitude of provoking independence of all the rest of the world. It is curious!" said Constance with an indescribable face,—"I feel that the independence of another is rapidly making a slave of me!—"

"What do you mean, Constance?" said Edith indignantly. But the others could do nothing but laugh.

Fleda did not wonder that Mr. Carleton made no more efforts to get her to ride, for the very next day after his last failure he had met her driving with Mr. Thorn. Fleda had been asked by Mr. Thorn's mother in such a way as made it impossible to get off; but it caused her to set a fresh seal of unkindness to Mrs. Evelyn's behaviour.

One evening when there was no other company at Mrs. Evelyn's, Mr. Stackpole was entertaining himself with a long dissertation upon the affairs of America, past, present, and future. It was a favourite subject; Mr. Stackpole always seemed to have more complacent enjoyment of his easy chair when he could succeed in making every American in the room sit uncomfortably. And this time, without any one to thwart him, he went on to his heart's content, disposing of the subject as one would strip a rose of its petals, with as much seeming nonchalance and ease, and with precisely the same design, to make a rose no rose. Leaf after leaf fell under Mr. Stackpole's touch, as if it had been a black frost. The American government was a rickety experiment; go to pieces presently,—American institutions an alternative between fallacy and absurdity, the fruit of raw minds and precocious theories;—American liberty a contradiction;— American character a compound of quackery and pretension;—American society (except at Mrs. Evelyn's) an anomaly;—American destiny the same with that of a Cactus or a volcano; a period of rest followed by a period of excitement; not however like the former making successive shoots towards perfection, but like the latter grounding every new face of things upon the demolition of that which went before. Smoothly and pleasantly Mr. Stackpole went on compounding this cup of entertainment for himself and his hearers, smacking his lips over it, and all the more, Fleda thought, when they made wry faces; throwing in a little truth, a good deal of fallacy, a great deal of perversion and misrepresentation; while Mrs. Evelyn listened and smiled, and half parried and half assented to his positions; and Fleda sat impatiently drumming upon her elbow with the fingers of her other hand, in the sheer necessity of giving some expression to her feelings. Mr. Stackpole at last got his finger upon the sore spot of American slavery, and pressed it hard.

"This is the land of the stars and the stripes!" said the gentleman in a little fit of virtuous indignation;—"This is the land where all are brothers!—where 'All men are born free and equal.'"

"Mr. Stackpole," said Fleda in a tone that called his attention,—"are you well acquainted with the popular proverbs of your country?"

"Not particularly," he said,—"he had never made it a branch of study."

"I am a great admirer of them."

He bowed, and begged to be excused for remarking that he didn't see the point yet.

"Do you remember this one, sir," said Fleda colouring a little,—"'Those that live in glass houses shouldn't throw stones?'"

"I have heard it; but pardon me,—though your remark seems to imply the contrary I am in the dark yet. What unfortunate points of vitrification have I laid open to your fire?"

"I thought they were probably forgotten by you, sir."

"I shall be exceedingly obliged to you if you will put me in condition to defend myself."

"I think nothing could do that, Mr. Stackpole. Under whose auspices and fostering care was this curse of slavery laid upon America?"

"Why—of course,—but you will observe, Miss Ringgan, that at that day the world was unenlightened on a great many points;—since then *we* have cast off the wrong which we then shared with the rest of mankind."

"Ay sir, but not until we had first repudiated it and Englishmen had desired to force it back upon us at the point of the sword. Four times" —

"But my dear Fleda," interrupted Mrs. Evelyn, "the English nation have no slaves nor slave-trade—they have put an end to slavery entirely everywhere under their flag."

"They were very slow about it," said Fleda. "Four times the government of Massachusetts abolished the slave-trade under their control, and four times the English government thrust it back upon them. Do you remember what Burke says about that?—in his speech on Conciliation with America?"

"It don't signify what Burke says about it," said Mr. Stackpole rubbing his chin,—"Burke is not the first authority—but Miss Ringgan, it is undeniable that slavery and the slave-trade, too, does at this moment exist in the interior of your own country."

"I will never excuse what is wrong, sir; but I think it becomes an Englishman to be very moderate in putting forth that charge."

"Why?" said he hastily;—"we have done away with it entirely in our own dominions;—wiped that stain clean off. Not a slave can touch British ground but he breathes free air from that minute."

"Yes, sir, but candour will allow that we are not in a condition in this country to decide the question by a *tour de force.*"

"What is to decide it then?" said he a little arrogantly.

"The progress of truth in public opinion."

"And why not the government—as well as our government?"

"It has not the power, you know, sir."

"Not the power! well, that speaks for itself."

"Nothing against us, on a fair construction," said Fleda patiently. "It is well known to those who understand the subject" —

"Where did you learn so much about it, Fleda?" said Mrs. Evelyn humourously.

"As the birds pick up their supplies, ma'am—here and there.—It is well known, Mr. Stackpole, that our constitution never could have been agreed upon if that question of slavery had not been by common consent left where it was—with the separate state governments."

"The separate state governments—well, why do not *they* put an end to it? The disgrace is only shifted."

"Of course they must first have the consent of the public mind of those states."

"Ah!—their consent!—and why is their consent wanting?"

"We cannot defend ourselves there," said Mrs. Evelyn;—"I wish we could."

"The disgrace at least is shifted from the whole to a part. But will you permit me," said Fleda, "to give another quotation from my despised authority, and remind you of an Englishman's testimony, that beyond a doubt that point of emancipation would never have been carried in parliament had the interests of even a part of the electors been concerned in it."

"It was done, however,—and done at the expense of twenty millions of money."

"And I am sure that was very noble," said Florence.

"It was what no nation but the English would ever have done," said Mrs. Evelyn.

"I do not wish to dispute it," said Fleda; "but still it was doing what did not touch the sensitive point of their own well-being."

"*We* think there is a little national honour concerned in it," said Mr. Stackpole dryly, stroking his chin again.

"So does every right-minded person," said Mrs. Evelyn; "I am sure I do."

"And I am sure so do I," said Fleda; "but I think the honour of a piece of generosity is considerably lessened by the fact that it is done at the expense of another."

"Generosity!" said Mr. Stackpole,—"it was not generosity, it was justice;—there was no generosity about it."

"Then it deserves no honour at all," said Fleda, "if it was merely that—the tardy execution of justice is but the removal of a reproach."

"We Englishmen are of opinion, however," said Mr. Stackpole contentedly, "that the removers of a reproach are entitled to some honour which those who persist in retaining it cannot claim."

"Yes," said Fleda, drawing rather a long breath,—"I acknowledge that; but I think that while some of these same Englishmen have shewn themselves so unwilling to have the condition of their own factory slaves ameliorated, they should be very gentle in speaking of wrongs which we have far less ability to rectify."

"Ah!—I like consistency," said Mr. Stackpole. "America shouldn't dress up poles with liberty caps till all who walk under are free to wear them. She cannot boast that the breath of her air and the breath of freedom are one."

"Can England?" said Fleda gently,—"when her own citizens are not free from the horrors of impressment?"

"Pshaw!" said Mr. Stackpole, half in a pet and half laughing,—"why, where did you get such a fury against England?—you are the first *fair* antagonist I have met on this side of the water."

"I wish I was a better one, sir," said Fleda laughing.

"Miss Ringgan has been prejudiced by an acquaintance with one or two unfortunate specimens," said Mrs. Evelyn.

"Ay!" said Mr. Stackpole a little bitterly,—"America is the natural birthplace of prejudice,—always was."

"Displayed, first, in maintaining the rights against the swords of Englishmen;—latterly, how, Mr. Stackpole?"

"It isn't necessary to enlighten *you* on any part of the subject," said he a little pointedly.

"Fleda, my dear, you are answered!" said Mrs. Evelyn, apparently with great internal amusement.

"Yet you will indulge me so far as to indicate what part of the subject you are upon?" said Fleda quietly.

"You must grant so much as that to so gentle a requisition, Mr. Stackpole," said the older lady.

"I venture to assume that you do not say that on your own account, Mrs. Evelyn?"

"Not at all—I agree with you, that Americans are prejudiced; but I think it will pass off, Mr. Stackpole, as they learn to know themselves and other countries better."

"But how do they deserve such a charge and such a defence? or how have they deserved it?" said Fleda.

"Tell her, Mr. Stackpole," said Mrs. Evelyn.

"Why," said Mr. Stackpole,—"in their absurd opposition to all the old and tried forms of things, and rancorous dislike of those who uphold them; and in their pertinacity on every point where they might be set right, and impatience of hearing the truth."

"Are they singular in that last item?" said Fleda.

"Now," said Mr. Stackpole, not heeding her,—"there's your treatment of the aborigines of this country—what do you call that, for a *free* people?"

"A powder magazine, communicating with a great one of your own somewhere else; so if you are a good subject, sir, you will not carry a lighted candle into it."

"One of our own—where?" said he.

"In India," said Fleda with a glance,—"and there are I don't know how many trains leading to it,—so better hands off, sir."

"Where did you pick up such a spite against us?" said Mr. Stackpole, drawing a little back and eying her as one would a belligerent mouse or cricket. "Will you tell me now that Americans are not prejudiced?"

"What do you call prejudice?" said Fleda smiling.

"O there is a great deal of it, no doubt, here, Mr. Stackpole," said Mrs. Evelyn blandly;—"but we shall grow out of it in time;—it is only the premature wisdom of a young people."

"And young people never like to hear their wisdom rebuked," said Mr Stackpole bowing.

"Fleda, my dear, what for is that little significant shake of your head?" said Mrs. Evelyn in her amused voice.

"A trifle, ma'am."

"Covers a hidden rebuke, Mrs. Evelyn, I have no doubt, for both our last remarks. What is it, Miss Fleda?—I dare say we can bear it."

"I was thinking, sir, that none would trouble themselves much about our foolscap if we had not once made them wear it."

"Mr. Stackpole, you are worsted!—I only wish Mr. Carleton had been here!" said Mrs. Evelyn, with a face of excessive delight.

"I wish he had," said Fleda, "for then I need not have spoken a word."

"Why," said Mr. Stackpole a little irritated, "you suppose he would have fought for you against me?"

"I suppose he would have fought for truth against anybody, sir," said Fleda.

"Even against his own interests?"

"If I am not mistaken in him," said Fleda, "he reckons his own and those of truth identical."

The shout that was raised at this by all the ladies of the family, made her look up in wonderment.

"Mr. Carleton,"—said Mrs. Evelyn,—"what do you say to that, sir."

The direction of the lady's eye made Fleda spring up and face about. The gentleman in question was standing quietly at the back of her chair, too quietly, she saw, to leave any doubt of his having been there some time. Mr. Stackpole uttered an ejaculation, but Fleda stood absolutely motionless, and nothing could be prettier than her colour.

"What do you say to what you have heard, Mr. Carleton?" said Mrs. Evelyn.

Fleda's eyes were on the floor, but she thoroughly appreciated the tone of the question.

"I hardly know whether I have listened with most pleasure or pain, Mrs. Evelyn."

"Pleasure!" said Constance.

"Pain!" said Mr. Stackpole.

"I am certain Miss Ringgan was pure from any intention of giving pain," said Mrs. Evelyn with her voice of contained fun. "She has no national antipathies, I am sure,—unless in the case of the Jews,—she is too charming a girl for that."

"Miss Ringgan cannot regret less than I a word that she has spoken," said Mr. Carleton looking keenly at her as she drew back and took a seat a little off from the rest.

"Then why was the pain?" said Mr. Stackpole.

"That there should have been any occasion for them, sir."

"Well I wasn't sensible of the occasion, so I didn't feel the pain," said Mr. Stackpole dryly, for the other gentleman's tone was almost haughtily significant. "But if I had, the pleasure of such sparkling eyes would have made me forget it. Good-evening, Mrs. Evelyn— good-evening, my gentle antagonist,—it seems to me you have learned, if it is permissible to alter one of your favorite proverbs, that it is possible to *break two windows* with one stone. However, I don't feel that I go away with any of mine shattered." —

"Fleda, my dear," said Mrs. Evelyn laughing,—"what do you say to that?"

"As he is not here I will say nothing to it, Mrs. Evelyn," said Fleda, quietly drawing off to the table with her work, and again in a tremor from head to foot.

"Why, didn't you see Mr. Carleton come in?" said Edith following her;—"I did—he came in long before you had done talking, and mamma held up her finger and made him stop; and he stood at the back of your chair the whole time listening. Mr. Stackpole didn't know he was there, either. But what's the matter with you?"

"Nothing—" said Fleda,—but she made her escape out of the room the next instant.

"Mamma," said Edith, "what ails Fleda?"

"I don't know, my love," said Mrs. Evelyn. "Nothing, I hope."

"There does, though," said Edith decidedly.

"Come here, Edith," said Constance, "and don't meddle with matters above your comprehension. Miss Ringgan has probably hurt her hand with throwing stones."

"Hurt her hand!" said Edith. But she was taken possession of by her eldest sister.

"That is a lovely girl, Mr. Carleton," said Mrs. Evelyn with an indescribable look—outwardly benign, but beneath that most keen in its scrutiny.

He bowed rather abstractedly.

"She will make a charming little farmer's wife, don't you think so?"

"Is that her lot, Mrs. Evelyn?" he said with a somewhat incredulous smile.

"Why no—not precisely,—" said the lady,—"you know in the country, or you do not know, the ministers are half farmers, but I suppose not more than half; just such a mixture as will suit Fleda, I should think. She has not told me in so many words, but it is easy to read so ingenuous a nature as hers, and I have discovered that there is a most deserving young friend of mine settled at Queechy that she is by no means indifferent to. I take it for granted that will be the end of it," said Mrs. Evelyn, pinching her sofa cushion in a great many successive places with a most composed and satisfied air.

But Mr. Carleton did not seem at all interested in the subject, and presently introduced another.

Chapter XXXV.

It is a hard matter for friends to meet; but mountains may be removed with earthquakes, and so encounter. — As You Like It.

"What have we to do to-night?" said Florence at breakfast the next morning.

"You have no engagement, have you?" said her mother.

"No mamma," said Constance arching her eyebrows, — "we are to taste the sweets of domestic life — you as head of the family will go to sleep in the dormeuse, and Florence and I shall take turns in yawning by your side."

"And what will Fleda do?" said Mrs. Evelyn laughing.

"Fleda, mamma, will be wrapped in remorseful recollections of having enacted a mob last evening and have enough occupation in considering how she shall repair damages."

"Fleda, my dear, she is very saucy," said Mrs. Evelyn, sipping her tea with great comfort.

"Why should we yawn to-night any more than last night?" said Fleda; a question which Edith would certainly have asked if she had not been away at school. The breakfast was too late for both her and her father.

"Last night, my dear, your fractious disposition kept us upon half breath; there wasn't time to yawn. I meant to have eased my breast by laughing afterwards, but that expectation was stifled."

"What stifled it?"

"I was afraid!—" said Constance with a little flutter of her person up and down in her chair.

"Afraid of what?"

"And besides you know we can't have our drawing-rooms filled with distinguished foreigners *every* evening we are not at home. I shall direct the fowling-piece to be severe in his execution of orders to-night and let nobody in. I forgot!"—exclaimed Constance with another flutter,—"it is Mr. Thorn's night!—My dearest mamma, will you consent to have the dormeuse wheeled round with its back to the fire?—and Florence and I will take the opportunity to hear little Edith's lessons in the next room—unless Mr Decatur comes. I must endeavour to make the Manton comprehend what he has to do."

"But what is to become of Mr. Evelyn?" said Fleda; "you make Mrs. Evelyn the head of the family very unceremoniously."

"Mr. Evelyn, my dear," said Constance gravely,—"makes a futile attempt semi-weekly to beat his brains out with a club; and every successive failure encourages him to try again; the only effect being a temporary decapitation of his family; and I believe this is the night on which he periodically turns a frigid eye upon their destitution."

"You are too absurd!" said Florence, reaching over for a sausage.

"Dear Constance!" said Fleda, half laughing, "why do you talk so?"

"Constance, behave yourself," said her mother.

"Mamma!" said the young lady,—"I am actuated by a benevolent desire to effect a diversion of Miss Ringgan's mind from its gloomy meditations, by presenting to her some more real subjects of distress."

"I wonder if you ever looked at such a thing," said Fleda.

"What 'such a thing'?"

"As a real subject of distress."

"Yes—I have one incessantly before me in your serious countenance. Why in the world, Fleda, don't you look like other people?"

"I suppose, because I don't feel like them."

"And why don't you? I am sure you ought to be as happy as most people."

"I think I am a great deal happier," said Fleda.

"Than I am?" said the young lady, with arched eyebrows. But they went down and her look softened in spite of herself at the eye and smile which answered her.

"I should be very glad, dear Constance, to know you were as happy as I."

"Why do you think I am not?" said the young lady a little tartly.

"Because no happiness would satisfy me that cannot last"

"And why can't it last?"

"It is not built upon lasting things."

"Pshaw!" said Constance, "I wouldn't have such a dismal kind of happiness as yours, Fleda, for anything."

"Dismal!" said Fleda smiling,—"because it can never disappoint me?—or because it isn't noisy?"

"My dear little Fleda!" said Constance in her usual manner,—"you have lived up there among the solitudes till you have got morbid ideas of life—which it makes me melancholy to observe. I am very much afraid they verge towards stagnation."

"No indeed!" said Fleda laughing; "but, if you please, with me the stream of life has flowed so quietly that I have looked quite to the bottom, and know how shallow it is, and growing shallower;—I could not venture my bark of happiness there; but with you it is like a spring torrent,—the foam and the roar hinder your looking deep into it."

Constance gave her a significant glance, a strong contrast to the earnest simplicity of Fleda's face, and presently inquired if she ever wrote poetry.

"Shall I have the pleasure some day of discovering your uncommon signature in the secular corner of some religious newspaper?"

"I hope not," said Fleda quietly.

Joe Manton just then brought in a bouquet for Miss Evelyn, a very common enlivener of the breakfast-table, all the more when, as in the present case, the sisters could not divine where it came from. It moved Fleda's wonder to see how very little the flowers were valued for their own sake; the probable cost, the probable giver, the probable éclat, were points enthusiastically discussed and thoroughly appreciated; but the sweet messengers themselves were carelessly set by for other eyes and seemed to have no attraction for those they were destined to. Fleda enjoyed them at a distance and could not help thinking that "Heaven sends almonds to those that have no teeth."

"This Camellia will just do for my hair to-morrow night!" said Florence;—"just what I want with my white muslin."

"I think I will go with you to-morrow, Florence," said Fleda;—"Mrs. Decatur has asked me so often."

"Well, my dear, I shall be made happy by your company," said Florence abstractedly, examining her bouquet,—"I am afraid it hasn't stem enough, Constance!—never mind—I'll fix it—where *is* the end of this myrtle?—I shall be very glad, of course, Fleda my dear, but—" picking her bouquet to pieces,—"I think it right to tell you, privately, I am afraid you will find it very stupid—"

"O I dare say she will not," said Mrs. Evelyn,—"she can go and try at any rate—she would find it very stupid with me here alone and Constance at the concert—I dare say she will find some there whom she knows."

"But the thing is, mamma, you see, at these conversaziones they never talk anything but French and German—I don't know—of *course* I should be delighted to have Fleda with me, and I have no doubt Mrs. Decatur would be very glad to have her—but I am afraid she won't enjoy herself."

"I do not want to go where I shall not enjoy myself," said Fleda quietly;—"that is certain."

"Of course, you know, dear, I would a great deal rather have you than not—I only speak for what I think would be for your pleasure."

"I would do just as I felt inclined, Fleda," said Mrs. Evelyn.

"I shall let her encounter the dullness alone, ma'am," said Fleda lightly.

But it was not in a light mood that she put on her bonnet after dinner and set out to pay a visit to her uncle at the library; she had resolved that she would not be near the dormeuse in whatsoever relative position that evening. Very, very quiet she was; her grave little face walked through the crowd of busy, bustling, anxious people, as if she had nothing in common with them; and Fleda felt that she had very little. Half unconsciously as she passed along the streets her eye scanned the countenances of that moving panorama; and the report it brought back made her draw closer within herself.

She wondered that her feet had ever tripped lightly up those library stairs.

"Ha! my fair Saxon," said the doctor;—"what has brought you down here to-day?"

"I felt in want of something fresh, uncle Orrin, so I thought I would come and see you."

"Fresh!" said he. "Ah you are pining for green fields, I know. But you little piece of simplicity, there are no green fields now at Queechy—they are two feet deep with snow by this time."

"Well I am sure *that* is fresh," said Fleda smiling.

The doctor was turning over great volumes one after another in a delightful confusion of business.

"When do you think you shall go north, uncle Orrin?"

"North?" said he—"what do you want to know about the north?"

"You said, you know, sir, that you would go a little out of your way to leave me at home."

"I won't go out of my way for anybody. If I leave you there, it will be in my way. Why you are not getting homesick?"

"No sir, not exactly,—but I think I will go with you when you go."

"That won't be yet awhile—I thought those people wanted you to stay till January."

"Ay, but suppose I want to do something else?"

He looked at her with a comical kind of indecision, and said,

"You don't know what you want!—I thought when you came in you needn't go further than the glass to see something fresh; but I believe the sea-breezes haven't had enough of you yet. Which part of you wants freshening?" he said in his mock-fierce way.

Fleda laughed and said she didn't know.

"Out of humour, I guess," said the doctor. "I'll talk to you!—Take this and amuse yourself awhile, with something that *isn't* fresh, till I get through, and then you shall go home with me."

Fleda carried the large volume into one of the reading rooms, where there was nobody, and sat down at the baize-covered table. But the book was not of the right kind—or her mood was notfor it failed to interest her. She sat nonchalantly turning over the leaves; but mentally she was busy turning over other leaves which had by far the most of her attention. The pages that memory read—the record of the old times passed in that very room, and the old childish light-hearted feelings that were, she thought, as much beyond recall. Those pleasant times, when the world was all bright and friends all fair, and the light heart had never been borne down by the pressure of care, nor sobered by disappointment, nor chilled by experience. The spirit will not spring elastic again from under that weight; and the flower that has closed upon its own sweetness will not open a second time to the world's breath. Thoughtfully, softly, she was touching and feeling of the bands that years had fastened about her heart—they would not be undone,—though so quietly and almost stealthily they had been bound there. She was remembering the shadows that one after another had been cast upon her life, till now one soft veil of a cloud covered the whole; no storm cloud certainly, but also there was nothing left of the glad sunlight that her young eyes rejoiced in. At Queechy the first shadow had fallen;—it was a good while before the next one, but then they came thick. There was the loss of some old comforts and advantages,—that could have been borne;—then consequent upon that, the annoyances and difficulties that had wrought such a change in her uncle, till Fleda could hardly look back and believe that he was the same person. Once manly, frank, busy, happy and making his family so;—now reserved, gloomy, irritable, unfaithful to his duty and selfishly throwing down the burden they must take up, but were far less able to bear. And so Hugh was changed too; not in loveliness of character and demeanour, nor even much in the always gentle and tender expression of countenance; but the animal spirits and frame, that should have had all the strong cherishing and bracing that affection and wisdom together could have applied, had been left to wear themselves out under trials his father had shrunk from and other trials his father had made. And Mrs. Rossitur,—it was hard for Fleda to remember the face she wore at Paris,—the bright eye and joyous corners of the mouth, that now were so utterly changed. All by his fault—that made it so hard to bear. Fleda had thought all this a hundred times; she went over it now as one looks at a thing one is well accustomed to; not with new sorrow, only in a subdued mood of mind just fit to make the most of it. The familiar place took her back to the time when it became familiar; she compared herself sitting there and feeling the whole world a blank, except for the two or three at home, with the child who had sat there years before in that happy time "when the feelings were young and the world was new."

Then the Evelyns—why should they trouble one so inoffensive and so easily troubled as her poor little self? They did not know all they were doing,—but if they had eyes they *must* see a little of it. Why could she not have been allowed to keep her old free simple feeling with everybody, instead of being hampered and constrained and miserable from this pertinacious putting of thoughts in her head that ought not to be there? It had made her unlike herself, she knew, in the company of several people. And perhaps *they* might be sharp-sighted enough to read it!—but even if not, how it had hindered her enjoyment. She had taken so much pleasure in the Evelyns last year, and in her visit,—well, she would go home and forget it, and maybe they would come to their right minds by the next time she saw them.

"What pleasant times we used to have here once, uncle Orrin!" she said with half a sigh, the other half quite made up by the tone in which she spoke. But it was not, as she thought, uncle Orrin that was standing by her side, and looking up as she finished speaking Fleda saw with a start that it was Mr. Carleton. There was such a degree of life and pleasantness in his eyes that, in spite of the start, her own quite brightened.

"That is a pleasure one may always command," he said, answering part of her speech.

"Ay, provided one has one's mind always under command," said Fleda. "It is possible to sit down to a feast with a want of appetite."

"In such a case, what is the best tonic?"

His manner, even in those two minutes, had put Fleda perfectly at her ease, ill-bred eyes and ears being absent. She looked up and answered, with such entire trust in him as made her forget that she had ever had any cause to distrust herself.

"For me," she said, — "as a general rule, nothing is better than to go out of doors—into the woods or the garden—they are the best fresheners I know of. I can do myself good there at times when books are a nuisance."

"You are not changed from your old self," he said.

The wish was strong upon Fleda to know whether *he* was, but it was not till she saw the answer in his face that she knew how plainly hers had asked the question. And then she was so confused that she did not know what the answer had been.

"I find it so too," he said. "The influences of pure nature are the best thing I know for some moods—after the company of a good horse."

"And you on his back, I suppose?"

"That was my meaning. What is the doubt thereupon?" said he laughing.

"Did I express any doubt?"

"Or my eyes were mistaken."

"I remember they never used to be that," said Fleda.

"What was it?"

"Why," said Fleda, thinking that Mr. Carleton had probably retained more than one of his old habits, for she was answering with her old obedience, — "I was doubting what the influence is in that case — worth analyzing, I think. I am afraid the good horse's company has little to do with it."

"What then do you suppose?" said he smiling.

"Why," said Fleda, — "it might be — but I beg your pardon, Mr. Carleton! I am astonished at my own presumption."

"Go on, and let me know why?" he said, with that happiness of manner which was never resisted. Fleda went on, reassuring her courage now and then with a glance.

"The relief *might* spring, sir, from the gratification of a proud feeling of independence, — or from a dignified sense of isolation, — or an imaginary riding down of opposition — or the consciousness of being master of what you have in hand."

She would have added to the general category, "the running away from oneself;" but the eye and bearing of the person before her forbade even such a thought as connected with him. He laughed, but shook his head.

"Perhaps then," said Fleda, "it may be nothing worse than the working off of a surplus of energy or impatience, that leaves behind no more than can be managed."

"You have learned something of human nature since I had the pleasure of knowing you," he said with a look at once amused and penetrating.

"I wish I hadn't," said Fleda.

Her countenance absolutely fell.

"I sometimes think," said he turning over the leaves of her book, "that these are the best companionship one can have—the world at large is very unsatisfactory."

"O how much!" said Fleda with a long breath. "The only pleasant thing that my eyes rested upon as I came through the streets this afternoon, was a huge bunch of violets that somebody was carrying. I walked behind them as long as I could."

"Is your old love for Queechy in full force?" said Mr. Carleton, still turning over the leaves, and smiling.

"I believe so—I should be very sorry to live here long—at home I can always go out and find society that refreshes me."

"You have set yourself a high standard," he said, with no displeased expression of the lips.

"I have been charged with that," said Fleda;—"but is it possible to set too high a standard, Mr. Carleton?"

"One may leave oneself almost alone in the world."

"Well, even then," said Fleda, "I would rather have only the image of excellence than be contented with inferiority."

"Isn't it possible to do both?" said he, smiling again.

"I don't know," said Fleda,—"perhaps I am too easily dissatisfied—I believe I have grown fastidious living alone—I have sometimes almost a disgust at the world and everything in it."

"I have often felt so," he said;—"but I am not sure that it is a mood to be indulged in—likely to further our own good or that of others."

"I am sure it is not," said Fleda;—"I often feel vexed with myself for it; but what can one do, Mr. Carleton?"

"Don't your friends the flowers help you in this?"

"Not a bit," said Fleda, —"they draw the other way; their society is so very pure and satisfying that one is all the less inclined to take up with the other."

She could not quite tell what to make of the smile with which he began to speak; it half abashed her.

"When I spoke a little while ago," said he, "of the best cure for an ill mood, I was speaking of secondary means simply—the only really humanizing, rectifying, peace-giving thing I ever tried was looking at time in the light of eternity, and shaming or melting my coldness away in the rays of the Sun of righteousness."

Fleda's eyes, which had fallen on her book, were raised again with such a flash of feeling that it quite prevented her seeing what was in his. But the feeling was a little too strong—the eyes went down, lower than ever, and the features shewed that the utmost efforts of self-command were needed to control them.

"There is no other cure," he went on in the same tone;—"but disgust and weariness and selfishness shrink away and hide themselves before a word or a look of the Redeemer of men. When we hear him say, 'I have bought thee—thou art mine,' it is like one of those old words of healing, 'Thou art loosed from thine infirmity,'—'Be thou clean,'—and the mind takes sweetly the grace and the command together, 'That he who loveth God love his brother also.'—Only the preparation of the gospel of peace can make our feet go softly over the roughness of the way."

Fleda did not move, unless her twinkling eyelashes might seem to contradict that.

"I need not tell you," Mr. Carleton went on a little lower, "where this medicine is to be sought."

"It is strange," said Fleda presently, "how well one may know and how well one may forget.—But I think the body has a great deal to do with it sometimes—these states of feeling, I mean."

"No doubt it has; and in these cases the cure is a more complicated matter. I should think the roses would be useful there?"

Fleda's mind was crossed by an indistinct vision of peas, asparagus, and sweet corn; she said nothing.

"An indirect remedy is sometimes the very best that can be employed. However it is always true that the more our eyes are fixed upon the source of light the less we notice the shadows that things we are passing fling across our way."

Fleda did not know how to talk for a little while; she was too happy. Whatever kept Mr. Carleton from talking, he was silent also. Perhaps it was the understanding of her mood.

"Mr. Carleton," said Fleda after a little time, "did you ever carry out that plan of a rose-garden that you were talking of a long while ago?"

"You remember it?" said he with a pleased look.—"Yes—that was one of the first things I set about after I went home—but I did not follow the regular fashion of arrangement that one of your friends is so fond of."

"I should not like that for anything," said Fleda,—"and least of all for roses."

"Do you remember the little shrubbery path that opened just in front of the library windows?—leading at the distance of half a mile to a long narrow winding glen?"

"Perfectly well!" said Fleda,—"through the wood of evergreens—I remember the glen very well."

"About half way from the house," said he smiling at her eyes, "a glade opens which merges at last in the head of the glen—I planted my roses there—the circumstances of the ground were very happy for disposing them according to my wish."

"And how far?"

"The roses?—O all the way, and some distance down the glen. Not a continuous thicket of them," he added smiling again,—"I wished each kind to stand so that its peculiar beauty should be fully relieved and appreciated; and that would have been lost in a crowd."

"Yes, I know it," said Fleda;—"one's eye rests upon the chief objects of attraction and the others are hardly seen,—they do not even serve as foils. And they must shew beautifully against that dark background of firs and larches!"

"Yes—and the windings of the ground gave me every sort of situation and exposure. I wanted room too for the different effects of masses of the same kind growing together and of fine individuals or groups standing alone where they could shew the full graceful development of their nature."

"What a pleasure!—What a beauty it must be!"

"The ground is very happy—many varieties of soil and exposure were needed for the plants of different habits, and I found or made them all. The rocky beginnings of the glen even furnished me with south walls for the little tea-roses, and the Macartneys and Musk roses,—the Banksias I kept nearer home."

"Do you know them all, Mr. Carleton?"

"Not quite," said he smiling at her.

"I have seen one Banksia—the Macartney is a name that tells me nothing."

"They are evergreens—with large white flowers—very abundant and late in the season, but they need the shelter of a wall with us."

"I should think you would say 'with *me*'," said Fleda. "I cannot conceive that the head-quarters of the Rose tribe should be anywhere else."

"One of the queens of the tribe is there, in the neighbourhood of the Macartneys—the difficult Rosa sulphurea—it finds itself so well accommodated that it condescends to play its part to perfection. Do you know that?"

"Not at all."

"It is one of the most beautiful of all, though not my favourite—it has large double yellow flowers shaped like the Provence—very superb, but as wilful as any queen of them all."

"Which is your favourite, Mr. Carleton?"

"Not that which shews itself most splendid to the eye, but which offers fairest indications to the fancy."

Fleda looked a little wistfully, for there was a smile rather of the eye than of the lips which said there was a hidden thought beneath.

"Don't you assign characters to your flowers?" said he gravely.

"Always!"

"That Rosa sulphurea is a haughty high-bred beauty that disdains even to shew herself beautiful unless she is pleased;—I love better what comes nearer home to the charities and wants of everyday life."

He had not answered her, Fleda knew; she thought of what he had said to Mrs. Evelyn about liking beauty but not *beauties*.

"Then," said he smiling again in that hidden way, "the head of the glen gave me the soil I needed for the Bourbons and French roses." —

"Bourbons?" — said Fleda.

"Those are exceeding fine — a hybrid between the Chinese and the Rose-à-quatre-saisons — I have not confined them all to the head of the glen; many of them are in richer soil, grafted on standards."

"I like standard roses," said Fleda, "better than any."

"Not better than climbers?"

"Better than any climbers I ever saw — except the Banksia."

"There is hardly a more elegant variety than that, though it is not strictly a climber; and indeed when I spoke I was thinking as much of the training roses. Many of the Noisettes are very fine. But I have the climbers all over — in some parts nothing else, where the wood closes in upon the path — there the evergreen roses or the Ayrshire cover the ground under the trees, or are trained up the trunks and allowed to find their own way through the branches down again — the Multiflora in the same manner. I have made the Boursault cover some unsightly rocks that were in my way. — Then in wider parts of the glade nearer home are your favourite standards — the Damask, and Provence, and Moss, which you know are varieties of the Centifolia, and the Noisette standards, some of them are very fine, and the Chinese roses, and countless hybrids and varieties of all these, with many Bourbons; — and your beautiful American yellow rose, and the Austrian briar and Eglantine, and the Scotch and white and Dog roses in their innumerable varieties change admirably well with the others, and relieve the eye very happily."

"Relieve the eye!" said Fleda, — "my imagination wants relieving! Isn't there — I have a fancy that there is — a view of the sea from some parts of that walk, Mr. Carleton?"

"Yes,—you have a good memory," said he smiling. "On one side the wood is rather dense, and in some parts of the other side; but elsewhere the trees are thinned off towards the south-west, and in one or two points the descent of the ground and some cutting have given free access to the air and free range to the eye, bounded only by the sea line in the distance—if indeed that can be said to bound anything."

"I haven't seen it since I was a child," said Fleda. "And for how long a time in the year is this literally a garden of roses, Mr. Carleton?"

"The perpetual roses are in bloom for eight months,—the Damask and the Chinese, and some of their varieties—the Provence roses are in blossom all the summer."

"Ah we can do nothing like that in this country," said Fleda shaking her head;—"our winters are unmanageable."

She was silent a minute, turning over the leaves of her book in an abstracted manner.

"You have struck out upon a grave path of reflection," said Mr. Carleton gently,—"and left me bewildered among the roses."

"I was thinking," said Fleda, looking up and laughing—"I was moralizing to myself upon the curious equalization of happiness in the world—I just sheered off from a feeling of envy, and comfortably reflected that one measures happiness by what one knows—not by what one does not know; and so that in all probability I have had near as much enjoyment in the little number of plants that I have brought up and cherished and know intimately, as you, sir, in your superb walk through fairyland."

"Do you suppose," said he laughing, "that I leave the whole care of fairyland to my gardener? No, you are mistaken—when the roses are to act as my correctors I find I must become theirs. I seldom go among them without a pruning knife and never without wishing for one. And you are certainly right so far,—that the plants on which I bestow most pains give me the most pleasure. There are some that no hand but mine ever touches, and those are by far the best loved of my eye."

A discussion followed, partly natural, partly moral, —on the manner of pruning various roses, and on the curious connection between care and complacency, and the philosophy of the same.

"The rules of the library are to shut up at sundown, sir," said one of the bookmen who had come into the room.

"Sundown!" exclaimed Fleda jumping up; —"is my uncle not here, Mr. Frost?"

"He has been gone half an hour, ma'am."

"And I was to have gone home with him —I have forgotten myself."

"If that is at all the fault of my roses,", said Mr. Carleton smiling, "I will do my best to repair it."

"I am not disposed to call it a fault," said Fleda tying her bonnet-strings, —"it is rather an agreeable thing once in a while. I shall dream of those roses, Mr. Carleton!"

"That would be doing them too much honour."

Very happily she had forgotten herself; and during all the walk home her mind was too full of one great piece of joy and indeed too much engaged with conversation to take up her own subject again. Her only wish was that they might not meet any of the Evelyns; — Mr. Thorn, whom they did meet, was a matter of entire indifference.

The door was opened by Dr. Gregory himself. To Fleda's utter astonishment Mr. Carleton accepted his invitation to come in. She went up stairs to take off her things in a kind of maze.

"I thought he would go away without my seeing him, and now what a nice time I have had!—in spite of Mrs. Evelyn—"

That thought slipped in without Fleda's knowledge, but she could not get it out again.

"I don't know how much it has been her fault either, but one thing is certain—I never could have had it at her house.—How very glad I am!—How *very* glad I am!—that I have seen him and heard all this from his own lips.—But how very funny that he will be here to tea"

"Well!" said the doctor when she came down,—"you *do* look freshened up, I declare. Here is this girl, sir, was coming to me a little while ago, complaining that she wanted something *fresh*, and begging me to take her back to Queechy, forsooth, to find it, with two feet of snow on the ground. Who wants to see you at Queechy?" he said, facing round upon her with a look half fierce, half quizzical.

Fleda laughed, but was vexed to feel that she could not help colouring and colouring exceedingly; partly from the consciousness of his meaning, and partly from a vague notion that somebody else was conscious of it too. Dr. Gregory, however, dashed right off into the thick of conversation with his guest, and kept him busily engaged till tea-time. Fleda sat still on the sofa, looking and listening with simple pleasure; memory served her up a rich entertainment enough. Yet she thought her uncle was the most heartily interested of the two in the conversation; there was a shade more upon Mr. Carleton, not than he often wore, but than he had worn a little while ago. Dr. Gregory was a great bibliopole, and in the course of the hour hauled out and made his guest overhaul no less than several musty old folios; and Fleda could not help fancying that he did it with an access of gravity greater even than the occasion called for. The grace of his manner, however, was unaltered; and at tea she did not know whether she had been right or not. Demurely as she sat there behind the tea-urn, for Dr. Gregory still engrossed all the attention of his guest as far as talking was concerned, Fleda was again inwardly smiling to herself at the oddity and the pleasantness of the chance that had brought those three together in such a quiet way, after all the weeks she had been seeing Mr. Carleton at a distance. And she enjoyed the conversation too; for though Dr. Gregory was a little fond of his hobby it was still conversation worthy the name.

"I have been so unfortunate in the matter of the drives," Mr. Carleton said, when he was about to take leave and standing before Fleda,—"that I am half afraid to mention it again."

"I could not help it, both those time, Mr. Carleton," said Fleda earnestly.

"Both the last?—or both the first?" said he smiling.

"The last?—" said Fleda.

"I have had the honour of making such an attempt twice within the last ten days——to my disappointment."

"It was not by my fault then either, sir," Fleda said quietly.

But he knew very well from the expression of her face a moment before where to put the emphasis her tongue would not make.

"Dare I ask you to go with me to-morrow?"

"I don't know," said Fleda with the old childish sparkle of her eye,— "but if you ask me, sir, I will go."

He sat down beside her immediately, and Fleda knew by his change of eye that her former thought had been right.

"Shall I see you at Mrs. Decatur's to-morrow?"

"No, sir."

"I thought I understood," said he in an explanatory tone, "from your friends the Miss Evelyns, that they were going."

"I believe they are, and I did think of it; but I have changed my mind, and shall stay at home with Mrs. Evelyn."

After some further conversation the hour for the drive was appointed, and Mr. Carleton took leave.

"Come for me twice and Mrs. Evelyn refused without consulting me!" thought Fleda. "What could make her do so?—How very rude he must have thought me! And how glad I am I have had an opportunity of setting that right."

So quitting Mrs. Evelyn her thoughts went off upon a long train of wandering over the afternoon's talk.

"Wake up!" said the doctor, laying his hand kindly upon her shoulder,—"you'll want something fresh again presently. What mine of profundity are you digging into now?"

Fleda looked up and came back from her profundity with a glance and smile as simple as a child's.

"Dear uncle Orrin, how came you to leave me alone in the library?"

"Was that what you were trying to discover?"

"Oh no, sir! But why did you, uncle Orrin? I might have been left utterly alone."

"Why," said the doctor, "I was going out, and a friend that I thought I could confide in promised to take care of you."

"A friend!—Nobody came near me," said Fleda.

"Then I'll never trust anybody again," said the doctor. "But what were you hammering at, mentally, just now?—come, you shall tell me."

"O nothing, uncle Orrin," said Fleda, looking grave again however;—"I was thinking that I had been talking too much to-day."

"Talking too much?—why whom have you been talking to?"

"O, nobody but Mr. Carleton."

"Mr. Carleton! why you didn't say six and a quarter words while he was here."

"No, but I mean in the library, and walking home."

"Talking too much! I guess you did," said the doctor;—"your tongue is like

'the music of the spheres, So loud it deafens human ears.'

How came you to talk too much? I thought you were too shy to talk at all in company."

"No sir, I am not;—I am not at all shy unless people frighten me. It takes almost nothing to do that; but I am very bold if I am not frightened."

"Were you frightened this afternoon?"

"No sir."

"Well, if you weren't frightened, I guess nobody else was," said the doctor.

CHAPTER XXXVI.

Whence came this?
This is some token from a newer friend.
Shakspeare.

The snow-flakes were falling softly and thick when Fleda got up the next morning.

"No ride for me to-day—but how very glad I am that I had a chance of setting that matter right. What could Mrs. Evelyn have been thinking of?—Very false kindness!—if I had disliked to go ever so much she ought to have made me, for my own sake, rather than let me seem so rude—it is true she didn't know *how* rude. O snow-flakes—how much purer and prettier you are than most things in this place!"

No one was in the breakfast parlour when Fleda came down, so she took her book and the dormeuse and had an hour of luxurious quiet before anybody appeared. Not a foot-fall in the house; nor even one outside to be heard, for the soft carpeting of snow which was laid over the streets. The gentle breathing of the fire the only sound in the room; while the very light came subdued through the falling snow and the thin muslin curtains, and gave an air of softer luxury to the apartment. "Money is pleasant," thought Fleda, as she took a little complacent review of all this before opening her book.—"And yet how unspeakably happier one may be without it than another with it. Happiness never was locked up in a purse yet. I am sure Hugh and I,—They must want me at home!—"

There was a little sober consideration of the lumps of coal and the contented looking blaze in the grate, a most essentially home-like thing,—and then Fleda went to her book and for the space of an hour turned over her pages without interruption. At the end of the hour "the fowling piece," certainly the noisiest of his kind, put his head in, but seeing none of his ladies took it and himself away again and left Fleda in peace for another half hour. Then appeared Mrs. Evelyn in her morning wrapper, and only stopping at the bell-handle, came up to the dormeuse and stooping down kissed Fleda's forehead, with so much tenderness that it won a look of most affectionate gratitude in reply.

"Fleda my dear, we set you a sad example. But you won't copy it. Joe, breakfast. Has Mr. Evelyn gone down town?"

"Yes, ma'am, two hours ago."

"Did it ever occur to you, Fleda my dear," said Mrs. Evelyn, breaking the lumps of coal with the poker in a very leisurely satisfied kind of a way, — "Did it ever occur to you to rejoice that you were not born a business man? What a life! — "

"I wonder how it compares with that of a business woman," said Fleda laughing. "There is an uncompromising old proverb which says

'Man's work is from sun to sun— But a woman's work is never done.'"

A saying which she instantly reflected was entirely beyond the comprehension of the person to whose consideration she had offered it.

And then came in Florence, rubbing her hands and knitting her eyebrows.

"Why don't you look as bright as the rest of the world, this morning," said Fleda.

"What a wretched storm!"

"Wretched! This beautiful snow! Here have I been enjoying it for this hour."

But Florence rubbed her hands and looked as if Fleda were no rule for other people.

"How horrid it will make the going out to-night, if it snows all day!"

"Then you can stay at home," said her mother composedly.

"Indeed I shall not, mamma!"

"Mamma!" said Constance now coming in with Edith,—"isn't breakfast ready? It strikes me that the fowling-piece wants polishing up. I have an indistinct impression that the sun would be upon the meridian if he was anywhere."

"Not quite so bad as that," said Fleda smiling;—"it is only an hour and a half since I came down stairs."

"You horrid little creature!—Mamma, I consider it an act of inhospitality to permit studious habits on the part of your guests. And I am surprised your ordinary sagacity has not discovered that it is the greatest impolicy towards the objects of your maternal care. We are labouring under growing disadvantages; for when we have brought the enemy to at long shot there is a mean little craft that comes in and unmans him in a close fight before we can get our speaking-trumpets up."

"Constance!—Do hush!" said her sister. "You are too absurd."

"Fact," said Constance gravely. "Capt. Lewiston was telling me the other night how the thing is managed; and I recognized it immediately and told him I had often seen it done!"

"Hold your tongue, Constance," said her mother smiling,—"and come to breakfast."

Half and but half of the mandate the young lady had any idea of obeying.

"I can't imagine what you are talking about, Constance!" said Edith.

"And then being a friend, you see," pursued Constance, "we can do nothing but fire a salute, instead of demolishing her."

"Can't you?" said Fleda. "I am sure many a time I have felt as if you had left me nothing but my colours."

"Except your prizes, my dear. I am sure I don't know about your being a friend either, for I have observed that you engage English and American alike."

"She is getting up her colours now," said Mrs. Evelyn in mock gravity, —"you can tell what she is."

"Blood-red!" said Constance. "A pirate!—I thought so,"—she exclaimed, with an ecstatic gesture. "I shall make it my business to warn everybody!"

"Oh Constance!" said Fleda, burying her face in her hands. But they all laughed.

"Fleda my dear, I would box her ears," said Mrs. Evelyn commanding herself. "It is a mere envious insinuation,—I have always understood those were the most successful colours carried."

"Dear Mrs. Evelyn!—"

"My dear Fleda, that is not a hot roll—you sha'n't eat it—Take this. Florence give her a piece of the bacon—Fleda my dear, it is good for the digestion—you must try it. Constance was quite mistaken in supposing yours were those obnoxious colours—there is too much white with the red—it is more like a very different flag."

"Like what then, mamma?" said Constance;—"a good American would have blue in it."

"You may keep the American yourself," said her mother.

"Only," said Fleda trying to recover herself, "there is a slight irregularity—with you the stars are blue and the ground white."

"My dear little Fleda!" exclaimed Constance jumping up and capering round the table to kiss her, "you are too delicious for anything; and in future I will be blind to your colours; which is a piece of self-denial I am sure nobody else will practise."

"Mamma," said Edith, "what *are* you all talking about? Can't Constance sit down and let Fleda eat her breakfast?"

"Sit down, Constance, and eat your breakfast!"

"I will do it, mamma, out of consideration for the bacon.—Nothing else would move me."

"Are you going to Mrs. Decatur's to-night, Fleda?"

"No, Edith, I believe not"

"I'm very glad; then there'll be somebody at home. But why don't you?"

"I think on the whole I had rather not."

"Mamma," said Constance, "you have done very wrong in permitting such a thing. I know just how it will be. Mr. Thorn and Mr. Stackpole will make indefinite voyages of discovery round Mrs. Decatur's rooms, and then having a glimmering perception that the light of Miss Ringgan's eyes is in another direction they will sheer off; and you will presently see them come sailing blandly in, one after the other, and cast anchor for the evening; when to your extreme delight Mr. Stackpole and Miss Ringgan will immediately commence fighting. I shall stay at home to see!" exclaimed Constance, with little bounds of delight up and down upon her chair which this time afforded her the additional elasticity of springs,—"I will not go. I am persuaded how it will be, and I would not miss it for anything."

"Dear Constance!" said Fleda, unable to help laughing through all her vexation,—"please do not talk so! You know very well Mr. Stackpole only comes to see your mother."

"He was here last night," said Constance in an extreme state of delight,—"with all the rest of your admirers—ranged in the hall, with their hats in a pile at the foot of the staircase as a token of their determination not to go till you came home; and as they could not be induced to come up to the drawing-room Mr. Evelyn was obliged to go down, and with some difficulty persuaded them to disperse."

Fleda was by this time in a state of indecision betwixt crying and laughing, assiduously attentive to her breakfast.

"Mr. Carleton asked me if you would go to ride with him again the other day, Fleda," said Mrs. Evelyn, with her face of delighted mischief,—"and I excused you; for I thought you would thank me for it."

"Mamma," said Constance, "the mention of that name rouses all the bitter feelings I am capable of! My dear Fleda—we have been friends—but if I see you abstracting my English rose"—

"Look at those roses behind you!" said Fleda.

The young lady turned and sprang at the word, followed by both her sisters; and for some moments nothing but a hubbub of exclamations filled the air,

"Joe, you are enchanting!—But did you ever *see* such flowers?—Oh those rose-buds!—"

"And these Camellias," said Edith,—"look, Florence, how they are cut—with such splendid long stems."

"And the roses too—all of them—see mamma, just cut from the bushes with the buds all left on, and immensely long stems—Mamma, these must have cost an immensity!—"

"That is what I call a bouquet," said Fleda, fain to leave the table too and draw near the tempting shew in Florence's hand.

"This is the handsomest you have had all winter, Florence," said Edith.

"Handsomest!—I never saw anything like it. I shall wear some of these to-night, mamma."

"You are in a great hurry to appropriate it," said Constance,—"how do you know but it is mine?"

"Which of us is it for, Joe?"

"Say it is mine, Joe, and I will vote you—the best article of your kind!" said Constance, with an inexpressible glance at Fleda.

"Who brought it, Joe?" said Mrs. Evelyn.

"Yes, Joe, who brought it? where did it come from, Joe?"

Joe had hardly a chance to answer.

"I really couldn't say, Miss Florence,—the man wasn't known to me."

"But did he say it was for Florence or for me?"

"No ma'am—he"—

"*Which* did he say it was for?"

"He didn't say it was either for Miss Florence or for you, Miss Constance; he—"

"But didn't he say who sent it?"

"No ma'am. It's"—

"Mamma here is a white moss that is beyond everything! with two of the most lovely buds—Oh!" said Constance clasping her hands and whirling about the room in comic ecstasy—"I sha'n't survive if I cannot find out where it is from!—"

"How delicious the scent of these tea-roses is!" said Fleda. "You ought not to mind the snow storm to-day after this, Florence. I should think you would be perfectly happy."

"I shall be, if I can contrive to keep them fresh to wear to-night. Mamma how sweetly they would dress me."

"They're a great deal too good to be wasted so," said Mrs. Evelyn; "I sha'n't let you do it."

"Mamma!—it wouldn't take any of them at all for my hair and the bouquet de corsage too—there'd be thousands left—Well Joe,—what are you waiting for?"

"I didn't say," said Joe, looking a good deal blank and a little afraid,—"I should have said—that the bouquet—is—"

"What is it?"

"It is—I believe, ma'am,—the man said it was for Miss Ringgan."

"For me!" exclaimed Fleda, her cheeks forming instantly the most exquisite commentary on the gift that the giver could have desired. She took in her hand the superb bunch of flowers from which the fingers of Florence unclosed as if it had been an icicle.

"Why didn't you say so before?" she inquired sharply; but the "fowling-piece" had wisely disappeared.

"I am very glad!" exclaimed Edith. "They have had plenty all winter, and you haven't had one—I am very glad it is yours, Fleda."

But such a shadow had come upon every other face that Fleda's pleasure was completely overclouded. She smelled at her roses, just ready to burst into tears, and wishing sincerely that they had never come.

"I am afraid, my dear Fleda," said Mrs. Evelyn quietly going on with her breakfast,—"that there is a thorn somewhere among those flowers."

Fleda was too sure of it. But not by any means the one Mrs. Evelyn intended.

"He never could have got half those from his own greenhouse, mamma," said Florence,—"if he had cut every rose that was in it; and he isn't very free with his knife either."

"I said nothing about anybody's greenhouse," said Mrs. Evelyn,— "though I don't suppose there is more than one Lot in the city they could have come from."

"Well," said Constance settling herself back in her chair and closing her eyes,—"I feel extinguished!——Mamma, do you suppose it possible that a hot cup of tea might revive me? I am suffering from a universal sense of unappreciated merit!—and nobody can tell what the pain is that hasn't felt it."

"I think you are extremely foolish, Constance," said Edith. "Fleda hasn't had a single flower sent her since she has been here and you have had them every other day. I think Florence is the only one that has a right to be disappointed."

"Dear Florence," said Fleda earnestly,—"you shall have as many of them as you please to dress yourself,—and welcome!"

"Oh no—of course not!—" Florence said,—"it's of no sort of consequence—I don't want them in the least, my dear. I wonder what somebody would think to see his flowers in my head!"

Fleda secretly had mooted the same question and was very well pleased not to have it put to the proof. She took the flowers up stairs after breakfast, resolving that they should not be an eye-sore to her friends; placed them in water and sat down to enjoy and muse over them in a very sorrowful mood. She again thought she would take the first opportunity of going home. How strange—out of their abundance of tributary flowers to grudge her this one bunch! To be sure it was a magnificent one. The flowers were mostly roses, of the rarer kinds, with a very few fine Camellias; all of them cut with a freedom that evidently had known no constraint but that of taste, and put together with an exquisite skill that Fleda felt sure was never possessed by any gardener. She knew that only one hand had had anything to do with them, and that the hand that had bought, not the one that had sold; and "How very kind!"—presently quite supplanted "How very strange!"—"How exactly like him,—and how singular that Mrs. Evelyn and her daughters should have supposed they could have come from Mr. Thorn." It was a moral impossibility that *he* should have put such a bunch of flowers together; while to Fleda's eye they so bore the impress of another person's character that she had absolutely been glad to get them out of sight for fear they might betray him. She hung over their varied loveliness, tasted and studied it, till the soft breath of the roses had wafted away every cloud of disagreeable feeling and she was drinking in pure and strong pleasure from each leaf and bud. What a very apt emblem of kindness and friendship she thought them; when their gentle preaching and silent sympathy could alone so nearly do friendship's work; for to Fleda there was both counsel and consolation in flowers. So she found it this morning. An hour's talk with them had done her a great deal of good, and when she dressed herself and went down to the drawing-room her grave little face was not less placid than the roses she had left; she would not wear even one of them down to be a disagreeable reminder. And she thought that still snowy day was one of the very pleasantest she had had in New York.

Florence went to Mrs. Decatur's; but Constance according to her avowed determination remained at home to see the fun. Fleda hoped most sincerely there would be none for her to see.

But a good deal to her astonishment, early in the evening Mr. Carleton walked in, followed very soon by Mr. Thorn. Constance and Mrs. Evelyn were forthwith in a perfect effervescence of delight, which as they could not very well give it full play promised to last the evening; and Fleda, all her nervous trembling awakened again, took her work to the table and endeavoured to bury herself in it. But ears could not be fastened as well as eyes; and the mere sound of Mrs. Evelyn's voice sometimes sent a thrill over her.

"Mr. Thorn," said the lady in her smoothest manner,—"are you a lover of floriculture, sir?"

"Can't say that I am, Mrs. Evelyn,—except as practised by others."

"Then you are not a connoisseur in roses?—Miss Ringgan's happy lot—sent her a most exquisite collection this morning, and she has been wanting to apply to somebody who could tell her what they are—I thought you might know.—O they are not here," said Mrs. Evelyn as she noticed the gentleman's look round the room;—"Miss Ringgan judges them too precious for any eyes but her own. Fleda, my dear, won't you bring down your roses to let Mr. Thorn tell us their names?"

"I am sure Mr. Thorn will excuse me, Mrs. Evelyn—I believe he would find it a puzzling task."

"The surest way, Mrs. Evelyn, would be to apply at the fountain head for information," said Thorn dryly.

"If I could get at it," said Mrs. Evelyn, (Fleda knew with quivering lips,)—"but it seems to me I might as well try to find the Dead Sea!"

"Perhaps Mr. Carleton might serve your purpose," said Thorn.

That gentleman was at the moment talking to Constance.

"Mr. Carleton—" said Mrs. Evelyn,—"are you a judge, sir?"

"Of what, Mrs. Evelyn?—I beg your pardon."

The lady's tone somewhat lowered.

"Are you a judge of roses, Mr. Carleton?"

"So far as to know a rose when I see it," he answered smiling, and with an imperturbable coolness that it quieted Fleda to hear.

"Ay, but the thing is," said Constance, "do you know twenty roses when you see them?"

"Miss Ringgan, Mr. Carleton," said Mrs. Evelyn, "has received a most beautiful supply this morning; but like a true woman she is not satisfied to enjoy unless she can enjoy intelligently—they are strangers to us all, and she would like to know what name to give them—Mr. Thorn suggested that perhaps you might help us out of our difficulty."

"With great pleasure, so far as I am able,—if my judgment may be exercised by daylight. I cannot answer for shades of green in the night time."

But he spoke with an ease and simplicity that left no mortal able to guess whether he had ever heard of a particular bunch of roses in his life before.

"You give me more of Eve in my character, Mrs. Evelyn, than I think belongs to me," said Fleda from her work at the far centre-table, which certainly did not get its name from its place in the room. "My enjoyment to-day has not been in the least troubled by curiosity."

Which none of the rest of the family could have affirmed.

"Do you mean to say, Mr. Carleton," said Constance, "that it is necessary to distinguish between shades of green in judging of roses?"

"It is necessary to make shades of distinction in judging of almost anything, Miss Constance. The difference between varieties of the same flower is often extremely nice."

"I have read of magicians," said Thorn softly, bending down towards Fleda's work,—"who did not need to see things to answer questions respecting them."

Fleda thought that was a kind of magic remarkably common in the world; but even her displeasure could not give her courage to speak. It gave her courage to be silent, however; and Mr. Thorn's best efforts in a conversation of some length could gain nothing but very uninterested rejoinders. A sudden pinch from Constance then made her look up and almost destroyed her self-possession as she saw Mr. Stackpole make his way into the room.

"I hope I find my fair enemy in a mollified humour," he said approaching them.

"I suppose you have repaired damages, Mr. Stackpole," said Constance,—"since you venture into the region of broken windows again."

"Mr. Stackpole declared there were none to repair," said Mrs. Evelyn from the sofa.

"More than I knew of," said the gentleman laughing—"there were more than I knew of; but you see I court the danger, having rashly concluded that I might as well know all my weak points at once."

"Miss Ringgan will break nothing to-night, Mr. Stackpole—she promised me she would not."

"Not even her silence?" said the gentleman.

"Is she always so desperately industrious?" said Mr. Thorn.

"Miss Ringgan, Mr. Stackpole," said Constance, "is subject to occasional fits of misanthropy, in which cases her retreating with her work to the solitude of the centre-table is significant of her desire to avoid conversation, — as Mr. Thorn has been experiencing."

"I am happy to see that the malady is not catching, Miss Constance."

"Mr. Stackpole!" said Constance, —"I am in a morose state of mind! — Miss Ringgan this morning received a magnificent bouquet of roses which in the first place I rashly appropriated to myself; and ever since I discovered my mistake I have been meditating the renouncing of society — it has excited more bad feelings than I thought had existence in my nature."

"Mr. Stackpole," said Mrs. Evelyn, "would you ever have supposed that roses could be a cause of discord?"

Mr. Stackpole looked as if he did not exactly know what the ladies were driving at.

"There have five thousand emigrants arrived at this port within a week!" said he, as if that were something worth talking about.

"Poor creatures! where will they all go?" said Mrs. Evelyn comfortably.

"Country's large enough," said Thorn.

"Yes, but such a stream of immigration will reach the Pacific and come back again before long: and then there will be a meeting of the waters! This tide of German and Irish will sweep over everything."

"I suppose if the land will not bear both, one party will have to seek other quarters," said Mrs. Evelyn with an exquisite satisfaction which Fleda could hear in her voice. "You remember the story of Lot and Abraham, Mr. Stackpole, — when a quarrel arose between them? — not about roses."

Mr. Stackpole looked as if women were—to say the least—incomprehensible.

"Five thousand a week!" he repeated.

"I wish there was a Dead Sea for them all to sheer off into!" said Thorn.

"If you had seen the look of grave rebuke that speech called forth, Mr. Thorn," said Constance, "your feelings would have been penetrated—if you have any."

"I had forgotten," he said, looking round with a bland change of manner,—"what gentle charities were so near me."

"Mamma!" said Constance with a most comic shew of indignation,—"Mr. Thorn thought that with Miss Ringgan he had forgotten all the gentle charities in the room!—I am of no further use to society!—I will trouble you to ring that bell, Mr. Thorn, if you please. I shall request candles and retire to the privacy of my own apartment!"

"Not till you have permitted me to expiate my fault!" said Mr. Thorn laughing.

"It cannot be expiated!—My worth will be known at some future day.—Mr. Carleton, *will* you have the goodness to summon our domestic attendant?"

"If you will permit me to give the order," he said smiling, with his hand on the bell. "I am afraid you are hardly fit to be trusted alone."

"Why?"

"May I delay obeying you long enough to give my reasons?"

"Yes."

"Because," said he coming up to her, "when people turn away from the world in disgust they generally find worse company in themselves."

"Mr. Carleton!—I would not sit still another minute, if curiosity didn't keep me. I thought solitude was said to be such a corrector?"

"Like a clear atmosphere—an excellent medium if your object is to take an observation of your position—worse than lost if you mean to shut up the windows and burn sickly lights of your own."

"Then according to that one shouldn't seek solitude unless one doesn't want it."

"No," said Mr. Carleton, with that eye of deep meaning to which Constance always rendered involuntary homage,—"every one wants it;—if we do not daily take an observation to find where we are, we are sailing about wildly and do not know whither we are going."

"An observation?" said Constance, understanding part and impatient of not catching the whole of his meaning.

"Yes," he said with a smile of singular fascination,—"I mean, consulting the unerring guides of the way to know where we are and if we are sailing safely and happily in the right direction—otherwise we are in danger of striking upon some rock or of never making the harbour; and in either case, all is lost."

The power of eye and smile was too much for Constance, as it had happened more than once before; her own eyes fell and for a moment she wore a look of unwonted sadness and sweetness, at what from any other person would have roused her mockery.

"Mr. Carleton," said she, trying to rally herself but still not daring to look up, knowing that would put it out of her power,—"I can't understand how you ever came to be such a grave person."

"What is your idea of gravity?" said he smiling. "To have a mind so at rest about the future as to be able to enjoy thoroughly all that is worth enjoying in the present?"

"But I can't imagine how *you* ever came to take up such notions."

"May I ask again, why not I?"

"O you know—you have so much to make you otherwise."

"What degree of present contentment ought to make one satisfied to leave that of the limitless future an uncertain thing?"

"Do you think it can be made certain?"

"Undoubtedly!—why not? the tickets are free—the only thing is to make sure that ours has the true signature. Do you think the possession of that ticket makes life a sadder thing? The very handwriting of it is more precious to me, by far, Miss Constance, than everything else I have."

"But you are a very uncommon instance," said Constance, still unable to look up, and speaking without any of her usual attempt at jocularity.

"No, I hope not," he said quietly.

"I mean," said Constance, "that it is very uncommon language to hear from a person like you."

"I suppose I know your meaning," he said after a minute's pause;— "but, Miss Constance, there is hardly a graver thought to me than that power and responsibility go hand in hand."

"It don't generally work so," said Constance rather uneasily.

"What are you talking about, Constance?" said Mrs. Evelyn.

"Mr. Carleton, mamma,—has been making me melancholy."

"Mr. Carleton," said Mrs. Evelyn, "I am going to petition that you will turn your efforts in another direction—I have felt oppressed all the afternoon from the effects of that funeral service I was attending—I am only just getting over it. The preacher seemed to delight in putting together all the gloomy thoughts he could think of."

"Yes!" said Mr. Stackpole, putting his hands in his pockets,—"it is the particular enjoyment of some of them, I believe, to do their best to make other people miserable."

Mr. Thorn said nothing, being warned by the impatient little hammering of Fleda's worsted needle upon the marble, while her eye was no longer considering her work, and her face rested anxiously upon her hand.

"There wasn't a thing," the lady went on,—"in anything he said, in his prayer or his speech,—there wasn't a single cheering or elevating consideration,—all he talked and prayed for was that the people there might be filled with a sense of their wickedness—"

"It's their trade, ma'am," said Mr. Stackpole,—"it's their trade! I wonder if it ever occurs to them to include themselves in that petition."

"There wasn't the slightest effort made in anything he said or prayed for,—and one would have thought that would have been so natural!—there was not the least endeavour to do away with that superstitious fear of death which is so common—and one would think it was the very occasion to do it;—he never once asked that we might be led to look upon it rationally and calmly.—It's so unreasonable, Mr. Stackpole—it is so dissonant with our views of a benevolent Supreme Being—as if it could be according to *his* will that his creatures should live lives of tormenting themselves—it so shews a want of trust in his goodness!"

"It's a relic of barbarism, ma'am," said Mr. Stackpole;—"it's a popular delusion—and it is like to be, till you can get men to embrace wider and more liberal views of things."

"What do you suppose it proceeds from?" said Mr. Carleton, as if the question had just occurred to him.

"I suppose, from false notions received from education, sir."

"Hardly," said Mr. Carleton;—"it is too universal. You find it everywhere; and to ascribe it everywhere to education would be but shifting the question back one generation."

"It is a root of barbarous ages," said Mr. Stackpole,—"a piece of superstition handed down from father to son—a set of false ideas which men are bred up and almost born with, and that they can hardly get rid of."

"How can that be a root of barbarism, which the utmost degree of intelligence and cultivation has no power to do away, nor even to lessen, however it may afford motive to control? Men may often put a brave face upon it and shew none of their thoughts to the world; but I think no one capable of reflection has not at times felt the influence of that dread."

"Men have often sought death, of purpose and choice," said Mr. Stackpole dryly and rubbing his chin.

"Not from the absence of this feeling, but from the greater momentary pressure of some other."

"Of course," said Mr. Stackpole, rubbing his chin still,—there is a natural love of life—the world could not get on if there was not."

"If the love of life is natural, the fear of death must be so, by the same reason."

"Undoubtedly," said Mrs. Evelyn, "it is natural—it is part of the constitution of our nature."

"Yes," said Mr. Stackpole, settling himself again in his chair with his hands in his pockets—"it is not unnatural, I suppose,—but then that is the first view of the subject—it is the business of reason to correct many impressions and prejudices that are, as we say, natural."

"And there was where my clergyman of to-day failed utterly," said Mrs. Evelyn;—"he aimed at strengthening that feeling and driving it down as hard as he could into everybody's mind—not a single lisp of anything to do it away or lessen the gloom with which we are, naturally as you say, disposed to invest the subject."

"I dare say he has held it up as a bugbear till it has become one to himself," said Mr. Stackpole.

"It is nothing more than the mere natural dread of dissolution," said Mr. Carleton.

"I think it is that," said Mrs. Evelyn,—"I think that is the principal thing."

"Is there not besides an undefined fear of what lies beyond—an uneasy misgiving that there may be issues which the spirit is not prepared to meet?"

"I suppose there is," said Mrs. Evelyn,—"but sir—"

"Why that is the very thing," said Mr. Stackpole,—"that is the mischief of education I was speaking of—men are brought up to it."

"You cannot dispose of it so, sir, for this feeling is quite as universal as the other; and so strong that men have not only been willing to render life miserable but even to endure death itself, with all the aggravation of torture, to smooth their way in that unknown region beyond."

"It is one of the maladies of human nature," said Mr. Stackpole,—
"that it remains for the progress of enlightened reason to dispel."

"What is the cure for the malady?" said Mr. Carleton quietly.

"Why sir!—the looking upon death as a necessary step in the course of our existence which simply introduces us from a lower to a higher sphere,—from a comparatively narrow to a wider and nobler range of feeling and intellect."

"Ay—but how shall we be sure that it is so?"

"Why Mr. Carleton, sir," said Mrs. Evelyn,—"do you doubt that? Do you suppose it possible for a moment that a benevolent being would make creatures to be anything but happy?"

"You believe the Bible, Mrs. Evelyn?" he said smiling slightly.

"Certainly, sir; but Mr. Carleton, the Bible I am sure holds out the same views of the goodness and glory of the Creator; you cannot open it but you find them on every page. If I could take such views of things as some people have," said Mrs. Evelyn, getting up to punch the fire in her extremity,—"I don't know what I should do!— Mr. Carleton, I think I would rather never have been born, sir!"

"Every one runs to the Bible!" said Mr. Stackpole. "It is the general armoury, and all parties draw from it to fight each other."

"True," said Mr. Carleton,—"but only while they draw partially. No man can fight the battle of truth but in the whole panoply; and no man so armed can fight any other."

"What do you mean, sir?"

"I mean that the Bible is not a riddle, neither inconsistent with itself; but if you take off one leg of a pair of compasses the measuring power is gone."

"But Mr. Carleton, sir," said Mrs. Evelyn,—"do you think that reading the Bible is calculated to give one gloomy ideas of the future?"

"By no means," he said with one of those meaning-fraught smiles,— "but is it safe, Mrs. Evelyn, in such a matter, to venture a single grasp of hope without the direct warrant of God's word?"

"Well, sir?"

"Well, ma'am,—that says, 'the soul that sinneth, it shall die.'"

"That disposes of the whole matter comfortably at once," said Mr. Stackpole.

"But, sir," said Mrs. Evelyn,—"that doesn't stand alone—the Bible everywhere speaks of the fulness and freeness of Christ's salvation?"

"Full and free as it can possibly be," he answered with something of a sad expression of countenance;—"but, Mrs. Evelyn, *never offered but with conditions.*"

"What conditions?" said Mr. Stackpole hastily.

"I recommend you to look for them, sir," answered Mr. Carleton, gravely;—"they should not be unknown to a wise man."

"Then you would leave mankind ridden by this nightmare of fear?— or what is your remedy?"

"There is a remedy, sir," said Mr. Carleton, with that dilating and darkening eye which shewed him deeply engaged in what he was thinking about;—"it is not mine. When men feel themselves lost and are willing to be saved in God's way, then the breach is made up— then hope can look across the gap and see its best home and its best friend on the other side—then faith lays hold on forgiveness and trembling is done—then, sin being pardoned, the sting of death is taken away and the fear of death is no more, for it is swallowed up in victory. But men will not apply to a physician while they think themselves well; and people will not seek the sweet way of safety by Christ till they know there is no other; and so, do you see, Mrs. Evelyn, that when the gentleman you were speaking of sought to-day to persuade his hearers that they were poorer than they thought they were, he was but taking the surest way to bring them to be made richer than they ever dreamed."

There was a power of gentle earnestness in his eye that Mrs Evelyn could not answer; her look fell as that of Constance had done, and there was a moment's silence.

Thorn had kept quiet, for two reasons—that he might not displease Fleda, and that he might watch her. She had left her work, and turning half round from the table had listened intently to the conversation, towards the last very forgetful that there might be anybody to observe her,—with eyes fixed, and cheeks flushing, and the corners of the mouth just indicating delight,—till the silence fell; and then she turned round to the table and took up her worsted-work. But the lips were quite grave now, and Thorn's keen eyes discerned that upon one or two of the artificial roses there lay two or three very natural drops.

"Mr. Carleton," said Edith, "what makes you talk such sober things?—you have set Miss Ringgan to crying."

"Mr. Carleton could not be better pleased than at such a tribute to his eloquence," said Mr. Thorn with a saturnine expression.

"Smiles are common things," said Mr. Stackpole a little maliciously; "but any man may be flattered to find his words drop diamonds."

"Fleda my dear," said Mrs. Evelyn, with that trembling tone of concealed ecstasy which always set every one of Fleda's nerves a jarring,—"you may tell the gentlemen that they do not always know when they are making an unfelicitous compliment—I never read what poets say about 'briny drops' and 'salt tears' without imagining the heroine immediately to be something like Lot's wife."

"Nobody said anything about briny drops, mamma," said Edith. "Why there's Florence!—"

Her entrance made a little bustle, which Fleda was very glad of. Unkind!—She was trembling again in every finger. She bent down over her canvas and worked away as hard as she could. That did not hinder her becoming aware presently that Mr. Carleton was standing close beside her.

"Are you not trying your eyes?" said he.

The words were nothing, but the tone was a great deal, there was a kind of quiet intelligence in it. Fleda looked up, and something in the clear steady self-reliant eye she met wrought an instant change in her feeling. She met it a moment and then looked at her work again with nerves quieted.

"Cannot I persuade them to be of my mind?" said Mr. Carleton, bending down a little nearer to their sphere of action.

"Mr. Carleton is unreasonable, to require more testimony of that this evening," said Mr. Thorn;—"his own must have been ill employed."

Fleda did not look up, but the absolute quietness of Mr. Carleton's manner could be felt; she felt it, almost with sympathetic pain. Thorn immediately left them and took leave.

"What are you searching for in the papers, Mr. Carleton?" said Mrs. Evelyn presently coming up to them.

"I was looking for the steamers, Mrs. Evelyn."

"How soon do you think of bidding us good-bye?"

"I do not know, ma'am," he answered coolly—"I expect my mother."

Mrs. Evelyn walked back to her sofa.

But in the space of two minutes she came over to the centre-table again, with an open magazine in her hand.

"Mr. Carleton," said the lady, "you must read this for me and tell me what you think of it, will you sir? I have been shewing it to Mr. Stackpole and he can't see any beauty in it, and I tell him it is his fault and there is some serious want in his composition. Now I want to know what you will say to it."

"An arbiter, Mrs. Evelyn, should be chosen by both parties."

"Read it and tell me what you think!" repeated the lady, walking away to leave him opportunity. Mr. Carleton looked it over.

"That is something pretty," he said putting it before Fleda. Mrs. Evelyn was still at a distance.

"What do you think of that print for trying the eyes?" said Fleda laughing as she took it. But he noticed that her colour rose a little.

"How do you like it?"

"I like it,—pretty well," said Fleda rather hesitatingly.

"You have seen it before?"

"Why?" Fleda said, with a look up at him at once a little startled and a little curious;—"what makes you say so?"

"Because—pardon me—you did not read it."

"Oh," said Fleda laughing, but colouring at the same time very frankly, "I can tell how I like some things without reading them very carefully."

Mr. Carleton looked at her, and then took the magazine again.

"What have you there, Mr. Carleton?" said Florence.

"A piece of English on which I was asking this lady's opinion, Miss Evelyn."

"Now, Mr. Carleton!" exclaimed Constance jumping up,—"I am going to ask you to decide a quarrel between Fleda and me about a point of English"—

"Hush, Constance!" said her mother,—"I want to speak to Mr. Carleton—Mr. Carleton, how do you like it?"

"Like what, mamma?" said Florence.

"A piece I gave Mr. Carleton to read. Mr. Carleton, tell how you like it, sir."

"But what is it, mamma?"

"A piece of poetry in an old Excelsior—'The Spirit of the Fireside.' Mr. Carleton, won't you read it aloud, and let us all hear—but tell me first what you think of it."

"It has pleased me particularly, Mrs. Evelyn."

"Mr. Stackpole says he does not understand it, sir."

"Fanciful," said Mr. Stackpole,—"it's a little fanciful—and I can't quite make out what the fancy is."

"It has been the misfortune of many good things before not to be prized, Mr. Stackpole," said the lady funnily.

"True, ma'am," said that gentleman rubbing his chin—"and the converse is also true unfortunately,—and with a much wider application."

"There is a peculiarity of mental development or training," said Mr. Carleton, "which must fail of pleasing many minds because of their

129

wanting the corresponding key of nature or experience. Some literature has a hidden freemasonry of its own."

"Very hidden indeed!" said Mr. Stackpole;—"the cloud is so thick that I can't see the electricity!"

"Mr. Carleton," said Mrs. Evelyn laughing, "I take that remark as a compliment, sir. I have always appreciated that writer's pieces—I enjoy them very much."

"Well, won't you please read it, Mr. Carleton?" said Florence, "and let us know what we are talking about."

Mr. Carleton obeyed, standing where he was by the centre-table.

"By the old hearthstone a Spirit dwells,
The child of bygone years,—
He lieth hid the stones amid,
And liveth on smiles and tears.

"But when the night is drawing on,
And the fire burns clear and bright,
He Cometh out and walketh about,
In the pleasant grave twilight.

"He goeth round on tiptoe soft,
And scanneth close each face;
If one in the room be sunk in gloom,
By him he taketh his place.

"And then with fingers cool and soft,
(Their touch who does not know)
With water brought from the well of Thought,
That was dug long years ago,

"He layeth his hand on the weary eyes—
They are closed and quiet now;—

And he wipeth away the dust of the day
Which had settled on the brow.

"And gently then he walketh away
And sits in the corner chair;
And the closed eyes swim—it seemeth to *him*
The form that once sat there.

"And whispered words of comfort and love
Fall sweet on the ear of sorrow;—
'Why weepest thou?—thou art troubled now,
But there cometh a bright to-morrow.

"'We too have passed over life's wild stream
In a frail and shattered boat,
But the pilot was sure—and we sailed secure
When we seemed but scarce afloat.

"'Though tossed by the rage of waves and wind,
The bark held together still,—
One arm was strong—it bore us along,
And has saved from every ill.'

"The Spirit returns to his hiding-place,
But his words have been like balm.
The big tears start—but the fluttering heart
Is soothed and softened and calm."

"I remember that," said Florence;—"it is beautiful."

"Who's the writer?" said Mr. Stackpole.

"I don't know," said Mrs. Evelyn,—"it is signed 'Hugh'—there have been a good many of his pieces in the Excelsior for a year past—and all of them pretty."

"Hugh!" exclaimed Edith springing forward, — "that's the one that wrote the Chestnuts! — Fleda, won't you read Mr. Carleton the Chestnuts?"

"Why no, Edith, I think not."

"Ah do! I like it so much, and I want him to hear it, — and you know mamma says they're all pretty. Won't you?"

"My dear Edith, you have heard it once already to day."

"But I want you to read it for me again."

"Let me have it, Miss Edith," said Mr. Carleton smiling, — "I will read it for you."

"Ah but it would be twice as good if you could hear her read it," said Edith, fluttering over the leaves of the magazine, — "she reads it so well. It's so funny — about the coffee and buckwheat cakes."

"What is that, Edith?" said her mother.

"Something Mr. Carleton is going to read for me, mamma."

"Don't you trouble Mr. Carleton."

"It won't trouble him, mamma — he promised of his own accord."

"Let us all have the benefit of it, Mr. Carleton," said the lady.

It is worthy of remark that Fleda's politeness utterly deserted her during the reading of both this piece and the last. She as near as possible turned her back upon the reader.

"Merrily sang the crickets forth
One fair October night; —
And the stars looked down, and the northern crown
Gave its strange fantastic light.

"A nipping frost was in the air,
On flowers and grass it fell;
And the leaves were still on the eastern hill
As if touched by a fairy spell.

"To the very top of the tall nut-trees
The frost-king seemed to ride;
With his wand he stirs the chestnut burs,
And straight they are opened wide
.

"And squirrels and children together dream
Of the coming winter's hoard;
And many, I ween, are the chestnuts seen
In hole or in garret stored.

"The children are sleeping in feather-beds —
Poor Bun in his mossy nest, —
He courts repose with his tail on his nose.
On the others warm blankets rest.

"Late in the morning the sun gets up
From behind the village spire;
And the children dream, that the first red gleam
Is the chestnut trees on fire!

"The squirrel had on when he first awoke
All the clothing he could command;
And his breakfast was light—he just took a bite
Of an acorn that lay at hand;

"And then he was off to the trees to work; —
While the children some time it takes
To dress and to eat what *they* think meet
Of coffee and buckwheat cakes.

"The sparkling frost when they first go out,
Lies thick upon all around;

And earth and grass, as they onward pass,
Give a pleasant crackling sound.

"O there is a heap of chestnuts, see!'
Cried the youngest of the train;
For they came to a stone where the squirrel had thrown
What he meant to pick up again.

"And two bright eyes from the tree o'erhead,
Looked down at the open bag
Where the nuts went in—and so to begin,
Almost made his courage flag.

"Away on the hill, outside the wood,
Three giant trees there stand;
And the chestnuts bright that hang in sight,
Are eyed by the youthful band.

"And one of their number climbs the tree,
And passes from bough to bough,—
And the children run—for with pelting fun
The nuts fall thickly now.

"Some of the burs are still shut tight,—
Some open with chestnuts three,—
And some nuts fall with no burs at all—
Smooth, shiny, as nuts should be.

"O who can tell what fun it was
To see the prickly shower!
To feel what a whack on head or back.
Was within a chestnut's power!—

"To run beneath the shaking tree,
And then to scamper away;
And with laughing shout to dance about
The grass where the chestnuts lay.

"With flowing dresses, and blowing hair,
And eyes that no shadow knew, —
Like the growing light of a morning bright—-
The dawn of the summer blue!

"The work was ended—the trees were stripped—
The children were 'tired of play.'
And they forgot (but the squirrel did not)
The wrong they had done that day."

Whether it was from the reader's enjoyment or good giving of these lines, or from Edith's delight in them, he was frequently interrupted with bursts of laughter.

"I can understand *that*" said Mr. Stackpole, "without any difficulty."

"You are not lost in the mysteries of chestnuting in open daylight," said Mrs. Evelyn.

"Mr. Carleton," said Edith, "wouldn't you have taken the squirrel's chestnuts?"

"I believe I should, Miss Edith,—if I had not been hindered."

"But what would have hindered you? don't you think it was right?"

"Ask your friend Miss Ringgan what she thinks of it," said he smiling.

"Now Mr. Carleton," said Constance as he threw down the magazine, "will you decide that point of English between Miss Ringgan and me?"

"I should like to hear the pleadings on both sides, Miss Constance."

"Well, Fleda, will you agree to submit it to Mr. Carleton?"

"I must know by what standards Mr. Carleton will be guided before I agree to any such thing," said Fleda.

"Standards! but aren't you going to trust anybody in anything without knowing what standards they go by?"

"Would that be a safe rule to follow in general?" said Fleda smiling.

"You won't be a true woman if you don't follow it, sooner or later, my dear Fleda," said Mrs. Evelyn. "Every woman must."

"The later the better, ma'am, I cannot help thinking."

"You will change your mind," said Mrs. Evelyn complacently.

"Mamma's notions, Mr. Stackpole, would satisfy any man's pride, when she is expatiating upon the subject of woman's dependence," said Florence.

"The dependence of affection," said Mrs. Evelyn. "Of course! It's their lot. Affection always leads a true woman to merge her separate judgment, on anything, in the judgment of the beloved object."

"Ay," said Fleda laughing, —"suppose her affection is wasted on an object that has none?"

"My dear Fleda!" said Mrs. Evelyn with a funny expression, —"that can never be, you know—don't you remember what your favourite Longfellow says—'affection never is wasted'?—Florence, my love, just hand me 'Evangeline' there—I want you to listen to it, Mr. Stackpole—here it is—

'Talk not of wasted affection; affection never was wasted;
If it enrich not the heart of another, its waters returning
Back to their springs shall fill them full of refreshment.
That which the fountain sends forth returns again to the fountain.'"

"How very plain it is that was written by a man!" said Fleda.

"Why?" said Mr. Carleton laughing.

"I always thought it was so exquisite!" said Florence.

"*I* was so struck with it," said Constance, "that I have been looking ever since for an object to waste *my* affections upon."

"Hush, Constance!" said her mother. "Don't you like it, Mr. Carleton?"

"I should like to hear Miss Ringgan's commentary," said Mr. Stackpole;—" I can't anticipate it. I should have said the sentiment was quite soft and tender enough for a woman."

"Don't you agree with it, Mr. Carleton," repeated Mrs. Evelyn.

"I beg leave to second Mr. Stackpole's motion," he said smiling.

"Fleda my dear, you must explain yourself,—the gentlemen are at a stand."

"I believe, Mrs. Evelyn," said Fleda smiling and blushing,—I am of the mind of the old woman who couldn't bear to see anything wasted."

"But the assertion is that it *isn't* wasted," said Mr. Stackpole.

"'That which the fountain sends forth returns again to the fountain,'" said Mrs. Evelyn.

"Yes, to flood and lay waste the fair growth of nature," said Fleda with a little energy, though her colour rose and rose higher.

"Did it never occur to you, Mrs. Evelyn, that the streams which fertilize as they flow do but desolate if their course be checked?"

"But your objection lies only against the author's figure," said Mr. Stackpole;—"come to the fact."

"I was speaking as he did, sir, of the fact under the figure—I did not mean to separate them."

Both the gentlemen were smiling, though with very different expression.

"Perhaps," said Mr. Carleton, "the writer was thinking of a gentler and more diffusive flow of kind feeling, which however it may meet with barren ground and raise no fruit there, is sure in due time to come back, heaven-refined, to refresh and replenish its source."

"Perhaps so," said Fleda with a very pleased answering look,—"I do not recollect how it is brought in—I may have answered rather Mrs. Evelyn than Mr. Longfellow."

"But granting that it is an error," said Mr. Stackpole, "as you understood it,—what shews it to have been made by a man?"

"Its utter ignorance of the subject, sir."

"You think *they* never waste their affections?" said he.

"By no means! but I think they rarely waste so much in any one direction as to leave them quite impoverished."

"Mr. Carleton, how do you bear that, sir?" said Mrs. Evelyn. "Will you let such an assertion pass unchecked?"

"I would not if I could help it, Mrs. Evelyn."

"That isn't saying much for yourself," said Constance;—"but Fleda my dear, where did you get such an experience of waste and desolation?"

"Oh, 'man is a microcosm,' you know," said Fleda lightly.

"But you make it out that only one-half of mankind can appropriate that axiom," said Mr. Stackpole. "How can a woman know *men's* hearts so well?"

"On the principle that the whole is greater than a part?" said Mr. Carleton smiling.

"I'll sleep upon that before I give my opinion," said Mr. Stackpole. "Mrs. Evelyn, good-evening!—"

"Well Mr. Carleton!" said Constance, "you have said a great deal for women's minds."

"Some women's minds," he said with a smile.

"And some men's minds," said Fleda. "I was speaking only in the general."

Her eye half unconsciously reiterated her meaning as she shook hands with Mr. Carleton. And without speaking a word for other people to hear, his look and smile in return were more than an answer. Fleda sat for some time after he was gone trying to think what it was in eye and lip which had given her so much pleasure. She could not make out anything but approbation,—the look of loving approbation that one gives to a good child; but she thought it had also something of that quiet intelligence—a silent communication of sympathy which the others in company could not share.

She was roused from her reverie by Mrs. Evelyn.

"Fleda my dear, I am writing to your aunt Lucy—have you any message to send?"

"No Mrs. Evelyn—I wrote myself to-day."

And she went back to her musings.

"I am writing about you, Fleda," said Mrs. Evelyn, again in a few minutes.

"Giving a good account, I hope, ma'am," said Fleda smiling.

"I shall tell her I think sea-breezes have an unfavourable effect upon you," said Mrs. Evelyn;—"that I am afraid you are growing pale; and that you have clearly expressed yourself in favour of a garden at Queechy rather than any lot in the city—or anywhere else;—so she had better send for you home immediately."

Fleda tried to find out what the lady really meant; but Mrs. Evelyn's delighted amusement did not consist with making the matter very plain. Fleda's questions did nothing but aggravate the cause of them, to her own annoyance; so she was fain at last to take her light and go to her own room.

She looked at her flowers again with a renewal of the first pleasure and of the quieting influence the giver of them had exercised over her that evening; thought again how very kind it was of him to send them, and to choose them so; how strikingly he differed from other people; how glad she was to have seen him again, and how more than glad that he was so happily changed from his old self. And then from that change and the cause of it, to those higher, more tranquilizing, and sweetening influences that own no kindred with earth's dust and descend like the dew of heaven to lay and fertilize it. And when she laid herself down to sleep it was with a spirit grave but simply happy; every annoyance and unkindness as unfelt now as ever the parching heat of a few hours before when the stars are abroad.

CHAPTER XXXVII.

A snake bedded himself under the threshold of a country house.
L'Estrange.

To Fleda's very great satisfaction Mr. Thorn was not seen again for several days. It would have been to her very great comfort too if he could have been permitted to die out of mind as well as out of sight; but he was brought up before her "lots of times," till poor Fleda almost felt as if she was really in the moral neighbourhood of the Dead Sea, every natural growth of pleasure was so withered under the barren spirit of raillery. Sea-breezes were never so disagreeable since winds blew; and nervous and fidgety again whenever Mr. Carleton was present, Fleda retreated to her work and the table and withdrew herself as much as she could from notice and conversation; feeling humbled,—feeling sorry and vexed and ashamed, that such ideas should have been put into her head, the absurdity of which, she thought, was only equalled by their needlessness. "As much as she could" she withdrew; but that was not entirely; now and then interest made her forget herself, and quitting her needle she would give eyes and attention to the principal speaker as frankly as he could have desired. Bad weather and bad roads for those days put riding out of the question.

One morning she was called down to see a gentleman, and came eschewing in advance the expected image of Mr. Thorn. It was a very different person.

"Charlton Rossitur! My dear Charlton, how do you do? Where did you come from?"

"You had better ask me what I have come for," he said laughing as he shook hands with her.

"What have you come for?"

"To carry you home."

"Home!" said Fleda.

"I am going up there for a day or two, and mamma wrote me I had better act as your escort, which of course I am most willing to do. See what mamma says to you."

"When are you going, Charlton?" said Fleda as she broke the seal of the note he gave her.

"To-morrow morning."

"That is too sudden a notice, Capt. Rossitur," said Mrs. Evelyn. "Fleda will hurry herself out of her colour, and then your mother will say there is something in sea-breezes that isn't good for her; and then she will never trust her within reach of them again,—which I am sure Miss Ringgan would be sorry for."

Fleda took her note to the window, half angry with herself that a kind of banter in which certainly there was very little wit should have power enough to disturb her. But though the shaft might be a slight one it was winged with a will; the intensity of Mrs. Evelyn's enjoyment in her own mischief gave it all the force that was wanting. Fleda's head was in confusion; she read her aunt's note three times over before she had made up her mind on any point respecting it.

"My Dearest Fleda,

Charlton is coming home for a day or two—hadn't you better take the opportunity to return with him? I feel as if you had been long away, my dear child—don't you feel so too? Your uncle is very desirous of seeing you; and as for Hugh and me we are but half ourselves. I would not still say a word about your coming home if it were for your good to stay; but I fancy from something in Mrs. Evelyn's letter that Queechy air will by this time do you good again; and opportunities of making the journey are very uncertain. My heart has grown lighter since I gave it leave to expect you. Yours, my darling,

L. R.

"P.S. I will write to Mrs. E. soon."

"What string has pulled these wires that are twitching me home?" thought Fleda, as her eyes went over and over the words which the feeling of the lines of her face would alone have told her were unwelcome. And why unwelcome? — "One likes to be moved by fair means and not by foul," was the immediate answer. "And besides, it is very disagreeable to be taken by surprise. Whenever, in any matter of my staying or going, did aunt Lucy have any wish but my pleasure?" Fleda mused a little while; and then with a perfect understanding of the machinery that had been at work, though an extremely vague and repulsed notion of the spring that had moved it, she came quietly out from her window and told Charlton she would go with him.

"But not to-morrow?" said Mrs. Evelyn composedly. "You will not hurry her off so soon as that, Capt. Rossitur?"

"Furloughs are the stubbornest things in the world, Mrs. Evelyn; there is no spirit of accommodation about them. Mine lies between to-morrow morning and one other morning some two days thereafter; and you might as soon persuade Atlas to change his place. Will you be ready, coz?"

"I will be ready," said Fleda; and her cousin departed.

"Now my dear Fleda" said Mrs. Evelyn, but it was with that funny face, as she saw Fleda standing thoughtfully before the fire, — you must be very careful in getting your things together — "

"Why, Mrs. Evelyn?"

"I am afraid you will leave something behind you, my love."

143

"I will take care of that, ma'am, and that I may I will go and see about it at once."

Very busy till dinner-time; she would not let herself stop to think about anything. At dinner Mr. Evelyn openly expressed his regrets for her going and his earnest wishes that she would at least stay till the holidays were over.

"Don't you know Fleda better, papa," said Florence, "than to try to make her alter her mind? When she says a thing is determined upon, I know there is nothing to do but to submit, with as good a grace as you can."

"I tried to make Capt. Rossitur leave her a little longer," said Mrs. Evelyn; "but he says furloughs are immovable, and his begins to-morrow morning—so he was immovable too. I should keep her notwithstanding, though, if her aunt Lucy hadn't sent for her."

"Well see what she wants, and come back again," said Mr. Evelyn.

"Thank you, sir," said Fleda smiling gratefully,—"I think not this winter."

"There are two or three of my friends that will be confoundedly taken aback," said Mr. Evelyn, carefully helping himself to gravy.

"I expect that an immediate depopulation of New York will commence," said Constance,—"and go on till the heights about Queechy are all thickly settled with elegant country-seats,—which is the conventional term for a species of mouse trap!"

"Hush, you baggage!" said her father. "Fleda, I wish you could spare her a little of your common-sense, to go through the world with."

"Papa thinks, you see, my dear, that you have *more than enough*— which is not perhaps precisely the compliment he intended."

"I take the full benefit of his and yours," said Fleda smiling.

After dinner she had just time to run down to the library to bid Dr. Gregory good-bye; her last walk in the city. It wasn't a walk she enjoyed much.

"Going to-morrow," said he. "Why I am going to Boston in a week— you had better stay and go with me."

"I can't now, uncle Orrin—I am dislodged—and you know there is nothing to do then but to go."

"Come and stay with me till next week."

But Fleda said it was best not, and went home to finish her preparations.

She had no chance till late, for several gentlemen spent the evening with them. Mr. Carleton was there part of the time, but he was one of the first to go; and Fleda could not find an opportunity to say that she should not see him again. Her timidity would not allow her to make one. But it grieved her.

At last she escaped to her own room, where most of her packing was still to do. By the time half the floor and all the bed was strewn with neat-looking piles of things, the varieties of her modest wardrobe, Florence and Constance came in to see and talk with her, and sat down on the floor too; partly perhaps because the chairs were all bespoken in the service of boxes and baskets, and partly to follow what seemed to be the prevailing style of things.

"What do you suppose has become of Mr. Thorn?" said Constance. "I have a presentiment that you will find him cracking nuts sociably with Mr. Rossitur or drinking one of aunt Lucy's excellent cups of coffee—in comfortable expectation of your return."

"If I thought that I should stay here," said Fleda. "My dear, those were *my* cups of coffee!"

"I wish I could make you think it then," said Constance.

145

"But you are glad to go home, aren't you, Fleda?" said Florence.

"She isn't!" said her sister. "She knows mamma contemplates making a grand entertainment of all the Jews as soon as she is gone. What *does* mamma mean by that, Fleda?—I observe you comprehend her with most invariable quickness."

"I should be puzzled to explain all that your mother means," said Fleda gently, as she went on bestowing her things in the trunk. "No—I am not particularly glad to go home—but I fancy it is time. I am afraid I have grown too accustomed to your luxury of life, and want knocking about to harden me a little."

"Harden you!" said Constance. "My dear Fleda, you are under a delusion. Why should any one go through an indurating process?— will you inform me?"

"I don't say that every one should," said Fleda,—"but isn't it well for those whose lot does not lie among soft things?"

There was extreme sweetness and a touching insinuation in her manner, and both the young ladies were silent for sometime thereafter watching somewhat wistfully the gentle hands and face that were so quietly busy; till the room was cleared again and looked remarkably empty with Fleda's trunk standing in the middle of it. And then reminding them that she wanted some sleep to fit her for the hardening process and must therefore send them away, she was left alone.

One thing Fleda had put off till then—the care of her bunch of flowers. They were beautiful still. They had given her a very great deal of pleasure; and she was determined they should be left to no servant's hands to be flung into the street. If it had been summer she was sure she could have got buds from them; as it was, perhaps she might strike some cuttings; at all events they should go home with her. So carefully taking them out of the water and wrapping the ends in some fresh earth she had got that very afternoon from her uncle's garden, Fleda bestowed them in the corner of her trunk that she had left for them, and went to bed, feeling weary in body, and in mind to the last degree quiet.

In the same mind and mood she reached Queechy the next afternoon. It was a little before January—just the same time that she had come home last year. As then, it was a bright day, and the country was again covered thick with the unspotted snow; but Fleda forgot to think how bright and fresh it was. Somehow she did not feel this time quite so glad to find herself there. It had never occurred to her so strongly before that Queechy could want anything.

This feeling flew away before the first glimpse of her aunt's smile, and for half an hour after Fleda would have certified that Queechy wanted nothing. At the end of that time came in Mr. Rossitur. His greeting of Charlton was sufficiently unmarked; but eye and lip wakened when he turned to Fleda.

"My dear child," he said, holding her face in both his hands,—how lovely you have grown!"

"That's only because you have forgotten her, father," said Hugh laughing.

It was a very lovely face just then. Mr. Rossitur gazed into it a moment and again kissed first one cheek and then the other, and then suddenly withdrew his hands and turned away, with an air— Fleda could not tell what to make of it—an air that struck her with an immediate feeling of pain; somewhat as if for some cause or other he had nothing to do with her or her loveliness. And she needed not to see him walk the room for three minutes to know that Michigan agencies had done nothing to lighten his brow or uncloud his character. If this had wanted confirmation Fleda would have found it in her aunt's face. She soon discovered, even in the course of the pleasant talkative hours before supper, that it was not brightened as she had expected to find it by her uncle's coming home; and her ears now caught painfully the occasional long breath, but half smothered, which told of a burden upon the heart but half concealed. Fleda supposed that Mr. Rossitur's business affairs at the West must have disappointed him; and resolved not to remember that Michigan was in the map of North America.

Still they talked on, through the afternoon and evening, all of them except him; he was moody and silent. Fleda felt the cloud overshadow sadly her own gayety; but Mrs. Rossitur and Hugh were accustomed to it, and Charlton was much too tall a light to come under any external obscuration whatever. He was descanting brilliantly upon the doings and prospects at Fort Hamilton where he was stationed, much to the entertainment of his mother and brother. Fleda could not listen to him while his father was sitting lost in something not half so pleasant as sleep in the corner of the sofa. Her eyes watched him stealthily till she could not bear it any longer. She resolved to bring the power of her sunbeam to bear, and going round seated herself on the sofa close by him and laid her hand on his arm. He felt it immediately. The arm was instantly drawn away to be put around her and Fleda was pressed nearer to his side, while the other hand took hers; and his lips were again on her forehead.

"And how do you like me for a farmer, uncle Rolf?" she said looking up at him laughingly, and then fearing immediately that she had chosen her subject ill. Not from any change in his countenance however,—that decidedly brightened up. He did not answer at once.

"My child—you make me ashamed of mankind!"

"Of the dominant half of them, sir, do you mean?" said Charlton,—"or is your observation a sweeping one?"

"It would sweep the greatest part of the world into the background, sir," answered his father dryly, "if its sense were the general rule."

"And what has Fleda done to be such a besom of desolation?"

Fleda's laugh set everybody else a going, and there was immediately more life and common feeling in the society than had been all day. They all seemed willing to shake off a weight, and even Fleda, in the endeavour to chase the gloom that hung over others, as it had often happened, lost half of her own.

"But still I am not answered," said Charlton when they were grave again. "What has Fleda done to put such a libel upon mankind?"

"You should call it a *label*, as Dr. Quackenboss does," said Fleda in a fresh burst,—"he says he never would stand being labelled!"—

"But come back to the point," said Charlton,—"I want to know what is the *label* in this case, that Fleda's doings put upon those of other people?"

"Insignificance," said his father dryly.

"I should like to know how bestowed," said Charlton.

"Don't enlighten him, uncle Rolf," said Fleda laughing,—"let my doings remain in safe obscurity,—please!"

"I stand as a representative of mankind," said Charlton, "and I demand an explanation."

"Look at what this slight frame and delicate nerves have been found equal to, and then tell me if the broad shoulders of all your mess would have borne half the burden or their united heads accomplished a quarter the results."

He spoke with sufficient depth of meaning, though now with no unpleasant expression. But Charlton notwithstanding rather gathered himself up.

"O uncle Rolf," said Fleda gently,—"nerves and muscles haven't much to do with it—after all you know I have just served the place of a mouth-piece. Seth was the head, and good Earl Douglass the hand."

"I am ashamed of myself and of mankind," Mr. Rossitur repeated, "when I see what mere weakness can do, and how proudly valueless strength is contended to be. You are looking, Capt. Rossitur,—but after all a cap and plume really makes a man taller only to the eye."

"When I have flung my plume in anybody's face, sir," said Charlton rather hotly, "it will be time enough to throw it back again."

Mrs. Rossitur put her hand on his arm and looked her remonstrance.

"Are you glad to be home again, dear Fleda?" she said turning to her.

But Fleda was making some smiling communications to her uncle and did not seem to hear.

"Fleda does it seem pleasant to be here again?"

"Very pleasant, dear aunt Lucy—though I have had a very pleasant visit too."

"On the whole you do not wish you were at this moment driving out of town in Mr. Thorn's cabriolet?" said her cousin.

"Not in the least," said Fleda coolly. "How did you know I ever did such a thing?"

"I wonder what should bring Mr. Thorn to Queechy at this time of year," said Hugh.

Fleda started at this confirmation of Constance's words; and what was very odd, she could not get rid of the impression that Mr. Rossitur had started too. Perhaps it was only her own nerves, but he had certainly taken away the arm that was round her.

"I suppose he has followed Miss Ringgan," said Charlton gravely.

"No," said Hugh, "he has been here some little time."

"Then he preceded her, I suppose, to see and get the sleighs in order."

"He did not know I was coming," said Fleda.

"Didn't!"

"No—I have not seen him for several days."

"My dear little cousin," said Charlton laughing,—"you are not a witch in your own affairs, whatever you may be in those of other people."

"Why, Charlton?"

"You are no adept in the art of concealment."

"I have nothing to conceal," said Fleda. "How do you know he is here, Hugh?"

"I was anxiously asked the other day," said Hugh with a slight smile, "whether you had come home; and then told that Mr. Thorn was in Queechy. There is no mistake about it, for my imformant had actually seen him, and given him the direction to Mr. Plumfield's, for which he was inquiring."

"The direction to Mr. Plumfield's!" said Fleda.

"What's your old friend Mr. Carleton doing in New York?" said Charlton.

"Is he there still?" said Mrs. Rossitur.

"As large as life," answered her son.

"Which, though you might not suppose it, aunt Lucy, is about the height of Capt. Rossitur, with—I should judge—a trifle less weight."

"Your eyes are observant!" said Charlton.

"Of a good many things," said Fleda lightly.

"He is *not* my height by half an inch," said Charlton;—"I am just six feet without my boots."

"An excellent height!" said Fleda,—"'your six feet was ever the only height.'"

"Who said that?" said Charlton.

"Isn't it enough that I say it?"

"What's he staying here for?"

"I don't know really," said Fleda. "It's very difficult to tell what people do things for."

"Have you seen much of him?" said Mrs. Rossitur.

"Yes ma'am—a good deal—he was often at Mrs. Evelyn's."

"Is he going to marry one of her daughters?"

"Oh no!" said Fleda smiling,—"he isn't thinking of such a thing;—not in America—I don't know what he may do in England."

"No!" said Charlton.—"I suppose he would think himself contaminated by matching with any blood in this hemisphere."

"You do him injustice," said Fleda, colouring;—"you do not know him, Charlton."

"You do?"

"Much better than that."

"And he is not one of the most touch-me-not pieces of English birth and wealth that ever stood upon their own dignity?"

"Not at all!" said Fleda;—"how people may be misunderstood!—he is one of the most gentle and kind persons I ever saw."

"To you!"

"To everybody that deserves it."

"Humph!—And not proud?"

"No, not as you understand it,"—and she felt it was very difficult to make him understand it, as the discovery involved a very offensive implication;—"he is too fine a character to be proud."

"That *is* arguing in a circle with a vengeance!" said Charlton.

"I know what you are thinking of," said Fleda, "and I suppose it passes for pride with a great many people who cannot comprehend it—he has a singular power of quietly rebuking wrong, and keeping impertinence at a distance—where Capt. Rossitur, for instance, I suppose, would throw his cap in a man's face, Mr. Carleton's mere silence would make the offender doff his and ask pardon."

The manner in which this was said precluded all taking offence.

"Well," said Charlton shrugging his shoulders,—"then I don't know what pride is—that's all!"

"Take care, Capt. Rossitur," said Fleda laughing,—"I have heard of such a thing as American pride before now."

"Certainly!" said Charlton, "and I'm quite willing—but it never reaches quite such a towering height on our side the water."

"I am sure I don't know how that may be," said Fleda, "but I know I have heard a lady, an enlightened, gentle-tempered American lady, so called,—I have heard her talk to a poor Irish woman with whom she had nothing in the world to do, in a style that moved my indignation—it stirred my blood!—and there was nothing whatever to call it out. 'All the blood of all the Howards,' I hope would not have disgraced itself so."

"What business have you to 'hope' anything about it?"

"None—except from the natural desire to find what one has a right to look for. But indeed I wouldn't take the blood of all the Howards for any security—pride as well as high-breeding is a thing of natural not adventitious growth—it belongs to character, not circumstance."

"Do you know that your favourite Mr. Carleton is nearly connected with those same Howards, and quarters their arms with his own?"

"I have a very vague idea of the dignity implied in that expression of 'quartering arms,' which comes so roundly out of your mouth, Charlton," said Fleda laughing. "No, I didn't know it. But in general I am apt to think that pride is a thing which reverses the usual rules of architecture, and builds highest on the narrowest foundations."

"What do you mean?"

"Never mind," said Fleda,—"if a meaning isn't plain it isn't worth looking after. But it will not do to measure pride by its supposed materials. It does not depend on them but on the individual. You everywhere see people assert that most of which they feel least sure, and then it is easy for them to conclude that where there is so much more of the reality there must be proportionably more of the assertion. I wish some of our gentlemen, and ladies, who talk of pride where they see and can see nothing but the habit of wealth—I wish they could see the universal politeness with which Mr. Carleton returns the salutes of his inferiors. Not more respectfully they lift their hats to him than he lifts his to them—unless when he speaks."

"You have seen it?"

"Often."

"Where?"

"In England—at his own place—among his own servants and dependents. I remember very well—it struck even my childish eyes."

"Well, after all, that is nothing still but a refined kind of haughtiness."

"It is a kind that I wish some of our Americans would copy," said Fleda.

"But dear Fleda," said Mrs. Rossitur, "all Americans are not like that lady you were talking of—it would be very unfair to make her a sample. I don't think I ever heard any one speak so in my life—you never heard me speak so."

"Dear aunt Lucy!—no,—I was only giving instance for instance. I have no idea that Mr. Carleton is a type of Englishmen in general—I wish he were. But I think it is the very people that cry out against superiority, who are the most happy to assert their own where they can; the same jealous feeling that repines on the one hand, revenges itself on the other."

"Superiority of what kind?" said Charlton stiffly.

"Of any kind—superiority of wealth, or refinement, or name, or standing. Now it does not follow that an Englishman is proud because he keeps liveried servants, and it by no means follows that an American lacks the essence of haughtiness because he finds fault with him for doing so."

"I dare say some of our neighbours think we are proud," said Hugh, "Because we use silver forks instead of steel."

"Because we're *too good for steel forks*, you ought to say," said Fleda. "I am sure they think so. I have been given to understand as much.

Barby, I believe, has a good opinion of us and charitably concludes that we mean right; but some other of our country friends would think I was far gone in uppishness if they knew that I never touch fish with a steel knife; and it wouldn't mend the matter much to tell them that the combination of flavours is disagreeable to me—it hardly suits the doctrine of liberty and equality that my palate should be so much nicer than theirs."

"Absurd!" said Charlton.

"Very," said Fleda; "but on which side, in all probability, is the pride?"

"It wasn't for liveried servants that I charged Mr. Carleton," said her cousin. "How do the Evelyns like this paragon of yours?"

"O everybody likes him," said Fleda smiling,—"except you and your friend Mr. Thorn."

"Thorn don't like him, eh?"

"I think not."

"What do you suppose is the reason?" said Charlton gravely.

"I don't think Mr. Thorn is particularly apt to like anybody," said Fleda, who knew very well the original cause of both exceptions but did not like to advert to it.

"Apparently you don't like Mr. Thorn?" said Mr. Rossitur, speaking for the first time.

"I don't know who does, sir, much,—except his mother."

"What is he?"

"A man not wanting in parts, sir, and with considerable force of character,—but I am afraid more for ill than for good. I should be very sorry to trust him with anything dear to me."

"How long were you in forming that opinion?" said Charlton looking at her curiously.

"It was formed, substantially, the first evening I saw him, and I hare never seen cause to alter it since."

The several members of the family therewith fell into a general muse, with the single exception of Hugh, whose eyes and thoughts seemed to be occupied with Fleda's living presence. Mr. Rossitur then requested that breakfast might be ready very early—at six o'clock.

"Six o'clock!" exclaimed Mrs. Rossitur.

"I have to take a long ride, on business, which must be done early in the day."

"When will you be back?"

"Not before night-fall."

"But going on *another* business journey!" said Mrs. Rossitur. "You have but just these few hours come home from one."

"Cannot breakfast be ready?"

"Yes, uncle Rolf," said Fleda bringing her bright face before him,—"ready at half-past five if you like—now that *I* am to the fore, you know."

He clasped her to his breast and kissed her again; but with a face so very grave that Fleda was glad nobody else saw it.

Then Charlton went, averring that he wanted at least a night and a half of sleep between two such journeys as the one of that day and the one before him on the next, —especially as he must resign himself to going without anything to eat. Him also Fleda laughingly promised that precisely half an hour before the stage time a cup of coffee and a roll should be smoking on the table, with whatever substantial appendages might be within the bounds of possibility, or the house.

"I will pay you for that beforehand with a kiss," said he.

"You will do nothing of the kind," said Fleda stepping back; —"a kiss is a favour taken, not given; and I am entirely ignorant what you have done to deserve it."

"You make a curious difference between me and Hugh," said Charlton, half in jest, half in earnest.

"Hugh is my brother, Capt. Rossitur," said Fleda smiling, —and that is an honour you never made any pretensions to."

"Come, you shall not say that any more," said he, taking the kiss that Fleda had no mind to give him.

Half laughing, but with eyes that were all too ready for something else, she turned again to Hugh when his brother had left the room and looked wistfully in his face, stroking back the hair from his temples with a caressing hand.

"You are just as you were when I left you! —" she said, with lips that seemed too unsteady to say more, and remained parted.

"I am afraid so are you," he replied; —"not a bit fatter. I hoped you would be."

"What have you been smiling at so this evening?"

"I was thinking how well you talked."

"Why Hugh! — You should have helped me — I talked too much."

"I would much rather listen," said Hugh. "Dear Fleda, what a different thing the house is with you in it!"

Fleda said nothing, except an inexplicable little shake of her head which said a great many things; and then she and her aunt were left alone. Mrs. Rossitur drew her to her bosom with a look so exceeding fond that its sadness was hardly discernible. It was mingled however with an expression of some doubt.

"What has made you keep so thin?"

"I have been very well, aunt Lucy, — thinness agrees with me."

"Are you glad to be home again, dear Fleda?"

"I am very glad to be with you, dear aunt Lucy!"

"But not glad to be home?"

"Yes I am," said Fleda, — "but somehow — I don't know — I believe I have got a little spoiled — it is time I was at home I am sure. — I shall be quite glad after a day or two, when I have got into the works again. I am glad now, aunt Lucy."

Mrs. Rossitur seemed unsatisfied, and stroked the hair from Fleda's forehead with an absent look.

"What was there in New York that you were so sorry to leave?"

"Nothing ma'am, in particular," — said Fleda brightly, — "and I am not sorry, aunt Lucy — I tell you I am a little spoiled with company and easy living — I am glad to be with you again."

Mrs. Rossitur was silent.

"Don't you get up to uncle Rolf's breakfast to-morrow, aunt Lucy."

"Nor you."

"I sha'n't unless I want to—but there'll be nothing for you to do, and you must just lie still. We will all have our breakfast together when Charlton has his."

"You are the veriest sunbeam that ever came into a house," said her aunt kissing her.

Chapter XXXVIII.

My flagging soul flies under her own pitch.

Dryden.

Fleda mused as she went up stairs whether the sun were a luminous body to himself or no, feeling herself at that moment dull enough. Bright, was she, to others? nothing seemed bright to her. Every old shadow was darker than ever. Her uncle's unchanged gloom,—her aunt's unrested face,—Hugh's unaltered delicate sweet look, which always to her fancy seemed to write upon his face, "Passing away!"—and the thickening prospects whence sprang the miasm that infected the whole moral atmosphere—alas, yes!—"Money is a good thing," thought Fleda;—"and poverty need not be a bad thing, if people can take it right;—but if they take it wrong!—"

With a very drooping heart indeed she went to the window. Her old childish habit had never been forgotten; whenever the moon or the stars were abroad Fleda rarely failed to have a talk with them from her window. She stood there now, looking out into the cold still night, with eyes just dimmed with tears—not that she lacked sadness enough, but she did lack spirit enough to cry. It was very still;—after the rattle and confusion of the city streets, that extent of snow-covered country where the very shadows were motionless—the entire absence of soil and of disturbance—the rest of nature—the breathlessness of the very wind—all preached a quaint kind of sermon to Fleda. By the force of contrast they told her what should be;—and there was more yet,—she thought that by the force of example they shewed what might be. Her eyes had not long travelled over the familiar old fields and fences before she came to the conclusion that she was home in good time,—she thought she had been growing selfish, or in danger of it; and she made up her mind she was glad to be back again among the rough things of life, where she could do so much to smooth them for others and her own spirit might grow to a polish it would never gain in the regions of ease and pleasure. "To do life's work!"—thought Fleda clasping her hands,—"no matter where—and mine is here. I am glad I am in my place again—I was forgetting I had one."

It was a face of strange purity and gravity that the moon shone upon, with no power to brighten as in past days; the shadows of life were upon the child's brow. But nothing to brighten it from within? One sweet strong ray of other light suddenly found its way through the shadows and entered her heart. "The Lord reigneth! let the earth be glad!"—and then the moonbeams pouring down with equal ray upon all the unevennesses of this little world seemed to say the same thing over and over. Even so! Not less equally his providence touches all,—not less impartially his faithfulness guides. "The Lord reigneth! let the earth be glad!" There was brightness in the moonbeams now that Fleda could read this in them; she went to sleep, a very child again, with these words for her pillow.

It was not six, and darkness yet filled the world, when Mr. Rossitur came down stairs and softly opened the sitting-room door. But the home fairy had been at work; he was greeted with such a blaze of cheerfulness as seemed to say what a dark place the world was everywhere but at home; his breakfast-table was standing ready, well set and well supplied; and even as he entered by one door Fleda pushed open the other and came in from the kitchen, looking as if she had some strange spirit-like kindred with the cheery hearty glow which filled both rooms.

"Fleda!—you up at this hour!"

"Yes, uncle Rolf," she said coming forward to put her hands upon his,—"you are not sorry to see me, I hope."

But he did not say he was glad; and he did not speak at all; he busied himself gravely with some little matters of preparation for his journey. Evidently the gloom of last night was upon him yet. But Fleda had not wrought for praise, and could work without encouragement; neither step nor hand slackened, till all she and Barby had made ready was in nice order on the table and she was pouring out a cup of smoking coffee.

"You are not fit to be up," said Mr. Rossitur, looking at her, —-"you are pale now, Put yourself in that arm chair, Fleda, and go to sleep — I will do this for myself."

"No indeed, uncle Rolf," she answered brightly, —"I have enjoyed getting breakfast very much at this out-of-the-way hour, and now I am going to have the pleasure of seeing you eat it. Suppose you were to take a cup of coffee instead of my shoulder."

He took it and sat down, but Fleda found that the pleasure of seeing him was to be a very qualified thing. He ate like a business man, in unbroken silence and gravity; and her cheerful words and looks got no return. It became an effort at length to keep either bright. Mr. Rossitur's sole remarks during breakfast were to ask if Charlton was going back that day, and if Philetus was getting the horse ready.

Mr. Skillcorn had been called in good time by Barby at Fleda's suggestion, and coming down stairs had opined discontentedly that "a man hadn't no right to be took out of bed in the morning afore he could see himself." But this, and Barby's spirited reply, that "there was no chance of his doing *that* at any time of day, so it was no use to wait,"—Fleda did not repeat. Her uncle was in no humour to be amused.

She expected almost that he would go off without speaking to her. But he came up kindly to where she stood watching him.

"You must bid me good-bye for all the family, uncle Rolf, as I am the only one here," she said laughing.

But she was sure that the embrace and kiss which followed were very exclusively for her. They made her face almost as sober as his own.

"There will be a blessing for you," said he, —"if there is a blessing anywhere!"

"If, uncle Rolf?" said Fleda, her heart swelling to her eyes.

He turned away without answering her.

Fleda sat down in the easy chair then and cried. But that lasted very few minutes; she soon left crying for herself to pray for him, that he might have the blessing he did not know. That did not stop tears. She remembered the poor man sick of the palsy who was brought in by friends to be healed, and that "Jesus seeing *their* faith, said unto the sick of the palsy, 'Son, thy sins be forgiven thee.'" It was a handle that faith took hold of and held fast while love made its petition. It was all she could do, she thought; *she* never could venture to speak to her uncle on the subject.

Weary and tired, tears and longing at length lost themselves in sleep. When she awaked she found the daylight broadly come, little King in her lap, the fire, instead of being burnt out, in perfect preservation, and Barby standing before it and looking at her.

"You ha'n't got one speck o' good by *this* journey to New York," was Miss Elster's vexed salutation.

"Do you think so?" said Fleda rousing herself. "*I* wouldn't venture to say as much as that, Barby."

"If you have, 'tain't in your cheeks," said Barby decidedly. "You look just as if you was made of anything that wouldn't stand wear, and that isn't the way you used to look."

"I have been up a good while without breakfast—my cheeks will be a better colour when I have had that, Barby—they feel pale."

The second breakfast was a cheerfuller thing. But when the second traveller was despatched, and the rest fell back upon their old numbers, Fleda was very quiet again. It vexed her to be so, but she could not change her mood. She felt as if she had been whirled along in a dream and was now just opening her eyes to daylight and reality. And reality—she could not help it—looked rather dull after dreamland. She thought it was very well she was waked up; but it cost her some effort to appear so. And then she charged herself with ingratitude, her aunt and Hugh were so exceedingly happy in her company.

"Earl Douglass is quite delighted with the clover hay, Fleda," said Hugh, as the three sat at an early dinner.

"Is he?" said Fleda.

"Yes,—you know he was very unwilling to cure it in your way—and he thinks there never was anything like it now."

"Did you ever see finer ham, Fleda?" inquired her aunt. "Mr. Plumfield says it could not be better."

"Very good!" said Fleda, whose thoughts had somehow got upon Mr. Carleton's notions about female education and were very busy with them.

"I expected you would have remarked upon our potatoes, before now," said Hugh. "These are the Elephants—have you seen anything like them in New York?"

"There cannot be more beautiful potatoes," said Mrs. Rossitur.

"We had not tried any of them before you went away, Fleda, had we?"

"I don't know, aunt Lucy!—no, I think not."

"You needn't talk to Fleda, mother," said Hugh laughing,—"she is quite beyond attending to all such ordinary matters—her thoughts have learned to take a higher flight since she has been in New York."

"It is time they were brought down then," said Fleda smiling; "but they have not learned to fly out of sight of home, Hugh."

"Where were they, dear Fleda?" said her aunt.

"I was thinking a minute ago of something I heard talked about in New York, aunt Lucy; and afterwards I was trying to find out by what possible or imaginable road I had got round to it."

"Could you tell?"

Fleda said no, and tried to bear her part in the conversation. But she did not know whether to blame the subjects which had been brought forward, or herself, for her utter want of interest in them. She went into the kitchen feeling dissatisfied with both.

"Did you ever see potatoes that would beat them Elephants?" said Barby.

"Never, certainly," said Fleda with a most involuntary smile.

"I never did," said Barby. "They beat all, for bigness and goodness both. I can't keep 'em together. There's thousands of 'em, and I mean to make Philetus eat 'em for supper—such potatoes and milk is good enough for him, or anybody. The cow has gained on her milk wonderful, Fleda, since she begun to have them roots fed out to her."

"Which cow?" said Fleda.

"Which cow?—why—the blue cow—there ain't none of the others that's giving any, to speak of," said Barby looking at her. "Don't you know,—the cow you said them carrots should be kept for?"

Fleda half laughed, as there began to rise up before her the various magazines of vegetables, grain, hay, and fodder, that for many weeks had been deliciously distant from her imagination.

"I made butter for four weeks, I guess, after you went away," Barby went on;—"just come in here and see—and the carrots makes it as yellow and sweet as June—I churned as long as I had anything to churn, and longer; and now we live on cream—you can make some cheesecakes just as soon as you're a mind to,—see! ain't that doing pretty well?—and fine it is,—put your nose down to it—"

"Bravely, Barby—and it is very sweet."

"You ha'n't left nothing behind you in New York, have you?" said Barby when they returned to the kitchen.

"Left anything! no,—what do you think I have left?"

"I didn't know but you might have forgotten to pack up your memory," said Barby dryly.

Fleda laughed; and then in walked Mr. Douglass.

"How d'ye do?" said he. "Got back again. I heerd you was hum, and so I thought I'd just step up and see. Been getting along pretty well?"

Fleda answered, smiling internally at the wide distance between her "getting along" and his idea of it.

"Well the hay's first-rate!" said Earl, taking off his hat and sitting down in the nearest chair;—"I've been feedin' it out, now, for a good spell, and I know what to think about it. We've been feedin' it out ever since some time this side o' the middle o' November;—I never see nothin' sweeter, and I don't want to see nothin' sweeter than it is! and the cattle eats it like May roses—they don't know how to thank you enough for it."

"To thank *you*, Mr. Douglass," said Fleda smiling.

"No," said he in a decided manner,—"I don't want no thanks for it, and I don't deserve none! 'Twa'n't thanks to none of *my* fore-sightedness that the clover wa'n't served the old way. I didn't like new notions—and I never did like new notions! and I never see much good of 'em;—but I suppose there's some on 'em that ain't moon-shine—my woman says there is, and I suppose there is, and after this clover hay I'm willin' to allow that there is! It's as sweet as a posie if you smell to it,—and all of it's cured alike; and I think, Fleda, there's a quarter more weight of it. I ha'n't proved it nor weighed it, but I've an eye and a hand as good as most folks', and I'll qualify to there being a fourth part more weight of it;—and it's a beautiful colour. The critters is as fond of it as you and I be of strawberries."

"Well that is satisfactory, Mr. Douglass," said Fleda. "How is Mrs. Douglass? and Catherine?"

"I ha'n't heerd 'em sayin' nothin' about it," he said,—"and if there was anythin' the matter I suppose they'd let me know. There don't much go wrong in a man's house without his hearin' tell of it. So I think. Maybe 'tain't the same in other men's houses. That's the way it is in mine."

"Mrs. Douglass would not thank you," said Fleda, wholly unable to keep from laughing. Earl's mouth gave way a very little, and then he went on.

"How be you?" he said. "You ha'n't gained much, as I see. I don't see but you're as poor as when you went away."

"I am very well, Mr. Douglass."

"I guess New York ain't the place to grow fat. Well, Fleda, there ha'n't been seen in the whole country, or by any man in it, the like of the crop of corn we took off that 'ere twenty-acre lot—they're all beat to hear tell of it—they won't believe me—Seth Plumfield ha'n't shewed as much himself—he says you're the best farmer in the state."

"I hope he gives you part of the credit, Mr. Douglass;—how much was there?

"I'll take my share of credit whenever I can get it," said Earl, "and I think it's right to take it, as long as you ha'n't nothing to be ashamed of; but I won't take no more than my share; and I will say I thought we was a goin' to choke the corn to death when we seeded the field in that way.—Well, there's better than two thousand bushel—more or less—and as handsome corn as I want to see;—there never was handsomer corn. Would you let it go for five shillings?—there's a man I've heerd of wants the hull of it."

"Is that a good price, Mr. Douglass? Why don't you ask Mr. Rossitur?"

"Do you s'pose Mr. Rossitur knows much about it?" inquired Earl with a curious turn of feature, between sly and contemptuous. "The less he has to do with that heap of corn the bigger it'll be—that's my idee, I ain't agoin' to ask him nothin'—you may ask him what you like to ask him—but I don't think he'll tell you much that'll make you and me wiser in the matter o' farmin'."

"But now that he is at home, Mr. Douglass, I certainly cannot decide without speaking to him."

"Very good!" said Earl uneasily,—"'tain't no affair of mine—as you like to have it so you'll have it—just as you please!—But now, Fleda, there's another thing I want to speak to you about—I want you to let me take hold of that 'ere piece of swamp land and bring it in. I knew a man that fixed a piece of land like that and cleared nigh a thousand dollars off it the first year."

"Which piece?" said Fleda.

"Why you know which 'tis—just the other side of the trees over there—between them two little hills. There's six or seven acres of it— nothin' in the world but mud and briars—will you let me take hold of it? I'll do the hull job if you'll give me half the profits for one year.—Come over and look at it, and I'll tell you—come! the walk won't hurt you, and it ain't fur."

All Fleda's inclinations said no, but she thought it was not best to indulge them. She put on her hood and went off with him; and was treated to a long and most implicated detail of ways and means, from which she at length disentangled the rationale of the matter and gave Mr. Douglass the consent he asked for, promising to gain that of her uncle.

169

The day was fair and mild, and in spite of weariness of body a certain weariness of mind prompted Fleda when she had got rid of Earl Douglass, to go and see her aunt Miriam. She went questioning with herself all the way for her want of good-will to these matters. True, they were not pleasant mind-work; but she tried to school herself into taking them patiently as good life-work. She had had too much pleasant company and enjoyed too much conversation, she said. It had unfitted her for home duties.

Mrs. Plumfield, she knew, was no better. But her eye found no change for the worse. The old lady was very glad to see her, and very cheerful and kind as usual.

"Well are you glad to be home again?" said aunt Miriam after a pause in the conversation.

"Everybody asks me that question," said Fleda smiling.

"Perhaps for the same reason I did—because they thought you didn't look very glad."

"I am glad—" said Fleda,—"but I believe not so glad as I was last year."

"Why not

"I suppose I had a pleasanter time, I have got a little spoiled, I believe, aunt Miriam," Fleda said with glistening eyes and an altering voice,—"I don't take up my old cares and duties kindly at first—I shall be myself again in a few days."

Aunt Miriam looked at her with that fond, wistful, benevolent look which made Fleda turn away.

"What has spoiled you, love?"

"Oh!—easy living and pleasure, I suppose—" Fleda said, but said with difficulty.

170

"Pleasure?"—said aunt Miriam, putting one arm gently round her. Fleda struggled with herself.

"It is so pleasant, aunt Miriam, to forget these money cares!—to lift one's eyes from the ground and feel free to stretch out one's hand—not to be obliged to think about spending sixpences, and to have one's mind at liberty for a great many things that I haven't time for here. And Hugh—and aunt Lucy—somehow things seem sad to me—"

Nothing could be more sympathizingly kind than the way in which aunt Miriam brought Fleda closer to her side and wrapped her in her arms.

"I am very foolish—" Fleda whispered,—"I am very wrong—I shall get over it—"

"I am afraid, dear Fleda," Mrs. Plumfield said after a pause,—"it isn't best for us always to be without sad things—though I cannot bear to see your dear little face look sad—but it wouldn't fit us for the work we have to do—it wouldn't fit us to stand where I stand now and look forward happily."

"Where you stand?" said Fleda raising her head.

"Yes, and I would not be without a sorrow I have ever known. They are bitter now, when they are present,—but the sweet fruit comes after."

"But what do you mean by 'where you stand'?"

"On the edge of life."

"You do not think so, aunt Miriam!" Fleda said with a terrified look. "You are not worse?"

"I don't expect ever to be better," said Mrs. Plumfield with a smile. "Nay, my love," she said, as Fleda's head went down on her bosom

171

again,—"not so! I do not wish it either, Fleda. I do not expect to leave you soon, but I would not prolong the time by a day. I would not have spoken of it now if I had recollected myself,—but I am so accustomed to think and speak of it that it came out before I knew it.—My darling child, it is nothing to cry for."

"I know it, aunt Miriam."

"Then don't cry," whispered aunt Miriam, when she had stroked Fleda's head for five minutes.

"I am crying for myself, aunt Miriam," said Fleda. "I shall be left alone."

"Alone, my dear child?"

"Yes—there is nobody but you that I feel I can talk to." She would have added that she dared not say a word to Hugh for fear of troubling him. But that pain at her heart stopped her, and pressing her hands together she burst into bitter weeping.

"Nobody to talk to but me?" said Mrs. Plumfield after again soothing her for some time,—"what do you mean, dear?"

"O—I can't say anything to them at home," said Fleda with a forced effort after voice;—"and you are the only one I can look to for help—Hugh never says anything—almost never—anything of that kind;—he would rather others should counsel him—"

"There is one friend to whom you may always tell everything, with no fear of wearying him,—of whom you may at all times ask counsel without any danger of being denied,—more dear, more precious, more rejoiced in, the more he is sought unto. Thou mayest lose friend after friend, and gain more than thou losest,—in that one."

"I know it," said Fleda;—"but dear aunt Miriam, don't you think human nature longs for some human sympathy and help too?"

"My sweet blossom!—yes—" said Mrs. Plumfield caressingly stroking her bowed head,—"but let him do what he will;—he hath said, 'I will never leave thee nor forsake thee.'"

"I know that too," said Fleda weeping. "How do people bear life that do not know it!"

"Or that cannot take the comfort of it. Thou art not poor nor alone while thou hast him to go to, little Fleda.—And you are not losing me yet, my child; you will have time, I think, to grow as well satisfied as I with the prospect."

"Is that possible,—for *others*?" said Fleda.

The mother sighed, as her son entered the room.

He looked uncommonly grave, Fleda thought. That did not surprise her, but it seemed that it did his mother, for she asked an explanation. Which however he did not give.

"So you've got back from New York," said he.

"Just got back, yesterday," said Fleda.

"Why didn't you stay longer?"

"I thought my friends at home would be glad to see me," said Fleda. "Was I mistaken?"

He made no answer for a minute, and then said,

"Is your uncle at home?"

"No," said Fleda, "he went away this morning on business, and we do not expect him home before night-fall. Do you want to see him?"

"No," said Seth very decidedly. "I wish he had staid in Michigan, or gone further west,—anywhere that Queechy'd never have heard of him."

"Why what has he done?" said Fleda, looking up half laughing and half amazed at her cousin. But his face was disagreeably dark, though she could not make out that the expression was one of displeasure. It did not encourage her to talk.

"Do you know a man in New York of the name of Thorn?" he said after standing still a minute or two.

"I know two men of that name," said Fleda, colouring and wondering.

"Is either on 'em a friend of your'n?"

"No."

"He ain't?" said Mr. Plumfield, giving the forestick on the fire an energetic kick which Fleda could not help thinking was mentally aimed at the said New Yorker.

"No certainly. What makes you ask?"

"O," said Seth dryly, "folks' tongues will find work to do;—I heerd say something like that—I thought you must take to him more than I do."

"Why what do you know of him?"

"He's been here a spell lately," said Seth,—"poking round; more for ill than for good, I reckon."

He turned and quitted the room abruptly; and Fleda bethought her that she must go home while she had light enough.

174

CHAPTER XXXIX.

Nothing could be more obliging and respectful than the lion's letter was, in appearance; but there was death in the true intent.—L'Estrange.

The landscape had grown more dark since Fleda came up the hill,—or else the eyes that looked at it. Both probably. It was just after sundown, and that is a very sober time of day in winter, especially in some states of the weather. The sun had left no largesses behind him; the scenery was deserted to all the coming poverty of night and looked grim and threadbare already. Not one of the colours of prosperity left. The land was in mourning dress; all the ground and even the ice on the little mill-ponds a uniform spread of white, while the hills were draperied with black stems, here just veiling the snow, and there on a side view making a thick fold of black. Every little unpainted workshop or mill shewed uncompromisingly all its forbidding sharpness of angle and outline darkening against the twilight. In better days perhaps some friendly tree had hung over it, shielding part of its faults and redeeming the rest. Now nothing but the gaunt skeleton of a friend stood there,—doubtless to bud forth again as fairly as ever should the season smile. Still and quiet all was, as Fleda's spirit, and in too good harmony with it; she resolved to choose the morning to go out in future. There was as little of the light of spring or summer in her own mind as on the hills, and it was desirable to catch at least a cheering reflection. She could rouse herself to no bright thoughts, try as she would; the happy voices of nature that used to speak to her were all hushed,—or her ear was deaf; and her eye met nothing that did not immediately fall in with the train of sad images that were passing through her mind and swell the procession. She was fain to fall back and stay herself upon these words, the only stand-by she could lay hold of;—

"To them who by patient continuance in well-doing seek for glory, and honour, and immortality, eternal life!"—

They toned with the scene and with her spirit exactly; they suited the darkening sky and the coming night; for "glory, honour, and immortality" are not now. They filled Fleda's mind, after they had once entered, and then nature's sympathy was again as readily given; each barren stern-looking hill in its guise of present desolation and calm expectancy seemed to echo softly, "patient continuance in well-doing." And the tears trembled then in Fleda's eyes; she had set her face, as the old Scotchman says, "in the right airth. [Footnote: quarter, direction]" "How sweet is the wind that bloweth out of the airth where Christ is!"

"Well," said Hugh, who entered the kitchen with her, "you have been late enough. Did you have a pleasant walk? You are pale, Fleda!"

"Yes, it was pleasant," said Fleda with one of her winning smiles, — "a kind of pleasant. But have you looked at the hills? They are exactly as if they had put on mourning—nothing but white and black—a crape-like dressing of black tree-stems upon the snowy face of the ground, and on every slope and edge of the hills the crape lies in folds. Do look at it when you go out! It has a most curious effect."

"Not pleasant, I should think," said Hugh.

"You'll see it is just as I have described it. No—not pleasant exactly—the landscape wants the sun to light it up just now—it is cold and wilderness looking. I think I'll take the morning in future. Whither are you bound?"

"I must go over to Queechy Run for a minute, on business—I'll be home before supper—I should have been back by this time but Philetus has gone to bed with a headache and I had to take care of the cows."

"Three times and out," said Barby. "I won't try again. I didn't know as anything would be too powerful for his head; but I find as sure as he has apple dumplin' for dinner he goes to bed for his supper and leaves the cows without none. And then Hugh has to take it. It has saved so many Elephants—that's one thing."

Hugh went out by one door and Fleda by another entered the breakfast-room; the one generally used in winter for all purposes. Mrs. Rossitur sat there alone in an easy-chair; and Fleda no sooner caught the outline of her figure than her heart sank at once to an unknown depth,—unknown before and unfathomable now. She was *cowering* over the fire,—her head sunk in her hands, so crouching, that the line of neck and shoulders instantly conveyed to Fleda the idea of fancied or felt degradation—there was no escaping it—how, whence, what, was all wild confusion. But the language of mere attitude was so unmistakable,—the expression of crushing pain was so strong, that after Fleda had fearfully made her way up beside her she could do no more. She stood there tongue-tied, spell-bound, present to nothing but a nameless chill of fear and heart-sinking. She was afraid to speak—afraid to touch her aunt, and abode motionless in the grasp of that dread for minutes. But Mrs. Rossitur did not stir a hair, and the terror of that stillness grew to be less endurable than any other.

Fleda spoke to her,—it did not win the shadow of a reply,—again and again. She laid her hand then upon Mrs. Rossitur's shoulder, but the very significant answer to that was a shrinking gesture of the shoulder and neck, away from the hand. Fleda growing desperate then implored an answer in words—prayed for an explanation— with an intensity of distress in voice and manner, that no one whose ears were not stopped with a stronger feeling could have been deaf to; but Mrs. Rossitur would not raise her head, nor slacken in the least the clasp of the fingers that supported it, that of themselves in their relentless tension spoke what no words could. Fleda's trembling prayers were in vain, in vain. Poor nature at last sought a woman's relief in tears—but they were heart-breaking, not heart-relieving tears—racking both mind and body more than they ought to bear, but bringing no cure. Mrs. Rossitur seemed as unconscious of her niece's mute agony as she had been of her agony of words; and it was from Fleda's own self-recollection alone that she fought off pain and roused herself above weakness to do what the time called for.

"Aunt Lucy," she said laying her hand upon her shoulder, and this time the voice was steady and the hand would not be shaken off, — "Aunt Lucy,—Hugh will be in presently—hadn't you better rouse yourself and go up stairs—for awhile?—till you are better?—and not let him see you so?—"

How the voice was broken and quivering before it got through!

The answer this time was a low long-drawn moan, so exceeding plaintive and full of pain that it made Fleda shake like an aspen. But after a moment she spoke again, bearing more heavily with her hand to mark her words.

"I am afraid he will be in presently—he ought not to see you now— Aunt Lucy, I am afraid it might do him an injury he might not get over—"

She spoke with the strength of desperation; her nerves were unstrung by fear, and every joint weakened so that she could hardly support herself. She had not however spoken in vain; one or two convulsive shudders passed over her aunt, and then Mrs. Rossitur suddenly rose turning her face from Fleda; neither would she permit her to follow her. But Fleda thought she had seen that one or two unfolded letters or papers of some kind, they looked like letters, were in her lap when she raised her head.

Left alone, Fleda sat down on the floor by the easy-chair and rested her head there; waiting,—she could do nothing else,—till her extreme excitement of body and mind should have quieted itself. She had a kind of vague hope that time would do something for her before Hugh came in. Perhaps it did; for though she lay in a kind of stupor, and was conscious of no change whatever, she was able when she heard him coming to get up and sit in the chair in an ordinary attitude. But she looked like the wraith of herself an hour ago.

"Fleda!" Hugh exclaimed as soon as he looked from the fire to her face,—"what is the matter?—what is the matter with you?"

"I am not very well—I don't feel very well," said Fleda speaking almost mechanically,—"I shall have a headache to-morrow—"

"Headache! But you look shockingly! what has happened to you? what is the matter, Fleda?"

"I am not ill—I shall be better by and by. There is nothing the matter with me that need trouble you, dear Hugh."

"Nothing the matter with you!" said he,—and Fleda might see how she looked in the reflection of his face,—"where's mother?"

"She is up-stairs—you mustn't go to her, Hugh!" said Fleda laying a detaining hand upon him with more strength than she thought she had,—"I don't want anything."

"Why mustn't I go to her?"

"I don't think she wants to be disturbed—"

"I must disturb her—"

"You musn't!—I know she don't—she isn't well—something has happened to trouble her—"

"What?"

"I don't know."

"And is that what has troubled you too?" said Hugh, his countenance changing as he gained more light on the subject;—"what is it, dear Fleda?"

"I don't know," repeated Fleda, bursting into tears. Hugh was quiet enough now, and sat down beside her, subdued and still, without even desiring to ask a question. Fleda's tears flowed violently, for a minute,—then she checked them, for his sake; and they sat motionless, without speaking to one another, looking into the fire and letting it die out before them into embers and ashes, neither stirring to put a hand to it. As the fire died the moonlight streamed in,—how very dismal the room looked!

"What do you think about having tea?" said Barby opening the door of the kitchen.

Neither felt it possible to answer her.

"Mr. Rossitur ain't come home, is he?"

"No," said Fleda shuddering.

"So I thought, and so I told Seth Plumfield just now—he was asking for him—My stars! ha'n't you no fire here? what did you let it go out for?"

Barby came in and began to build it up.

"It's growing cold I can tell you, so you may as well have something in the chimney to look at. You'll want it shortly if you don't now."

"Was Mr. Plumfield here, did you say, Barby?"

"Yes."

"Why didn't he come in?"

"I s'pose he hadn't a mind to," said Barby. "Twa'n't for want of being asked. I did the civil thing by him if he didn't by me;—but he said he didn't want to see anybody but Mr. Rossitur."

Did not wank to see anybody but Mr. Rossitur, when he had distinctly said he did not wish to see him? Fleda felt sick, merely from the mysterious dread which could fasten upon nothing and therefore took in everything.

"Well what about tea?" concluded Barby, when the fire was going according to her wishes. "Will you have it, or will you wait longer?"

"No—we won't wait—we will have it now, Barby," said Fleda, forcing herself to make the exertion; and she went to the window to put down the hangings.

The moonlight was very bright, and Fleda's eye was caught in the very act of letting down the curtain, by a figure in the road slowly passing before the courtyard fence. It paused a moment by the horse-gate, and turning paced slowly back till it was hid behind the rose acacias. There was a clump of shrubbery in that corner thick enough even in winter to serve for a screen. Fleda stood with the curtain in her hand, half let down, unable to move, and feeling almost as if the very currents of life within her were standing still too. She thought, she was almost sure, she knew the figure; it was on her tongue to ask Hugh to come and look, but she checked that. The form appeared again from behind the acacias, moving with the same leisurely pace the other way towards the horse-gate. Fleda let down the curtain, then the other two quietly, and then left the room and stole noiselessly out at the front door, leaving it open that the sound of it might not warn Hugh what she was about, and stepping like a cat down the steps ran breathlessly over the snow to the courtyard gate. There waited, shivering in the cold but not feeling it for the cold within,—while the person she was watching stood still a lew moments by the horse-gate and came again with leisurely steps towards her.

"Seth Plumfield!"—said Fleda, almost as much frightened at the sound of her own voice as he was. He stopped immediately, with a start, and came up to the little gate behind which she was standing. But said nothing.

"What are you doing here?"

"You oughtn't to be out without anything on," said he, —"you're fixing to take your death."

He had good reason to say so. But she gave him no more heed than the wind.

"What are you waiting here for? What do you want?"

"I have nothing better to do with my time," said he; —"I thought I'd walk up and down here a little. You go in!"

"Are you waiting to see uncle Rolf?" she said, with teeth chattering.

"You mustn't stay out here," said he earnestly—"you're like nothing but a spook this minute—I'd rather see one, or a hull army of 'em. Go in, go in!"

"Tell me if you want to see him, Seth."

"No I don't—I told you I didn't."

"Then why are you waiting for him?"

"I thought I'd see if he was coming home to-night—I had a word to say if I could catch him before he got into the house."

"*Is* he coming home to-night?" said Fleda.

"I don't know!" said he looking at her. "Do you?"

Fleda burst open the gate between them and putting her hands on his implored him to tell her what was the matter. He looked singularly disturbed; his fine eye twinkled with compassion; but his face, never a weak one, shewed no signs of yielding now.

"The matter is," said he pressing hard both her hands, "that you are fixing to be down sick in your bed by to-morrow. You mustn't stay another second."

182

"Come in then."

"No—not to-night."

"You won't tell me!—"

"There is nothing I can tell you—Maybe there'll be nothing to tell—
Run in, run in, and keep quiet."

Fleda hurried back to the house, feeling that she had gone to the
limit of risk already. Not daring to show herself to Hugh in her
chilled state of body and mind she went into the kitchen.

"Why what on earth's come over you?" was Barby's terrified
ejaculation when she saw her.

"I have been out and got myself cold—"

"Cold!" said Barby,—"you're looking dreadful! What on earth ails
you, Fleda?"

"Don't ask me, Barby," said Fleda hiding her face in her hands and
shivering,—"I made myself very cold just now—Aunt Lucy doesn't
feel very well and I got frightened," she added presently.

"What's the matter with her?"

"I don't know—if you'll make me a cup of tea I'll take it up to her,
Barby."

"You put yourself down there," said Barby placing her with gentle
force in a chair,—"you'll do no such a thing till I see you look as if
there was some blood in you. I'll take it up myself."

But Fleda held her, though with a hand much too feeble indeed for
any but moral suasion. It was enough. Barby stood silently and very
anxiously watching her, till the fire had removed the outward chill at
least. But even that took long to do, and before it was well done

Fleda again asked for the cup of tea. Barby made it without a word, and Fleda went to her aunt with it, taking her strength from the sheer emergency. Her knees trembled under her as she mounted the stairs, and once a glimpse of those words flitted across her mind,— "patient continuance in well-doing." It was like a lightning flash in a dark night shewing the way one must go. She could lay hold of no other stay. Her mind was full of one intense purpose—to end the suspense.

She gently tried the door of her aunt's room; it was unfastened, and she went in. Mrs. Rossitur was lying on the bed; but her first mood had changed, for at Fleda's soft word and touch she half rose up and putting both arms round her waist laid her face against her. There were no tears still, only a succession of low moans, so inexpressibly weak and plaintive that Fleda's nature could hardly bear them without giving way. A more fragile support was never clung to. Yet her trembling fingers, in their agony moved caressingly among her aunt's hair and over her brow as she begged her—when she could, she was not able at first—to let her know the cause that was grieving her. The straightened clasp of Mrs. Rossitur's arms and her increased moaning gave only an answer of pain. But Fleda repeated the question. Mrs. Rossitur still neglecting it, then made her sit down upon the bed, so that she could lay her head higher, on Fleda's bosom; where she hid it, with a mingling of fondness given and asked, a poor seeking for comfort and rest, that wrung her niece's heart.

They sat so for a little time; Fleda hoping that her aunt would by degrees come to the point herself. The tea stood cooling on the table, not even offered; not wanted there.

"Wouldn't you feel better if you told me, dear aunt Lucy?" said Fleda, when they had been for a little while perfectly still. Even the moaning had ceased.

"Is your uncle come home?" whispered Mrs. Rossitur, but so low that Fleda could but half catch the words.

"Not yet."

"What o'clock is it?"

"I don't know—not early—it must be near eight.—Why?"

"You have not heard anything of him?"

"No—nothing."

There was silence again for a little, and then Mrs. Rossitur said in a low fearful whisper,

"Have you seen anybody round the house?"

Fleda's thoughts flew to Seth, with that nameless fear to which she could give neither shape nor direction, and after a moment's hesitation she said,

"What do you mean?"

"Have you?" said Mrs. Rossitur with more energy.

"Seth Plumfield was here a little while ago."

Her aunt had the clew that she had not, for with a half scream, half exclamation, she quitted Fleda's arms and fell back upon the pillows, turning from her and hiding her face there. Fleda prayed again for her confidence, as well as the weakness and the strength of fear could do; and Mrs. Rossitur presently grasping a paper that lay on the bed held it out to her, saying only as Fleda was about quitting the room, "Bring me a light."

Fleda left the letter there and went down to fetch one. She commanded herself under the excitement and necessity of the moment,—all but her face; that terrified Barby exceedingly. But she spoke with a strange degree of calmness; told her Mrs. Rossitur was not alarmingly ill; that she did not need Barby's services and wished to see nobody but herself and didn't want a fire. As she was passing through the hall again Hugh came out of the sitting-room to ask after his mother. Fleda kept the light from her face.

"She does not want to be disturbed—I hope she will be better to-morrow."

"What is the matter, Fleda?"

"I don't know yet."

"And you are ill yourself, Fleda!—you are ill!—"

"No—I shall do very well—never mind me. Hugh, take some tea—I will be down by and by."

He went back, and Fieda went up stairs. Mrs. Rossitur had not moved. Fleda set down the light and herself beside it, with the paper her aunt had given her. It was a letter.

"Queechy, *Thursday*—

"It gives me great concern, my dear madam, to be the means of bringing to you a piece of painful information—but it cannot be long kept from your knowledge and you may perhaps learn it better from me than by any other channel. May I entreat you not to be too much alarmed, since I am confident the cause will be of short duration.

"Pardon me for what I am about to say.

"There are proceedings entered into against Mr. Rossitur—there are writs out against him—on the charge of having, some years ago, endorsed my father's name upon a note of his own giving.—Why it has lain so long I cannot explain. There is unhappily no doubt of the fact.

"I was in Queechy some days ago, on business of my own, when I became aware that this was going on—my father had made no

186

mention of it to me. I immediately took strict measures—I am happy to say I believe with complete success,—to have the matter kept a profound secret. I then made my way as fast as possible to New York to confer on the subject with the original mover of it—unfortunately I was disappointed. My father had left for a neighbouring city, to be absent several days. Finding myself too late to prevent, as I had hoped to do, any open steps from being taken at Queechy, I returned hither immediately to enforce secrecy of proceedings and to assure you, madam, that my utmost exertions shall not be wanting to bring the whole matter to a speedy and satisfactory termination. I entertain no doubt of being able to succeed entirely—even to the point of having the whole transaction remain unknown and unsuspected by the world. It is so entirely as yet, with the exception of one or two law-officers whose silence I have means of procuring.

"May I confess that I am not entirely disinterested? May the selfishness of human nature ask its reward, and own its moving spring? May I own that my zeal in this cause is quickened by the unspeakable excellencies of Mr. Rossitur's lovely niece—which I have learned to appreciate with my whole *heart*—and be forgiven?— And may I hope for the kind offices and intercession of the lady I have the honour of addressing, with her niece Miss Ringgan, that my reward,—the single word of encouragement I ask for,—may be given me?—Having that, I will promise anything—I will guaranty the success of any enterprise, however difficult, to which she may impel me,—and I will undertake that the matter which furnishes the painful theme of this letter shall never more be spoken or thought of, by the world, or my father, or by Mrs. Rossitur's

obliged, grateful, and faithful servant, Lewis Thorn."

Fleda felt as she read as if icicles were gathering about her heart. The whirlwind of fear and distress of a little while ago which could take no definite direction, seemed to have died away and given place to a dead frost—the steady bearing down of disgrace and misery, inevitable, unmitigable, unchangeable; no lessening, no softening of that blasting power, no, nor ever any rising up from under it; the landscape could never be made to smile again. It was the fall of a bright star from their home constellation; but alas! the star was fallen long ago, and the failure of light which they had deplored was all too easily accounted for; yet now they knew that no restoration was to be hoped. And the mother and son—what would become of them? And the father—what would become of him? what further distress was in store?—*Public* disgrace?—and Fleda bowed her head forward on her clasped hands with the mechanical, vain endeavour to seek rest or shelter from thought. She made nothing of Mr. Thorn's professions; she took only the facts of his letter; the rest her eye had glanced over as if she had no concern with it, and it hardly occurred to her that she had any. But the sense of his words she had taken in, and knew, better perhaps than her aunt, that there was nothing to look for from his kind offices. The weight on her heart was too great just then for her to suspect as she did afterwards that he was the sole mover of the whole affair.

As the first confusion of thought cleared away, two images of distress loomed up and filled the view,—her aunt, broken under the news, and Hugh still unknowing to them; her own separate existence Fleda was hardly conscious of. Hugh especially,—how was he to be told, and how could he bear to hear? with his most sensitive conformation of both physical and moral nature. And if an arrest should take place there that night!—Fleda shuddered, and unable to go on thinking rose up and went to her aunt's bedside. It had not entered her mind till the moment she read Mr. Thorn's letter that Seth Plumfield was sheriff for the county. She was shaking again from head to foot with fear. She could not say anything—the touch of her lips to the throbbing temples, soft and tender as sympathy itself, was all she ventured.

"Have you heard anything of him?" Mrs. Rossitur whispered.

"No—I doubt if we do at all to-night."

There was a half breathed "Oh!—" of indescribable pain and longing; and with a restless change of position Mrs. Rossitur gathered herself up on the bed and sat with her head leaning on her knees. Fleda brought a large cloak and put it round her.

"I am in no danger," she said, —"I wish I were!"

Again Fleda's lips softly, tremblingly, touched her cheek.

Mrs. Rossitur put her arm round her and drew her down to her side, upon the bed; and wrapped half of the big cloak about her; and they sat there still in each other's arms, without speaking or weeping, while quarter after quarter of an hour passed away, —nobody knew how many. And the cold bright moonlight streamed in on the floor, mocking them.

"Go!" whispered Mrs. Rossitur at last, —"go down stairs and take care of yourself—and Hugh."

"Won't you come?"

Mrs. Rossitur shook her head.

"Mayn't I bring you something?—do let me!"

But Mrs. Rossitur's shake of the head was decisive. Fleda crawled off the bed, feeling as if a month's illness had been making its ravages upon her frame and strength. She stood a moment to collect her thoughts; but alas, thinking was impossible; there was a palsy upon her mind. She went into her own room and for a minute kneeled down, —not to form a petition in words, she was as much beyond that; it was only the mute attitude of appeal, the pitiful outward token of the mind's bearing, that could not be forborne, a silent uttering of the plea she had made her own in happy days. There was something of comfort in the mere feeling of doing it; and there was more in one or two words that even in that blank came to her mind; —"*Like as a father pitieth his children, so the Lord pitieth them that fear him;*" and she again recollected that "Providence runneth not upon broken wheels." Nothing could be darker than the prospect before her, and these things did not bring light; but they gave her a sure stay to hold on by and keep her feet; a bit of strength to preserve from utterly fainting. Ah! the storehouse must be filled and the mind well familiarized with what is stored in it while yet the days are bright, or it will never be able to find what it wants in the dark.

Fleda first went into the kitchen to tell Barby to fasten the doors and not sit up.

"I don't believe uncle Rolf will be home to-night; but if he comes I will let him in."

Barby looked at her with absolutely a face of distress; but not daring to ask and not knowing how to propose anything, she looked in silence.

"It must be nine o'clock now," Fleda went on.

"And how long be you going to sit up?" said Barby.

"I don't know—a while yet."

"You look proper for it!" said Barby half sorrowfully and half indignantly;—"you look as if a straw would knock you down this minute. There's sense into everything. You catch me a going to bed and leaving you up! It won't do me no hurt to sit here the hull night; and I'm the only one in the house that's fit for it, with the exception of Philetus, and the little wit he has by day seems to forsake him at night. All the light that ever gets into his head, *I* believe, comes from the outside; as soon as ever that's gone he shuts up his shutters. He's been snoozing a'ready now this hour and a half. Go yourself off to bed, Fleda," she added with a mixture of reproach and kindness, "and leave me alone to take care of myself and the house too."

Fleda did not remonstrate, for Barby was as determined in her way as it was possible for anything to be. She went into the other room without a particle of notion what she should say or do.

Hugh was walking up and down the floor—a most unusual sign of perturbation with him. He met and stopped her as she came in.

"Fleda, I cannot bear it. What is the matter?—Do you know?'" he said as her eyes fell.

"Yes. ——"

"What is it?"

She was silent and tried to pass on to the fire. But he stayed her.

"What is it?" he repeated.

"Oh I wish I could keep it from you!" said Fleda bursting into tears.

He was still a moment, and then bringing her to the arm-chair made her sit down, and stood himself before her, silently waiting, perhaps because he could not speak, perhaps from the accustomed gentle endurance of his nature. But Fleda was speechless too.

"You are keeping me in distress," he said at length.

"I cannot end the distress, dear Hugh," said Fleda.

She saw him change colour and he stood motionless still.

"Do you remember," said Fleda, trembling even to her voice,— "what Rutherford says about Providence 'not running on broken wheels'?"

He gave her no answer but the intent look of expectation. Its intentness paralyzed Fleda. She did not know how to go on. She rose from her chair and hung upon his shoulder.

"Believe it now, if you can—for oh, dear Hugh!—we have something to try it."

"It is strange my father don't come home," said he, supporting her with tenderness which had very little strength to help it,—"we want him very much."

Whether or not any unacknowledged feeling prompted this remark, some slight involuntary movement of Fleda's made him ask suddenly,

"Is it about him?"

He had grown deadly pale and Fleda answered eagerly,

"Nothing that has happened to-day—it is not anything that has happened to-day—he is perfectly well, I trust and believe."

"But it is about him?"

Fleda's head sank, and she burst into such an agony of tears that Hugh's distress was for a time divided.

"When did it happen, Fleda?"

"Years ago."

"And what?"

Fleda hesitated still, and then said,

"It was something he did, Hugh."

"What?"

"He put another person's name on the back of a note he gave."

She did not look up, and Hugh was silent for a moment.

"How do you know?"

"Mr. Thorn wrote it to aunt Lucy—it was Mr. Thorn's father."

Hugh sat down and leaned his head on the table. A long, long, time passed,—unmeasured by the wild coursing of thought to and fro.

Then Fleda came and knelt down at the table beside him, and put her arm round his neck.

"Dear Hugh," she said—and if ever love and tenderness and sympathy could be distilled in tones, such drops were those that fell upon the mind's ear,—"can't you look up at me?"

He did then, but he did not give her a chance to look at him. He locked his arms about her, bringing her close to his breast; and for a few minutes, in utter silence, they knew what strange sweetness pure affection can mingle even in the communion of sorrow. There were tears shed in those minutes that, bitter as they seemed at the time, Memory knew had been largely qualified with another admixture.

"Dear Hugh," said Fleda,—"let us keep what we can—won't you go to bed and rest?"

He looked dreadfully as if he needed it. But the usual calmness and sweetness of his face was not altered;—it was only deepened to very great sadness. Mentally, Fleda thought, he had borne the shock better than his mother; for the bodily frame she trembled. He had not answered and she spoke again.

"You need it worse than I, poor Fleda"

"I will go too presently—I do not think anybody will be here tonight."

"Is—Are there—Is this what has taken him away?" said Hugh.

Her silence and her look told him, and then laying her cheek again alongside of his she whispered, how unsteadily, "We have only one help, dear Hugh."

They were still and quiet again for minutes, counting the pulses of pain; till Fleda came back to her poor wish "to keep what they could." She mixed a restorative of wine and water, which however little desired, she felt was necessary for both of them, and Hugh went up stairs. She staid a few minutes to prepare another glass with particular care for her aunt. It was just finished, and taking her candle she had bid Barby good-night, when there came a loud rap at the front door. Fleda set down candle and glass, from the quick inability to hold them as well as for other reasons; and she and Barby stood and looked at each other, in such a confusion of doubt and dread that some little time had passed before either stirred even her eyes. Barby then threw down the tongs with which she had begun to make preparations for covering up the fire and set off to the front.

"You mustn't open the door, Barby," cried Fleda, following her. "Come in here and let us look out of one of the windows."

Before this could be reached however, there was another prolonged repetition of the first thundering burst. It went through Fleda's heart, because of the two up stairs who must hear it.

Barby threw up the sash.

"Who's there?"

"Is this Mr. Rossitur's place?" enquired a gruff voice.

"Yes, it is."

"Well will you come round and open the door?"

"Who wants it open?"

"A lady wants it open?"

"A lady!—what lady?"

"Down yonder in the carriage."

"What lady? who is she?"

"I don't know who she is—she wanted to come to Mr. Rossitur's place—will you open the door for her?"

Barby and Fleda both now saw a carriage standing in the road.

"We must see who it is first," whispered Fleda.

"When the lady comes I'll open the door," was Barby's ultimatum.

The man withdrew to the carriage; and after a few moments of intense watching Fleda and Barby certainly saw something in female apparel enter the little gate of the court-yard and come up over the bright moonlit snow towards the house, accompanied by a child; while the man with whom they had had the interview came behind transformed into an unmistakeable baggage-carrier.

Chapter XL.

Zeal was the spring whence flowed her hardiment.
Fairfax.

Barby undid bolt and lock and Fleda met the traveller in the hall. She was a lady; her air and dress shewed that, though the latter was very plain.

"Does Mr. Rossitur live here?" was her first word.

Fleda answered it, and brought her visitor into the sitting room. But the light falling upon a form and face that had seen more wear and tear than time, gave her no clue as to the who or what of the person before her. The stranger's hurried look round the room seemed to expect something.

"Are they all gone to bed?"

"All but me," said Fleda.

"We have been delayed—we took a wrong road—we've been riding for hours to find the place—hadn't the right direction."—Then looking keenly at Fleda, from whose vision an electric spark of intelligence had scattered the clouds, she said;

"I am Marion Rossitur."

"I knew it!" said Fleda, with lips and eyes that gave her already a sister's welcome; and they were folded in each other's arms almost as tenderly and affectionately, on the part of one at least, as if there had really been the relationship between them. But more than surprise and affection struck Fleda's heart.

"And where are they all, Fleda? Can't I see them?"

"You must wait till I have prepared them—Hugh and aunt Lucy are not very well. I don't know that it will do for you to see them at all to-night, Marion."

"Not to-night! They are not ill?"

"No—only enough to be taken care of—not ill. But it would be better to wait"

"And my father?"

"He is not at home."

Marion exclaimed in sorrow, and Fleda to hide the look that she felt was on her face stooped down to kiss the child. He was a remarkably fine-looking manly boy.

"That is your cousin Fleda," said his mother.

"No—*aunt* Fleda," said the person thus introduced—"don't put me off into cousindom, Marion. I am uncle Hugh's sister—and so I am your aunt Fleda. Who are you?"

"Rolf Rossitur Schwiden."

Alas how wide are the ramifications of evil! How was what might have been very pure pleasure utterly poisoned and turned into bitterness. It went through Fleda's heart with a keen pang when she heard that name and looked on the very fair brow that owned it, and thought of the ineffaceable stain that had come upon both. She dared look at nobody but the child. He already understood the melting eyes that were making acquaintance with his, and half felt the pain that gave so much tenderness to her kiss, and looked at her with a grave face of awakening wonder and sympathy. Fleda was glad to have business to call her into the kitchen.

"Who is it?" was Barby's immediate question.

"Aunt Lucy's daughter."

"She don't look much like her!" said Barby intelligently.

"They will want something to eat, Barby."

"I'll put the kettle on. It'll boil directly. I'll go in there and fix up the fire."

A word or two more, and then Fleda ran up to speak to her aunt and Hugh.

Her aunt she found in a state of agitation that was frightful. Even Fleda's assurances, with all the soothing arts she could bring to bear were some minutes before they could in any measure tranquillize her. Fleda's own nerves were in no condition to stand another shock when she left her and went to Hugh's door. But she could get no answer from him though she spoke repeatedly.

She did not return to her aunt's room. She went down stairs and brought up Barby and a light from thence.

Hugh was lying senseless and white; not whiter than his adopted sister as she stood by his side. Her eye went to her companion.

"Not a bit of it!" said Barby—"he's in nothing but a faint—just run down stairs and get the vinegar bottle, Fleda—the pepper vinegar.— Is there any water here?—"

Fleda obeyed; and watched, she could do little more, the efforts of Barby, who indeed needed no help, with the cold water, the vinegar, and rubbing of the limbs. They were for sometime unsuccessful; the fit was a severe one; and Fleda was exceedingly terrified before any signs of returning life came to reassure her.

"Now you go down stairs and keep quiet!" said Barby, when Hugh was fairly restored and had smiled a faint answer to Fleda's kiss and explanations,—"Go, Fleda! you ain't fit to stand. Go and sit down some place, and I'll be along directly and see how the fire burns. Don't you s'pose Mis' Rossitur could come in and sit in this easy-chair a spell without hurting herself?"

It occurred to Fleda immediately that it might do more good than harm to her aunt if her attention were diverted even by another cause of anxiety. She gently summoned her, telling her no more than was necessary to fit her for being Hugh's nurse; and in a very few minutes she and Barby were at liberty to attend to other claims upon them. But it sank into her heart, "Hugh will not get over this!"—and when she entered the sitting-room, what Mr. Carleton years before had said of the wood-flower was come true in its fullest extent—"a storm-wind had beaten it to the ground."

She was able literally to do no more than Barby had said, sit down and keep herself quiet. Miss Elster was in her briskest mood; flew in and out; made up the fire in the sitting-room and put on the kettle in the kitchen, which she had been just about doing when called to see Hugh. The much-needed supper of the travellers must be still waited for; but the fire was burning now, the room was cosily warm and bright, and Marion drew up her chair with a look of thoughtful contentment. Fleda felt as if some conjuror had been at work here for the last few hours—the room looked so like and felt so unlike itself.

"Are you going to be ill too, Fleda?" said Marion suddenly. "You are looking—very far from well!"

"I shall have a headache to-morrow," said Fleda quietly. "I generally know the day beforehand."

"Does it always make you look so?"

"Not always—I am somewhat tired."

"Where is my father gone?"

"I don't know.—Rolf, dear," said Fleda bending forward to the little fellow who was giving expression to some very fidgety impatience,—"what is the matter? what do you want?"

The child's voice fell a little from its querulousness towards the sweet key in which the questions had been put, but he gave utterance to a very decided wish for "bread and butter."

"Come here," said Fleda, reaching out a hand and drawing him, certainly with no force but that of attraction, towards her easy-chair,—"come here and rest yourself in this nice place by me—see, there is plenty of room for you;—and you shall have bread and butter and tea, and something else too, I guess, just as soon as Barby can get it ready."

"Who is Barby?" was the next question, in a most uncompromising tone of voice.

"You saw the woman that came in to put wood on the fire—that was Barby—she is very good and kind and will do anything for you if you behave yourself."

The child muttered, but so low as to shew some unwillingness that his words should reach the ears that were nearest him, that "he wasn't going to behave himself."

Fleda did not choose to hear; and went on with composing observations till the fair little face she had drawn to her side was as bright as the sun and returned her smile with interest.

"You have an admirable talent at moral suasion, Fleda," said the mother half smiling;—"I wish I had it."

"You don't need it so much here."

"Why not?"

"It may do very well for me, but I think not so well for you."

"Why?—what do you mean? I think it is the only way in the world to bring up children—the only way fit for rational beings to be guided."

Fleda smiled, though the faintest indication that lips could give, and shook her head,—ever so little.

"Why do you do that?—tell me."

"Because in my limited experience," said Fleda as she passed her fingers through the boy's dark locks of hair,—"in every household where 'moral suasion' has been the law, the children have been the administrators of it. Where is your husband?"

"I have lost him—years ago—" said Marion with a quick expressive glance towards the child. "I never lost what I at first thought I had, for I never had it. Do you understand?"

Fleda's eyes gave a sufficient answer.

"I am a widow—these five years—in all but what the law would require," Marion went on. "I have been alone since then—except my child. He was two years old then; and since then I have lived such a life, Fleda!—"

"Why didn't you come home?"

"Couldn't—the most absolute reason in the world. Think of it!— Come home! It was as much as I could do to stay there!"

Those sympathizing eyes were enough to make her go on.

"I have wanted everything—except trouble. I have done everything—except ask alms. I have learned, Fleda, that death is not the worst form in which distress can come."

Fleda felt stung, and bent down her head to touch her lips to the brow of little Rolf.

"Death would have been a trifle!" said Marion. "I mean,—not that *I* should have wished to leave Rolf alone in the world; but if I had been left—I mean I would rather wear outside than inside mourning."

Fleda looked up again, and at her.

"O I was so mistaken, Fleda!" she said clasping her hands,—"so mistaken!—in everything;—so disappointed,—in all my hopes. And the loss of my fortune was the cause of it all."

Nay verily! thought Fleda; but she said nothing; she hung her head again; and Marion after a pause went on to question her about an endless string of matters concerning themselves and other people, past doings and present prospects, till little Rolf soothed by the uninteresting soft murmur of voices fairly forgot bread and butter and himself in a sound sleep, his head resting upon Fleda.

"Here is one comfort for you, Marion," she said looking down at the dark eyelashes which lay on a cheek rosy and healthy as ever seven years old knew;—"he is a beautiful child, and I am sure, a fine one."

"It is thanks to his beauty that I have ever seen home again," said his mother.

Fleda had no heart this evening to speak words that were not necessary; her eyes asked Marion to explain herself.

"He was in Hyde Park one day—I had a miserable lodging not far from it, and I used to let him go in there, because he must go somewhere, you know,—I couldn't go with him—"

"Why not?"

"Couldn't!—Oh Fleda!—I have seen changes!—He was there one afternoon, alone, and had got into difficulty with some bigger boys — a little fellow, you know,—he stood his ground man-fully, but his strength wasn't equal to his spirit, and they were tyrannizing over him after the fashion of boys, who are I do think the ugliest creatures in creation!" said Mme. Schwiden, not apparently reckoning her own to be of the same gender,—"and a gentleman who was riding by stopped and interfered and took him out of their hands, and then asked him his name,—struck I suppose with his appearance. Very kind, wasn't it? men so seldom bother themselves about what becomes of children, I suppose there were thousands of others riding by at the same time."

"Very kind," Fleda said.

"When he heard what his name was he gave his horse to his servant and walked home with Rolf; and the next day he sent me a note, speaking of having known my father and mother and asking permission to call upon me.—I never was so mortified, I think, in my life," said Marion after a moment's hesitation.

"Why?" said Fleda, not a little at a loss to follow out the chain of her cousin's reasoning.

"Why I was in such a sort of a place—you don't know, Fleda; I was working then for a fancy store-keeper, to support myself—living in a miserable little two rooms.—If it had been a stranger I wouldn't have cared so much, but somebody that had known us in different times—I hadn't a thing in the world to answer the note upon but a half sheet of letter paper."

Fleda's lips sought Rolf's forehead again, with a curious rush of tears and smiles at once. Perhaps Marion had caught the expression of her countenance, for she added with a little energy,

"It is nothing to be surprised at—you would have felt just the same; for I knew by his note, the whole style of it, what sort of a person it must be."

"My pride has been a good deal chastened," Fleda said gently.

"I never want *mine* to be, beyond minding everything," said Marion; "and I don't believe yours is. I don't know why in the world I did not refuse to see him—I had fifty minds to—but he had won Rolf's heart, and I was a little curious, and it was something strange to see the face of a friend, any better one than my old landlady, so I let him come."

"Was *she* a friend?" said Fleda.

"If she hadn't been I should not have lived to be here—the best soul that ever was; but still, you know, she could do nothing for me but be as kind as she could live;—this was something different. So I let him come, and he came the next day."

Fleda was silent, a little wondering that Marion should be so frank with her, beyond what she had ever been in former years; but as she guessed, Mme. Schwiden's heart was a little opened by the joy of finding herself at home and the absolute necessity of talking to somebody; and there was a further reason which Fleda could not judge of, in her own face and manner. Marion needed no questions and went on again after stopping a moment.

"I was so glad in five minutes,—I can't tell you, Fleda,—that I had let him come. I forget entirely about how I looked and the wretched place I was in. He was all that I had supposed, and a great deal more, but somehow he hadn't been in the room three minutes before I didn't care at all for all the things I had thought would trouble me. Isn't it strange what a witchery some people have to make you forget everything but themselves!"

"The reason is, I think, because that is the only thing they forget," said Fleda, whose imagination however was entirely busy with the *singular* number.

"I shall never forget him," said Marion. "He was very kind to me—I cannot tell how kind—though I never realized it till afterwards; at the time it always seemed only a sort of elegant politeness which he could not help. I never saw so elegant a person. He came two or three times to see me and he took Rolf out with him I don't know how often, to drive; and he sent me fruit—such fruit!—and game, and flowers; and I had not had anything of the kind, not even seen it, for so long—I can't tell you what it was to me. He said he had known my father and mother well when they were abroad."

"What, was his name?" said Fleda quickly.

"I don't know—he never told me—and I never could ask him. Don't you know there are some people you can't do anything with but just what they please? There wasn't the least thing like stiffness—you never saw anybody less stiff,—but I never dreamed of asking him questions except when he was out of sight. Why, do you know him?" she said suddenly.

"When you tell me who he was I'll tell you," said Fleda smiling.

"Have you ever heard this story before?"

"Certainly not!"

"He is somebody that knows us very well," said Marion, "for he asked after every one of the family in particular."

"But what had all this to do with your getting home?"

"I don't wonder you ask. The day after his last visit came a note saying that he owed a debt in my family which it had never been in his power to repay; that he could not give the enclosure to my father, who would not recognize the obligation; and that if I would permit him to place it in my hands I should confer a singular favour upon him."

"And what was the enclosure?"

"Five hundred pounds."

Fleda's head went down again and tears dropped fast upon little Rolf's shoulder.

"I suppose my pride has been a little broken too," Marion went on, "or I shouldn't have kept it. But then if you saw the person, and the whole manner of it—I don't know how I could ever have sent it back. Literally I couldn't, though, for I hadn't the least clue. I never saw or heard from him afterwards."

"When was this, Marion?"

"Last spring."

"Last spring!—then what kept you so long?"

"Because of the arrival of eyes that I was afraid of. I dared not make the least move that would show I could move. I came off the very first packet after I was free."

"How glad you must be!" said Fleda.

"Glad!—"

"Glad of what, mamma?" said Rolf, whose dreams the entrance of Barby had probably disturbed.

"Glad of bread and butter," said his mother; "wake up—here it is."

The young gentleman declared, rubbing his eyes, that he did not want it now; but however Fleda contrived to dispel that illusion, and bread and butter was found to have the same dulcifying properties at Queechy that it owns in all the rest of the world. Little Rolf was completely mollified after a hearty meal and was put with his mother to enjoy most unbroken slumbers in Fleda's room. Fleda herself, after a look at Hugh, crept to her aunt's bed; whither Barby very soon despatched Mrs. Rossitur, taking in her place the arm-chair and the watch with most invincible good-will and determination; and sleep at last took the joys and sorrows of that disturbed household into its kind custody.

Fleda was the first one awake, and was thinking how she should break the last news to her aunt, when Mrs. Rossitur put her arms round her and after a most affectionate look and kiss, spoke to what she supposed had been her niece's purpose.

"You want taking care of more than I do, poor Fleda!"

"It was not for that I came," said Fleda;—"I had to give up my room to the travellers."

"Travellers!—"

A very few words more brought out the whole, and Mrs. Rossitur sprang out of bed and rushed to her daughter's room.

Fleda hid her face in the bed to cry—for a moment's passionate indulgence in weeping while no one could see. But a moment was all. There was work to do and she must not disable herself. She slowly got up, feeling thankful that her headache did not announce itself with the dawn, and that she would be able to attend to the morning affairs and the breakfast, which was something more of a circumstance now with the new additions to the family. More than that she knew from sure signs she would not be able to accomplish.

It was all done and done well, though with what secret flagging of mind and body nobody knew or suspected. The business of the day was arranged, Barby's course made clear, Hugh visited and smiled upon; and then Fleda set herself down in the breakfast-room to wear out the rest of the day in patient suffering. Her little spaniel, who seemed to understand her languid step and faint tones and know what was coming, crept into her lap and looked up at her with a face of equal truth and affection; and after a few gentle acknowledging touches from the loved hand, laid his head on her knees, and silently avowed his determination of abiding her fortunes for the remainder of the day.

They had been there for some hours. Mrs. Rossitur and her daughter were gathered in Hugh's room; whither Rolf also after sundry expressions of sympathy for Fleda's headache, finding it a dull companion, had departed. Pain of body rising above pain of mind had obliged as far as possible even thought to be still; when a loud rap at the front door brought the blood in a sudden flush of pain to Fleda's face. She knew instinctively what it meant.

She heard Barby's distinct accents saying that somebody was "not well." The other voice was more smothered. But in a moment the door of the breakfast-room opened and Mr. Thorn walked in.

The intensity of the pain she was suffering effectually precluded Fleda from discovering emotion of any kind. She could not move. Only King lifted up his head and looked at the intruder, who seemed shocked, and well he might. Fleda was in her old headache position; bolt upright on the sofa, her feet on the rung of a chair while her hands supported her by their grasp upon the back of it. The flush had passed away leaving the deadly paleness of pain, which the dark rings under her eyes shewed to be well seated.

"Miss Ringgan!" said the gentleman, coming up softly as to something that frightened him,—"my dear Miss Fleda!—I am distressed!—You are very ill—can nothing be done to relieve you?"

Fleda's lips rather than her voice said, "Nothing."

"I would not have come in on any account to disturb you if I had known—I did not understand you were more than a trifle ill—"

Fleda wished he would mend his mistake, as his understanding certainly by this time was mended. But that did not seem to be his conclusion of the best thing to do.

"Since I am here,—can you bear to hear me say three words? without too much pain?—I do not ask you to speak"—

A faint whispered "yes" gave him leave to go on. She had never looked at him. She sat like a statue; to answer by a motion of her head was more than could be risked.

He drew up a chair and sat down, while King looked at him with eyes of suspicious indignation.

"I am not surprised," he said gently, "to find you suffering. I knew how your sensibilities must feel the shock of yesterday—I would fain have spared it you—I will spare you all further pain on the same score if possible—Dear Miss Ringgan, since I am here and time is precious may I say one word before I cease troubling you—take it for granted that you were made acquainted with the contents of my letter to Mrs. Rossitur?—with *all* the contents?—were you?"

Again Fleda's lips almost voicelessly gave the answer.

"Will you give me what I ventured to ask for?" said he gently,—"the permission to work *for you?* Do not trouble those precious lips to speak—the answer of these fingers will be as sure a warrant to me as all words that could be spoken that you do not deny my request."

He had taken one of her hands in his own. But the fingers lay with unanswering coldness and lifelessness for a second in his clasp and then were drawn away and took determinate hold of the chair-back. Again the flush came to Fleda's cheeks, brought by a sharp pain,—oh, bodily and mental too!—and after a moment's pause, with a distinctness of utterance that let him know every word, she said,

"A generous man would not ask it, sir."

Thorn sprang up, and several times paced the length of the room, up and down, before he said anything more. He looked at Fleda, but the flush was gone again, and nothing could seem less conscious of his presence. Pain and patience were in every line of her face, but he could read nothing more, except a calmness as unmistakably written. Thorn gave that face repeated glances as he walked, then stood still and read it at leisure. Then he came to her side again and spoke in a different voice.

"You are so unlike anybody else," he said, "that you shall make me unlike myself. I will do freely what I hoped to do with the light of your smile before me. You shall hear no more of this affair, neither you nor the world—I have the matter perfectly in my own hands—it shall never raise a whisper again. I will move heaven and earth rather than fail—but there is no danger of my failing. I will try to prove myself worthy of your esteem even where a man is most excusable for being selfish."

He took one of her cold hands again,—Fleda could not help it without more force than she cared to use, and indeed pain would by this time almost have swallowed up other sensation if every word and touch had not sent it in a stronger throb to her very finger ends. Thorn bent his lips to her hand, twice kissed it fervently, and then left her; much to King's satisfaction, who thereupon resigned himself to quiet slumbers.

His mistress knew no such relief. Excitement had dreadfully aggravated her disorder, at a time when it was needful to banish even thought as far as possible. Pain effectually banished it now, and Barby coming in a little after Mr. Thorn had gone found her quite unable to speak and scarce able to breathe, from agony. Barby's energies and fainting remedies were again put in use; but pain reigned triumphant for hours, and when its hard rule was at last abated Fleda was able to do nothing but sleep like a child for hours more.

Towards a late tea-time she was at last awake, and carrying on a very one-sided conversation with Rolf, her own lips being called upon for little more than a smile now and then. King, not able to be in her lap, had curled himself up upon a piece of his mistress's dress and as close within the circle of her arms as possible, where Fleda's hand and his head were on terms of mutual satisfaction.

"I thought you wouldn't permit a dog to lie in your lap," said Marion.

"Do you remember that?" said Fleda with a smile. "Ah I have grown tender-hearted, Marion, since I have known what it was to want comfort myself. I have come to the conclusion that it is best to let everything have all the enjoyment it can in the circumstances. King crawled into my lap one day when I had not spirits enough to turn him out, and he has kept the place ever since.—Little King!"—In answer to which word of intelligence King looked in her face and wagged his tail, and then earnestly endeavoured to lick all her fingers. Which however was a piece of comfort she would not give him.

"Fleda," said Barby putting her head in, "I wish you'd just step out here and tell me which cheese you'd like to have cut."

"What a fool!" said Marion. "Let her cut them all if she likes."

"She is no fool," said Fleda. She thought Barby's punctiliousness however a little ill-timed, as she rose from her sofa and went into the kitchen.

"Well you *do* look as if you wa'n't good for nothing but to be taken care of!" said Barby. "I wouldn't have riz you up if it hadn't been just tea-time, and I knowed you couldn't stay quiet much longer;"—and with a look which explained her tactics she put into Fleda's hand a letter directed to her aunt.

"Philetus gave it to me," she said, without a glance at Fleda's face,—"he said it was give to him by a spry little shaver who wa'n't a mind to tell nothin' about himself."

"Thank you, Barby!" was Fleda's most grateful return; and summoning her aunt up-stairs she took her into her own room and locked the door before she gave her the letter which Barby's shrewdness and delicacy had taken such care should not reach its owner in a wrong way. Fleda watched her as her eye ran over the paper and caught it as it fell from her fingers.

"My Dear Wife,

"That villain Thorn has got a handle of me which he will not fail to use—you know it all I suppose, by this time—It is true that in an evil hour, long ago, when greatly pressed, I did what I thought I should surely undo in a few days—The time never came—I don't know why he has let it lie so long, but he has taken it up now, and he will push it to the extreme—There is but one thing left for me—I shall not see you again. The rascal would never let me rest, I know, in any spot that calls itself American ground.

"You will do better without me than with me.

"R. R."

Fleda mused over the letter for several minutes, and then touched her aunt who had fallen on a chair with her head sunk in her hands.

"What does he mean?" said Mrs. Rossitur, looking up with a perfectly colourless face.

"To leave the country."

"Are you sure? is that it?" said Mrs. Rossitur, rising and looking over the words again;—"He would do anything, Fleda—"

"That is what he means, aunt Lucy;—don't you see he says he could not be safe anywhere in America?"

Mrs. Rossitur stood eying with intense eagerness for a minute or two the note in her niece's hand.

"Then he is gone! now that it is all settled!—And we don't know where—and we can't get word to him—"

Her cheek which had a little brightened became perfectly white again.

"He isn't gone yet—he can't be—he cannot have left Queechy till to-day—he will be in New York for several days yet probably."

"New York!—it may be Boston?"

"No, he would be more likely to go to New York—I am sure he would—he is accustomed to it."

"We might write to both places," said poor Mrs. Rossitur. "I will do it and send them off at once."

"But he might not get the letters," said Fleda thoughtfully,—"he might not dare to ask at the post-office."

His wife looked at that possibility, and then wrung her hands.

"Oh why didn't he give us a clew!"

Fleda put an arm round her affectionately and stood thinking; stood trembling might as well be said, for she was too weak to be standing at all.

"What can we do, dear Fleda?" said Mrs. Rossitur in great distress. "Once out of New York and we can get nothing to him! If he only knew that there is no need, and that it is all over!—"

"We must do everything, aunt Lucy," said Fleda thoughtfully, "and I hope we shall succeed yet. We will write, but I think the most hopeful other thing we could do would be to put advertisements in the newspapers—he would be very likely to see them."

"Advertisements!—But you couldn't—what would you put in?"

"Something that would catch his eye and nobody's else—*that* is easy, aunt Lucy."

"But there is nobody to put them in, Fleda,—you said uncle Orrin was going to Boston—"

"He wasn't going there till next week, but he was to be in Philadelphia a few days before that—the letter might miss him."

"Mr. Plumfield!—Couldn't he?"

But Fleda shook her head.

"Wouldn't do, aunt Lucy—he would do all he could, but he don't know New York nor the papers—he wouldn't know how to manage it—he don't know uncle Rolf—shouldn't like to trust it to him."

"Who then?—there isn't a creature we could ask—"

Fleda laid her cheek to her poor aunt's and said,

"I'll do it."

"But you must be in New York to do it, dear Fleda,—you can't do it here."

"I will go to New York."

"When?"

"To-morrow morning."

"But dear Fleda, you can't go alone! I can't let you, and you're not fit to go at all, my poor child!—" and between conflicting feelings Mrs. Rossitur sat down and wept without measure.

"Listen, aunt Lucy," said Fleda, pressing a hand on her shoulder,—"listen, and don't cry so!—I'll go and make all right, if efforts can do it. I am not going alone—I'll get Seth to go with me; and I can sleep in the cars and rest nicely in the steamboat—I shall feel happy and well when I know that I am leaving you easier and doing all that can be done to bring uncle Rolf home. Leave me to manage, and don't say anything to Marion,—it is one blessed thing that she need not know anything about all this. I shall feel better than if I were at home and had trusted this business to any other hands."

"*You* are the blessing of my life," said Mrs. Rossitur.

"Cheer up, and come down and let us have some tea," said Fleda, kissing her; "I feel as if that would make me up a little; and then I'll write the letters. I sha'n't want but very little baggage; there'll be nothing to pack up."

Philetus was sent up the hill with a note to Seth Plumfield, and brought home a favorable answer. Fleda thought as she went to rest that it was well the mind's strength could sometimes act independently of its servant the body, hers felt so very shattered and unsubstantial.

CHAPTER XLI.

I thank you for your company; but good faith, I had as lief
have been myself alone. — As You Like It.

The first thing next morning Seth Plumfield came down to say that
he had seen Dr. Quackenboss the night before and had chanced to
find out that he was going to New York too, this very day; and
knowing that the doctor would be just as safe an escort as himself,
Seth had made over the charge of his cousin to him; "calculating," he
said, "that it would make no difference to Fleda and that he had
better stay at home with his mother."

Fleda said nothing and looked as little as possible of her
disappointment, and her cousin went away wholly unsuspecting of
it.

"Seth Plumfield ha'n't done a smarter thing than that in a good
while," Barby remarked satirically as he was shutting the door. "I
should think he'd ha' hurt himself."

"I dare say the doctor will take good care of me," said Fleda;—"as
good as he knows how."

"Men beat all!" said Barby impatiently.—"The little sense there is
into them!—"

Fleda's sinking heart was almost ready to echo the sentiment; but
nobody knew it.

Coffee was swallowed, her little travelling bag and bonnet on the
sofa; all ready. Then came the doctor.

"My dear Miss Ringgan!—I am most happy of this delightful
opportunity—I had supposed you were located at home for the
winter. This is a sudden start."

"Is it sudden to you, Dr. Quackenboss?" said Fleda.

"Why—a—not disagreeably so," said the doctor smiling;—"nothing could be that in the present circumstances,—but I—a—I hadn't calculated upon it for much of a spell beforehand."

Fleda was vexed, and looked,—only unconversable.

"I suppose," said the doctor after a pause,—"that we have not much time to waste—a—in idle moments. Which route do you intend to travel?"

"I was thinking to go by the North River, sir."

"But the ice has collected,—I am afraid,—"

"At Albany, I know; but when I came up there was a boat every other day, and we could get there in time by the stage—this is her day."

"But we have had some pretty tight weather since, if you remember," said the doctor; "and the boats have ceased to connect with the stage. We shall have to go to Greenfield to take the Housatonic which will land us at Bridgeport on the Sound"

"Have we time to reach Greenfield this morning?"

"Oceans of time?" said the doctor delightedly; "I've got my team here and they're jumping out of their skins with having nothing to do and the weather—they'll carry us there as spry as grasshoppers— now, if you're ready, my dear Miss Ringgan!"

There was nothing more but to give and receive those speechless lip-messages that are out of the reach of words, and Mrs. Rossitur's half-spoken last charge, to take care of *herself*; and with these seals upon her mission Fleda set forth and joined the doctor; thankful for one foil to curiosity in the shape of a veil and only wishing that there were any invented screen that she could place between her and hearing.

"I hope your attire is of a very warm description," said the doctor as he helped her into the wagon;—"it friz pretty hard last night and I don't think it has got out of the notion yet. If I had been consulted in any other—a—form, than that of a friend, I should have disapprobated, if you'll excuse me, Miss Ringgan's travelling again before her 'Rose of Cassius' there was in blow. I hope you have heard no evil tidings? Dr.—a—Gregory, I hope, is not taken ill?"

"I hope not, sir," said Fleda.

"He didn't look like it. A very hearty old gentleman. Not very old either, I should judge. Was he the brother of your mother or your father?"

"Neither, sir."

"Ah!—I misunderstood—I thought, but of course I was mistaken,—I thought I heard you speak to him under the title of uncle. But that is a title we sometimes give to elderly people as a term of familiarity— there is an old fellow that works for me,—he has been a long time in our family, and we always call him 'uncle Jenk.'"

Fleda was ready to laugh, cry, and be angry, in a breath. She looked straight before her and was mum.

"That 'Rose of Cassius' is a most exquisite thing!" said the doctor, recurring to the cluster of bare bushy stems in the corner of the garden. "Did Mr. Rossitur bring it with him when he came to his present residence?"

"Yes sir."

"Where is Mr. Rossitur now?"

Fleda replied, with a jump of her heart, that business affairs had obliged him to be away for a few days.

"And when does he expect to return?" said the doctor.

"I hope he will be home as soon as I am," said Fleda.

"Then you do not expect to remain long in the city this time?"

"I shall not have much of a winter at home if I do," said Fleda. "We are almost at January."

"Because," said the doctor, "in that case I should have no higher gratification than in attending upon your motions. I—a—beg you to believe, my dear Miss Ringgan, that it would afford me the—a— most particular—it would be most particularly grateful to me to wait upon you to—a—the confines of the world."

Fleda hastened to assure her officious friend that the time of her return was altogether uncertain; resolving rather to abide a guest with Mrs. Pritchard than to have Dr. Quackenboss hanging upon her motions every day of her being there. But in the mean time the doctor got upon Capt. Rossitur's subject; then came to Mr. Thorn; and then wanted to know the exact nature of Mr. Rossitur's business affairs in Michigan; through all which matters poor Fleda had to run the gauntlet of questions, interspersed with gracious speeches which she could bear even less well. She was extremely glad to reach the cars and take refuge in seeming sleep from the mongrel attentions, which if for the most part prompted by admiration owned so large a share of curiosity. Her weary head and heart would fain have courted the reality of sleep, as a refuge from more painful thoughts and a feeling of exhaustion that could scarcely support itself; but the restless roar and jumble of the rail-cars put it beyond her power. How long the hours were—how hard to wear out, with no possibility of a change of position that would give rest; Fleda would not even raise her head when they stopped, for fear of being talked to; how trying that endless noise to her racked nerves. It came to an end at last, though Fleda would not move for fear they might be only taking in wood and water.

"Miss Ringgan!" said the doctor in her ear,—"my dear Miss Ringgan!—we are here!—"

"Are we?" said Fleda, looking up;—"what other name has the place, doctor?"

"Why Bridgeport," said the doctor,—"we're at Bridgeport—now we have leave to exchange conveyances. A man feels constrained after a prolonged length of time in a place. How have you enjoyed the ride?"

"Not very well—it has seemed long. I am glad we are at the end of it!"

But as she rose and threw back her veil the doctor looked startled.

"My dear Miss Ringgan!—are you faint?"

"No sir."

"You are not well, indeed!—I am very sorry—the ride has been—Take my arm!—Ma'am," said the doctor touching a black satin cloak which filled the passage-way,—"will you have the goodness to give this lady a passport?"

But the black satin cloak preferred a straightforward manner of doing this, so their egress was somewhat delayed. Happily faintness was not the matter.

"My dear Miss Ringgan!" said the doctor as they reached the ground and the outer air,—"what was it?—the stove too powerful? You are looking—you are of a dreadfully delicate appearance!"

"I had a headache yesterday," said Fleda; "it always leaves me with a disagreeable reminder the next day. I am not ill."

But he looked frightened, and hurried her, as fast as he dared, to the steamboat; and there proposed half a dozen restoratives; the simplest of which Fleda took, and then sought delicious rest from him and from herself on the cushions of a settee. Delicious!—though she was alone, in the cabin of a steamboat, with strange forms and noisy tongues around her, the closed eyelids shut it out all; and she had time but for one resting thought of "patient continuance in well-doing," and one happy heart-look up to him who has said that he cares for his children, a look that laid her anxieties down there,—when past misery and future difficulty faded away before a sleep that lasted till the vessel reached her moorings and was made fast.

She was too weary and faint even to think during the long drive up to Bleecker-st. She was fain to let it all go—the work she had to do and the way she must set about it, and rest in the assurance that nothing could be done that night. She did not so much as hear Dr. Quackenboss's observations, though she answered a few of them, till, at the door, she was conscious of his promising to see her to-morrow and of her instant conclusion to take measures to see nobody.

How strange everything seemed. She walked through the familiar hall, feeling as if her acquaintance with every old thing was broken. There was no light in the back parlour, but a comfortable fire.

"Is my—is Dr. Gregory at home?" she asked of the girl who had let her in.

"No ma'am; he hasn't got back from Philadelphia."

"Tell Mrs. Pritchard a lady wants to see her."

Good Mrs. Pritchard was much more frightened than Dr. Quackenboss had been when she came into the back parlour to see "a lady" and found Fleda in the great arm-chair taking off her things. She poured out questions, wonderings and lamentings, not "in a breath" but in a great many; quite forgot to be glad to see her, she looked so dreadfully; and "what *had* been the matter?" Fleda answered her,—told of yesterday's illness and to-day's journey; and met all her shocked enquiries with so composed a face and such a calm smile and bearing, that Mrs. Pritchard was almost persuaded not to believe her eyes.

"My uncle is not at home?"

"O no, Miss Fleda! I suppose he's in Philadelphy—but his motions is so little to be depended on that I never know when I have him; maybe he'll stop going through to Boston, and maybe no, and I don't know when; so anyhow I had to have a fire made and this room all ready; and ain't it lucky it was ready for you to-night!—and now he ain't here you can have the great chair all to yourself and make yourself comfortable—we can keep warmer here, I guess, than you can in the country," said the good housekeeper, giving some skilful admonishing touches to the fire;—"and you must just sit there and read and rest, and see if you can't get back your old looks again. If I thought it was *that* you came for I'd be happy. I never *did* see such a change in any one in five days!—"

She stood looking down at her guest with a face of very serious concern, evidently thinking much more than she chose to give utterance to.

"I am tired, Mrs. Pritchard," said Fleda, smiling up at her.

"I wish you had somebody to take care of you, Miss Fleda, that wouldn't let you tire yourself. It's a sin to throw your strength away so—and you don't care for looks nor nothing else when it's for other people. You're looking just as handsome, too, for all," she said, her mouth giving way a little, as she stooped down to take off Fleda's overshoes, "but that's only because you can't help it. Now what is there you'd like to have for supper!—just say and you shall have it—whatever would seem best—because I mightn't hit the right thing?"

Fleda declared her indifference to everything but a cup of tea, and her hostess bustled away to get that and tax her own ingenuity and kindness for the rest. And leaning her weary head back in the lounge

Fleda tried to think,—but it was not time yet; she could only feel; feel what a sad change had come over her since she had sat there last; shut her eyes and wish she could sleep again.

But Mrs. Pritchard's hospitality must be gone through with first.

The nicest of suppers was served in the bright little parlour and her hostess was a compound of care and good will; nothing was wanting to the feast but a merry heart. Fleda could not bring that, so her performance was unsatisfactory and Mrs. Pritchard was distressed. Fleda went to her own room promising better doings to-morrow.

She awoke in the morning to the full burden of care and sorrow which sheer weakness and weariness the day before had in part laid down; to a quicker sense of the state of things than she had had yet. The blasting evil that had fallen upon them,—Fleda writhed on her bed when she thought of it. The sternest, cruellest, most inflexible, grasp of distress. Poverty may be borne, death may be sweetened, even to the survivors; but *disgrace*—Fleda hid her head, as if she would shut the idea out with the light. And the ruin it had wrought. Affection killed at the root,—her aunt's happiness withered, for this world,—Hugh's life threatened,—the fair name of his family gone,— the wear and weariness of her own spirit,—but that had hardly a thought. Himself?—oh no one could tell what a possible wreck, now that self-respect and the esteem of others, those two safe-guards of character, were lost to him. "So much security has any woman in a man without religion;" she remembered those words of her aunt Miriam now; and she thought if Mr. Thorn had sought an ill wind to blow upon his pretensions he could not have pitched them better. What fairer promise, without religion, could be than her uncle had given? Reproach had never breathed against his name, and no one less than those who knew him best could fancy that he had ever given it occasion. And who could have more at stake?—and the stake was lost—that was the summing up thought.

No, it was not,—for Fleda's mind presently sprang beyond,—to the remedy; and after a little swift and earnest flitting about of thought over feasibilities and contingencies, she jumped up and dressed herself with a prompt energy which shewed a mind made up to its course. And yet when she came down to the parlour, though bending herself with nervous intentness to the work she had to do, her fingers and her heart were only stayed in their trembling by some of the happy assurances she had been fleeing to; —

"Commit thy works unto the Lord, and all thy thoughts shall be established." —

"In all thy ways acknowledge Him: He shall direct they paths." —

—Assurances, not indeed that her plans should meet with success, but that they should have the issue best for them.

She was early, but the room was warm and in order and the servant had left it. Fleda sought out paper and pencil and sat down to fashion the form of an advertisement, — the first thing to be done. She had no notion how difficult a thing till she came to do it.

"*R. R. is entreated to communicate with his niece at the old place in Bleecker-street, on business of the greatest importance.*"

"It will not do," said Fleda to herself as she sat and looked at it, — "there is not enough to catch his eye; and there is *too much* if it caught anybody else's eye; — 'R. R.', and 'his niece,' and 'Bleecker-street,' — that would tell plain enough."

"*Dear uncle, F. has followed you here on business of the greatest importance. Pray let her see you — she is at the old place.*"

"It will not do," thought Fleda again, — "there is still less to catch his eye — I cannot trust it. And if I were to put 'Queechy' over it, that would give the clue to the Evelyns and everybody. But I had better risk anything rather than his seeing it —"

The miserable needlessness of the whole thing, the pitiful weighing of sorrow against sorrow, and shame against shame overcame her for a little; and then dashing away the tears she had no time for and locking up the strong box of her heart, she took her pencil again.

"*Queechy*.

"*Let me see you at the old place. I have come here on urgent business* for you. *Do not deny me, for H—-'s sake!*"

With a trifle of alteration she thought this would do; and went on to make a number of fair copies of it for so many papers, This was done and all traces of it out of the way before Mrs. Pritchard came in and the breakfast; and after bracing herself with coffee, though the good housekeeper was still sadly dissatisfied with her indifference to some more substantial brace in the shape of chickens and ham, Fleda prepared herself inwardly and outwardly to brave the wind and the newspaper offices, and set forth. It was a bright keen day; she was sorry; she would it had been cloudy. It seemed as if she could not hope to escape some eyes in such an atmosphere.

She went to the library first, and there requested the librarian, whom she knew, to bring her from the reading-room the files of morning and evening papers. They were many more than she had supposed; she had not near advertisements enough. Paper and ink were at hand however, and making carefully her list of the various offices, morning and evening separate, she wrote out a copy of the notice for each of them.

The morning was well on by the time she could leave the library. It was yet far from the fashionable hour, however, and sedulously shunning the recognition of anybody, in hopes that it would be one step towards her escaping theirs, she made her way down the bright thoroughfare as far as the City Hall, and then crossed over the Park and plunged into a region where it was very little likely she would see a face that she knew. She saw nothing else either that she knew; in spite of having studied the map of the city in the library she was forced several times to ask her way, as she visited office after office, of the evening papers first, till she had placed her notice with each one of them. Her courage almost failed her, her heart did quite, after two or three. It was a trial from which her whole nature shrank, to go among the people, to face the eyes, to exchange talk with the lips, that were at home in those purlieus; look at them she did not. Making her slow way through the choked narrow streets, where the mere confusion of business was bewildering, — very, to any one come from Queechy; among crowds, of what mixed and doubtful character, hurrying along and brushing with little ceremony past her; edging by loitering groups that filled the whole sidewalk, or perhaps edging through them, groups whose general type of character was sufficiently plain and unmixed; entering into parley with clerk after clerk who looked at such a visiter as an anomaly, — poor Fleda almost thought so too, and shrank within herself; venturing hardly her eyes beyond her thick veil, and shutting her ears resolutely as far as possible to all the dissonant rough voices that helped to assure her she was where she ought not to be. Sometimes she felt that it was *impossible* to go on and finish her task; but a thought or two nerved her again to plunge into another untried quarter or make good her entrance to some new office through a host of loungers and waiting news-boys collected round the door. Sometimes in utter discouragement she went on and walked to a distance and came back, in the hope of a better opportunity. It was a long business; and she often had to wait. The end of her list was reached at last, and the paper was thrown away; but she did not draw free breath till she had got to the west side of Broadway again, and turned her back upon them all.

It was late then, and the street was thinned of a part of its gay throng. Completely worn, in body as well as mind, with slow faltering steps, Fleda moved on among those still left; looking upon them with a curious eye as if they and she belonged to different classes of beings; so very far her sobered and saddened spirit seemed to herself from their stir of business and gayety; if they had been a train of lady-flies or black ants Fleda would hardly have felt that she had less in common with them. It was a weary long way up to Bleecker-street, as she was forced to travel it.

The relief was unspeakable to find herself within her uncle's door with the sense that her dreaded duty was done, and well and thoroughly. Now her part was to be still and wait. But with the relief came also a reaction from the strain of the morning. Before her weary feet had well mounted the stairs her heart gave up its control; and she locked herself in her room to yield to a helpless outpouring of tears which she was utterly unable to restrain, though conscious that long time could not pass before she would be called to dinner. Dinner had to wait.

"Miss Fleda," said the housekeeper in a vexed tone when the meal was half over, —"I didn't know you ever did any thing wrong."

"You are sadly mistaken, Mrs. Pritchard," said Fleda half lightly, half sadly.

"You're looking not a bit better than last night, and if anything rather worse," Mrs. Pritchard went on. "It isn't right, Miss Fleda. You oughtn't to ha' set the first step out of doors, I know you oughtn't, this blessed day; and you've been on your feet these seven hours, — and you shew it! You're just ready to drop."

"I will rest to-morrow," said Fleda, —"or try to."

"You are fit for nothing but bed," said the housekeeper, —"and you've been using yourself, Miss Fleda, as if you had the strength of an elephant. Now do you think you've been doing right?"

Fleda would have made some cheerful answer, but she was not equal to it; she had lost all command of herself, and she dropped knife and fork to burst into a flood of exceeding tears. Mrs. Pritchard equally astonished and mystified, hurried questions, apologies, and consolations, one upon another; and made up her mind that there was something mysterious on foot about which she had better ask no questions. Neither did she, from that time. She sealed up her mouth, and contented herself with taking the best care of her guest that she possibly could. Needed enough, but all of little avail.

The reaction did not cease with that day. The next, Sunday, was spent on the sofa, in a state of utter prostration. With the necessity for exertion the power had died. Fleda could only lie upon the cushions, and sleep helplessly, while Mrs. Pritchard sat by, anxiously watching her; curiosity really swallowed up in kind feeling. Monday was little better, but towards the after part of the day the stimulant of anxiety began to work again, and Fleda sat up to watch for a word from her uncle, But none came, and Tuesday morning distressed Mrs. Pritchard with its want of amendment. It was not to be hoped for, Fleda knew, while this fearful watching lasted. Her uncle might not have seen the advertisement—he might not have got her letter— he might be even then setting sail to quit home forever. And she could do nothing but wait. Her nerves were alive to every stir; every touch of the bell made her tremble; it was impossible to read, to lie down, to be quiet or still anywhere. She had set the glass of expectancy for one thing in the distance; and all things else were a blur or a blank.

They had sat down to dinner that Tuesday, when a ring at the door which had made her heart jump was followed—yes, it was,—by the entrance of the maid-servant holding a folded bit of paper in her hand. Fleda did not wait to ask whose it was; she seized it and saw; and sprang away up stairs. It was a sealed scrap of paper, that had been the back of a letter, containing two lines without signature.

"I will meet you *at Dinah's*—if you come there alone about sundown."

Enough! Dinah was an old black woman who once had been a very attached servant in Mr. Rossitur's family, and having married and become a widow years ago, had set up for herself in the trade of a washerwoman, occupying an obscure little tenement out towards Chelsea. Fleda had rather a shadowy idea of the locality, though remembering very well sundry journeys of kindness she and Hugh had made to it in days gone by. But she recollected it was in Sloman-street and she knew she could find it; and dropping upon her knees poured out thanks too deep to be uttered and too strong to be even thought without a convulsion of tears. Her dinner after that was but a mental thanksgiving; she was hardly conscious of anything beside;

and a thankful rejoicing for all her weary labours. Their weariness was sweet to her now. Let her but see him;—the rest was sure.

Chapter XLII.

How well appaid she was her bird to find.
Sidney.

Fleda counted the minutes till it wanted an hour of sundown; and then avoiding Mrs. Pritchard made her escape out of the house. A long walk was before her and the latter part of it through a region which she wished to pass while the light was good. And she was utterly unable to travel at any but a very gentle rate. So she gave herself plenty of time.

It was a very bright afternoon and all the world was astir. Fleda shielded herself with a thick veil and went up one of the narrow streets, not daring to venture into Broadway; and passing Waverly Place which was almost as bright, turned down Eighth-street. A few blocks now and she would be out of all danger of meeting any one that knew her. She drew her veil close and hurried on. But the proverb saith "a miss is as good as a mile," and with reason; for if fate wills the chances make nothing. As Fleda set her foot down to cross Fifth Avenue she saw Mr. Carleton on the other side coming up from Waverly Place. She went as slowly as she dared, hoping that he would pass without looking her way, or be unable to recognize her through her thick wrapper. In vain, — she soon saw that she was known; he was waiting for her, and she must put up her veil and speak to him.

"Why I thought you had left New York," said he; — "I was told so."

"I had left it — I have left it, sir," said Fleda; — "I have only come back for a day or two —"

"Have you been ill?" he said with a sudden change of tone, the light in his eye and smile giving place to a very marked gravity.

Fleda would have answered with a half smile, but such a sickness of heart came over her that speech failed and she was very near bursting into tears. Mr. Carleton looked at her earnestly a moment, and then put the hand which Fleda had forgotten he still held, upon his arm and began to walk forward gently with her. Something in the grave tenderness with which this was done reminded Fleda irresistibly of the times when she had been a child under his care; and somehow her thoughts went off on a tangent back to the further days of her mother and father and grandfather, the other friends from whom she had had the same gentle protection, which now there was no one in the world to give her. And their images did never seem more winning fair than just then, — when their place was left most especially empty. Her uncle she had never looked up to in the same way, and whatever stay he had been was cut down. Her aunt leaned upon *her*; and Hugh had always been more of a younger than an elder brother. The quick contrast of those old happy childish days was too strong; the glance back at what she had had, made her feel the want. Fleda blamed herself, reasoned and fought with herself;—but she was weak in mind and body, her nerves were unsteady yet, her spirits unprepared for any encounter or reminder of pleasure; and though vexed and ashamed she *could* not hold her head up, and she could not prevent tear after tear from falling as they went along; she could only hope that nobody saw them.

Nobody spoke of them. But then nobody said anything; and the silence at last frightened her into rousing herself She checked her tears and raised her head; she ventured no more; she dared not turn her face towards her companion. He looked at her once or twice, as if in doubt whether to speak or not.

"Are you not going beyond your strength?" he said at length gently.

Fleda said no, although in a tone that half confessed his suspicion. He was silent again, however, and she cast about in vain for something to speak of; it seemed to her that all subjects of conversation in general had been packed up for exportation, neither eye nor memory could light upon a single one. Block after block was passed, the pace at which he walked, and the manner of his care for her, alone shewing that he knew what a very light hand was resting upon his arm.

"How pretty the curl of blue smoke is from that chimney," he said.

It was said with a tone so carelessly easy that Fleda's heart jumped for one instant in the persuasion that he had seen and noticed nothing peculiar about her.

"I know it," she said eagerly,—"I have often thought of it— especially here in the city—"

"Why is it? what is it?—"

Fleda's eye gave one of its exploratory looks at his, such as he remembered from years ago, before she spoke.

"Isn't it contrast?—or at least I think that helps the effect here."

"What do you make the contrast?" he said quietly.

"Isn't it," said Fleda with another glance, "the contrast of something pure and free and upward-tending, with what is below it. I did not mean the mere painter's contrast. In the country smoke is more picturesque, but in the city I think it has more character."

"To how many people do you suppose it ever occurred that smoke had a character?" said he smiling.

"You are laughing at me, Mr. Carleton? perhaps I deserve it."

"You do not think that," said he with a look that forbade her to think it. "But I see you are of Lavater's mind, that everything has a physiognomy?"

"I think he was perfectly right," said Fleda. "Don't you, Mr. Carleton?"

"To some people, yes!—But the expression is so subtle that only very nice sensibilities, with fine training, can hope to catch it; therefore to the mass of the world Lavater would talk nonsense."

"That is a gentle hint to me. But if I talk nonsense I wish you would set me right, Mr. Carleton;—I am very apt to amuse myself with tracing out fancied analogies in almost everything, and I may carry it too far—too far—to be spoken of wisely. I think it enlarges one's field of pleasure very much. Where one eye is stopped, another is but invited on."

"So," said Mr. Carleton, "while that puff of smoke would lead one person's imagination only down the chimney to the kitchen fire, it would take another's——where did yours go?" said he suddenly turning round upon her.

Fleda met his eye again, without speaking; but her look had perhaps more than half revealed her thought, for she was answered with a smile so intelligent and sympathetic that she was abashed.

"How very much religion heightens the enjoyments of life," Mr. Carleton said after a while.

Fieda's heart throbbed an answer; she did not speak.

"Both in its direct and indirect action. The mind is set free from influences that narrowed its range and dimmed its vision; and refined to a keener sensibility, a juster perception, a higher power of appreciation, by far, than it had before. And then, to say nothing of religion's own peculiar sphere of enjoyment, technically religious,—what a field of pleasure it opens to its possessor in the world of moral beauty, most partially known to any other,—and the fine but exquisite analogies of things material with things spiritual,—those *harmonies of Nature*, to which, talk as they will, all other ears are deaf!"

"You know," said Fleda with full eyes that she dared not shew, "how Henry Martyn said that he found he enjoyed painting and music so much more after he became a Christian."

"I remember. It is the substituting a just medium for a false one—it is putting nature within and nature without in tune with each other, so that the chords are perfect now which were jarring before."

"And yet how far people would be from believing you, Mr. Carleton."

"Yes—they are possessed with the contrary notion. But in all the creation nothing has a one-sided usefulness;—what a reflection it would be upon the wisdom of its author if godliness alone were the exception—if it were not 'profitable for the life that now is, as well as for that which is to come'!"

"They make that work the other way, don't they?" said Fleda.—"Not being able to see how thorough religion should be for anybody's happiness, they make use of your argument to conclude that it is not what the Bible requires. How I have heard that urged—that God intended his creatures to be happy—as a reason why they should disobey him. They lay hold on the wrong end of the argument and work backwards."

"Precisely.

"'God intended his creatures to be happy.

"'Strict obedience would make them unhappy.

"'Therefore, he does not intend them to obey.'"

"They never put it before them quite so clearly," said Fleda.

"They would startle at it a little. But so they would at the right stating of the case."

"And how would that be, Mr. Carleton?"

"It might be somewhat after this fashion—

"'God requires nothing that is not for the happiness of his people —

"'He requires perfect obedience —

"'Therefore perfect obedience is for their happiness'

"But unbelief will not understand that. Did it ever strike you how much there is in those words 'Come and see'? — All that argument can do, after all, is but to persuade to that. Only faith will submit to terms and enter the narrrow gate; and only obedience knows what the prospect is on the other side."

"But isn't it true, Mr. Carleton, that the world have some cause for their opinion? — judging as they do by the outside? The peculiar pleasures of religion, as you say, are out of sight, and they do not always find in religious people that enlargement and refinement of which you were speaking."

"Because they make unequal comparisons. Recollect that, as God has declared, the ranks of religion are not for the most part filled from the wise and the great. In making your estimate you must measure things equal in other respects. Compare the same man with himself before he was a Christian or with his unchristianized fellows — and you will find invariably the refining, dignifying, ennobling, influence of true religion; the enlarged intelligence and the greater power of enjoyment."

"And besides those causes of pleasure-giving that you mentioned," said Fleda, — "there is a mind at ease; and how much that is alone. If I may judge others by myself, — the mere fact of being unpoised — unresting — disables the mind from a thousand things that are joyfully relished by one entirely at ease."

"Yes," said he, — "do you remember that word — 'The stones of the field shall be at peace with thee'?"

"I am afraid people would understand you as little as they would me, Mr. Carleton," said Fleda laughing.

He smiled, rather a prolonged smile, the expression of which Fleda could not make out; she felt that *she* did not quite understand him.

"I have thought," said he after a pause, "that much of the beauty we find in many things is owing to a hidden analogy—the harmony they make with some unknown string of the mind's harp which they have set a vibrating. But the music of that is so low and soft that one must listen very closely to find out what it is."

"Why that is the very theory of which I gave you a smoky illustration a little while ago," said Fleda. "I thought I was on safe ground, after what you said about the characters of flowers, for that was a little—"

"Fanciful?" said he smiling.

"What you please," said Fleda colouring a little,—"I am sure it is true. The theory, I mean. I have many a time felt it, though I never put it in words. I shall think of that."

"Did you ever happen to see the very early dawn of a winter's morning?" said he.

But he laughed the next instant at the comical expression of Fleda's face as it was turned to him.

"Forgive me for supposing you as ignorant as myself. I have seen it—once."

"Appreciated it, I hope, that time?" said Fleda.

"I shall never forget it."

"And it never wrought in you a desire to see it again?"

"I might see many a dawn," said he smiling, "without what I saw then. It was very early—and a cloudy morning, so that night had still almost undisturbed possession of earth and sky; but in the south-

236

eastern quarter, between two clouds, there was a space of fair white promise, hardly making any impression upon the darkness but only set off by it. And upon this one bright spot in earth or heaven, rode the planet of the morning—the sun's forerunner—bright upon the brightness. All else was dusky—except where overhead the clouds had parted again and shewed a faint old moon, glimmering down upon the night it could no longer be said to 'rule'."

"Beautiful!" said Fleda. "There is hardly any time I like so well as the dawn of a winter morning with an old moon in the sky. Summer weather has no beauty like it—in some things."

"Once," continued Mr, Carleton, "I should have seen no more than I have told you—the beauty that every cultivated eye must take in. But now, methought I saw the dayspring that has come upon a longer night—and from out of the midst of it there was the fair face of the morning star looking at me with its sweet reminder and invitation—looking over the world with its aspect of triumphant expectancy;—there was its calm assurance of the coming day,—its promise that the star of hope which now there were only a few watching eyes to see, should presently be followed by the full beams of the Sun of righteousness making the kingdoms of the world his own.—Your memory may bring to you the words that came to mine,—the promise 'to him that overcometh', and the beauty of the lips that made it—the encouragement to 'patient continuance in well-doing', 'till the day break and the shadows flee away.'—And there on the other hand was the substituted light of earth's wisdom and inventions, dominant yet, but waning and soon to be put out for ever."

Fleda was crying again, and perhaps that was the reason why Mr. Carleton was silent for some time. She was very sorry to shew herself so weak, but she could not help it; part of his words had come too close. And when she had recovered again she was absolutely silent too, for they were nearing Sloman-street and she could not take him there with her. She did not know what to say, nor what he would think; and she said not another word till they came to the corner. There she must stop and speak.

"I am very much obliged to you, Mr. Carleton," she said drawing her hand from his arm, "for taking care of me all this disagreeable way — I will not give you any more trouble."

"You are not going to dismiss me?" said he looking at her with a countenance of serious anxiety.

"I must," said Fleda ingenuously, — "I have business to attend to here —"

"But you will let me have the pleasure of waiting for you?"

"O no," said Fleda hesitating and flushing, — "thank you, Mr. Carleton, — but pray do not — I don't know at all how long I may be detained."

He bowed, she thought gravely, and turned away, and she entered the little wretched street; with a strange feeling of pain that she could not analyze. She did not know where it came from, but she thought if there only had been a hiding-place for her she could have sat down and wept a whole heartful. The feeling must be kept back now, and it was soon forgotten in the throbbing of her heart at another thought which took entire possession.

The sun was not down, there was time enough, but it was with a step and eye of hurried anxiety that Fleda passed along the little street, for fear of missing her quest or lest Dinah should have changed her domicil. Yet would her uncle have named it for their meeting if he had not been sure of it? It was very odd he should have appointed that place at all, and Fleda was inclined to think he must have seen Dinah by some chance, or it never would have come into his head. Still her eye passed unheeding over all the varieties of dinginess and misery in her way, intent only upon finding that particular dingy cellar-way which used to admit her to Dinah's premises. It was found at last, and she went in.

The old woman, herself most unchanged, did not know the young lady, but well remembered the little girl whom Fleda brought to her mind. And then she was overjoyed to see her, and asked a multitude of questions, and told a long story of her having met Mr. Rossitur in the street the other day "in the last place where she'd have looked to see him;" and how old he had grown, and how surprised she had been to see the grey hairs in his head. Fleda at last gave her to understand that she expected him to meet her there and would like to see him alone; and the good woman immediately took her work into another apartment, made up the fire and set up the chairs, and leaving her assured Fleda she would lock up the doors "and not let no one come through."

It was sundown, and later, Fleda thought, and she felt as if every pulse was doing double duty. No matter—if she were shattered and the work done. But what work!—Oh the needlessness, the cruelty, the folly of it! And how much of the ill consequences she might be unable after all to ward off. She took off her hat, to relieve a nervous smothered feeling; and walked, and sat down; and then sat still, from trembling inability to do anything else. Dinah's poor little room, clean though it was, looked to her the most dismal place in the world from its association with her errand; she hid her face on her knees that she might have no disagreeableness to contend with but that which could not be shut out.

It had lain there some time, till a sudden felling of terror at the growing lateness made her raise it to look at the window. Mr. Rossitur was standing still before her, he must have come in very softly,—and looking,—oh Fleda had not imagined him looking so changed. All was forgotten,—the wrong, and the needlessness, and the indignation with which she had sometimes thought of it; Fleda remembered nothing but love and pity, and threw herself upon his neck with such tears of tenderness and sympathy, such kisses of forgiveness and comfort-speaking, as might have broken a stouter heart than Mr. Rossitur's. He held her in his arms for a few minutes, passively suffering her caresses, and then gently unloosing her hold placed her on a seat; sat down a little way off, covered his face and groaned aloud.

Fleda could not recover herself at once. Then shaking off her agitation she came and knelt down by his side and putting one arm over his shoulder laid her cheek against his forehead. Words were beyond reach, but his forehead was wet with her tears; and kisses, of soft entreaty, of winning assurance, said all she could say.

"What did you come here for, Fleda?" said Mr. Rossitur at length, without changing his position.

"To bring you home, uncle Rolf."

"Home!" said he, with an accent between bitterness and despair.

"Yes, for it's all over, it's all forgotten—there is no more to be said about it at all," said Fleda, getting her words out she didn't know how.

"What is forgotten?" said he harshly.

"All that you would wish, sir," replied Fleda softly and gently;— "there is no more to be done about it; and I came to tell you if possible before it was too late. Oh I'm so glad!—" and her arms and her cheek pressed closer as fresh tears stopped her voice.

"How do you know, Fleda?" said Mr. Rossitur raising his head and bringing hers to his shoulder, while his arms in turn enclosed her.

Fleda whispered, "He told me so himself."

"Who?"

"Mr. Thorn."

The words were but just spoken above her breath. Mr. Rossitur was silent for some time.

"Are you sure you understood him?"

"Yes, sir; it could not have been spoken plainer."

"Are you quite sure he meant what he said, Fleda?"

"Perfectly sure, uncle Rolf! I know he did."

"What stipulation did he make beforehand?"

"He did it without any stipulation, sir."

"What was his inducement then? If I know him he is not a man to act without any."

Fleda's cheek was dyed, but except that she gave no other answer.

"Why has it been left so long?" said her uncle presently.

"I don't know, sir—he said nothing about that. He promised that neither we nor the world should hear anything more of it."

"The world?" said Mr. Rossitur.

"No sir, he said that only one or two persons had any notion of it and that their secrecy he had the means of securing."

"Did he tell you anything more?"

"Only that he had the matter entirely under his control and that never a whisper of it should be heard again, No promise could be given more fully and absolutely."

Mr. Rossitur drew a long breath, speaking to Fleda's ear very great relief, and was silent.

"And what reward is he to have for this, Fleda?" he said after some musing.

"All that my hearty thanks and gratitude can give, as far as I am concerned, sir."

"Is that what he expects, Fleda?"

"I cannot help what he expects," said Fleda, in some distress.

"What have you engaged yourself to, my child?"

"Nothing in the world, uncle Rolf!" said Fleda earnestly—"nothing in the world. I haven't engaged myself to anything. The promise was made freely, without any sort of stipulation."

Mr. Rossitur looked thoughtful and disquieted. Fleda's tears were pouring again.

"I will not trust him," he said,—"I will not stay in the country!"

"But you will come home, uncle?" said Fleda, terrified.

"Yes my dear child—yes my dear child!" he said tenderly, putting his arms round Fleda again and kissing, with an earnestness of acknowledgment that went to her heart, her lips and brow,—"you shall do what you will with me; and when I go, we will all go together."

From Queechy! From America!—But she had no time for that thought now.

"You said 'for Hugh's sake,'" Mr. Rossitur observed after a pause, and with some apparent difficulty;—"what of him?"

"He is not well, uncle Rolf," said Fleda,—"and I think the best medicine will be the sight of you again."

Mr. Rossitur looked pale and was silent a moment.

"And my wife?" he said.

His face, and the thought of those faces at home, were too much for Fleda; she could not help it; "Oh, uncle Rolf," she said, hiding her face, "they only want to see you again now!"

Mr. Rossitur leaned his head in his hands and groaned; and Fleda could but cry; she felt there was nothing to say.

"It was for Marion," he said at length;—"it was when I was hard pressed and I was fearful if it were known that it might ruin her prospects.—I wanted that miserable sum—only four thousand dollars—that fellow Schwiden asked to borrow it of me for a few days, and to refuse would have been to confess all. I dared not try my credit, and I just madly took that step that proved irretrievable— I counted at the moment upon funds that were coming to me only the next week, sure, I thought, as possible,—but the man cheated me, and our embarrassments thickened from that time; that thing has been a weight—oh a weight of deadening power!—round my neck ever since. I have died a living death these six years!—"

"I know it, dear uncle—I know it all!" said Fleda, bringing the sympathizing touch of her cheek to his again.

"The good that it did has been unspeakably overbalanced by the evil—even long ago I knew that."

"The good that it did"! It was no time *then* to moralize, but he must know that Marion was at home, or he might incautiously reveal to her what happily there was no necessity for her ever knowing. And the story must give him great and fresh pain——

"Dear uncle Rolf!" said Fleda pressing closer to him, "we may be happier than we have been in a long time, if you will only take it so. The cloud upon you has been a cloud upon us."

"I know it!" he exclaimed,—"a cloud that served to shew me that my jewels were diamonds!"

"You have an accession to your jewels, uncle Rolf."

"What do you mean?"

"I mean," said Fleda trembling, "that there are two more at home."

He held her back to look at her.

"Can't you guess who?"

"No!" said he. "What do you mean?"

"I must tell you, because they know nothing, and needn't know, of all this matter."

"What are you talking about?"

"Marion is there——"

"Marion!" exclaimed Mr. Rossitur, with quick changes of expression,—" Marion!—At Queechy!—and her husband?"

"No sir,—a dear little child."

"Marion!—and her husband—where is he?"

Fleda hesitated.

"I don't know—I don't know whether she knows—"

"Is he dead?"

"No sir—"

Mr. Rossitur put her away and got up and walked, or strode, up and down, up and down, the little apartment. Fleda dared not look at him, even by the faint glimmer that came from the chimney.

But abroad it was perfectly dark—the stars were shining, the only lamps that illumined the poor little street, and for a long time there had been no light in the room but that of the tiny wood fire. Dinah never could be persuaded of the superior cheapness of coal. Fleda came at last to her uncle's side and putting her arm within his said,

"How soon will you set off for home, uncle Rolf?"

"To-morrow morning."

"You must take the boat to Bridgeport now—you know the river is fast."

"Yes I know——"

"Then I will meet you at the wharf, uncle Rolf,—at what o'clock?"

"My dear child," said he, stopping and passing his hand tenderly over her cheek, "are you fit for it to-morrow? You had better stay where you are quietly for a few days—you want rest."

"No, I will go home with you," said Fleda, "and rest there. But hadn't we better let Dinah in and bid her good bye? for I ought to be somewhere else to get ready."

Dinah was called, and a few kind words spoken, and with a more substantial remembrance, or reward, from Fleda's hand, they left her.

Fleda had the support of her uncle's arm till they came within sight of the house, and then he stood and watched her while she went the rest of the way alone.

Anything more white and spirit-looking, and more spirit-like in its purity and peacefulness, surely did not walk that night. There was music in her ear, and abroad in the star-light, more ethereal than Ariel's, but she knew where it came from; it was the chimes of her heart that were ringing; and never a happier peal, nor never had the mental atmosphere been more clear for their sounding. Thankfulness,—that was the oftenest note,—swelling thankfulness for her success,—joy for herself and for the dear ones at home,—generous delight at having been the instrument of their relief,—the harmonies of pure affections, without any grating now,—the hope well grounded she thought, of improvement in her uncle and better times for them all,—a childlike peace that was at rest with itself and the world,—these were mingling and interchanging their music, and again and again in the midst of it all, faith rang the last chime in heaven.

CHAPTER XLIII.

As some lone bird at day's departing hour
Sings in the sunbeam of the transient shower,
Forgetful though its wings are wet the while.

Bowles.

Happily possessed with the notion that there was some hidden mystery in Fleda's movements, Mrs. Pritchard said not a word about her having gone out, and only spoke in looks her pain at the imprudence of which she had been guilty. But when Fleda asked to have a carriage ordered to take her to the boat in the morning, the good housekeeper could not hold any longer.

"Miss Fleda," said she with a look of very serious remonstrance, —"I don't know what you're thinking of, but I know you're fixing to kill yourself. You are no more fit to go to Queechy to-morrow than you were to be out till seven o'clock this evening; and if you saw yourself you wouldn't want me to say any more. There is not the least morsel of colour in your face, and you look as if you had a mind to get rid of your body altogether as fast as you can! You want to be in bed for two days running, now this minute."

"Thank you, dear Mrs. Pritchard," said Fleda smiling; "you are very careful of me; but I must go home to-morrow, and go to bed afterwards."

The housekeeper looked at her a minute in silence, and then said, "Don't, dear Miss Fleda!"—with an energy of entreaty which brought the tears into Fleda's eyes. But she persisted in desiring the carriage; and Mrs. Pritchard was silenced, observing however that she shouldn't wonder if she wasn't able to go after all. Fleda herself was not without a doubt on the subject before the evening was over. The reaction, complete now, began to make itself felt; and morning settled the question. She was not able even to rise from her bed.

The housekeeper was, in a sort, delighted; and Fleda was in too passive a mood of body and mind to have any care on the subject. The agitation of the past days had given way to an absolute quiet that seemed as if nothing could ever ruffle it again, and this feeling was seconded by the extreme prostration of body. She was a mere child in the hands of her nurse, and had, Mrs. Pritchard said, "if she wouldn't mind her telling,—the sweetest baby-face that ever had so much sense belonging to it."

The morning was half spent in dozing slumbers, when Fleda heard a rush of footsteps, much lighter and sprightlier than good Mrs. Pritchard's, coming up the stairs and pattering along the entry to her room; and with little ceremony in rushed Florence and Constance Evelyn. They almost smothered Fleda with their delighted caresses, and ran so hard their questions about her looks and her illness, that she was well nigh spared the trouble of answering.

"You horrid little creature!" said Constance,—"why didn't you come straight to our house? just think of the injurious suspicions you have exposed us to!—to say nothing of the extent of fiction we have found ourselves obliged to execute. I didn't expect it of you, little Queechy."

Fleda kept her pale face quiet on the pillow, and only smiled her incredulous curiosity.

"But when did you come back, Fleda?" said Miss Evelyn.

"We should never have known a breath about your being here," Constance went on. "We were sitting last night in peaceful unconsciousness of there being any neglected calls upon our friendship in the vicinity, when Mr. Carleton came in and asked for you. Imagine our horror!—we said you had gone out early in the afternoon and had not returned."

"You didn't say that!" said Fleda colouring.

"And he remarked at some length," said Constance, "upon the importance of young ladies having some attendance when they are out late in the evening, and that you in particular were one of those persons—he didn't say, but he intimated, of a slightly volatile disposition,—whom their friends ought not to lose sight of."

"But what brought you to town again, Fleda?" said the elder sister.

"What makes you talk so, Constance?" said Fleda.

"I haven't told you the half!" said Constance demurely. "And then mamma excused herself as well as she could, and Mr. Carleton said very seriously that he knew there was a great element of head-strongness in your character—he had remarked it, he said, when you were arguing with Mr. Stackpole."

"Constance, be quiet!" said her sister. "*Will* you tell me, Fleda, what you have come to town for? I am dying with curiosity."

"Then it's inordinate curiosity, and ought to be checked, my dear," said Fleda smiling.

"Tell me!"

"I came to take care of some business that could not very well be attended to at a distance."

"Who did you come with?"

"One of our Queechy neighbours that I heard was coming to New York."

"Wasn't your uncle at home?"

"Of course not. If he had been, there would have been no need of my stirring."

"But was there nobody else to do it but you?"

"Uncle Orrin away, you know; and Charlton down at his post—Fort Hamilton, is it?—I forget which fort—he is fast there."

"He is not so very fast," said Constance, "for I see him every now and then in Broadway shouldering Mr. Thorn instead of a musket; and he has taken up the distressing idea that it is part of his duty to oversee the progress of Florence's worsted-work—(I've made over that horrid thing to her, Fleda)—or else his precision has been struck with the anomaly of blue stars on a white ground, and he is studying that,—I don't know which,—and so every few nights he rushes over from Governor's Island, or somewhere, to prosecute enquiries. Mamma is quite concerned about him—she says he is wearing himself out."

The mixture of amusement, admiration, and affection, with which the other sister looked at her and laughed with her was a pretty thing to see.

"But where is your other cousin,—Hugh?" said Florence.

"He was not well."

"Where is your uncle?"

"He will be at home to-day I expect; and so should I have been—I meant to be there as soon as he was,—but I found this morning that I was not well enough,—to my sorrow."

"You were not going alone!"

"O no—a friend of ours was going to-day."

"I never saw anybody with so many friends!" said Florence. "But you are coming to us now, Fleda. How soon are you going to get up?"

"O by to-morrow," said Fleda smiling;—"but I had better stay where I am the little while I shall be here—I must go home the first minute I can find an opportunity."

"But you sha'n't find an opportunity till we've had you," said Constance. "I'm going to bring a carriage for you this afternoon. I could bear the loss of your friendship, my dear, but not the peril of my own reputation. Mr. Carleton is under the impression that you are suffering from a momentary succession of fainting fits, and if we were to leave you here in an empty house to come out of them at your leisure, what would he think of us?"

What would he think!—Oh world! Is this it?

But Fleda was not able to be moved in the afternoon; and it soon appeared that nature would take more revenge than a day's sleep for the rough handling she had had the past week. Fleda could not rise from her bed the next morning; and instead of that a kind of nondescript nervous fever set in; nowise dangerous, but very wearying. She was nevertheless extremely glad of it, for it would serve to explain to all her friends the change of look which had astonished them. They would make it now the token of coming, not of past, evil. The rest she took with her accustomed patience and quietness, thankful for everything after the anxiety and the relief she had just before known.

Dr. Gregory came home from Philadelphia in the height of her attack, and aggravated it for a day or two with the fear of his questioning. But Fleda was surprised at his want of curiosity. He asked her indeed what she had come to town for, but her whispered answer of "Business," seemed to satisfy him, for he did not inquire what the business was. He did ask her furthermore what had made her get sick; but this time he was satisfied more easily still, with a very curious sweet smile which was the utmost reply Fleda's wits at the moment could frame. "Well, get well," said he kissing her heartily once or twice, "and I won't quarrel with you about it."

The getting well however promised to be a leisurely affair. Dr. Gregory staid two or three days, and then went on to Boston, leaving Fleda in no want of him.

Mrs. Pritchard was the tenderest and carefullest of nurres. The Evelyns did everything *but* nurse her. They sat by her, talked to her, made her laugh, and not seldom made her look sober too, with their wild tales of the world and the world's doings. But they were indeed very affectionate and kind, and Fleda loved them for it. If they wearied her sometimes with their talk, it was a change from the weariness of fever and silence that on the whole was useful.

She was quieting herself one morning, as well as she could, in the midst of both, lying with shut eyes against her pillow, and trying to fix her mind on pleasant things, when she heard Mrs. Pritchard open the door and come in. She knew it was Mrs. Pritchard, so she didn't move nor look. But in a moment, the knowledge that Mrs. Pritchard's feet had stopped just by the bed, and a strange sensation of something delicious saluting her made her open her eyes; when they lighted upon a huge bunch of violets, just before them and in most friendly neighbourhood to her nose. Fleda started up, and her "Oh!" fairly made the housekeeper laugh; it was the very quintessence of gratification.

"Where did you get them?"

"I didn't get them indeed, Miss Fleda," said the housekeeper gravely, with an immense amount of delighted satisfaction.

"Delicious!—Where did they come from?"

"Well they must have come from a greenhouse, or hot-house, or something of that kind, Miss Fleda,—these things don't grow nowhere out o' doors at this time."

Mrs. Pritchard guessed Fleda had got the clue, from her quick change of colour and falling eye. There was a quick little smile too; and "How kind!" was upon the end of Fleda's tongue, but it never got any further. Her energies, so far as expression was concerned, seemed to be concentrated in the act of smelling. Mrs. Pritchard stood by.

"They must be put in water," said Fleda,—"I must have a dish for them—Dear Mrs. Pritchard, will you get me one?"

The housekeeper went smiling to herself. The dish was brought, the violets placed in it, and a little table at Fleda's request was set by the side of the bed close to her pillow, for them to stand upon. And Fleda lay on her pillow and looked at them.

There never were purer-breathed flowers than those. All the pleasant associations of Fleda's life seemed to hang about them, from the time when her childish eyes had first made acquaintance with violets, to the conversation in the library a few days ago; and painful things stood aloof; they had no part. The freshness of youth, and the sweetness of spring-time, and all the kindly influences which had ever joined with both to bless her, came back with their blessing in the violets' reminding breath. Fleda shut her eyes and she felt it; she opened her eyes, and the little double blue things smiled at her good humouredly and said, "Here we are—you may shut them again." And it was curious how often Fleda gave them a smile back as she did so.

Mrs. Pritchard thought Fleda lived upon the violets that day rather than upon food and medicine; or at least, she said, they agreed remarkably well together. And the next day it was much the same.

"What will you do when they are withered?" she said that evening. "I shall have to see and get some more for you."

"Oh they will last a great while," said Fleda smiling.

But the next morning Mrs. Pritchard came into her room with a great bunch of roses, the very like of the one Fleda had had at the Evelyns'. She delivered them with a sort of silent triumph, and then as before stood by to enjoy Fleda and the flowers together. But the degree of

Fleda's wonderment, pleasure, and gratitude, made her reception of them, outwardly at least, this time rather grave.

"You may throw the others away now, Miss Fleda," said the housekeeper smiling.

"Indeed I shall not!—"

"The violets, I suppose, is all gone," Mrs. Pritchard went on;—but I never *did* see such a bunch of roses as that since I lived anywhere.— They have made a rose of you, Miss Fleda."

"How beautiful!—" was Fleda's answer.

"Somebody—he didn't say who—desired to know particularly how Miss Ringgan was to-day."

"Somebody is *very* kind!" said Fleda from the bottom of her heart. "But dear Mrs. Pritchard, I shall want another dish."

Somebody was kind, she thought more and more; for there came every day or two the most delicious bouquets, every day different. They were *at least* equal in their soothing and refreshing influences to all the efforts of all the Evelyns and Mrs. Pritchard put together. There never came any name with them, and there never was any need. Those bunches of flowers certainly had a physiognomy; and to Fleda were (not the flowers but the choosing, cutting, and putting of them together) the embodiment of an amount of grace, refined feeling, generosity, and kindness, that her imagination never thought of in connection with but one person. And his kindness was answered, perhaps Mrs. Pritchard better than Fleda guessed how well, from the delighted colour and sparkle of the eye with which every fresh arrival was greeted as it walked into her room. By Fleda's order the bouquets were invariably put out of sight before the Evelyns made their first visit in the morning, and not brought out again till all danger of seeing them any more for the day was past. The regular coming of these floral messengers confirmed Mrs. Pritchard in her mysterious surmises about Fleda, which were still further strengthened by this incomprehensible order; and at last she got so into the spirit of the thing that if she heard an untimely ring at the door she would catch up a glass of flowers and run as if they had been contraband, without a word from anybody.

The Evelyns wrote to Mrs. Rossitur, by Fleda's desire, so as not to alarm her; merely saying that Fleda was not quite well, and that they meant to keep her a little while to recruit herself; and that Mrs. Rossitur must send her some clothes. This last clause was tha particular addition of Constance.

The fever lasted a fortnight, and then went off by degrees, leaving her with a very small portion of her ordinary strength. Fleda was to go to the Evelyns as soon as she could bear it; at present she was only able to come down to the little back parlour and sit in the doctor's arm chair, and eat jelly, and sleep, and look at Constance, and when Constance was not there look at her flowers. She could hardly bear a book as yet. She hadn't a bit of colour in her face, Mrs. Pritchard said, but she looked better than when she came to town; and to herself the good housekeeper added, that she looked happier too. No doubt that was true. Fleda's principal feeling, ever since she lay down in her bed, had been thankfulness; and now that the ease of returning health was joined to this feeling, her face with all its subdued gravity was as untroubled in its expression as the faces of her flowers.

She was disagreeably surprised one day, after she had been two or three days down stairs, by a visit from Mrs. Thorn. In her well-grounded dread of seeing one person Fleda had given strict orders that no *gentleman* should be admitted; she had not counted upon this invasion. Mrs. Thorn had always been extremely kind to her, but though Fleda gave her credit for thorough good-heartedness, and a true liking for herself, she could not disconnect her attentions from another thought, and therefore always wished them away; and never had her kind face been more thoroughly disagreeable to Fleda than when it made its appearance in the doctor's little back parlour on this occasion. With even more than her usual fondness, or Pleda's excited imagination fancied so, Mrs. Thorn lavished caresses upon her, and finally besought her to go out and take the air in her carriage. Fleda tried most earnestly to get rid of this invitation, and was gently unpersuadable, till the lady at last was brought to promise that she should see no creature during the drive but herself. An ominous promise! but Fleda did not know any longer how, to refuse without hurting a person for whom she had really a grateful regard. So she went. And doubted afterwards exceedingly whether she had done well.

She took special good care to see nobody again till she went to the Evelyns. But then precautions were at an end. It was no longer possible to keep herself shut up. She had cause, poor child, the very first night of her coming, to wish herself back again.

This first evening she would fain have pleaded weakness as her excuse and gone to her room, but Constance laid violent hands on her and insisted that she should stay at least a little while with them. And she seemed fated to see all her friends in a bevy. First came Charlton; then followed the Decaturs, whom she knew and liked very well, and engrossed her, happily before her cousin had time to make any enquiries; then came Mr. Carleton; then Mr. Stackpole. Then Mr. Thorn, in expectation of whom Fleda's breath had been coming and going painfully all the evening. She could not meet him without a strange mixture of embarrassment and confusion with the gratitude she wished to express, an embarrassment not at all lessened by the air of happy confidence with which he came forward to her. It carried an intimation that almost took away the little strength she had. And if anything could have made his presence more intolerable, it was the feeling she could not get rid of that it was the cause why Mr. Carleton did not come near her again; though she prolonged her stay in the drawing-room in the hope that he would. It proved to be for Mr. Thorn's benefit alone.

"Well you staid all the evening after all," said Constance as they were going up stairs.

"Yes—I wish I hadn't," said Fleda. "I wonder when I shall be likely to find a chance of getting back to Queechy."

"You're not fit yet, so you needn't trouble yourself about it," said Constance. "We'll find you plenty of chances."

Fleda could not think of Mr. Thorn without trembling. His manner meant—so much more than it had any right, or than she had counted upon. He seemed—she pressed her hands upon her face to get rid of the impression—he seemed to take for granted precisely that which she had refused to admit; he seemed to reckon as paid for that which she had declined to set a price upon. Her uncle's words and manner came up in her memory. She could see nothing best to do but to get home as fast as possible. She had no one here to fall back upon. Again that vision of father and mother and grandfather flitted across her fancy; and though Fleda's heart ended by resting down on that foundation to which it always recurred, it rested with a great many tears.

For several days she denied herself absolutely to morning visitors of every kind. But she could not entirely absent herself from the drawing-room in the evening; and whenever the family were at home there was a regular levee. Mr. Thorn could not be avoided then. He was always there, and always with that same look and manner of satisfied confidence. Fleda was as grave, as silent, as reserved, as she could possibly be and not be rude; but he seemed to take it in excellent good part, as being half indisposition and half timidity. Fleda set her face earnestly towards home, and pressed Mrs. Evelyn to find her an opportunity, weak or strong, of going there; but for those days as yet none presented itself.

Mr. Carleton was at the house almost as often as Mr. Thorn, seldom staying so long however, and never having any more to do with Fleda than he had that first evening. Whenever he did come in contact with her, he was, she thought, as grave as he was graceful. That was to be sure his common manner in company, yet she could not help thinking there was some difference since the walk they had taken together, and it grieved her.

CHAPTER XLIV.

The beat-laid schemes o' mice and men
Gang aft agley.

Burns.

After a few days Charlton verified what Constance had said about his not being very *fast* at Fort Hamilton, by coming again to see them one morning. Fleda asked him if he could not get another furlough to go with her home, but he declared he was just spending one which was near out; and he could not hope for a third in some time; he must be back at his post by the day after to-morrow.

"When do you want to go, coz?"

"I would to-morrow, if I had anybody to go with me," said Fleda sighing.

"No you wouldn't," said Constance,—"you are well enough to go out now, and you forget we are all to make Mrs. Thorn happy to-morrow night."

"I am not," said Fleda.

"Not? you can't help yourself; you must; you said you would."

"I did not indeed."

"Well then I said it for you, and that will do just as well. Why my dear, if you don't—just think!—the Thorns will be in a state—I should prefer to go through a hedge of any description rather than meet the trying demonstrations which will encounter me on every side."

"I am going to Mrs. Decatur's," said Fleda;—"she invited me first, and I owe it to her, she has asked me so often and so kindly."

"I shouldn't think you'd enjoy yourself there," said Florence; "they don't talk a bit of English these nights. If I was going, my dear, I would act as your interpreter, but my destiny lies in another direction."

"If I cannot make anybody understand my French I will get somebody to condescend to my English," said Fleda.

"Why do you talk French?" was the instant question from both mouths.

"Unless she has forgotten herself strangely," said Charlton. "Talk! she will talk to anybody's satisfaction—that happens to differ from her; and I think her tongue cares very little which language it wags in. There is no danger about Fleda's enjoying herself, where people are talking."

Fleda laughed at him, and the Evelyns rather stared at them both.

"But we are all going to Mrs. Thorn's? you can't go alone?"

"I will make Charlton take me," said Fleda,—"or rather I will take him, if he will let me. Will you, Charlton? will you take care of me to Mrs. Decatur's to-morrow night?"

"With the greatest pleasure, my dear coz, but I have another engagement in the course of the evening."

"Oh that is nothing," said Fleda;—"if you will only go with me, that is all I care for. You needn't stay but ten minutes. And you can call for me," she added, turning to the Evelyns,—"as you come back from Mrs. Thorn's."

To this no objection could be made, and the ensuing raillery Fleda bore with steadiness at least if not with coolness; for Charlton heard it, and she was distressed.

She went to Mrs. Decatur's the next evening in greater elation of spirits than she had known since she left her uncle's; delighted to be missing from the party at Mrs. Thorn's, and hoping that Mr. Lewis would be satisfied with this very plain hint of her mind. A little pleased too to feel quite free, alone from too friendly eyes, and ears that had too lively a concern in her sayings and doings. She did not in the least care about going to Mrs. Decatur's; her joy was that she was not at the other place. But there never was elation so outwardly quiet. Nobody would have suspected its existence.

The evening was near half over when Mr. Carleton came in. Fleda had half hoped he would be there, and now immediately hoped she might have a chance to see him alone and to thank him for his flowers; she had not been able to do that yet. He presently came up to speak to her just as Charlton, who had found attraction enough to keep him so long, came to tell he was going.

"You are looking better," said the former, as gravely as ever, but with an eye of serious interest that made the word something.

"I am better," said Fleda gratefully.

"So much better that she is in a hurry to make herself worse," said her cousin. "Mr. Carleton, you are a professor of medicine, I believe,—I have an indistinct impression of your having once prescribed a ride on horseback for somebody;—wouldn't you recommend some measure of prudence to her consideration?"

"In general," Mr. Carleton answered gravely; "but in the present case I could not venture upon any special prescription, Capt. Rossitur."

"As for instance, that she should remain in New York till she is fit to leave it?—By the way, what brought you here again in such a hurry, Fleda? I haven't heard that yet."

The question was rather sudden. Fleda was a little taken by surprise; her face shewed some pain and confusion both. Mr. Carleton prevented her answer, she could not tell whether with design.

"What imprudence do you charge your cousin with, Capt. Rossitur?"

"Why she is in a great hurry to get back to Queechy, before she is able to go anywhere—begging me to find an escort for her. It is lucky I can't. I didn't know I ever should be glad to be 'posted up' in this fashion, but I am."

"You have not sought very far, Capt. Rossitur," said the voice of Thorn behind him. "Here is one that will be very happy to attend Miss Fleda, whenever she pleases."

Fleda's shocked start and change of countenance was seen by more eyes than one pair. Thorn's fell, and a shade crossed his countenance too, for an instant, that Fleda's vision was too dazzled to see. Mr. Carleton moved away.

"Why are *you* going to Queechy?" said Charlton astonished.

His friend was silent a moment, perhaps for want of power to speak. Fleda dared not look at him.

"It is not impossible,—unless this lady forbid me. I am not a fixture."

"But what brought you here, man, to offer your services?" said Charlton;—"most ungallantly leaving so many pairs of bright eyes to shine upon your absence."

"Mr. Thorn will not find himself in darkness here, Capt. Rossitur," said Mrs. Decatur.

"It's my opinion he ought, ma'am," said Charlton.

"It is my opinion every man ought, who makes his dependance on gleams of sunshine," said Mr. Thorn rather cynically. "I cannot say I was thinking of brightness before or behind me."

"I should think not," said Charlton;—"you don't look as if you had seen any in a good while."

"A light goes out every now and then," said Thorn, "and it takes one's eyes some time to get accustomed to it. What a singular world we live in, Mrs. Decatur!"

"That is so new an idea," said the lady laughing, "that I must request an explanation."

"What new experience of its singularity has your wisdom made?" sid his friend. "I thought you and the world knew each other's faces pretty well before."

"Then you have not heard the news?"

"What news?"

"Hum—I suppose it is not about yet," said Thorn composedly. "No—you haven't heard it."

"But what, man?" said Charlton,—"let's hear your news, for I must be off."

"Why—but it is no more than rumour yet—but it is said that strange things are coming to light about a name that used to be held in very high respect."

"In this city?"

"In this city?—yes—it is said proceedings are afoot against one of our oldest citizens, on charge of a very grave offence."

"Who?—and what offence? what do you mean?"

"Is it a secret, Mr. Thorn?" said Mrs. Decatur.

"If you have not heard, perhaps it is as well not to mention names too soon;—if it comes out it will be all over directly; possibly the family may hush it up, and in that case the less said the better; but those have it in hand that will not let it slip through their fingers."

Mrs. Decatur turned away, saying "how shocking such things were;" and Thorn, with a smile which did not however light up his face, said,

"You may be off, Charlton, with no concern for the bright eyes you leave behind you—I will endeavour to atone for my negligence elsewhere, by my mindfulness of them."

"Don't excuse you," said Charlton;—but his eye catching at the moment another attraction opposite in the form of man or woman, instead of quitting the room he leisurely crossed it to speak to the new-comer; and Thorn with an entire change of look and manner pressed forward and offered his arm to Fleda, who was looking perfectly white. If his words had needed any commentary it was given by his eye as it met hers in speaking the last sentence to Mrs. Decatur. No one was near whom she knew and Mr. Thorn led her out to a little back room where the gentlemen had thrown off their cloaks, where the air was fresher, and placing her on a seat stood waiting before her till she could speak to him.

"What do you mean, Mr. Thorn?" Fleda looked as much as said, when she could meet his face.

"I may rather ask you what *you* mean, Miss Fleda," he answered gravely.

Fleda drew breath painfully.

"I mean nothing," she said lowering her head again, —"I have done nothing—"

"Did you think I meant nothing when I agreed to do all you wished?"

"I thought you said you would do it freely," she said, with a tone of voice that might have touched anybody, there was such a sinking of heart in it.

"Didn't you understand me?"

"And is it all over now?" said Fleda after a pause.

"Not yet—but it soon may be. A weak hand may stop it now,—it will soon be beyond the power of the strongest."

"And what becomes of your promise that it should no more be heard of?" said Fleda, looking up at him with a colourless face but eyes that put the question forcibly nevertheless.

"Is any promise bound to stand without its conditions?"

"I made no conditions," said Fleda quickly.

"Forgive me,—but did you not permit me to understand them?"

"No!—or if I did I could not help it."

"Did you say that you wished to help it?" said he gently.

"I must say so now, then, Mr. Thorn," said Fleda withdrawing the hand he had taken;—"I did not mean or wish you to think so, but I was too ill to speak—almost to know what I did—It was not my fault—"

"You do not make it mine, that I chose such a time, selfishly, I grant, to draw from your lips the words that are more to me than life?"

"Cannot you be generous?" —*for once*, she was very near saying.

"Where you are concerned, I do not know how."

Fleda was silent a moment, and then bowed her face in her hands.

"May I not ask that question of you?" said he, bending down and endeavouring to remove them;—"will you not say—or look—that word that will make others happy beside me?"

"I cannot, sir."

"Not for their sakes?" he said calmly.

"Can you ask me to do for theirs what I would not for my own?"

"Yes—for mine," he said, with a meaning deliberateness.

Fleda was silent, with a face of white determination.

"It will be beyond *eluding*, as beyond recall, the second time. I may seem selfish—I am selfish—but dear Miss Ringgan you do not see all,—you who make me so can make me anything else with a touch of your hand—it is selfishness that would be bound to your happiness, if you did but entrust it to me."

Fleda neither spoke nor looked at him and rose up from her chair.

"Is this *your* generosity?" he said, pointedly though gently.

"That is not the question now, sir," said Fleda, who was trembling painfully. "I cannot do evil that good may come."

"But *evil*?" said he detaining her,—"what evil do I ask of you?—to *remove* evil, I do."

Fleda clasped her hands, but answered calmly,

"I cannot make any pretences, sir;—I cannot promise to give what is not in my power."

"In whose power then?" said he quickly.

A feeling of indignation came to Fleda's aid, and she turned away. But he stopped her still.

"Do you think I do not understand?" he said with a covert sneer that had the keenness and hardness, and the brightness, of steel.

"*I* do not, sir," said Fleda.

"Do you think I do not know whom you came here to meet?"

Fleda's glance of reproach was a most innocent one, but it did not check him.

"Has that fellow renewed his old admiration of you?" he went on in the same tone.

"Do not make me desire his old protection," said Fleda, her gentle face roused to a flush of displeasure.

"Protection!" said Charlton coming in,—"who wants protection? here it is—protection from what? my old friend Lewis? what the deuce does this lady want of protection, Mr. Thorn?"

It was plain enough that Fleda wanted it, from the way she was drooping upon his arm.

"You may ask the lady herself," said Thorn, in the same tone he had before used,—"I have not the honour to be her spokesman."

"She don't need one," said Charlton,—"I addressed myself to you—speak for yourself, man."

"I am not sure that it would be her pleasure I should," said Thorn. "Shall I tell this gentleman, Miss Ringgan, who needs protection, and from what?—"

Fleda raised her head, and putting her hand on his arm looked a concentration of entreaty—lips were sealed.

"Will you give me," said he gently taking the hand in his own, "your sign manual for Capt. Rossitur's security? It is not too late.—Ask it of her, sir!"

"What does this mean?" said Charlton looking from his cousin to his friend.

"You shall have the pleasure of knowing, sir, just so soon as I find it convenient."

"I will have a few words with you on this subject, my fine fellow," said Capt. Rossitur, as the other was preparing to leave the room.

"You had better speak to somebody else," said Thorn. "But I am ready."

Charlton muttered an imprecation upon his absurdity, and turned his attention to Fleda, who needed it. And yet desired anything else. For a moment she had an excuse for not answering his questions in her inability; and then opportunely Mrs. Decatur came in to look after her; and she was followed by her daughter. Fleda roused all her powers to conceal and command her feelings; rallied herself; said she had been a little weak and faint; drank water, and declared herself able to go back into the drawing-room. To go home would have been her utmost desire, but at the instant her energies were all bent to the one point of putting back thought and keeping off suspicion. And in the first hurry and bewilderment of distress the dread of finding herself alone with Charlton till she had had time to collect her thoughts would of itself have been enough to prevent her accepting the proposal.

She entered the drawing-room again on Mrs. Decatur's arm, and had stood a few minutes talking or listening, with that same concentration of all her faculties upon the effort to bear up outwardly, when Charlton came up to ask if he should leave her.

Fleda made no objection, and he was out of her sight, far enough to be beyond reach or recall, when it suddenly struck her that she ought not to have let him go without speaking to him,—without entreating him to see her in the morning before he saw Thorn. The sickness of this new apprehension was too much for poor Fleda's power of keeping up. She quietly drew her arm from Mrs. Decatur's, saying that she would sit down; and sought out a place for herself apart from the rest by an engraving stand; where for a little while, not to seem unoccupied, she turned over print after print that she did not see. Even that effort failed at last; and she sat gazing at one of Sir Thomas Lawrence's bright-faced children, and feeling as if in herself the tides of life were setting back upon their fountain preparatory to being still forever. She became sensible that some one was standing beside the engravings, and looked up at Mr. Carleton.

"Are you ill?" he said, very gently and tenderly.

The answer was a quick motion of Fleda's hand to her head, speaking sudden pain, and perhaps sudden difficulty of self-command. She did not speak.

"Will you have anything?"

A whispered "no."

"Would you like to return to Mrs. Evelyn's?—I have a carriage here."

With a look of relief that seemed to welcome him as her good angel, Pleda instantly rose up, and took the arm he offered her. She would have hastened from the room then, but he gently checked her pace; and Fleda was immediately grateful for the quiet and perfect shielding from observation that his manner secured her. He went with her up the stairs, and to the very door of the dressing-room. There Fleda hurried on her shoes and mufflers in trembling fear that some one might come and find her, gained Mr. Carleton's arm again, and was placed in the carriage.

The drive was in perfect silence, and Fleda's agony deepened and strengthened with every minute. She had freedom to think, and thought did but carry a torch into chamber after chamber of misery. There seemed nothing to be done. She could not get hold of Charlton; and if she could? — Nothing could be less amenable than his passions to her gentle restraints. Mr. Thorn was still less approachable or manageable, except in one way, that she did not even think of. His insinuations about Mr. Carleton did not leave even a tinge of embarrassment upon her mind; they were cast from her as insulting absurdities, which she could not think of a second time without shame.

The carriage rolled on with them a long time without a word being said. Mr. Carleton knew that she was not weeping nor faint. But as the light of the lamps was now and then cast within the carriage he saw that her face looked ghastly; and he saw too that its expression was not of a quiet sinking under sorrow, nor of an endeavour to bear up against it, but a wild searching gaze into the darkness of *possibilities*. They had near reached Mrs. Evelyn's.

"I cannot see you so," he said, gently touching the hand which lay listlessly beside him. "You are ill!"

Again the same motion of the other hand to her face, the quick token of great pain suddenly stirred.

"For the sake of old times, let me ask," said he, "can nothing be done?"

Those very gentle and delicate tones of sympathy and kindness Were too much to bear. The hand was snatched away to be pressed to her face. Oh that those old times were back again, and she a child that could ask his protection! — No one to give it now.

He was silent a moment. Fleda's head bowed beneath the mental pressure.

"Has Dr. Gregory returned?"

The negative answer was followed by a half-uttered exclamation of longing, — checked midway, but sufficiently expressive of her want.

"Do you trust me?" he said after another second of pausing.

"Perfectly!" said Fleda amidst her tears, too much excited to know what she was saying, and in her simplicity half forgetting that she was not a child still; — "more than any one in the world!"

The few words he had spoken, and the manner of them, had curiously borne her back years in a minute; she seemed to be under his care more than for the drive home. He did not speak again for a minute; when he did his tone was very quiet and lower than before.

"Give me what a friend *can* have in charge to do for you, and it shall be done."

Fleda raised her head and looked out of the window in a silence of doubt. The carriage stopped at Mrs. Evelyn's.

"Not now," said Mr. Carleton, as the servant was about to open the door; — "drive round the square — till I speak to you."

Fleda was motionless and almost breathless with uncertainty. If Charlton could be hindered from meeting Mr. Thorn — But how, could Mr. Carleton effect it? — But there was that in him or in his manner which invariably created confidence in his ability, or fear of it, even in strangers; and how much more in her who had a childish but very clear recollection of several points in his character which confirmed the feeling. And might not something be done, through his means, to facilitate her uncle's escape? of whom she seemed to herself now the betrayer. — But to tell him the story I — a person of his high nice notions of character — what a distance it would put even between his friendship and her, — but that thought was banished instantly, with one glance at Mr. Thorn's imputation of ungenerousness. To sacrifice herself to *him* would not have been generosity, — to lower herself in the esteem of a different character, she felt, called for it. There was time even then too for one swift thought of the needlessness and bitter fruits of wrong-doing. But here they were;—should she make them known?—and trouble Mr. Carleton, friend though he were, with these miserable matters in which he had no concern?—She sat with a beating heart and a very troubled brow, but a brow as easy to read as a child's. It was the trouble of anxious questioning. Mr. Carleton watched it for a little while,—undecided as ever, and more pained.

"You said you trusted me," he said quietly, taking her hand again.

"But—I don't know what you could do, Mr. Carleton," Fleda said with a trembling voice.

"Will you let me be the judge of that?"

"I cannot bear to trouble you with these miserable things—"

"You cannot," said he with that same quiet tone, "but by thinking and saying so. I can have no greater pleasure than to take pains for you."

Fleda heard these words precisely and with the same simplicity as a child would have heard them, and answered with a very frank burst of tears,—soon, as soon as possible, according to her custom, driven back; though even in the act of quieting herself they broke forth again as uncontrollably as at first. But Mr. Carleton had not long to wait. She raised her head again after a short struggle, with the wonted look of patience sitting upon her brow, and wiping away her tears paused merely for breath and voice. He was perfectly silent.

"Mr. Carleton, I will tell you," she began;—"I hardly know whether I ought or ought not,—" and her hand went to her forehead for a moment,—"but I cannot think to-night—and I have not a friend to apply to—"

She hesitated; and then went on, with a voice that trembled and quavered sadly.

"Mr. Thorn has a secret—of my uncle's—in his power—which he promised—without conditions—to keep faithfully; and now insists that he will not—but upon conditions—"

"And cannot the conditions be met?"

"No—and—O I may as well tell you at once?" said Fleda in bitter sorrow,—"it is a crime that he committed—"

"Mr. Thorn?"

"No—oh no!" said Fleda weeping bitterly,—"not he—"

Her agitation was excessive for a moment; then she threw it off, and spoke more collectedly, though with exceeding depression of manner.

"It was long ago—when he was in trouble—he put Mr. Thorn's name to a note, and never was able to take it up;—and nothing was ever heard about it till lately; and last week he was going to leave the country, and Mr. Thorn promised that the proceedings should be entirely given up; and that was why I came to town, to find uncle Rolf and bring him home; and I did, and he is gone; and now Mr. Thorn says it is all going on again and that he will not escape this time;—and I have done it!—"

Fleda writhed again in distress.

"Thorn promised without conditions?"

"Certainly—he promised freely—and now he insists upon them; and you see uncle Rolf would have been safe out of the country now, if it hadn't been for me—"

"I think I can undo this snarl," said Mr. Carleton calmly.

"But that is not all," said Fleda, a little quieted;—"Charlton came in this evening when we were talking, and he was surprised to find me so, and Mr. Thorn was in a very ill humour, and some words passed between them; and Charlton threatened to see him again; and Oh if he does!" said poor Fleda,—"that will finish our difficulties!—for Charlton is very hot, and I know how it will end—how it must end"

"Where is your cousin to be found?"

"I don't know where he lodges when he is in town."

"You did not leave him at Mrs. Decatur's. Do you know where he is this evening?"

"Yes!" said Fleda, wondering that she should have heard and remembered,—"he said he was going to meet a party of his brother officers at Mme. Fouché's—a sister-in-law of his Colonel, I believe."

"I know her. This note—was it the name of the young Mr. Thorn, or of his father that was used?"

"Of his father!—"

"Has *he* appeared at all in this business?"

"No," said Fleda, feeling for the first time that there was something notable about it.

"What sort of person do you take him to be?"

"Very kind—very pleasant, always, he has been to me, and I should think to everybody,—very unlike the son"

Mr. Carleton had ordered the coachman back to Mrs. Evelyn's.

"Do you know the amount of the note? It may be desirable that I should not appear uninformed."

"It was for four thousand dollars" Fleda said in the low voice of shame.

"And when given?"

"I don't know exactly—but six years ago—some time in the winter of '43, it must have been."

He said no more till the carriage stopped; and then before handing her out of it, lifted her hand to his lips. That carried all the promise Fleda wanted from him. How oddly, how curiously, her hand kept the feeling of that kiss upon it all night.

Chapter XLV.

Heat not a furnace for your friend so hot
That it may singe yourself.

Shakspeare.

Mr. Carleton went to Mme. Fouché's, who received most graciously, as any lady would, his apology for introducing himself unlooked-for, and begged that he would commit the same fault often. As soon as practicable he made his way to Charlton, and invited him to breakfast with him the next morning.

Mrs. Carleton always said it never was known that Guy was refused anything he had a mind to ask. Charlton, though taken by surprise, and certainly not too much prepossessed in his favour, was won by an influence that where its owner chose to exert it was generally found irresistible; and not only accepted the invitation, but was conscious to himself of doing it with a good deal of pleasure. Even when Mr. Carleton made the further request that Capt. Rossitur would in the mean time see no one on business, of any kind, intimating that the reason would then be given, Charlton though startling a little at this restraint upon his freedom of motion could do no other than give the desired promise, and with the utmost readiness.

Guy then went to Mr. Thorn's.—It was by this time not early.

"Mr. Lewis Thorn—is he at home?"

"He is, sir," said the servant admitting him rather hesitatingly.

"I wish to see him a few moments on business."

"It is no hour for business," said the voice of Mr. Lewis from over the balusters;—"I can't see anybody to-night."

"I ask but a few minutes," said Mr. Carleton. "It is important."

"It may be any thing!" said Thorn. "I won't do business after twelve o'clock."

Mr. Carleton desired the servant to carry his card, with the same request, to Mr, Thorn the elder.

"What's that?" said Thorn as the man came up stairs,—"my father?—Pshaw! *he* can't attend to it—Well, walk up, sir, if you please!—may as well have it over and done with it."

Mr. Carleton mounted the stairs and followed the young gentleman into an apartment to which he rapidly led the way.

"You've no objections to this, *I* suppose?" Thorn remarked as he locked the door behind them.

"Certainly not," said Mr. Carleton coolly, taking out the key and putting it in his pocket;—"my business is private—it needs no witnesses."

"Especially as it so nearly concerns yourself," said Thorn sneeringly.

"Which part of it, sir?" said Mr. Carleton with admirable breeding. It vexed at the same time that it constrained Thorn.

"I'll let you know presently!" he said, hurriedly proceeding to the lower end of the room where some cabinets stood, and unlocking door after door in mad haste.

The place had somewhat the air of a study, perhaps Thorn's private room. A long table stood in the middle of the floor, with materials for writing, and a good many books were about the room, in cases and on the tables, with maps and engravings and portfolios, and a nameless collection of articles, the miscellaneous gathering of a man of leisure and some literary taste.

Their owner presently came back from the cabinets with tokens of a very different kind about him.

"There, sir!" he said, offering to his guest a brace of most inhospitable-looking pistols,—"take one and take your stand, as soon as you please—nothing like coming to the point at once!"

He was heated and excited even more than his manner indicated. Mr. Carleton glanced at him and stood quietly examining the pistol he had taken. It was all ready loaded.

"This is a business that comes upon me by surprise," he said calmly,—"I don't know what I have to do with this, Mr. Thorn."

"Well I do," said Thorn, "and that's enough. Take your place, sir! You escaped me once, but"—and he gave his words dreadful emphasis,—"you won't do it the second time!"

"You do not mean," said the other, "that your recollection of such an offence has lived out so many years?"

"No sir! no sir!" said Thorn,—"it is not that. I despise it, as I do the offender. You have touched me more nearly."

"Let me know in what," said Mr. Carleton turning his pistol's mouth down upon the table and leaning on it.

"You know already,—what do you ask me for?" said Thorn who was foaming,—"if you say you don't you lie heartily. I'll tell you nothing but out of *this*—"

"I have not knowingly injured you, sir,—in a whit."

"Then a Carleton may be a liar," said Thorn, "and you are one—dare say not the first. Put yourself there, sir, will you?"

"Well," said Guy carelessly,—"if it is decreed that I am to fight of course there's no help for it; but as I have business on hand that might not be so well done afterwards I must beg your attention to that in the first place."

"No, sir," said Thorn,—"I'll attend to nothing—I'll hear nothing from you. I know you!—I'll not hear a word. I'll see to the business!—Take your stand."

"I will not have anything to do with pistols," said Mr. Carleton coolly, laying his out of his hand;—"they make too much noise."

"Who cares for the noise?" said Thorn. "It won't hurt you; and the door is locked."

"But people's ears are not," said Guy.

Neither tone nor attitude nor look had changed in the least its calm gracefulness. It began to act upon Thorn.

"Well, in the devil's name, have your own way," said he, throwing down his pistol too, and going back to the cabinets at the lower end of the room,—"there are rapiers here, if you like them better—I don't,—the shortest the best for me,—but here they are—take your choice."

Guy examined them carefully for a few minutes, and then laid them both, with a firm hand upon them, on the table.

"I will choose neither, Mr. Thorn, till you have heard me. I came here to see you on the part of others—I should be a recreant to my charge if I allowed you or myself to draw me into anything that might prevent my fulfilling it. That must be done first."

Thorn looked with a lowering brow on the indications of his opponent's eye and attitude; they left him plainly but one course to take.

"Well speak and have done," he said as in spite of himself;—but I know it already."

"I am here as a friend of Mr. Rossitur."

"Why don't you say a friend of somebody else, and come nearer the truth?" said Thorn.

There was an intensity of expression in his sneer, but pain was there as well as anger; and it was with even a feeling of pity that Mr. Carleton answered,

"The truth will be best reached, sir, if I am allowed to choose my own words."

There was no haughtiness in the steady gravity of this speech, whatever there was in the quiet silence he permitted to follow. Thorn did not break it.

"I am informed of the particulars concerning this prosecution of Mr. Rossitur—I am come here to know if no terms can be obtained."

"No!" said Thorn,—"no terms—I won't speak of terms. The matter will be followed up now till the fellow is lodged in jail, where he deserves to be."

"Are you aware, sir, that this, if done, will be the cause of very great distress to a family who have *not* deserved it?"

"That can't be helped," said Thorn. "Of course!—it must cause distress, but you can't act upon that. Of course when a man turns rogue he ruins his family—that's part of his punishment—and a just one."

"The law is just," said Mr. Carleton,—"but a friend may be merciful."

"I don't pretend to be a friend," said Thorn viciously,—"and I have no cause to be merciful. I like to bring a man to public shame when he has forfeited his title to anything else; and I intend that Mr.

Rossitur shall become intimately acquainted with the interior of the State's Prison."

"Did it ever occur to you that public shame *might* fall upon other than Mr. Rossitur? and without the State Prison?"

Thorn fixed a somewhat startled look upon the steady powerful eye of his opponent, and did not like its meaning.

"You must explain yourself, sir," he said haughtily.

"I am acquainted with *all* the particulars of this proceeding, Mr. Thorn. If it goes abroad, so surely will they."

"She told you, did she?" said Thorn in a sudden flash of fury.

Mr. Carleton was silent, with his air of imperturbable reserve, telling and expressing nothing but a cool independence that put the world at a distance.

"Ha!" said Thorn,—"it is easy to see why our brave Englishman comes here to solicit 'terms' for his honest friend Rossitur—he would not like the scandal of franking letters to Sing Sing. Come, sir," he said snatching up the pistol,—"our business is ended—come, I say! or I won't wait for you."

But the pistol was struck from his baud.

"Not yet," said Mr. Carleton calmly,—"you shall have your turn at these,—mind, I promise you;—but my business must be done first— till then, let them alone!"

"Well what is it?" said Thorn impatiently. "Rossitur will be a convict, I tell you; so you'll have to give up all thoughts of his niece, or pocket her shame along with her. What more have you got to say? that's all your business, I take it."

"You are mistaken, Mr. Thorn," said Mr. Carleton gravely.

"Am I? In what?"

"In every position of your last speech."

"It don't affect your plans and views, I suppose, personally, whether this prosecution is continued or not?"

"It does not in the least."

"It is indifferent to you, I suppose, what sort of a Queen consort you carry to your little throne of a provinciality down yonder?"

"I will reply to you, sir, when you come back to the subject," said Mr. Carleton coldly.

"You mean to say that your pretensions have not been in the way of mine?"

"I have made none, sir."

"Doesn't she like you?"

"I have never asked her."

"Then what possessed her to tell you all this to-night?"

"Simply because I was an old friend and the only one at hand, I presume."

"And you do not look for any reward of your services, of course?"

"I wish for none, sir, but her relief."

"Well, it don't signify," said Thorn with a mixture of expressions in his face,—"if I believed you, which I don't,—it don't signify a hair what you do, when once this matter is known. I should never think of advancing *my* pretensions into a felon's family."

"You know that the lady in whose welfare you take so much interest will in that case suffer aggravated distress as having been the means of hindering Mr. Rossitur's escape,"

"Can't help it," said Thorn, beating the table with a ruler;—"so she has; she must suffer for it. It isn't my fault."

"You are willing then to abide the consequences of a full disclosure of all the circumstances?—for part will not come out without the whole?"

"There is happily nobody to tell them," said Thorn with a sneer.

"Pardon me—they will not only be told, but known thoroughly in all the circles in this country that know Mr. Thorn's name."

"*The lady*" said Thorn in the same tone, "would hardly relish such a publication of *her* name—*her welfare* would be scantily advantaged by it."

"I will take the risk of that upon myself," said Mr. Carleton quietly; "and the charge of the other."

"You dare not!" said Thorn. "You shall not go alive out of this room to do it! Let me have it, sir! you said you would—"

His passion was at a fearful height, for the family pride which had been appealed to felt a touch of fear, and his other thoughts were confirmed again, besides the dim vision of a possible thwarting of all his plans. Desire almost concentrated itself upon revenge against the object that threatened them. He had thrown himself again towards the weapons which lay beyond his reach, but was met and forcibly withheld from them.

"Stand back!" said Mr. Carleton. "I said I would, but I am not ready;—finish this business first."

"What is there to finish?" said Thorn furiously;—"you will never live to do anything out of these doors again—you are mocking yourself."

"My life is not in your hands, sir, and I will settle this matter before I put it in peril. If not with you, with Mr. Thorn your father, to whom it more properly belongs."

"You cannot leave the room to see him," said Thorn sneeringly.

"That is at my pleasure," said the other,—"unless hindered by means I do not think you will use."

Thorn was silent.

"Will you yield anything of justice, once more, in favour of this distressed family?"

"That is, yield the whole, and let the guilty go free."

"When the punishment of the offender would involve that of so many unoffending, who in this case would feel it with peculiar severity."

"He deserves it, if it was only for the money he has kept me out of— he ought to be made to refund what he has stolen, if it took the skin off his back!"

"That part of his obligation," said Mr. Carleton, "I am authorized to discharge, on condition of having the note given up. I have a cheque with me which I am commissioned to fill up, from one of the best names here. I need only the date of the note, which the giver of the cheque did not know."

Thorn hesitated, again tapping the table with the ruler in a troubled manner. He knew by the calm erect figure before him and the steady eye he did not care to meet that the threat of disclosure would be kept. He was not prepared to brave it,—in case his revenge should fail;—and if it did not——

"It is deuced folly," he said at length with a half laugh,—"for I shall have it back again in five minutes, if my eye don't play me a trick,— however, if you will have it so—I don't care. There are chances in all things—"

He went again to the cabinets, and presently brought the endorsed note. Mr. Carleton gave it a cool and careful examination, to satisfy himself of its being the true one; and then delivered him the cheque; the blank duly filled up.

"There are chances in nothing, sir," he said, as he proceeded to burn the note effectually in the candle.

"What do you mean?"

"I mean that there is a Supreme Disposer of all things, who among the rest has our lives in his hand. And now, sir, I will give you that chance at my life for which you have been so eagerly wishing."

"Well take your place," said Thorn seizing his pistol,—"and take your arms—put yourself at the end of the table——!"

"I shall stand here," said Mr. Carleton, quietly folding his arms;— "you may take your place where you please."

"But you are not armed!" said Thorn impatiently,—"why don't you get ready? what are you waiting for?"

"I have nothing to do with arms," said Mr. Carleton smiling; "I have no wish to hurt you, Mr. Thorn; I bear you no ill-will. But you may do what you please with me."

"But you promised!" said Thorn in desperation.

"I abide by my promise, sir."

Thorn's pistol hand fell; he looked *dreadfully*. There was a silence of several minutes.

"Well?"—said Mr. Carleton looking up and smiling.

"I can do nothing unless you will," said Thorn hoarsely, and looking hurriedly away.

"I am at your pleasure, sir! But on my own part I have none to gratify."

There was silence again, during which Thorn's face was pitiable in its darkness. He did not stir.

"I did not come here in enmity, Mr. Thorn," said Guy after a little approaching him;—"I have none now. If you believe me you will throw away the remains of yours and take my hand in pledge of it."

Thorn was ashamed and confounded, in the midst of passions that made him at the moment a mere wreck of himself. He inwardly drew back exceedingly from the proposal. But the grace with which the words were said wrought upon all the gentlemanly character that belonged to him, and made it impossible not to comply. The pistol was exchanged for Mr. Carleton's hand.

"I need not assure you," said the latter, "that nothing of what we have talked of to-night shall ever be known or suspected, in any quarter, unless by your means."

Thorn's answer was merely a bow, and Mr. Carleton withdrew, his quondam antagonist lighting him ceremoniously to the door.

It was easy for Mr. Carleton the next morning to deal with his guest at the break fast-table.

The appointments of the service were such as of themselves to put Charlton in a good humour, if he had not come already provided with that happy qualification; and the powers of manner and conversation which his entertainer brought into play not only put them into the background of Capt. Rossitur's perceptions but even made him merge certain other things in fascination, and lose all thought of what probably had called him there. Once before, he had known Mr. Carleton come out in a like manner, but this time he forgot to be surprised.

The meal was two thirds over before the business that had drawn them together was alluded to.

"I made an odd request of you last night, Capt. Rossitur," said his host;—"you haven't asked for an explanation."

"I had forgotten all about it," said Rossitur candidly. "I am *inconséquent* enough myself not to think everything odd that requires an explanation."

"Then I hope you will pardon me if mine seem to touch upon what is not my concern. You had some cause to be displeased with Mr. Thorn's behaviour last night?"

Who told you as much?—was in Rossitur's open eyes, and upon his tongue; but few ever asked naughty questions of Mr Carleton. Charlton's eyes came back, not indeed to their former dimensions, but to his plate, in silence.

"He was incomprehensible," he said after a minute,—"and didn't act like himself—I don't know what was the matter. I shall call him to account for it."

"Capt. Rossitur, I am going to ask you a favour."

"I will grant it with the greatest pleasure," said Charlton,—"if it lie within my power."

"A wise man's addition," said Mr. Carleton,—"but I trust you will not think me extravagant. I will hold myself much obliged to you if you will let Mr. Thorn's folly, or impertinence, go this time without notice."

Charlton absolutely laid down his knife in astonishment; while at the same moment this slight let to the assertion of his dignity roused it to uncommon pugnaciousness.

"Sir—Mr. Carleton—" he stammered,—"I would be very happy to grant anything in my power,—but this, sir,—really goes beyond it."

"Permit me to say," said Mr. Carleton, "that I have myself seen Thorn upon the business that occasioned his discomposure, and that it has been satisfactorily arranged; so that nothing more is to be gained or desired from a second interview."

Who gave you authority to do any such thing?—was again in Charlton's eyes, and an odd twinge crossed his mind; but as before his thoughts were silent.

"*My* part of the business cannot have been arranged," he said,—"for it lies in a question or two that I must put to the gentleman myself."

"What will that question or two probably end in?" said Mr. Carleton significantly.

"I can't tell!" said Rossitur,—"depends on himself—it will end according to his answers."

"Is his offence so great that it cannot be forgiven upon my entreaty?"

"Mr. Carleton!" said Rossitur,—"I would gladly pleasure you, sir, but you see, this is a thing a man owes to himself."

"What thing, sir?"

"Why, not to suffer impertinence to be offered him with impunity."

"Even though the punishment extend to hearts at home that must feel it far more heavily than the offender?"

"Would you suffer yourself to be insulted, Mr. Carleton?" said Rossitur, by way of a mouth stopper.

"Not if I could help it," said Mr. Carleton smiling;—"but if such a misfortune happened, I don't know how it would be repaired by being made a matter of life and death."

"But honour might," said Rossitur.

"Honour is not reached, Capt. Rossitur. Honour dwells in a strong citadel, and a squib against the walls does in no wise affect their security."

"But also it is not consistent with honour to sit still and suffer it."

"Question. The firing of a cracker, I think, hardly warrants a sally."

"It calls for chastisement though," said Rossitur a little shortly.

"I don't know that," said Mr. Carleton gravely. "We have it on the highest authority that it is the glory of man to *pass by* a transgression."

"But you can't go by that," said Charlton a little fidgeted;—"the world wouldn't get along so;—men must take care of themselves."

"Certainly. But what part of themselves is cared for in this resenting of injuries?"

"Why, their good name!"

"As how affected?—pardon me."

"By the world's opinion," said Rossitur,—"which stamps every man with something worse than infamy who cannot protect his own standing."

"That is to say," said Mr. Carleton seriously,—"that Capt. Rossitur will punish a fool's words with death, or visit the last extremity of distress upon those who are dearest to him, rather than leave the world in any doubt of his prowess."

"Mr. Carleton!" said Rossitur colouring. "What do you mean by speaking so, sir?"

"Not to displease you, Capt. Rossitur."

"Then you count the world's opinion for nothing?"

"For less than nothing—compared with the regards I have named."

"You would brave it without scruple?"

"I do not call him a brave man who would not, sir."

"I remember," said Charlton half laughing,—"you did it yourself once; and I must confess I believe nobody thought you lost anything by it."

"But forgive me for asking," said Mr. Carleton,—"is this terrible world a party to *this* matter? In the request which I made,—and which I have not given up, sir,—do I presume upon any more than the sacrifice of a little private feeling?"

"Why, yes,—" said Charlton looking somewhat puzzled, "for I promised the fellow I would see to it, and I must keep my word."

"And you know how that will of necessity issue."

"I can't consider that, sir; that is a secondary matter. I must do what I told him I would."

"At all hazards?" said Mr. Carleton.

"What hazards?"

"Not hazard, but certainty,—of incurring a reckoning far less easy to deal with."

"What, do you mean with yourself?" said Rossitur.

"No sir," said Mr. Carleton, a shade of even sorrowful expression crossing his face;—"I mean with one whose displeasure is a more weighty matter;—one who has declared very distinctly, 'Thou shalt not kill.'"

"I am sorry for it," said Rossitur after a disturbed pause of some minutes,—"I wish you had asked me anything else; but we can't take this thing in the light you do, sir. I wish Thorn had been in any spot of the world but at Mrs. Decatur's last night, or that Fleda hadn't taken me there; but since he was, there is no help for it,—I must make him account for his behaviour, to her as well as to me. I really don't know how to help it, sir."

"Let me beg you to reconsider that," Mr. Carleton said with a smile which disarmed offence,—"for if you will not help it, I must."

Charlton looked in doubt for a moment and then asked "how he would help it?"

"In that case, I shall think it my duty to have you bound over to keep the peace."

He spoke gravely now, and with that quiet tone which always carries conviction. Charlton stared unmistakably and in silence.

"You are not in earnest?" he then said.

"I trust you will permit me to leave you forever in doubt on that point," said Mr. Carleton, with again a slight giving way of the muscles of his face.

"I cannot indeed," said Rossitur. "Do you mean what you said just now?"

"Entirely."

"But Mr. Carleton," said Rossitur, flushing and not knowing exactly how to take him up, — "is this the manner of one gentleman towards another?"

He had not chosen right, for he received no answer but an absolute quietness which needed no interpretation. Charlton was vexed and confused, but somehow it did not come into his head to pick a quarrel with his host, in spite of his irritation. That was perhaps because he felt it to be impossible.

"I beg your pardon," he said, most unconsciously verifying Fleda's words in his own person, — "but Mr. Carleton, do me the favour to say that I have misunderstood your words. They are incomprehensible to me, sir."

"I must abide by them nevertheless, Capt. Rossitur," Mr. Carleton answered with a smile. "I will not permit this thing to be done, while, as I believe, I have the power to prevent it. You see," he said, smiling again, — "I put in practice my own theory."

Charlton looked exceedingly disturbed, and maintained a vexed and irresolute silence for several minutes, realizing the extreme disagreeableness of having more than his match to deal with.

"Come, Capt. Kossitur," said the other turning suddenly round upon him, — "say that you forgive me what you know was meant in no disrespect to you?"

"I certainly should not," said Rossitur, yielding however with a half laugh, "if it were not for the truth of the proverb that it takes two to make a quarrel."

"Give me your hand upon that. And now that the question of honour is taken out of your hands, grant not to me but to those for whom I ask it, your promise to forgive this man."

Charlton hesitated, but it was difficult to resist the request, backed as it was with weight of character and grace of manner, along with its intrinsic reasonableness; and he saw no other way so expedient of getting out of his dilemma.

"I ought to be angry with somebody," he said, half laughing and a little ashamed;—"if you will point out any substitute for Thorn I will let him go—since I cannot help myself—with pleasure."

"I will bear it," said Mr. Carleton lightly. "Give me your promise for Thorn and hold me your debtor in what amount you please."

"Very well—I forgive him," said Rossitur;—"and now Mr. Carleton I shall have a reckoning with you some day for this."

"I will meet it. When you are next in England you shall come down to—— shire, and I will give you any satisfaction you please."

They parted in high good-humour; but Charlton looked grave as he went down the staircase; and very oddly all the way down to Whitehall his head was running upon the various excellencies and perfections of his cousin Fleda.

CHAPTER XLVI

There is a fortune coming
Towards you, dainty, that will take thee thus,
And set thee aloft.

Ben Jonson.

That day was spent by Fleda in the never-failing headache which was sure to visit her after any extraordinary nervous agitation or too great mental or bodily trial. It was severe this time, not only from the anxiety of the preceding night but from the uncertainty that weighed upon her all day long. The person who could have removed the uncertainty came indeed to the house, but she was too ill to see anybody.

The extremity of pain wore itself off with the day, and at evening she was able to leave her room and come down stairs. But she was ill yet, and could do nothing but sit in the corner of the sofa, with her hair unbound, and Florence gently bathing her head with cologne.

Anxiety as well as pain had in some measure given place to exhaustion, and she looked a white embodiment of endurance which gave a shock to her friends' sympathy. Visitors were denied, — and Constance and Edith devoted their eyes and tongues at least to her service, if they could do no more.

It happened that Joe Manton was out of the way, holding an important conference with a brother usher next door, a conference that he had no notion would be so important when he began it; when a ring on his own premises summoned one of the maid-servants to the door. She knew nothing about "not at home," and unceremoniously desired the gentleman to "walk up," — "the ladies were in the drawing-room."

The door had been set wide open for the heat, and Fleda was close in the corner behind it; gratefully permitting Florence's efforts with the cologne, which yet she knew could avail nothing but the kind feelings of the operator; for herself patiently waiting her enemy's time. Constance was sitting on the floor looking at her.

"I can't conceive how you can bear so much," she said at length.

Fleda thought, how little she knew what was borne!

"Why you could bear it I suppose if you had to," said Edith philosophically.

"She knows she looks most beautiful," said Florence, softly passing her cologned hands down over the smooth hair; — "she knows

"'Il faut souffrir pour être belle.'"

"La migraine ne se guérit avec les douceurs," said Mr. Carleton entering; — "try something sharp, Miss Evelyn."

"Where are we to get it?" said Constance springing up, and adding in a most lack-a-daisical aside to her mother, "(Mamma! — the fowling piece!) — Our last vinegar hardly comes under the appellation; and you don't expect to find anything volatile in this house, Mr. Carleton?"

He smiled.

"Have you none for grave occasions, Miss Constance?"

"I won't retort the question about 'something sharp,'" said Constance arching her eyebrows, "because it is against my principles to make people uncomfortable; but you have certainly brought in some medicine with you, for Miss Ringgan's cheeks a little while ago were as pure as her mind — from a tinge of any sort — and now, you see — "

"My dear Constance," said her mother, "Miss Ringgan's cheeks will stand a much better chance if you come away and leave her in peace. How can she get well with such a chatter in her ears."

"Mr. Carleton and I, mamma, are conferring upon measures of relief,—and Miss Ringgan gives token of improvement already."

"For which I am very little to be thanked," said Mr. Carleton. "But I am not a bringer of bad news, that she should look pale at the sight of me."

"Are you a bringer of any news?" said Constance, "O do let us have them, Mr. Carleton!—I am dying for news—I haven't heard a bit to-day."

"What is the news, Mr. Carleton?" said her mother's voice, from the more distant region of the fire.

"I believe there are no general news, Mrs. Evelyn."

"Are there any particular news?" said Constance.—"I like particular news infinitely the best!"

"I am sorry, Miss Constance, I have none for you. But—will this headache yield to nothing?"

"Fleda prophesied that it would to time," said Florence;—"she Would not let us try much beside."

"And I must confess there has been no volatile agency employed at all," said Constance;—"I never knew time have less of it; and Fleda seemed to prefer him for her physician."

"He hasn't been a good one to-day," said Edith nestling affectionately to her side. "Isn't it better, Fleda?"—for she had covered her eyes with her hand.

"Not just now," said Fleda softly.

"It is fair to change physicians if the first fails," said Mr. Carleton. "I have had a slight experience in headache-curing,—if you will permit me, Miss Constance, I will supersede time and try a different prescription."

He went out to seek it; and Fleda leaned her head in her hand and tried to quiet the throbbing heart every pulsation of which was felt so keenly at the seat of pain. She knew from Mr. Carleton's voice and manner,—she *thought* she knew,—that he had exceeding good tidings for her; once assured of that she would soon be better; but she was worse now.

"Where is Mr. Carleton gone?" said Mrs. Evelyn.

"I haven't the least idea, mamma—he has ventured upon an extraordinary undertaking and has gone off to qualify himself, I suppose. I can't conceive why he didn't ask Miss Ringgan's permission to change her physician, instead of mine."

"I suppose he knew there was no doubt about that." said Edith, hitting the precise answer of Fleda's thoughts.

"And what should make him think there was any doubt about mine?" said Constance tartly.

"O you know," said her sister, "you are so odd nobody can tell what you will take a fancy to."

"You are—extremely liberal in your expressions, at least, Miss Evelyn,—I must say," said Constance, with a glance of no doubtful meaning.—"Joe—did you let Mr. Carleton in?"

"No, ma'am."

"Well let him in next time; and don't let in anybody else."

Whereafter the party relapsed into silent expectation.

It was not many minutes before Mr. Carleton returned.

"Tell your friend, Miss Constance," he said putting an exquisite little vinaigrette into her hand,—"that I have nothing worse for her than that."

"Worse than this!" said Constance examining it. "Mr. Carleton—I doubt exceedingly whether smelling this will afford Miss Ringgan any benefit."

"Why, Miss Constance?"

"Because—it has made me sick only to look at it!"

"There will be no danger for her," be said smiling.

"Won't there?—Well, Fleda my dear—here, take it," said the young lady;—"I hope you are differently constituted from me, for I feel a sudden pain since I saw it;—but as you keep your eyes shut and so escape the sight of this lovely gold chasing, perhaps it will do you no mischief."

"It will do her all the more good for that," said Mrs. Evelyn.

The only ears that took the benefit of this speech were Edith's and Mr. Carleton's; Fleda's were deafened by the rush of feeling. She very little knew what she was holding. Mr. Carleton stood with rather significant gravity watching the effect of his prescription, while Edith beset her mother to know why the outside of the vinaigrette being of gold should make it do Fleda any more good; the disposing of which question effectually occupied Mrs. Evelyn's attention for some time.

"And pray how long is it since you took up the trade of a physician, Mr. Carleton?" said Constance.

"It is—just about nine years, Miss Constance," he answered gravely.

But that little reminder, slight as it was, overcame the small remnant of Fleda's self-command; the vinaigrette fell from her hands and her face was hid in them; whatever became of pain, tears must flow.

"Forgive me," said Mr. Carleton gently, bending down towards her, "for speaking when I should have been silent.—Miss Evelyn, and Miss Constance, will you permit me to order that my patient be left in quiet."

And he took them away to Mrs. Evelyn's quarter, and kept them all three engaged in conversation, too busily to trouble Fleda with any attention; till she had had ample time to try the effect of the quiet and of the vinegar both. Then he went himself to look after her.

"Are you better?" said he, bending down and speaking low.

Fleda opened her eyes and gave him, what a look!—of grateful feeling. She did not know the half that was in it; but he did. That she was better was a very small item.

"Ready for the coffee?" said he smiling.

"O no," whispered Fleda,—"it don't matter about that—never mind the coffee!"

But he went back with his usual calmness to Mrs. Evelyn and begged that she would have the goodness to order a cup of rather strong coffee to be made.

"But Mr. Carleton, sir," said that lady,—"I am not at all sure that it would be the best thing for Miss Ringgan—if she is better,—I think it would do her far more good to go to rest and let sleep finish her cure, before taking something that will make sleep impossible."

"Did you ever hear of a physician, Mrs. Evelyn," he said smiling, "that allowed his prescriptions to be interfered with? I must beg you will do me this favour."

"I doubt very much whether it will be a favour to Miss Ringgan," said Mrs. Evelyn, —"however—"

And she rang the bell and gave the desired order, with a somewhat disconcerted face. But Mr. Carleton again left Fleda to herself and devoted his attention to the other ladies, with so much success, though with his usual absence of effort, that good humour was served long before the coffee.

Then indeed he played the physician's part again; made the coffee himself and saw it taken, according to his own pleasure; skilfully however seeming all the while, except to Fleda, to be occupied with everything else. The group gathered round her anew; she was well enough to bear their talk by this time; by the time the coffee was drunk quite well.

"Is it quite gone?" asked Edith.

"The headache?—yes."

"You will owe your physician a great many thanks, my dear Fleda," said Mrs. Evelyn.

Fleda's only answer to this, however, was by a very slight smile; and she presently left the room to go up stairs and arrange her yet disarranged hair.

"That is a very fine girl," remarked Mrs. Evelyn, preparing half a cup of coffee for herself in a kind of amused abstraction, —"my friend Mr. Thorn will have an excellent wife of her."

"Provided she marries him," said Constance somewhat shortly.

"I am sure I hope she won't," said Edith, —"and I don't believe she will."

"What do you think of his chances of success, Mr. Carleton?"

"Your manner of speech would seem to imply that they are very good, Mrs. Evelyn," he answered coolly.

"Well don't you think so?" said Mrs. Evelyn, coming back to her seat with her coffee-cup, and apparently dividing her attention between it and her subject,—"It's a great chance for her—most girls in her circumstances would not refuse it—I think he's pretty sure of his ground."

"So I think," said Florence.

"It don't prove anything, if he is," said Constance dryly. "I hate people who are always sure of their ground!"

"What do you think, Mr. Carleton?" said Mrs. Evelyn, taking little satisfied sips of her coffee.

"May I ask, first, what is meant by the 'chance' and what by the 'circumstances.'"

"Why Mr. Thorn has a fine fortune, you know, and he is of an excellent family—there is not a better family in the city—and very few young men of such pretensions would think of a girl that has no name nor standing."

"Unless she had qualities that would command them," said Mr. Carleton.

"But Mr. Carleton, sir," said the lady,—"do you think that can be? do you think a woman can fill gracefully a high place in society if she has had disadvantages in early life to contend with that were calculated to unfit her for it?"

"But mamma," said Constance,—"Fleda don't shew any such thing."

"No, she don't shew it," said Mrs. Evelyn,—"but I am not talking of Fleda—I am talking of the effect of early disadvantages. What do you think, Mr. Carleton?"

"Disadvantages of what kind, Mrs. Evelyn?"

"Why, for instance—the strange habits of intercourse, on familiar terms, with rough and uncultivated people,—such intercourse for years—in all sorts of ways,—in the field and in the house,—mingling with them as one of them—it seems to me it must leave its traces on the mind and on the habits of acting and thinking?"

"There is no doubt it does," he answered with an extremely unconcerned face.

"And then there's the actual want of cultivation," said Mrs. Evelyn, warming;—"time taken up with other things, you know,—usefully and properly, but still taken up,—so as to make much intellectual acquirement and accomplishments impossible; it can't be otherwise, you know,—neither opportunity nor instructors; and I don't think anything can supply the want in after life—it isn't the mere things themselves which may be acquired—the mind should grow up in the atmosphere of them—don't you think so, Mr. Carleton?"

He bowed.

"Music, for instance, and languages, and converse with society, and a great many things, are put completely beyond reach;—Edith, my dear, you are not to touch the coffee,—nor Constance either,—no I will not let you,—And there could not be even much reading, for want of books if for nothing else. Perhaps I am wrong, but I confess I don't see how it is possible in such a case"—

She checked herself suddenly, for Fleda with the slow noiseless step that weakness imposed had come in again and stood by the centre-table.

"We are discussing a knotty question, Miss Ringgan," said Mr. Carleton with a smile, as he brought a bergère for her; "I should like to have your voice on it."

There was no seconding of his motion. He waited till she had seated herself and then went on.

"What in your opinion is the best preparation for wearing prosperity well?"

A glance at Mrs. Evelyn's face which was opposite her, and at one or two others which had undeniably the air of being *arrested*, was enough for Fleda's quick apprehension. She knew they had been talking of her. Her eyes stopped short of Mr. Carleton's and she coloured and hesitated. No one spoke.

"By prosperity you mean—?"

"Rank and fortune," said Florence, without looking up.

"Marrying a rich man, for instance," said Edith, "and having one's hands full."

This peculiar statement of the case occasioned a laugh all round, but the silence which followed seemed still to wait upon Fleda's reply.

"Am I expected to give a serious answer to that question?" she said a little doubtfully.

"Expectations are not stringent things," said her first questioner smiling. "That waits upon your choice."

"They are horridly stringent, *I* think," said Constance. "We shall all be disappointed if you don't, Fleda my dear."

"By wearing it 'well' you mean, making a good use of it?"

"And gracefully," said Mrs. Evelyn.

"I think I should say then," said Fleda after some little hesitation and speaking with evident difficulty,—"Such an experience as might teach one both the worth and the worthlessness of money."

Mr. Carleton's smile was a sufficiently satisfied one; but Mrs. Evelyn retorted,

"The *worth* and the *worthlessness!*—Fleda my dear, I don't understand—"

"And what experience teaches one the worth and what the worthlessness of money?" said Constance;—"Mamma is morbidly persuaded that I do not understand the first—of the second I have an indefinite idea from never being able to do more than half that I want with it."

Fleda smiled and hesitated again, in a way that shewed she would willingly be excused, but the silence left her no choice but to speak.

"I think," she said modestly, "that a person can hardly understand the true worth of money,—the ends it can best subserve,—that has not been taught it by his own experience of the want; and—"

"What follows?" said Mr. Carleton.

"I was going to say, sir, that there is danger, especially when people have not been accustomed to it, that they will greatly overvalue and misplace the real worth of prosperity; unless the mind has been steadied by another kind of experience, and has learnt to measure things by a higher scale."

"And how when they *have* been accustomed to it?" said Florence.

"The same danger, without the 'especially'," said Fleda, with a look that disclaimed any assuming.

"One thing is certain," said Constance,—"you hardly ever see *les nouveaux riches* make a graceful use of anything.—Fleda my dear, I am seconding all of your last speech that I understand. Mamma, I perceive, is at work upon the rest."

"I think we ought all to be at work upon it," said Mrs. Evelyn, "for Miss Ringgan has made it out that there is hardly anybody here that is qualified to wear prosperity well."

"I was just thinking so," said Florence.

Fleda said nothing, and perhaps her colour rose a little.

"I will take lessons of her," said Constance, with eyebrows just raised enough to neutralize the composed gravity of the other features, —"as soon as I have an amount of prosperity that will make it worth while."

"But I don't think," said Florence, "that a graceful use of things is consistent with such a careful valuation and considering of the exact worth of everything—it's not my idea of grace."

"Yet *propriety* is an essential element of gracefulness, Miss Evelyn."

"Well," said Florence, —"certainly; but what then?"

"Is it attainable, in the use of means, without a nice knowledge of their true value?"

"But, Mr. Carleton, I am sure I have seen improper things—things improper in a way—gracefully done?"

"No doubt; but, Miss Evelyn," said he smiling "the impropriety did not in those cases, I presume, attach itself to the other quality. The graceful *manner* was strictly proper to its ends, was it not, however the ends might be false?"

"I don't know," said Florence;—"you have gone too deep for me. But do you think that close calculation, and all that sort of thing, is likely to make people use money, or anything else, gracefully? I never thought it did."

"Not close calculation alone," said Mr. Carleton.

"But do you think it is *consistent* with gracefulness?"

"The largest and grandest views of material things that man has ever taken, Miss Evelyn, stand upon a basis of the closest calculation."

Florence worked at her worsted and looked very dissatisfied.

"O Mr. Carleton," said Constance as he was going, —"don't leave your vinaigrette—there it is on the table."

He made no motion to take it up.

"Don't you know, Miss Constance, that physicians seldom like to have anything to do with their own prescriptions?"

"It's very suspicious of them," said Constance; —"but you must take it, Mr. Carleton, if you please, for I shouldn't like the responsibility of its being left here; and I am afraid it would be dangerous to our peace of mind, besides."

"I shall risk that," he said laughing. "Its work is not done."

"And then, Mr. Carleton," said Mrs. Evelyn, and Fleda knew with what a look, —"you know physicians are accustomed to be paid when their prescriptions are taken."

But the answer to this was only a bow, so expressive in its air of haughty coldness that any further efforts of Mrs. Evelyn's wit were chilled for some minutes after he had gone.

Fleda had not seen this. She had taken up the vinaigrette, and was thinking with acute pleasure that Mr. Carleton's manner last night and to-night had returned to all the familiar kindness of old times. Not as it had been during the rest of her stay in the city. She could be quite contented now to have him go back to England, with this pleasant remembrance left her. She sat turning over the vinaigrette, which to her fancy was covered with hieroglyphics that no one else could read; of her uncle's affair, of Charlton's danger, of her own distress, and the kindness which had wrought its relief, more penetrating and pleasant than even the fine aromatic scent which fairly typified it, — Constance's voice broke in upon her musings.

"Isn't it awkward?" she said as she saw Fleda handling and looking at the pretty toy, — "Isn't it awkward? I sha'n't have a bit of rest now for fear something will happen to that. I hate to have people do such things!"

"Fleda my dear," said Mrs. Evelyn, — "I wouldn't handle it, my love; you may depend there is some charm in it—some mischievous hidden influence, — and if you have much to do with it I am afraid you will find a gradual coldness stealing over you, and a strange forgetfulness of Queechy, and you will perhaps lose your desire ever to go back there any more."

The vinaigrette dropped from Fleda's fingers, but beyond a heightened colour and a little tremulous gravity about the lip, she gave no other sign of emotion.

"Mamma," said Florence laughing, — "you are too bad!"

"Mamma," said Constance, "I wonder how any tender sentiment for you can continue to exist in Fleda's breast! — By the way, Fleda, my dear, do you know that we have heard of two escorts for you? but I only tell you because I know you'll not be fit to travel this age."

"I should not be able to travel to-morrow," said Fleda.

"They are not going to-morrow," said Mrs. Evelyn quietly.

"Who are they?"

"Excellent ones," said Mrs. Evelyn. "One of them is your old friend Mr. Olmney,"

"Mr. Olmney!" said Fleda. "What has brought him to New York?"

"Really," said Mrs. Evelyn laughing,—"I do not know. What should keep him away? I was very glad to see him, for my part. Maybe he has come to take you home."

"Who is the other?" said Fleda.

"That's another old friend of yours—Mrs. Renney."

"Mrs. Renney?—who is she?" said Fleda.

"Why don't you know? Mrs. Renney—she used to live with your aunt Lucy in some capacity—years ago,—when she was in New York,—housekeeper, I think; don't you remember her?"

"Perfectly, now," said Fleda. "Mrs. Renney!—"

"She has been housekeeper for Mrs. Schenck these several years, and she is going somewhere out West to some relation, her brother, I believe, to take care of his family; and her road leads her your way."

"When do they go, Mrs. Evelyn?"

"Both the same day, and both the day after to-morrow. Mr. Olmney takes the morning train, he says, unless you would prefer some other,—I told him you were very anxious to go,—and Mrs. Renney goes in the afternoon. So there's a choice for you."

"Mamma," said Constance, "Fleda is not fit to go at all, either time."

"I don't think she is," said Mrs. Evelyn. "But she knows best what she likes to do."

Thoughts and resolutions came swiftly one after another into Fleda's mind and were decided upon in as quick succession. First, that she must go the day after to-morrow, at all events. Second, that it should not be with Mr. Olmney. Third, that to prevent that, she must not see him in the mean time, and therefore—yes, no help for it,—must refuse to see any one that called the next day; there was to be a party

307

in the evening, so then she would be safe. No doubt Mr. Carleton would come, to give her a more particular account of what he had done, and she wished unspeakably to hear it; but it was not possible that she should make an exception in his favour and admit him alone. That could not be. If friends would only be simple and straightforward and kind,—one could afford to be straightforward too;—but as it was she must not do what she longed to do and they would be sure to misunderstand. There was indeed the morning of the day following left her if Mr. Olmney did not take it into his head to stay. And it might issue in her not seeing Mr. Carleton at all, to bid good-bye and thank him? He would not think her ungrateful, he knew better than that, but still—Well! so much for kindness!—

"What *are* you looking so grave about?" said Constance.

"Considering ways and means," Fleda said with a slight smile.

"Ways and means of what?"

"Going."

"You don't mean to go the day after to-morrow?"

"Yes."

"It's too absurd for anything! You sha'n't do it."

"I must indeed."

"Mamma," said Constance, "if you permit such a thing, I shall hope that memory will be a fingerboard of remorse to you, pointing to Miss Ringgan's pale cheeks."

"I shall charge it entirely upon Miss Ringgan's own fingerboard," said Mrs. Evelyn, with her complacently amused face. "Fleda, my dear,—shall I request Mr. Olmney to delay his journey for a day or two, my love, till you are stronger?"

"Not at all, Mrs. Evelyn! I shall go then;—if I am not ready in the morning I will take Mrs. Renney in the afternoon—I would quite as lief go with her."

"Then I will make Mr. Olmney keep to his first purpose," said Mrs. Evelyn.

Poor Fleda, though with a very sorrowful heart, kept her resolutions, and for very forlornness and weariness slept away a great part of the next day. Neither would she appear in the evening, for fear of more people than one. It was impossible to tell whether Mrs. Evelyn's love of mischief would not bring Mr. Olmney there, and the Thorns, she knew, were invited. Mr. Lewis would probably absent himself, but Fleda could not endure even the chance of seeing his mother. She wanted to know, but dared not ask, whether Mr. Carleton had been to see her. What if to-morrow morning should pass without her seeing him? Fleda pondered this uncertainty a little, and then jumped out of bed and wrote him the heartiest little note of thanks and remembrance that tears would let her write; sealed it, and carried it herself to the nearest branch of the despatch post the first thing next morning.

She took a long look that same morning at the little vinaigrette which still lay on the centre-table, wishing very much to take it up stairs and pack it away among her things. It was meant for her she knew, and she wanted it as a very pleasant relic from the kind hands that had given it; and besides, he might think it odd if she should slight his intention. But how odd it would seem to him if he knew that the Evelyns had half appropriated it. And appropriate it anew, in another direction, she could not. She could not without their knowledge, and they would put their own absurd construction on what was a simple matter of kindness; she could not brave it.

The morning, a long one it was, had passed away; Fleda had just finished packing her trunk, and was sitting with a faint-hearted feeling of body and mind, trying to rest before being called to her early dinner, when Florence came to tell her it was ready.

"Mr. Carleton was here awhile ago," she said, "and he asked for you; but mamma said you were busy; she knew you had enough to tire you without coming down stairs to see him. He asked when you thought of going."

"What did you tell him?"

"I told him, 'O you were not gone yet!'—it's such a plague to be bidding people good-bye—*I* always want to get rid of it. Was I right?"

Fleda said nothing, but in her heart she wondered what possible concern it could be of her friends if Mr. Carleton wanted to see her before she went away. She felt it was unkind—they did not know how unkind, for they did not understand that he was a very particular friend and an old friend—they could not tell what reason there was for her wishing to bid him good-bye. She thought she should have liked to do it, very much.

Chapter XLVII.

Methought I was—there is no man can tell what. Methought
I was, and methought I had,—But man is but a patched fool,
if he will offer to say what methought I had.—Midsummer
Night's Dream.

Mrs. Evelyn drove down to the boat with Fleda and did not leave her
till she was safely put in charge of Mrs. Renney. Fleda immediately
retreated to the innermost depths of the ladies' cabin, hoping to find
some rest for the body at least if not forgetfulness for the mind.

The latter was not to be. Mrs. Renney was exceeding glad to see her
and bent upon knowing what had become of her since those days
when they used to know each other.

"You're just the same, Miss Fleda, that you used to be—you're very
little altered—I can see that—though you're looking a good deal
more thin and pale—you had very pretty roses in your cheeks in
those times.—Yes, I know, I understood Mrs. Evelyn to say you had
not been well; but allowing for that I can see you are just yourself
still—I'm glad of it. Do you recollect, Miss Fleda, what a little thing
you was then?"

"I recollect, very well," said Fleda.

"I'm sure of another thing—you're just as good as you used to be,"
said the housekeeper looking at her complacently. "Do you
remember how you used to come into my room to see me make
jelly? I see it as well as if it was yesterday;—and you used to beg me
to let you squeeze the lemons; and I never could refuse you, because
you never did anything I didn't want you to; and do you mind how I
used to tie you up in a big towel for fear you would stain your dress
with the acid, and I'd stand and watch to see you putting all your
strength to squeeze 'em clean, and be afraid that Mrs. Rossitur
would be angry with me for letting you spoil your hands, but you
used to look up and smile at me so, I couldn't help myself but let you

do just whatever you had a mind. You don't look quite so light and bright as you did in those times; but to be sure, you ain't feeling well! See here—just let me pull some of these things onto this settee, and you put yourself down there and rest—pillows—let's have another pillow,—there, how's that?"

Oh if Fleda might have silenced her! She thought it was rather hard that she should have two talkative companions on this journey of all others. The housekeeper paused no longer than to arrange her couch and see her comfortably laid down.

"And then Mr. Hugh would come in to find you and carry you away—he never could bear to be long from you. How is Mr. Hugh, Miss Fleda? he used to be always a very delicate looking child. I remember you and him used to be always together—he was a very sweet boy! I have often said I never saw such another pair of children. How does Mr. Hugh have his health, Miss Fleda?"

"Not very well, just now," said Fleda gently, and shutting her eyes that they might reveal less.

There was need; for the housekeeper went on to ask particularly after every member of the family, and where they had been living, and as much as she conveniently could about how they had been living. She was very kind through it all, or she tried to be; but Fleda felt there was a difference since the time when her aunt kept house in State street and Mrs. Renney made jellies for her. When her neighbours' affairs were exhausted Mrs. Renney fell back upon her own, and gave Fleda a very circumstantial account of the occurrences that were drawing her westward; how so many years ago her brother had married and removed thither; how lately his wife had died; what in general was the character of his wife, and what, in particular, the story of her decease; how many children were left without care, and the state of her brother's business which demanded a great deal; and how finally, she, Mrs. Renney, had received and accepted an invitation to go on to Belle Rivière and be housekeeper de son chef. And as Fleda's pale worn face had for some time given her no sign of attention the housekeeper then hoped she was asleep, and placed herself so as to screen her and have herself a good view of everything that was going on in the cabin.

But poor Fleda was not asleep, much as she rejoiced in being thought so. Mind and body could get no repose, sadly as the condition of both called for it. Too worn to sleep, perhaps;—too down-hearted to rest. She blamed herself for it, and told over to herself the causes, the recent causes, she had of joy and gratitude; but it would not do. Grateful she could be and was; but tears that were not the distillation of joy came with her gratitude; came from under the closed eyelid in spite of her; the pillow was wet with them. She excused herself, or tried to, with thinking that she was weak and not very well, and that her nerves had gone through so much for a few days past it was no wonder if a reaction left her without her usual strength of mind. And she could not help thinking there had been a want of kindness in the Evelyns to let her come away to-day to make such a journey, at such a season, under such guardianship. But it was not all that; she knew it was not. The journey was a small matter; only a little piece of disagreeableness that was well in keeping with her other meditations. She was going home and home had lost all its fair-seeming; its honours were withered. It would be pleasant indeed to be there again to nurse Hugh; but nurse him for what?—life or death?—she did not like to think; and beyond that she could fix upon nothing at all that looked bright in the prospect; she almost thought herself wicked, but she could not. If she might hope that her uncle would take hold of his farm like a man, and redeem his character and his family's happiness on the old place,—that would have been something; but he had declared a different purpose, and Fleda knew him too well to hope that he would be better than his word. Then they must leave the old homestead, where at least the associations of happiness clung, and go to a strange land. It looked desolate to Fleda, wherever it might be. Leave Queechy!—that she loved unspeakably beyond any other place in the world; where the very hills had been the friends of her childhood, and where she had seen the maples grow green and grow red through as many-coloured changes of her own fortunes; the woods where the shade of her grandfather walked with her and where the presence even of her father could be brought back by memory; where the air was sweeter and the sunlight brighter, by far, than in any other place, for both had some strange kindred with the sunny days of long ago. Poor Fleda turned her face from Mrs. Renney, and leaving doubtful prospects and withering comforts for a while as it were out of sight, she wept the fair outlines and the red maples of Queechy as if they had been all she had to regret. They had never disappointed her. Their countenance had comforted her many a time, under many a sorrow. After all, it was only fancy choosing at which shrine the whole offering of sorrow should be made. She knew that many of the tears that fell were due to some other. It was in vain to tell herself they were selfish; mind and body were in no condition to struggle with anything.

It had fallen dark some time, and she had wept and sorrowed herself into a half-dozing state, when a few words spoken near aroused her.

"It is snowing," —was said by several voices.

"Going very slow, ain't we?" said Fleda's friend in a suppressed voice.

"Yes, 'cause it's so dark, you see; the Captain dursn't let her run."

Some poor witticism followed from a third party about the 'Butterfly's' having run herself off her legs the first time she ever ran at all; and then Mrs. Renney went on.

"Is the storm so bad, Hannah?"

"Pretty thick—can't see far ahead—I hope we'll make out to find our way in—that's all I care for."

"How far are we?"

"Not half way yet—I don't know—depends on what headway we make, you know;—there ain't much wind yet, that's a good thing."

"There ain't any danger, is there?"

This of course the chambermaid denied, and a whispered colloquy followed which Fleda did not try to catch. A new feeling came upon her weary heart,—a feeling of fear. There was a sad twinge of a wish that she were out of the boat and safe back again with the Evelyns, and a fresh sense of the unkindness of letting her come away that afternoon so attended. And then with that sickness of heart the forlorn feeling of being alone, of wanting some one at hand to depend upon, to look to. It is true that in case of real danger none such could be a real protection,—and yet not so neither, for strength and decision can live and make live where a moment's faltering will kill, and weakness must often falter of necessity. "All the ways of the Lord are mercy and truth" to his people; she thought of that, and yet she feared, for his ways are often what we do not like. A few moments of sick-heartedness and trembling,—and then Fleda mentally folded her arms about a few other words of the Bible and laid her head down in quiet again.—*"The Lord is my refuge and my fortress; my God; in him will I trust."*

And then what comes after,—*"He shall cover thee with his feathers, and under his wings shalt thou trust; his truth shall be thy shield and buckler."*

Fleda lay quiet till she was called to tea.

"Bless me, how pale you are!" said the housekeeper, as Fleda raised herself up at this summons,—"do you feel very bad, Miss Fleda?"

Fleda said no.

"Are you frighted?" said the housekeeper;—"there's no need of that—Hannah says there's no need—we'll be in by and by."

"No, Mrs. Renney," said Fleda smiling. "I believe I am not very strong yet."

The housekeeper and Hannah both looked at her with strangely touched faces, and again begged her to try the refreshment of tea. But Fleda would not go down, so they served her up there with great zeal and tenderness. And then she waited patiently and watched the people in the cabin, as they sat gossiping in groups or stupefying in solitude; and thought how miserable a thing is existence where religion and refinement have not taught the mind to live in somewhat beyond and above its every-day concern.

Late at night the boat arrived safe at Bridgeport. Mrs. Renney and Fleda had resolved to stay on board till morning, when the former promised to take her to the house of a sister she had living in the town; as the cars would not leave the place till near eleven o'clock. Kest was not to be hoped for meantime in the boat, on the miserable couch which was the best the cabin could furnish; but Fleda was so thankful to have finished the voyage in safety that she took thankfully everything else, even lying awake. It was a wild night. The wind rose soon after they reached Bridgeport, and swept furiously over the boat, rattling the tiller chains and making Fleda so nervously alive to possibilities that she got up two or three times to see if the boat were fast to her moorings. It was very dark, and only by a fortunately placed lantern she could see a bit of the dark wharf and one of the posts belonging to it, from which the lantern never budged; so at last, quieted or tired out, nature had her rights, and she slept.

It was not refreshing rest after all, and Fleda was very glad that Mrs. Renney's impatience for something comfortable made her willing to be astir as early as there was any chance of finding people up in the town. Few were abroad when they left the boat, they two. Not a foot had printed the deep layer of snow that covered the wharf. It had fallen thick during the night. Just then it was not snowing; the clouds seemed to have taken a recess, for they hung threatening yet; one uniform leaden canopy was over the whole horizon.

"The snow ain't done yet," said Mrs. Renney.

"No, but the worst of our journey is over," said Fleda. "I am glad to be on the land."

"I hope we'll get something to eat here," said Mrs. Renney as they stepped along over the wharf. "They ought to be ashamed to give people such a mess, when it's just as easy to have things decent. My! how it has snowed. I declare, if I'd ha' known I'd ha' waited till somebody had tracked a path for us. But I guess it's just as well we didn't,—you look as like a ghost as you can, Miss Fleda. You'll be better when you get some breakfast. You'd better catch on to my arm—I'll waken up the seven sleepers but what I'll have something to put life into you directly."

Fleda thanked her but declined the proffered accommodation, and followed her companion in the narrow beaten path a few travellers had made in the street, feeling enough like a ghost, if want of flesh and blood reality were enough. It seemed a dream that she was walking through the grey light and the empty streets of the little town; everything looked and felt so wild and strange.

If it was a dream she was soon waked out of it. In the house where they were presently received and established in sufficient comfort, there was such a little specimen of masculine humanity as never shewed his face in dream land yet; a little bit of reality enough to bring any dreamer to his senses. He seemed to have been brought up on stove heat, for he was ail glowing yet from a very warm bed he had just tumbled out of somewhere, and he looked at the pale thin stranger by his mother's fireplace as if she were an anomaly in the comfortable world. If he could have contented himself with looking!—but he planted himself firmly on the rug just two feet from Fleda, and with a laudable and most persistent desire to examine into the causes of what he could not understand he commenced inquiring,

"Are you cold?—say! Are you cold?—say!"—in a tone most provokingly made up of wonder and dulness. In vain Fleda answered him, that she was not very cold and would soon not be cold at all by that good fire;—the question came again, apparently in all its freshness, from the interrogator's mind,—"Are you cold?—say!—"

And silence and words, looking grave and laughing, were alike thrown away. Fleda shut her eyes at length and used the small remnant of her patience to keep herself quiet till she was called to breakfast. After breakfast she accepted the offer of her hostess to go up stairs and lie down till the cars were ready; and there got some real and much needed refreshment of sleep and rest.

It lasted longer than she bad counted upon. For the cars were not ready at eleven o'clock; the snow last night had occasioned some perplexing delays. It was not till near three o'clock that the often-despatched messenger to the dépôt brought back word that they might go as soon as they pleased. It pleased Mrs. Renney to be in a great hurry, for her baggage was in the cars she said, and it would be dreadful if she and it went different ways; so Fleda and her companion hastened down to the station house and choose their places some time before anybody else thought of coming. They had a long, very tiresome waiting to go through, and room for some uneasy speculations about being belated and a night journey. But Fleda was stronger now, and bore it all with her usual patient submission. At length, by degrees the people dropped in and filled the cars, and they get off.

"How early do you suppose we shall reach Greenfield?" said Fleda.

"Why we ought to get there between nine and ten o'clock, I should think," said her companion. "I hope the snow will hold up till we get there,"

Fleda thought it a hope very unlikely to be fulfilled. There were as yet no snow-flakes to be seen near by, but at a little distance the low clouds seemed already to enshroud every clump of trees and put a mist about every hill. They surely would descend more palpably soon.

It was pleasant to be moving swiftly on again towards the end of their journey, if Fleda could have rid herself of some qualms about the possible storm and the certain darkness; they might not reach Greenfield by ten o'clock; and she disliked travelling in the night at any time. But she could do nothing, and she resigned herself anew to the comfort and trust she had built upon last night. She had the seat next the window, and with a very sober kind of pleasure watched the pretty landscape they were flitting by—misty as her own prospects,—darkening as they?—no, she would not allow that thought. "'Surely I know that it shall be well with them that fear God;' and I can trust him." And she found a strange sweetness in that naked trust and clinging of faith, that faith never tried never knows. But the breath of daylight was already gone, though the universal spread of snow gave the eye a fair range yet, white, white, as far as the view could reach, with that light misty drapery round everything in the distance and merging into the soft grey sky; and every now and then as the wind served, a thick wreath of white vapour came by from the engine and hid all, eddying past the windows and then skimming off away over the snowy ground from which it would not lift; a more palpable veil for a moment of the distant things,—and then broken, scattered, fragmentary, lovely in its frailty and evanishing. It was a pretty afternoon, but a sober; and the bare black solitary trees near hand which the cars flew by, looked to Fleda constantly like finger-posts of the past; and back at their bidding her thoughts and her spirits went, back and forward, comparing, in her own mental view, what had once been so gay and genial with its present bleak and chill condition. And from this, in sudden contrast, came a strangely fair and bright image of Heaven— its exchange of peace for all this turmoil,—of rest for all this weary bearing up of mind and body against the ills that beset both,—of its quiet home for this unstable strange world where nothing is at a stand-still—of perfect and pure society for the unsatisfactory and wearying friendships that the most are here. The thought came to Fleda like one of those unearthly clear Northwestern skies from which a storm cloud has rolled away, that seem almost to mock Earth with their distance from its defilement and agitations. "Truly I know that it shall be well with them that fear God!"—She could remember Hugh,—she could not think of the words without him,— and yet say them with the full bounding assurance. And in that weary and uneasy afternoon her mind rested and delighted itself with two lines of George Herbert, that only a Christian can well understand,—

"Thy power and love,—my love and trust, Make one place everywhere."

But the night fell, and Fleda at last could see nothing but the dim rail fences they were flying by, and the reflection from some stationary lantern on the engine or one of the forward cars, that always threw a bright spot of light on the snow. Still she kept her eyes fastened out of the window; anything but the view *inboard*. They were going slowly now, and frequently stopping; for they were out of time, and some other trains were to be looked out for. Nervous work; and whenever they stopped the voices which at other times were happily drowned in the rolling of the car-wheels, rose and jarred in discords far less endurable. Fleda shut her ears to the words, but it was easy enough without words to understand the indications of coarse and disagreeable natures in whose neighbourhood she disliked to find herself; of whose neighbourhood she exceedingly disliked to be reminded. The muttered oath, the more than muttered jest, the various laughs that tell so much of head or heart emptiness,—the shadowy but sure tokens of that in human nature which one would not realize and which one strives to forget;—Fleda shrank within herself and would gladly have stopped her ears; did sometimes covertly. Oh if home could be but reached, and she out of this atmosphere! how well she resolved that never another time, by any motive, of delicacy or otherwise, she would be tempted to trust herself in the like again without more than womanly protection. The hours rolled wearily on; they heard nothing of Greenfield yet.

They came at length to a more obstinate stop than usual. Fleda took her hands from her ears to ask what was the matter.

"I don't know," said Mrs. Renney. "I hope they won't keep us a great while waiting here."

The door swung open and the red comforter and tarpaulin hat of one of the brakemen shewed itself a moment. Presently after "Can't get on"—was repeated by several voices in the various tones of assertion, interrogation, and impatience. The women folks, having nobody to ask questions of, had nothing for it but to be quiet and use their ears.

"Can't get on!" said another man coming in,—"there's nothing but snow out o' doors—track's all foul."

A number of people instantly rushed out to see.

"Can't get on any further to-night?" asked a quiet old gentleman of the news-bringer.

"Not another inch, sir;—worse off than old Dobbs was in the mill-pond,—we've got half way but we can't turn and go back."

"And what are we going to do?" said an unhappy wight not quick in drawing conclusions.

"I s'pose we'll all be stiff by the morning," answered the other gravely,—"unless the wood holds out, which ain't likely."

How much there is in even a cheery tone of voice, Fleda was sorry when this man took his away with him. There was a most uncheering confusion of tongues for a few minutes among the people he had left, and then the car was near deserted; everybody went out to bring his own wits to bear upon the obstacles in the way of their progress. Mrs. Renney observed that she might as well warm her feet while she could, and went to the stove for the purpose.

Poor Fleda felt as if she had no heart left. She sat still in her place and leaned her head upon the back of the deserted chair before her, in utter inability to keep it up. The night journey was bad enough, but *this* was more than she had counted upon. Danger, to be sure, there might be none in standing still there all night, unless perhaps the danger of death from the cold;—she had heard of such things;—but to sit there till morning among all those people and obliged to hear their unloosed tongues,—Fleda felt almost that she could not bear it,—a most forlorn feeling, with which came anew a keen reflection upon the Evelyns for having permitted her to run even the hazard of such trouble. And in the morning, if well it came, who would take care of them in all the subsequent annoyance and difficulty of getting out of the snow? —

It must have taken very little time for these thoughts to run through her head, for half a minute had not flown when the vacant seat beside her was occupied and a hand softly touched one of hers which lay in her lap. Fleda started up in terror, — to have the hand taken and her eye met by Mr. Carleton.

"Mr. Carleton! — O sir, how glad I am to see you!" — was said by eye and cheek as unmistakably as by word.

"Have you come from the clouds?"

"I might rather ask that question of you," said he smiling.

"You have been invisible ever since the night when I had the honour of playing the part of your physician."

"I could not help it, sir, — I was sure you would believe it. I wanted exceedingly to see you and to thank you — as well as I could — but I was obliged to leave it — "

She could hardly say so much. Her swimming eye gave him more thanks than he wanted. But she scolded herself vigorously and after a few minutes was able to look and speak again.

"I hoped you would not think me ungrateful, sir, but in case you might, I wrote to let you know that you were mistaken."

"You wrote to me!" said he.

"Yes, sir — yesterday morning — at least it was put in the post yesterday morning."

"It was more unnecessary than you are aware off," he said with a smile and turning one of his deep looks away from her.

"Are we fast here for all night, Mr. Carleton?" she said presently.

"I am afraid so—I believe so—I have been out to examine and the storm is very thick."

"You need not look so about it for me," said Fleda;—"I don't care for it at all now."

And a long-drawn breath half told how much she had cared for it, and what a burden was gone.

"You look very little like breasting hardships," said Mr. Carleton, bending on her so exactly the look of affectionate care that she had often had from him when she was a child, that Fleda was very near overcome again.

"O you know," she said, speaking by dint of great force upon herself,—"You know the will is everything, and mine is very good"

But he looked extremely unconvinced and unsatisfied.

"I am so comforted to see you sitting there, sir," Fleda went on gratefully,—"that I am sure I can bear patiently all the rest."

His eye turned away and she did not know what to make of his gravity. But a moment after he looked again and spoke with his usual manner.

"That business you entrusted to me," he said in a lower tone,—"I believe you will have no more trouble with it."

"So I thought!—so I gathered—the other night,—" said Fleda, her heart and her face suddenly full of many things.

"The note was given up—I saw it burned."

Fleda's two hands clasped each other mutely.

"And will he be silent?"

"I think he will choose to be so—for his own sake."

The only sake that would avail in that quarter, Fleda knew. How had Mr. Carleton ever managed it!

"And Charlton?" she said after a few minutes' tearful musing.

"I had the pleasure of Capt. Rossitur's company to breakfast, the next morning,—and I am happy to report that there is no danger of any trouble arising there."

"How shall I ever thank you, sir!" said Fleda with trembling lips.

His smile was so peculiar she almost thought he was going to tell her. But just then Mrs. Renney having accomplished the desirable temperature of her feet, came back to warm her ears, and placed herself on the next seat; happily not the one behind but the one before them, where her eyes were thrown away; and the lines of Mr. Carleton's mouth came back to their usual quiet expression.

"You were in particular haste to reach home?" he asked.

Fleda said no, not in the abstract; it made no difference whether to-day or to-morrow.

"You had heard no ill news of your cousin?"

"Not at all, but it is difficult to find an opportunity of making the journey, and I thought I ought to come yesterday."

He was silent again; and the baffled seekers after ways and means who had gone out to try arguments upon the storm, began to come pouring back into the car. And bringing with them not only their loud and coarse voices with every shade of disagreeableness aggravated by ill-humour, but also an average amount of snow upon their hats and shoulders, the place was soon full of a reeking atmosphere of great coats. Fleda was trying to put up her window, but Mr. Carleton gently stopped her and began bargaining with a neighbouring fellow-traveller for the opening of his.

"Well, sir, I'll open it if you wish it," said the man civilly, "but they say we sha'n't have nothing to make fires with more than an hour or two longer;—so maybe you'll think we can't afford to let any too much cold in."

The gentleman however persisting in his wish and the wish being moreover backed with those arguments to which every grade of human reason is accessible, the window was opened. At first the rush of fresh air was a great relief; but it was not very long before the raw snowy atmosphere which made its way in was felt to be more dangerous, if it was more endurable, than the close pent-up one it displaced. Mr. Carleton ordered the window closed again; and Fleda's glance of meek grateful patience was enough to pay any reasonable man for his share of the suffering. *Her* share of it was another matter. Perhaps Mr. Carleton thought so, for he immediately bent himself to reward her and to avert the evil, and for that purpose brought into play every talent of manner and conversation that could beguile the time and make her forget what she was among. If success were his reward he had it. He withdrew her attention completely from all that was around her, and without tasking it; she could not have borne that. He did not seem to task himself; but without making any exertion he held her eye and ear and guarded both from communication with things disagreeable. He knew it. There was not a change in her eye's happy interest, till in the course of the conversation Fleda happened to mention Hugh, and he noticed the saddening of the eye immediately afterwards.

"Is he ill?" said Mr. Carleton.

"I don't know," said Fleda faltering a little,—"he was not—very,— but a few weeks ago—"

Her eye explained the broken sentences which there in the neighbourhood of other ears she dared not finish.

"He will be better after he has seen you," said Mr. Carleton gently.

"Yes—"

A very sorrowful and uncertain "yes," with an "if" in the speaker's mind which she did not bring out.

"Can you sing your old song yet, —" said Mr. Carleton softly, —

"'Yet one thing secures us. Whatever betide?'"

But Fleda burst into tears.

"Forgive me," he whispered earnestly, —"for reminding you of that, —you did not need it, and I have only troubled you."

"No sir, you have not," said Fleda, —"it did not trouble me—and Hugh knows it better than I do. I cannot bear anything to-night, I believe—"

"So you have remembered that, Mr. Carleton?" she said a minute after.

"Do you remember that?" said he, putting her old little Bible into her hand.

Fleda seized it, but she could hardly bear the throng of images that started up around it. The smooth worn cover brought so back the childish happy days when it had been her constant companion—the shadows of the Queechy of old, and Cynthia and her grandfather; and the very atmosphere of those times when she had led a light-hearted strange wild life all alone with them, reading the Encyclopædia and hunting out the wood-springs. She opened the book and slowly turned over the leaves where her father's hand had drawn those lines, of remark and affection, round many a passage, — the very look of them she knew; but she could not see it now, for her eyes were dim and tears were dropping fast into her lap, —she hoped Mr. Carleton did not see them, but she could not help it; she could only keep the book out of the way of being blotted. And there were other and later associations she had with it too,—how dear!—how tender!—how grateful!

Mr. Carleton was quite silent for a good while—till the tears had ceased; then he bent towards her so as to be heard no further off.

"It has been for many years my best friend and companion," he said in a low tone.

Fleda could make no answer, even by look.

"At first," he went on softly, "I had a strong association of you with it; but the time came when I lost that entirely, and itself quite swallowed up the thought of the giver."

A quick glance and smile told how well Fleda understood, how heartily she was pleased with that. But she instantly looked away again.

"And now," said Mr. Carleton after a pause,—"for some time past, I have got the association again; and I do not choose to have it so. I have come to the resolution to put the book back into your hands and not receive it again, unless the giver go with the gift."

Fleda looked up, a startled look of wonder, into his face, but the dark eye left no doubt of the meaning of his words; and in unbounded confusion she turned her own and her attention, ostensibly, to the book in her hand, though sight and sense were almost equally out of her power. For a few minutes poor Fleda felt as if all sensation had retreated to her finger-ends. She turned the leaves over and over, as if willing to cheat herself or her companion into the belief that she had something to think of there, while associations and images of the past were gone with a vengeance, swallowed up in a tremendous reality of the present; and the book, which a minute ago was her father's Bible, was now—what was it?—something of Mr. Carleton's which she must give back to him. But still she held it and looked at it—conscious of no one distinct idea but that, and a faint one besides that he might like to be repossessed of his property in some reasonable time—time like everything else was in a whirl; the only steady thing in creation seemed to be that perfectly still and moveless figure by her side—till her trembling fingers admonished her they would not be able to hold anything much longer; and gently and slowly, without looking, her hand put the book back towards Mr. Carleton. That both were detained together she knew but hardly felt;—the thing was that she had given it!—

There was no other answer; and there was no further need that Mr. Carleton should make any efforts for diverting her from the scene and the circumstances where they were. Probably he knew that, for he made none. He was perfectly silent for a long time, and Fleda was deaf to any other voice that could be raised, near or far. She could not even think.

Mrs. Renney was happily snoring, and most of the other people had descended into their coat collars, or figuratively speaking had lowered their blinds, by tilting over their hats in some uncomfortable position that signified sleep; and comparative quiet had blessed the place for some time; as little noticed indeed by Fleda as noise would have been. The sole thing that she clearly recognized in connection with the exterior world was that clasp in which one of her hands lay. She did not know that the car had grown quiet, and that only an occasional grunt of ill-humour, or waking-up colloquy, testified that it was the unwonted domicile of a number of human beings who were harbouring there in a disturbed state of mind. But this state of things could not last. The time came that had been threatened, when their last supply of extrinsic warmth was at an end. Despite shut windows, the darkening of the stove was presently followed by a very sensible and fast-increasing change of temperature; and this addition to their causes of discomfort roused every one of the company from his temporary lethargy. The growl of dissatisfied voices awoke again, more gruff than before; the spirit of jesting had long languished and now died outright, and in its stead came some low and deep and bitter-spoken curses. Poor Mrs. Renney shook off her somnolency and shook her shoulders, a little business shake, admonitory to herself to keep cool; and Fleda came to the consciousness that some very disagreeable chills were making their way over her.

"Are you warm enough?" said Mr. Carleton suddenly, turning to her.

"Not quite," said Fleda hesitating, —"I feel the cold a little. Please don't, Mr. Carleton!—" she added earnestly as she saw him preparing to throw off his cloak, the identical black fox which Constance had described with so much vivacity; —"pray do not! I am not very cold—I can bear a little—I am not so tender as you think me; I do not need it, and you would feel the want very much after wearing it.—I won't put it on."

But he smilingly bade her "stand up," stooping down and taking one of her hands to enforce his words, and giving her at the same time the benefit of one of those looks of good humoured wilfulness to which his mother always yielded, and to which Fleda yielded instantly, though with a colour considerably heightened at the slight touch of peremptoriness in his tone.

"You are not offended with me, Elfie?" he said in another manner, when she had sat down again and he was arranging the heavy folds of the cloak.

Offended!—A glance answered.

"You shall have everything your own way," he whispered gently, as he stooped down to bring the cloak under her feet, —"*except yourself.*"

What good care should be taken of that exception was said in the dark eye at which Fleda hardly ventured half a glance. She had much ado to command herself.

She was shielded again from all the sights and sounds within reach. She was in a maze. The comfort of the fur cloak was curiously mixed with the feeling of something else, of which that was an emblem, —a surrounding of care and strength which would effectually be exerted for her protection,—somewhat that Fleda had not known for many a long day,—the making up of the old want. Fleda had it in her heart to cry like a baby. Such a dash of sunlight had fallen at her feet that she hardly dared look at it for fear of being dazzled; but she could not look anywhere that she did not see the reflection.

In the mean time the earful of people settled again into sullen quietude. The cold was not found propitious to quarrelling. Those who could subsided anew into lethargy, those who could not gathered in their outposts to make the best defence they might of the citadel. Most happily it was not an extreme night; cold enough to be very disagreeable and even (without a fur cloak) dangerous; but not enough to put even noses and ears in immediate jeopardy. Mr. Carleton had contrived to procure a comfortable wrapper for Mrs. Renney from a Yankee who for the sake of being "a warm man" as to his pockets was willing to be cold otherwise for a time. The rest of the great coats and cloaks which were so alert and erect a little while ago were doubled up on every side in all sorts of despondent attitudes. A dull quiet brooded over the assembly; and Mr. Carleton walked up and down the vacant space. Once he caught an anxious glance from Fleda, and came immediately to her side.

"You need not be troubled about me," be said with a most genial smile;—"I am not suffering—never was further from it in my life."

Fleda could neither answer nor look.

"There are not many hours of the night to wear out," he said. "Can't you follow your neighbour's example?"

She shook her head.

"This watching is too hard for you. You will have another headache to-morrow."

"No—perhaps not," she said with a grateful look up.

"You do not feel the cold now, Elfie?"

"Not at all—not in the least—I am perfectly comfortable—I am doing very well—"

He stood still, and the changing lights and shades on Fleda's cheek grew deeper.

"Do you know where we are, Mr. Carleton?"

"Somewhere between a town the name of which I have forgotten and a place called Quarrenton, I think; and Quarrenton, they tell me, is but a few miles from Greenfield. Our difficulties will vanish, I hope, with the darkness."

He walked again, and Fleda mused, and wondered at herself in the black fox. She did not venture another look, though her eye took in nothing very distinctly but the outlines of that figure passing up and down through the car. He walked perseveringly; and weariness at last prevailed over everything else with Fleda; she lost herself with her head leaning against the bit of wood between the windows.

The rousing of the great coats, and the growing gray light, roused her before her uneasy sleep had lasted an hour. The lamps were out, the car was again spotted with two long rows of window-panes, through which the light as yet came but dimly. The morning had dawned at last, and seemed to have brought with it a fresh accession of cold, for everybody was on the stir. Fleda put up her window to get a breath of fresh air and see how the day looked.

A change of weather had come with the dawn. It was not fine yet. The snowing had ceased, but the clouds hung overhead still, though not with the leaden uniformity of yesterday; they were higher and broken into many a soft grey fold, that promised to roll away from the sky by and by. The snow was deep on the ground; every visible thing lapped in a thick white covering; a still, very grave, very pretty winter landscape, but somewhat dreary in its aspect to a trainful of people fixed in the midst of it out of sight of human habitation. Fleda felt that, but only in the abstract; to her it did not seem dreary; she enjoyed the wild solitary beauty of the scene very much, with many a grateful thought of what might have been. As it was, she left difficulties entirely to others.

As soon as it was light the various inmates of the strange dormitory gathered themselves up and set out on foot for Quarrenton. By one of them Mr. Carleton sent an order for a sleigh, which in as short a time as possible arrived, and transported him and Fleda and Mrs. Renney, and one other ill-bestead woman, safely to the little town of Quarrenton.

CHAPTER XLVIII.

Welcome the sour cup of prosperity! Affliction may one day smile again, and till then, Sit thee down, sorrow! — Love's Labour Lost.

It had been a wild night, and the morning looked scared. Perhaps it was only the particular locality, for if ever a place shewed bleak and winter stricken the little town of Quarrenton was in that condition that morning. The snow overlaid and enveloped everything, except where the wind had been at work; and the wind and the grey clouds seemed the only agencies abroad. Nor a ray of sunlight to relieve the uniform sober tints, the universal grey and white, only varied where a black house-roof, partially cleared, or a blacker bare-branched tree, gave it a sharp interruption. There was not a solitary thing that bore an indication of comfortable life, unless the curls of smoke that went up from the chimneys; and Fleda was in no condition to study their physiognomy.

A little square hotel, perched alone on a rising ground, looked the especial bleak and unpromising spot of the place. It bore however the imposing title of the Pocahontas; and there the sleigh set them down.

They were ushered up-stairs into a little parlour furnished in the usual style, with one or two articles a great deal too showy for the place and a general dearth as to the rest. A lumbering mahogany sofa, that shewed as much wood and as little promise as possible; a marble-topped centre-table; chairs in the minority and curtains minus; and the hearth-rug providently turned bottom upwards. On the centre-table lay a pile of Penny Magazines, a volume of selections of poetry from various good authors, and a sufficient complement of newspapers. The room was rather cold, but of that the waiter gave a reasonable explanation in the fact that the fire had not been burning long.

Furs however might be dispensed with, or Fleda thought so; and taking off her bonnet she endeavoured to rest her weary head against the sharp-cut top of the sofa-back, which seemed contrived expressly to punish and forbid all attempts at ease-seeking. The mere change of position was still comparative ease. But the black fox had not done duty yet. Its ample folds were laid over the sofa, cushion-back and all, so as at once to serve for pillow and mattress, and Fleda being gently placed upon it laid her face down again upon the soft fur, which gave a very kindly welcome not more to the body than to the mind. Fleda almost smiled as she felt that. The furs were something more than a pillow for her cheek—they were the soft image of somewhat for her mind to rest on. But entirely exhausted, too much for smiles or tears, though both were near, she resigned herself as helplessly as an infant to the feeling of rest; and in five minutes was in a state of dreamy unconsciousness.

Mrs. Renney, who had slept a great part of the night, courted sleep anew in the rocking-chair, till breakfast should be ready; the other woman had found quarters in the lower part of the house; and Mr. Carleton stood still with folded arms to read at his leisure the fair face that rested so confidingly upon the black fur of his cloak, looking so very fair in the contrast. It was the same face he had known in time past,—the same, with only an alteration that had added new graces but had taken away none of the old. Not one of the soft outlines had grown hard under Time's discipline; not a curve had lost its grace or its sweet mobility; and yet the hand of Time had been there; for on brow and lip and cheek and eyelid there was that nameless grave composure which said touchingly that hope had long ago clasped hands with submission. And perhaps, that if hope's anchor had not been well placed, ay, even where it could not be moved, the storms of life might have beaten even hope from her ground and made a clean sweep of desolation over all she had left. Not the storms of the last few weeks. Mr. Carleton saw and understood their work in the perfectly colourless and thin cheek. But these other finer drawn characters had taken longer to write. He did not know the instrument, but he read the hand-writing, and came to his own resolutions therefrom.

Yet if not untroubled she had remained unspotted by the world; that was as clear as the other. The slight eyebrow sat with its wonted calm purity of outline just where it used; the eyelid fell as quietly; the forehead above it was as unruffled; and if the mouth had a subdued gravity that it had taken years to teach, it had neither lost any of the sweetness nor any of the simplicity of childhood. It was a strange picture that Mr. Carleton was looking at, — strange for its rareness. In this very matter of simplicity, that the world will never leave those who belong to it. Half sitting and half reclining, she had given herself to rest with the abandonment and self-forgetfulness of a child; her attitude had the very grace of a child's unconsciousness; and her face shewed that even in placing herself there she had lost all thought of any other presence or any other eyes than her own; even of what her hand and cheek lay upon, and what it betokened. It meant something to Mr. Carleton too; and if Fleda could have opened her eyes she would have seen in those that were fixed upon her a happy promise for her future life. She was beyond making any such observations; and Mrs. Renney gave no interruption to his till the breakfast bell rang.

Mr. Carleton had desired the meal to be served in a private room. But he was met with a speech in which such a confusion of arguments endeavoured to persuade him to be of another mind, that he had at last given way. It was asserted that the ladies would have their breakfast a great deal quicker and a great deal hotter with the rest of the company; and in the same breath that it would be a very great favour to the house if the gentleman would not put them to the inconvenience of setting a separate table; the reasons of which inconvenience were set forth in detail, or would have been if the gentleman would have heard them; and desirous especially of haste, on Fleda's account, Mr. Carleton signified his willingness to let the house accommodate itself. Following the bell a waiter now came to announce and conduct them to their breakfast.

Down the stairs, through sundry narrow turning passages, they went to a long low room at one corner of the house; where a table was spread for a very nondescript company, as it soon proved, many of their last night's companions having found their way thither. The two *ladies*, however, were given the chief posts at the head, as near as possible to a fiery hot stove, and served with tea and coffee from a neighbouring table by a young lady in long ringlets who was there probably for their express honour. But alas for the breakfast! They might as good have had the comfort of a private room, for there was none other to be had. Of the tea and coffee it might be said as once it was said of two bad roads—"whichever one you take you will wish you had taken the other;" the beefsteak was a problem of impracticability; and the chickens—Fleda could not help thinking that a well-to-do rooster which she saw flapping his wings in the yard, must in all probability be at that very moment endeavouring to account for a sudden breach in his social circle; and if the oysters had been some very fine ladies they could hardly have retained less recollection of their original circumstances. It was in vain to try to eat or to drink; and Fleda returned to her sofa with even an increased appetite for rest, the more that her head began to take its revenge for the trials to which it had been put the past day and night.

She had closed her eyes again in her old position. Mrs. Renney was tying her bonnet-strings. Mr. Carleton was pacing up and down.

"Aren't you going to get ready, Miss Ringgan?" said the former.

"How soon will the cars be here?" exclaimed Fleda starting up.

"Presently," said Mr. Carleton; "but," said he, coming up to her and taking her hands,—"I am going to prescribe for you again—will you let me?"

Fleda's face gave small promise of opposition.

"You are not fit to travel now. You need some hours of quiet rest before we go any further."

"But when shall we get home?" said Fleda.

"In good time—not by the railroad—there is a nearer way that will take us to Queechy without going through Greenfield. I have ordered a room to be made ready for you—will you try if it be habitable?"

Fleda submitted; and indeed there was in his manner a sort of gentle determination to which few women would have opposed themselves; besides that her head threatened to make a journey a miserable business.

"You are ill now," said Mr. Carleton. "Cannot you induce your companion to stay and attend you?"

"I don't want her," said Fleda.

Mr. Carleton however mooted the question himself with Mrs. Renney, but she represented to him, though with much deference, that the care of her property must oblige her to go where and when it went. He rang and ordered the housekeeper to be sent.

Presently after a young lady in ringlets entered the room, and first taking a somewhat leisurely survey of the company, walked to the window and stood there looking out. A dim recollection of her figure and air made Fleda query whether she were not the person sent for; but it was several minutes before it came into Mr. Carleton's head to ask if she belonged to the house.

"I do, sir," was the dignified answer.

"Will you shew this lady the room prepared for her? And take care that she wants nothing."

The owner of the ringlets answered not, but turning the front view of them full upon Fleda seemed to intimate that she was ready to act as her guide. She hinted however that the rooms were very *airy* in winter and that Fleda would stand a better chance of comfort where she was. But this Fleda would not listen to, and followed her adviser to the half warmed and certainly very airy apartment which had been got ready for her. It was probably more owing to something in her own appearance than to Mr. Carleton's word of admonition on the subject that her attendant was really assiduous and kind.

"Be you of this country?" she said abruptly, after her good offices as Fleda thought were ended, and she had just closed her eyes.

She opened them again and said "yes."

"Well, that ain't in the parlour, is he?"

"What?" said Fleda.

"One of our folks?"

"An American, you mean?—No."

"I thought he wa'n't—What is he?"

"He is English."

"Is he your brother?"

"No."

The young lady gave her a good look out of her large dark eyes, and remarking that "she thought they didn't look much like," left the room.

The day was spent by poor Fleda between pain and stupor, each of which acted in some measure to check the other; too much exhausted for nervous pain to reach the height it sometimes did, while yet that was sufficient to prevent stupor from sinking into sleep. Beyond any power of thought or even fancy, with only a dreamy succession of images flitting across her mind, the hours passed she knew not how; that they did pass she knew from her handmaid in the long curls who was every now and then coming in to look at her and give her fresh water; it needed no ice. Her handmaid told her that the cars were gone by—that it was near noon—then that it was past noon.

There was no help for it; she could only lie still and wait; it was long past noon before she was able to move; and she was looking ill enough yet when she at last opened the door of the parlour and slowly presented herself.

Mr. Carleton was there alone, Mrs. Renney having long since accompanied her baggage. He came forward instantly and led Fleda to the sofa, with such gentle grave kindness that she could hardly bear it; her nerves had been in an unsteady state all day. A table was set and partially spread with evidently much more care than the one of the morning; and Fleda sat looking at it afraid to trust herself to look anywhere else. For years she had been taking care of others; and now there was something so strange in this feeling of being cared for, that her heart was full. Whatever Mr. Carleton saw or suspected of this, it did not appear. On the contrary his manner and his talk on different matters was as cool, as quiet, as graceful, as if neither he nor Fleda had anything particular to think of; avoiding even an allusion to whatever might in the least distress her. Fleda thought she had a great many reasons to be grateful to him, but she never thanked him for anything more than at that moment she thanked him for the delicacy which so regarded her delicacy and put her in a few minutes completely at her ease as she could be.

The refreshments were presently brought, and Fleda was served with them in a way that went as far as possible towards making them satisfactory; but though a great improvement upon the morning they furnished still but the substitute for a meal. There was a little pause then after the horses were ordered.

"I am afraid you have wanted my former prescription to-day," said Mr. Carleton, after considering the little-improved colour of Fleda's face.

"I have indeed."

"Where is it?"

Fleda hesitated, and then in a little confusion said she supposed it was lying on Mrs. Evelyn's centre-table.

"How happens that?" said he smiling.

"Because—I could not help it, Mr. Carleton," said Fleda with no little difficulty;—"I was foolish—I could not bring it away."

He understood and was silent.

"Are you fit to bear a long ride in the cold?" he said compassionately a few minutes after.

"Oh yes!—It will do me good."

"You have had a miserable day, have you not?"

"My head has been pretty bad,—" said Fleda a little evasively.

"Well, what would you have?" said he lightly;—"doesn't that make a miserable day of it?"

Fleda hesitated and coloured,—and then conscious that her cheeks were answering for her, coloured so exceedingly that she was fain to put both her hands up to hide what they only served the more plainly to shew. No advantage was taken. Mr. Carleton said nothing; she could not see what answer might be in his face. It was only by a peculiar quietness in his tone whenever he spoke to her afterwards that Fleda knew she had been thoroughly understood. She dared not lift her eyes.

They had soon employment enough around her. A sleigh and horses better than anything else Quarrenton had been known to furnish, were carrying her rapidly towards home; the weather had perfectly cleared off, and in full brightness and fairness the sun was shining upon a brilliant world. It was cold indeed, though the only wind was that made by their progress; but Fleda had been again unresistingly wrapped in the furs and was for the time beyond the reach of that or any other annoyance. She eat silently and quietly enjoying; so quietly that a stranger might have questioned there being any enjoyment in the case. It was a very picturesque broken country, fresh-covered with snow; and at that hour, late in the day, the lights and shadows were a constantly varying charm to the eye. Clumps of evergreens stood out in full disclosure against the white ground; the bare branches of neighbouring trees, in all their barrenness, had a wild prospective or retrospective beauty peculiar to themselves. On the wavy white surface of the meadow-land, or the steep hill-sides, lay every variety of shadow in blue and neutral tint; where they lay not the snow was too brilliant to be borne. And afar off, through a heaven bright and cold enough to hold the canopy over Winter's head, the ruler of the day was gently preparing to say good-bye to the world. Fleda's eye seemed to be new set for all forms of beauty, and roved from one to the other, as grave and bright as nature itself.

For a little way Mr. Carleton left her to her musings and was as silent as she. But then he gently drew her into a conversation that broke up the settled gravity of her face and obliged her to divide her attention between nature and him, and his part of it he knew how to manage. But though eye and smile constantly answered him he could win neither to a straightforward bearing.

They were about a mile from Queechy when Pleda suddenly exclaimed,

"O Mr. Carleton, please stop the sleigh I—"

The horses were stopped.

"It is only Earl Douglass—our farmer," Fleda said in explanation,— "I want to ask how they are at home."

In answer to her nod of recognition Mr. Douglass came to the side of the vehicle; but till he was there, close, gave her no other answer by word or sign; when there, broke forth his accustomed guttural,

"How d'ye do!"

"How d'ye do, Mr. Douglass," said Fleda. "How are they all at home?"

"Well, there ain't nothin' new among 'em, as I've heerd on," said Earl, diligently though stealthily at the same time qualifying himself to make a report of Mr. Carleton,—"I guess they'll be glad to see you. *I* be."

"Thank you, Mr. Douglass. How is Hugh?"

"He ain't nothin' different from what he's been for a spell back—at least I ain't heerd that he was.—Maybe he is, but if he is I han't heerd speak of it, and if he was, I think I should ha' heerd speak of it. He *was* pretty bad a spell ago—about when you went away—but he's been better sen. So they say. I ha'n't seen him.—Well Flidda," he added with somewhat of a sly gleam in his eye,—"do you think you're going to make up your mind to stay to hum this time?"

"I have no immediate intention of running away, Mr. Douglass," said Fleda, her pale cheeks turning rose as she saw him looking curiously up and down the edges of the black fox. His eye came back to hers with a good-humoured intelligence that she could hardly stand.

"It's time you was back," said he. "Your uncle's to hum,—but he don't do me much good, whatever he does to other folks—nor himself nother, as far as the farm goes; there's that corn"—

"Very well, Mr. Douglass," said Fleda,—"I shall be at home now and I'll see about it."

"*Very* good!" said Earl as he stepped back,—"Queechy can't get along without you, that's no mistake."

They drove on a few minutes in silence.

"Aren't you thinking, Mr. Carleton," said Fleda, "that my countrymen are a strange mixture?"

"I was not thinking of them at all at this moment. I believe such a notion has crossed my mind."

"It has crossed mine very often," said Fleda.

"How do you read them? what is the basis of it?"

"I think,—the strong self-respect which springs from the security and importance that republican institutions give every man. But," she added colouring, "I have seen very little of the world and ought not to judge."

"I have no doubt you are quite right," said Mr. Carleton smiling. "But don't you think an equal degree of self-respect may consist with giving honour where honour is due?"

"Yes—" said Fleda a little doubtfully,—"where religion and not republicanism is the spring of it."

"Humility and not pride," said he. "Yes—you are right."

"My countrymen do yield honour where they think it is due," said Fleda; "especially where it is not claimed. They must give it to reality, not to pretension. And I confess I would rather see them a little rude in their independence than cringing before mere advantages of external position;—even for my own personal pleasure."

"I agree with you, Elfie,—putting perhaps the last clause out of the question."

"Now that man," said Fleda, smiling at his look,—"I suppose his address must have struck you as very strange; and yet there was no want of respect under it. I am sure he has a true thorough respect and even regard for me, and would prove it on any occasion."

"I have no doubt of that."

"But it does not satisfy you?"

"Not quite. I confess I should require more from any one under my control."

"Oh nobody is under control here," said Fleda. "That is, I mean, individual control. Unless so far as self-interest comes in. I suppose that is all-powerful here as elsewhere."

"And the reason it gives less power to individuals is that the greater freedom of resources makes no man's interest depend so absolutely on one other man. That is a reason you cannot regret. No—your countrymen have the best of it, Elfie. But do you suppose that this is a fair sample of the whole country?"

"I dare not say that," said Fleda. "I am afraid there is not so much intelligence and cultivation everywhere. But I am sure there are many parts of the land that will bear a fair comparison with it."

"It is more than I would dare say for my own land."

"I should think—" Fleda suddenly stopped.

"What?—" said Mr. Carleton gently.

"I beg your pardon, sir,—I was going to say something very presumptuous."

"You cannot," he said in the same tone.

"I was going to say," said Fleda blushing, "that I should think there might be a great deal of pleasure in raising the tone of mind and character among the people,—as one could who had influence over a large neighbourhood."

His smile was very bright in answer.

"I have been trying that, Elfie, for the last eight years."

Fleda's eye looked now eagerly in pleasure and in curiosity for more. But he was silent.

"I was thinking a little while ago," he said, "of the time once before when I rode here with you—when you were beginning to lead me to the problem I have been trying to work out ever since.—When I left you in Paris I went to resolve with myself the question, What I had to do in the world?—Your little Bible was my invaluable help. I had read very little of it when I threw aside all other books; and my problem was soon solved. I saw that the life has no honour nor value which is not spent to the glory of God. I saw the end I was made for—the happiness I was fitted for—the dignity to which even a fallen creature may rise, through his dear Redeemer and surety."

Fleda's eyes were down now. Mr. Carleton was silent a moment, watching one or two bright witnesses that fell from them.

"The next conclusion was easy,—that my work was at home.—I have wanted my good fairy," Mr. Carleton went on smiling. "But I hope she will be contented to carry the standard of Christianity, without that of republicanism."

"But Christianity tends directly to republicanism, Mr. Carleton," said Fleda, trying to laugh.

"I know that," said he smiling, "and I am willing to know it. But the leaven of truth is one thing, and the powder train of the innovator is another."

Fleda sat thinking that she had very little in common with the layers of powder trains. She did not know the sleigh was passing Deepwater Lake, till Mr. Carleton said,—

"I am glad, my dear Elfie, for your sake, that we are almost at the end of your journey."

"I should think you might be glad for your own sake, Mr. Carleton."

"No—my journey is not ended—"

"Not?"

"No—it will not be ended till I get back to New York, or rather till I find myself here again—I shall make very little delay there—"

"But you will not go any further to-night?" said Fleda, her eye this time meeting his fully.

"Yes—I must take the first train to New York. I have some reason to expect my mother by this steamer."

"Back to New York!" said Fleda. "Then taking care of me has just hindered you in your business."

But even as she spoke she read the truth in his eye and her own fell in confusion.

"My business?" said he smiling;—"you know it now, Elfie. I arrived at Mrs. Evelyn's just after you had quitted it, intending to ask you to take the long talked of drive; and learned to my astonishment that you had left the city, and as Edith kindly informed me, under no better guardianship than that in which I found you. I was just in time to reach the boat."

"And you were in the boat night before last?"

"Certainly."

"I should have felt a great deal easier if I had known that," said Fleda.

"So should I," said he, "but you were invisible, till I discerned you in the midst of a crowd of people before me in the car."

Fleda was silent till the sleigh stopped and Mr. Carleton had handed her out.

"What's going to be done

"I will send somebody down to help you with it," said Fleda. "It is too heavy for one alone."

"Well I reckon it is," said he. "I guess you didn't know I was a cousin, did you?"

"No," said Fleda.

"I believe I be."

"Who are you?"

"I am Pierson Barnes. I live to Quarrenton for a year back. Squire Joshua Springer's your uncle, ain't he?"

"Yes, my father's uncle."

"Well he's mine too. His sister's my mother."

"I'll send somebody to help you, Mr. Barnes."

She took Mr. Carleton's arm and walked half the way up to the house without daring to look at him.

"Another specimen of your countrymen," he said smiling.

There was nothing but quiet amusement in the tone, and there was not the shadow of anything else in his face. Fleda looked, and thanked him mentally, and drew breath easier. At the house door he made a pause.

"You are coming in, Mr. Carleton?"

"Not now."

"It is a long drive to Greenfield, Mr. Carleton;—you must not turn away from a country house till we have shewn ourselves unworthy to live in it. You will come in and let us give you something more substantial than those Quarrenton oysters. Do not say no," she said earnestly as she saw a refusal in his eye,—"I know what you are thinking of, but they do not know that you have been told anything—it makes no difference."

She laid her gentle detaining hand, as irresistible in its way as most things, upon his arm, and he followed her in.

Only Hugh was in the sitting-room, and he was in a great easy-chair by the fire. It struck to Fleda's heart; but there was no time but for a flash of thought. He had turned his face and saw her. Fleda meant to have controlled herself and presented Mr. Carleton properly, but Hugh started up, he saw nothing but herself, and one view of the ethereal delicacy of his face made Fleda for a moment forget everything but him. They were in each other's arms, and then still as death. Hugh was unconscious that a stranger was there, and though Fleda was very conscious that one was there who was no stranger,— there was so much in both hearts, so much of sorrow and joy, and gratitude and tenderness, on the one part and on the other, so much that even if they had been alone lips could only have said silently,— that for a little while they kissed each other and wept in a passionate attempt to speak what their hearts were too full of.

Fleda at last whispered to Hugh that somebody else was there and turned to make as well as she might the introduction. But Mr. Carleton did not need it, and made his own with that singular talent which in all circumstances, wherever he chose to exert it, had absolute power. Fleda saw Hugh's countenance change, with a kind of pleased surprise, and herself stood still under the charm for a minute; then she recollected she might be dispensed with. She took up her little spaniel who was in an agony of gratulation at her feet, and went out into the kitchen.

"Well do you mean to say you are here at last?" said Barby, her grey eyes flashing pleasure as she came forward to take the half hand which, owing to King's monopoly, was all Fleda had to give her. "Have you come home to stay, Fleda?"

"I am tired enough to be quiet," said Fleda. "But dear Barby, what have you got in the house?—I want supper as quickly as it can be had."

"Well you do look dreadful bad," said Barby eying her. "Why there ain't much particular, Fleda; nobody's had any heart to eat lately; I thought I might a'most as well save myself the fuss of getting victuals. Hugh lives like a bird, and Mis' Rossitur ain't much better, and I think all of 'em have been keeping their appetites till you came back; 'cept Philetus and me; we keep it up pretty well. Why you're come home hungry, ain't you?"

"No, not I," said Fleda, "but there's a gentleman here that came with me that must have something before he goes away again. What have you Barby?"

"Who is he?" said Barby.

"A friend that took care of me on the way—I'll tell you about it,—but in the mean time, supper, Barby."

"Is he a New Yorker, that one must be curious for?"

"As curious as you like," said Fleda, "but he is not a New Yorker."

"Where *is* he from, then?" said Barby, who was busily putting on the tea-kettle.

"England."

"England!" said Barby facing about. "Oh if he's an Englishman I don't care for him, Fleda."

"But you care for me," said Fleda laughing; "and for my sake don't let our hospitality fail to somebody who has been very kind to me, if he is an Englishman; and he is in haste to be off."

"Well I don't know what we're a going to give him," said Barby looking at her. "There ain't much in the pantry besides cold pork and beans that Philetus and me made our dinner on—they wouldn't have it in there, and eat nothing but some pickerel the doctor sent down—and cold fish ain't good for much."

"None of them left uncooked?"

"Yes, there's a couple—he sent a great lot—I guess he thought there was more in the family—but two ain't enough to go round; they're little ones."

"No, but put them down and I'll make an omelette. Just get the things ready for me, Barby, will you, while I run up to see aunt Lucy. The hens have begun to lay?"

"La yes—Philetus fetches in lots of eggs—he loves 'em, I reckon—but you ain't fit this minute to do a thing but rest, Fleda."

"I'll rest afterwards. Just get the things ready for me, Barby, and an apron; and the table—I'll be down in a minute. And Barby, grind some coffee, will you?"

But as she turned to run up stairs, her uncle stood in her way, and the supper vanished from Fleda's head. His arms were open and she was silently clasped in them, with so much feeling on both sides that thought and well nigh strength for anything else on her part was gone. His smothered words of deep blessing overcame her. Fleda could do nothing but sob, in distress, till she recollected Barby. Putting her arms round his neck then she whispered to him that Mr. Carleton was in the other room and shortly explained how he came to be there, and begged her uncle would go in and see him till supper should be ready. Enforcing this request with a parting kiss on his cheek, she ran off up stairs. Mr. Rossitur looked extremely moody and cloudy for a few minutes, and then went in and joined his guest. Mrs. Rossitur and her daughter could not be induced to shew themselves.

Little Rolf, however, had no scruples of any kind. He presently edged himself into the room to see the stranger whom he no sooner saw than with a joyous exclamation he bounded forward to claim an old friend.

"Why, Mr. Carleton," exclaimed Mr. Rossitur in surprise, "I was not aware that this young gentleman had the honour of your acquaintance."

"But I have!" said Rolf.

"In London, sir, I had that pleasure," said Mr. Carleton.

"I think it was *I* had the pleasure," said Rolf, pounding one hand upon Mr. Carleton's knee.

"Where is your mother?"

"She wouldn't come down," said Rolf,—"but I guess she will when she knows who is here—"

And he was darting away to tell her, when Mr. Carleton, within whose arms he stood, quietly restrained him, and told him he was going away presently, but would come again and see his mother another time.

"Are you going back to England, sir?"

"By and by."

"But you will come here again first?"

"Yes—if Mr. Rossitur will let me."

"Mr. Carleton knows he commands his own welcome," said that gentleman somewhat stately. "Go and tell your aunt Fleda that tea is ready, Rolf."

"She knows," said Rolf. "She was making an omelette—I guess it was for this gentleman!"

Whose name he was not clear of yet. Mr. Rossitur looked vexed, but Hugh laughed and asked if his aunt gave him leave to tell that. Rolf entered forthwith into discussion on this subject, while Mr. Carleton who had not seemed to hear it engaged Mr. Rossitur busily in another; till the omelette and Fleda came in. Rolf's mind however was ill at ease.

"Aunt Fleda," said he, as soon as she had fairly taken her place at the head of the table, "would you mind my telling that you made the omelette for this gentleman?"

Fleda cast a confused glance first at the person in question and then round the table, but Mr. Carleton without looking at her answered instantly,

"Don't you understand, Rolf, that the same kindness which will do a favour for a friend will keep him in ignorance of it?"

Rolf pondered a moment and then burst forth,

"Why, sir, wouldn't you like it as well for knowing she made it?"

It was hardly in human gravity to stand this. Fleda herself laughed, but Mr. Carleton as unmoved as possible answered him, "Certainly not!"—and Rolf was nonplussed.

The supper was over. Hugh had left the room, and Mr. Rossitur had before that gone out to give directions about Mr. Carleton's horses. He and Fleda were left alone.

"I have something against you, fairy," said he lightly, taking her hand and putting it to his lips. "You shall not again do me such honour as you have done me to-day—I did not deserve it, Elfie."

The last words were spoken half reproachfully. Fleda stood a moment motionless, and then by some curious revulsion of feeling put both her hands to her face and burst into tears.

She struggled against them, and spoke almost immediately,

"You will think me very foolish, Mr. Carleton,—I am ashamed of myself—but I have lived here so long in this way,—my spirits have grown so quieted by different things,—that it seems sometimes as if I could not bear anything.—I am afraid—"

"Of what, my dear Elfie?"

But she did not answer, and her tears came again.

"You are weary and spent," he said gently, repossessing himself of one of her hands. "I will ask you another time what you are afraid of, and rebuke all your fears."

"I deserve nothing but rebuke now," said Fleda.

But her hand knew, by the gentle and quiet clasp in which it lay, that there was no disposition to give it.

"Do not speak to me for a minute," she said hastily as she heard some one coming.

She went to the window and stood there looking out till Mr. Carleton came to bid her good-bye.

"Will you permit me to say to Mrs. Evelyn," he said in a low tone, "that you left a piece of your property in her house and have commissioned me to bring it you?"

"Yes—" said Fleda, hesitating and looking a little confused,—"but—will you let me write a note instead, Mr. Carleton?"

"Certainly!—but what are you thinking of, Elfie? what grave doubt is lying under your brow?"

All Fleda's shadows rolled away before that clear bright eye.

"I have found by experience," she said, smiling a little but looking down,—"that whenever I tell my secret thoughts to anybody I have some reason afterwards to be sorry for it."

"You shall make me an exception to your rule, however, Elfie."

Fleda looked up, one of her looks half questioning, half fearing, and then answered, a little hesitating,

"I was afraid, sir, that if you went to Mrs. Evelyn's on that errand—I was afraid you would shew them you were displeased."

"And what then?" said he quietly.

"Only—that I wanted to spare them what always gives me a cold chill."

"Gives you!" said Mr. Carleton.

"No sir—only by sympathy—I thought my agency would be the gentlest."

"I see I was right," she said, looking up as he did not answer,—"they don't deserve it,—not half so much as you think. They talk—they don't know what. I am sure they never meant half they said—never meant to annoy me with it, I mean,—and I am sure they have a true love for me; they have shewn it in a great many ways. Constance especially never shewed me anything else. They have been very kind to me; and as to letting me come away as they did, I suppose they thought I was in a greater hurry to get home than I really was—and they would very likely not have minded travelling so themselves; I am so different from them that they might in many things judge me by themselves and yet judge far wrong."

Fleda was going on, but she suddenly became aware that the eye to which she was speaking had ceased to look at the Evelyns, even in imagination, and she stopped short.

"Will you trust me, after this, to see Mrs. Evelyn without the note?" said he smiling.

But Fleda gave him her hand very demurely without raising her eyes again, and he went.

Barby who had come in to clear away the table took her stand at the window to watch Mr. Carleton drive off. Fleda had retreated to the fire. Barby looked in silence till the sleigh was out of sight.

"Is he going back to England now?" she said coming back to the table.

"No."

Barby gathered a pile of plates together and then enquired,

"Is he going to settle in America?"

"Why no, Barby! What makes you ask such a thing?"

"I thought he looked as if he had dressed himself for a cold climate," said Barby dryly.

Fleda sat down by Hugh's easy-chair and laid her head on his breast.

"I like your Mr. Carleton very much," Hugh whispered after awhile.

"Do you?" said Fleda, a little wondering at Hugh's choice of that particular pronominal adjective.

"Very much indeed. But he has changed, Fleda?"

"Yes—in some things—some great things."

"He says he is coming again," said Hugh.

Fleda's heart beat. She was silent.

"I am very glad," repeated Hugh, "I like him very much. But you won't leave me, Fleda,—will you?"

"Leave you?" said Fleda looking at him.

"Yes," said Hugh smiling, and drawing her head down again;—I always thought what he came over here for. But you will stay with me while I want you, Fleda?"

"While you want me!" said Fleda again.

"Yes.—It won't be long."

"What won't be long?"

"I," said Hugh quietly. "Not long. I am very glad I shall not leave you alone, dear Fleda—very glad!—promise me you will not leave me any more."

"Don't talk so, dear Hugh!"

"But it is true, Fleda," said Hugh gently. "I know it. I sha'n't be here but a little while. I am so glad you are come home, dear Fleda!—You will not let anybody take you away till I am gone first?"

Fleda drew her arm close around Hugh's neck and was still,—still even to his ear,—for a good while. A hard battle must be fought, and she must not be weak, for his sake and for everybody's sake. Others of the family had come or were coming into the room. Hugh waited till a short breath, but freer drawn, told him he might speak.

356

"Fleda—" he whispered.

"What?"

"I am very happy.—I only want your promise about that."

"I can't talk to you, Hugh."

"No, but promise me."

"What?"

"That you will not let anybody take you away while I want you."

"I am sure he would not ask it," said Fleda, hiding her cheeks and eyes at once in his breast.

CHAPTER XLIX.

Do you think I shall not love a sad Pamela as well as a joyful?
Sidney.

Mr. Carleton came back without his mother; she had chosen to put
off her voyage till spring. He took up his quarters at Montepoole,
which, far though it was, was yet the nearest point where his notions
of ease could have freedom enough.

One would have thought that saw him, — those most nearly
concerned almost did think, — that in his daily coming to Queechy
Mr. Carleton sought everybody's pleasure rather than his own. He
was Fleda's most gentle and kind assistant in taking care of Hugh,
soon dearly valued by the sick one, who watched for and welcomed
his coming as a bright spot in the day; and loved particularly to have
Mr. Carleton's hand do anything for him. Rather than almost any
other. His mother's was too feeling; Fleda's Hugh often feared was
weary; and his father's, though gentle to him as to an infant, yet
lacked the mind's training. And though Marion was his sister in
blood, Guy was his brother in better bonds. The deep blue eye that
little Fleda had admired Hugh learned to love and rest on singularly.

To the rest of the family Mr. Carleton's influence was more soothing
and cheering than any cause beside. To all but the head of it. Even
Mrs. Rossitur, after she had once made up her mind to see him,
could not bear to be absent when he was in the house. The dreaded
contrast with old times gave no pain, either to her or Marion. Mr.
Carleton forgot so completely that there was any difference that they
were charmed into forgetting it too. But Mr. Rossitur's pride lay
deeper, or had been less humbled by sorrow; the recollections that
his family let slip never failed to gall him when Mr. Carleton was
present; and if now and then for a moment these were banished by
his guest's graces of mind and manner, the next breath was a sigh for
the circles and the pleasures they served to recall, now seeming for
ever lost to him. Mr. Carleton perceived that his company gave pain
and not pleasure to his host and for that reason was the less in the

house, and made his visits to Hugh at times when Mr. Rossitur was not in the way. Fleda he took out of the house and away with him, for her good and his own.

To Fleda the old childish feeling came back, that she was in somebody's hands who had a marvellous happy way of managing things about her and even of managing herself. A kind of genial atmosphere, that was always doing her good, yet so quietly and so skilfully that she could only now and then get a chance even to look her thanks. Quietly and efficiently he was exerting himself to raise the tone of her mind, to brighten her spirits, to reach those sober lines that years of patience had drawn round her eye and mouth, and charm them away. So gently, so indirectly, by efforts so wisely and gracefully aimed, he set about it, that Fleda did not know what he was doing; but *he* knew. He knew when he saw her brow unbend and her eye catch its old light sparkle, that his conversation and the thoughts and interests with which he was rousing her mind or fancy, were working, and would work all he pleased. And though the next day he might find the old look of patient gravity again, he hardly wished it not there, for the pleasure of doing it away. Hugh's anxious question to Fleda had been very uncalled for, and Fleda's assurance was well-grounded; that subject was never touched upon.

Fleda's manner with Mr. Carleton was peculiar and characteristic. In the house, before others, she was as demure and reserved as though he had been a stranger; she never placed herself near him, nor entered into conversation with him, unless when he obliged her; but when they were alone there was a frank confidence and simplicity in her manner that most happily answered the high-bred delicacy that had called it out.

One afternoon of a pleasant day in March Fleda and Hugh were sitting alone together in the sick room. Hugh was weaker than usual, but not confined to his bed; he was in his great easy-chair which had been moved up-stairs for him again. Fleda had been repeating hymns.

"You are tired," Hugh said.

"No—"

"There's something about you that isn't strong," said Hugh fondly. "I wonder where is Mr. Carleton to-day. It is very pleasant, isn't it?"

"Very pleasant, and warm; it is like April; the snow all went off yesterday, and the ground is dry except in spots."

"I wish he would come and give you a good walk. I have noticed how you always come back looking so much brighter after one of your walks or rides with him."

"What makes you think so, dear Hugh?" said Fleda a little troubled.

"Only my eyes," said Hugh smiling. "It does me as much good as you, Fleda."

"I *never* want to go and leave you, Hugh."

"I am very glad there is somebody to take you. I wish he would come. You want it this minute."

"I don't think I shall let him take me if he comes."

"Whither? and whom?" said another voice.

"I didn't know you were there, sir," said Fleda suddenly rising.

"I am but just here—Rolf admitted me as he passed out."

Coming in between them and still holding the hand of one Mr. Carleton bent down towards the other.

"How is Hugh, to-day?"

It was pleasant to see, that meeting of eyes,—the grave kindliness on the one side, the confident affection on the other. But the wasted features said as plainly as the tone of Hugh's gentle reply, that he was passing away,—fast.

"What shall I do for you?"

"Take Fleda out and give her a good walk. She wants it."

"I will, presently. You are weary—what shall I do to rest you?"

"Nothing—" said Hugh, closing his eyes with a very placid look;— "unless you will put me in mind of something about heaven, Mr. Carleton."

"Shall I read to you?—Baxter,—or something else?"

"No—just give me something to think of while you're gone,—as you have done before, Mr. Carleton."

"I will give you two or three of the Bible bits on that subject; they are but hints and indications you know—rather rays of light that stream out from the place than any description of it; but you have only to follow one of these indications and see whither it will lead you. The first I recollect is that one spoken to Abraham, 'Fear not—I am thy shield, and thy exceeding great reward.'"

"Don't go any further, Mr. Carleton," said Hugh with a smile. "Fleda—do you remember?"

They sat all silent, quite silent, all three, for nobody knew how long.

"You were going to walk," said Hugh without looking at them.

Fleda however did not move till a word or two from Mr. Carleton had backed Hugh's request; then she went.

"Is she gone?" said Hugh. "Mr. Carleton, will you hand me that little desk."

It was his own. Mr. Carleton brought it. Hugh opened it and took out a folded paper which he gave to Mr. Carleton, saying that he thought he ought to have it.

"Do you know the handwriting, sir?"

"No."

"Ah she has scratched it so. It is Fleda's."

Hugh shut his eyes again and Mr. Carleton seeing that he had settled himself to sleep went to the window with the paper. It hardly told him anything he did not know before, though set in a fresh light.

"Cold blew the east wind
And thick fell the rain,
I looked for the tops
Of the mountains in vain;
Twilight was gathering
And dark grew the west,
And the woodfire's crackling
Toned well with the rest.

"Speak fire and tell me—
Thy flickering flame
Fell on me in years past—
Say, am I the same?
Has my face the same brightness
In those days it wore?—
My foot the same lightness
As it crosses the floor?

"Methinks there are changes—
Am weary to-night,—
I once was as tireless
As the bird on her flight;
My bark in full measure
Threw foam from the prow;—

Not even for pleasure
Would I care to move now.

"Tis not the foot only
That lieth thus still, —
I am weary in spirit,
I am listless in will.
My eye vainly peereth
Through the darkness, to find
Some object that cheereth —
Some light for the mind.

"What shadows come o'er me —
What things of the past, —
Bright things of my childhood
That fled all too fast,
The scenes where light roaming
My foot wandered free,
Come back through the gloamin' —
Come all back to me.

"The cool autumn evening,
The fair summer morn, —
The dress and the aspect
Some dear ones have worn, —
The sunshiny places —
The shady hill-side —
The words and the faces
That might not abide. —

"Die out little fire —
Ay, blacken and pine! —
So have paled many lights
That were brighter than thine.
I can quicken thy embers
Again with a breath,
But the others lie cold
In the ashes of death."

Mr. Carleton had read near through the paper before Fleda came in.

"I have kept you a long time, Mr. Carleton," she said coming up to the window; "I found aunt Lucy wanted me."

But she saw with a little surprise the deepening eye which met her, and which shewed, she knew, the working of strong feeling. Her own eye went to the paper in search of explanation.

"What have you there?—Oh, Mr. Carleton," she said, putting her hand over it,—"Please to give it to me!"

Fleda's face was very much in earnest. He took the hand but did not give her the paper, and looked his refusal.

"I am ashamed you should see that!—who gave it to you?"

"You shall wreak your displeasure on no one but me," he said smiling.

"But have you read it?"

"Yes."

"I am very sorry!"

"I am very glad, my dear Elfie."

"You will think—you will think what wasn't true,—it was just a mood I used to get into once in a while—I used to be angry with myself for it, but I could not help it—one of those listless fits would take me now and then—"

"I understand it, Elfie."

"I am very sorry you should know I ever felt or wrote so."

"Why?"

"It was very foolish and wrong—"

"Is that a reason for my not knowing it?"

"No—not a good one—But you have read it now,—won't you let me have it?"

"No—I shall ask for all the rest of the portfolio, Elfie," he said as he put it in a place of security.

"Pray do not!" said Fleda most unaffectedly.

"Why?"

"Because I remember Mrs. Carleton says you always have what you ask for."

"Give me permission to put on your bonnet, then," said he laughingly, taking it from her hand.

The air was very sweet, the footing pleasant. The first few steps of the walk were made by Fleda in silence, with eager breath and a foot that grew lighter as it trod.

"I don't think it was a right mood of mind I had when I wrote that," she said. "It was morbid. But I couldn't help it.—Yet if one could keep possession of those words you quoted just now, I suppose one never would have morbid feelings, Mr. Carleton?"

"Perhaps not; but human nature has a weak hold of anything, and many things may make it weaker."

"Mine is weak," said Fleda. "But it is possible to keep firm hold of those words, Mr. Carleton?"

"Yes—by strength that is not human nature's—And after all the firm hold is rather that in which we are held, or ours would soon fail. The very hand that makes the promise its own must be nerved to grasp it. And so it is best, for it keeps us looking off always to the Author and Finisher of our faith."

"I love those words," said Fleda. "But Mr. Carleton, how shall one be *sure* that one has a right to those other words—those I mean that you told to Hugh? One cannot take the comfort of them unless one is *sure*."

Her voice trembled.

"My dear Elfie, the promises have many of them their *double*—stamped with the very same signet—and if that sealed counterpart is your own, it is the sure earnest and title to the whole value of the promise."

"Well—in this case?" said Fleda eagerly.

"In this case,—God says, 'I am thy shield, and thy exceeding great reward.' Now see if your own heart can give the countersign,—'*Thou art my portion, O Lord!*'"

Fleda's head sank instantly and almost lay upon his arm.

"If you have the one, my dear Elfie, the other is yours—it is the note of hand of the maker of the promise—sure to be honoured. And if you want proof here it is,—and a threefold cord is not soon broken.—'Because he hath set his love upon me, therefore will I deliver him: I will set him on high, because he hath known my name. He shall call upon me, and I will answer him; I will be with him in trouble; I will deliver him, and honour him. With long life will I satisfy him, and shew him my salvation.'"

There was a pause of some length. Fleda had lifted up her head, but walked along very quietly, not seeming to care to speak.

"Have you the countersign, Elfie?"

Fleda flashed a look at him, and only restrained herself from weeping again.

"Yes.—But so I had then, Mr. Carleton—only sometimes I got those fits of feeling—I forgot it, I suppose."

"When were these verses written?"

"Last fall;—uncle Rolf was away, and aunt Lucy unhappy,—and I believe I was tired—I suppose it was that."

For a matter of several rods each was busy with his own musings. But Mr. Carleton bethought himself.

"Where are you, Elfie?"

"Where am I?"

"Yes—Not at Queechy?"

"No indeed," said Fleda laughing. "Far enough away."

"Where?"

"At Paris—at the Marché des Innocens."

"How did you get to Paris?"

"I don't know—by a bridge of associations, I suppose, resting one end on last year, and the other on the time when I was eleven years old."

"Very intelligible," said Mr. Carleton smiling.

"Do you remember that morning, Mr. Carleton?—when you took Hugh and me to the Marché des Innocens?"

"Perfectly."

"I have thanked you a great many times since for getting up so early that morning."

"I think I was well paid at the time. I remember I thought I had seen one of the prettiest sights I had even seen in Paris."

"So I thought!" said Fleda. "It has been a pleasant picture in my imagination ever since."

There was a curious curl in the corners of Mr. Carleton's mouth which made Fleda look an inquiry — a look so innocently wistful that his gravity gave way.

"My dear Elfie!" said he, "you are the very child you were then."

"Am I?" said Fleda. "I dare say I am, for I feel so. I have the very same feeling I used to have then, that I am a child, and you taking the care of me into your own hands."

"One half of that is true, and the other half nearly so."

"How good you always were to me!" Fleda said with a sigh.

"Not necessary to balance the debtor and creditor items on both sides," he said with a smile, "as the account bids fair to run a good while."

A silence again, during which Fleda is clearly *not* enjoying the landscape nor the fine weather.

"Elfie, — what are you meditating?"

She came back from her meditations with a very frank look.

"I was thinking, — Mr. Carleton, — of your notions about female education."

"Well? — "

They had paused upon a rising ground. Fleda hesitated, and then looked up in his face.

"I am afraid you will find me wanting, and when you do, will you put me in the way of being all you wish me to be?"

Her look was ingenuous and tender, equally. He gave her no answer, except by the eye of grave intentness that fixed hers till she could meet it no longer and her own fell. Mr. Carleton recollected himself.

"My dear Elfie," said he, and whatever the look had meant Elfie was at no loss for the tone now,—"what do you consider yourself deficient in?"

Fleda spoke with a little difficulty.

"I am afraid in a good many things—in general reading,—and in what are called accomplishments—"

"You shall read as much as you please by and by," said he, "provided you will let me read with you; and as for the other want, Elfie, it is rather a source of gratification to me."

Elfie very naturally asked why?

"Because as soon as I have the power I shall immediately constitute myself your master in the arts of riding and drawing, and in any other art or acquisition you may take a fancy to, and give you lessons diligently."

"And will there be gratification in that?" said Fleda.

His answer was by a smile. But he somewhat mischievously asked her, "Will there not?"—and Fleda was quiet.

CHAPTER L.

Friends, I sorrow not to leave ye;
If this life an exile be,
We who leave it do but journey
Homeward to our family.

Spanish Ballad.

The first of April came.

Mr. Rossitur had made up his mind not to abide at Queechy, which only held him now by the frail thread of Hugh's life. Mr. Carleton knew this, and had even taken some steps towards securing for him a situation in the West Indies. But it was unknown to Fleda; she had not heard her uncle say anything on the subject since she came home; and though aware that their stay was a doubtful matter, she still thought it might be as well to have the garden in order. Philetus could not be trusted to do everything wisely of his own head, and even some delicate jobs of hand could not be safely left to his skill; if the garden was to make any headway Fleda's head and hand must both be there, she knew. So as the spring opened she used to steal away from the house every morning for an hour or two, hardly letting her friends know what she was about, to make sure that peas and potatoes and radishes and lettuce were in the right places at the right times, and to see that the later and more delicate vegetables were preparing for. She took care to have this business well over before the time that Mr. Carleton ever arrived from the Pool.

One morning she was busy in dressing the strawberry beds, forking up the ground between the plants and filling the vacancies that the severe winter or some irregularities of fall dressing had made. Mr. Skillcorn was rendering a somewhat inefficient help, or perhaps amusing himself with seeing how she worked. The little old silver-grey hood was bending down over the strawberries, and the fork was going at a very energetic rate.

"Philetus—"

"Marm!"

"Will you bring me that bunch of strawberry plants that lies at the corner of the beds, in the walk?—and my trowel?"

"I will!—" said Mr. Skillcorn.

It was another hand however that brought them and laid them beside her; but Fleda very intent upon her work and hidden under her close hood did not find it out. She went on busily putting in the plants as she found room for them, and just conscious, as she thought, that Philetus was still standing at her side she called upon him from time to time, or merely stretched out her hand, for a fresh plant as she had occasion for it.

"Philetus," she said at length, raising her voice a little that it might win to him round the edge of her hood without turning her face,—"I wish you would get the ground ready for that other planting of potatoes—you needn't stay to help me any longer."

"'Tain't me, I guess," said the voice of Philetus on the other side of her.

Fleda looked in astonishment to make sure that it really was Mr. Skillcorn proceeding along the garden path in that quarter, and turning jumped up and dropped her trowel and fork, to have her hands otherwise occupied. Mr. Skillcorn walked off leisurely towards the potato ground, singing to himself in a kind of consolatory aside,—

"I cocked up my beaver, and who but I!—
The lace in my hat was so gallant and so gay,
That I flourished like a king in his own countray."

"There is one of your countrymen that is an odd variety, certainly," said Mr. Carleton, looking after him with a very comic expression of eye.

"Is he not!" said Fleda. "And hardly a common one. There never was a line more mathematically straight than the course of Philetus's ideas; they never diverge, I think, to the right hand or the left, a jot from his own self-interest."

"You will be an invaluable help to me, Elfie, if you can read my English friends as closely."

"I am afraid you will not let me come as close to them," said Fleda laughing.

"Perhaps not. I shouldn't like to pay too high a premium for the knowledge. How is Hugh, to-day?"

Fleda answered with a quick change of look and voice that he was much as usual.

"My mother has written me that she will be here by the Europa, which is due to-morrow—I must set off for New York this afternoon; therefore I came so early to Queechy."

Fleda was instinctively pulling off her gardening gloves, as they walked towards the house.

"Aunt Miriam wants to see you, Mr. Carleton—she begged I would ask you to come there some time—"

"With great pleasure—shall we go there now, Elfie?"

"I will be ready in five minutes."

Mrs. Rossitur was alone in the breakfast-room when they went in. Hugh she reported was asleep, and would be just ready to see Mr.

Carleton by the time they got back. They stood a few minutes talking, and then Fleda went to get ready.

Both pair of eyes followed her as she left the room and then met with perfect understanding.

"Will you give your child to me, Mrs. Rossitur?" said the gentleman.

"With all my heart!" exclaimed Mrs. Rossitur bursting into tears,— "even if I were left alone entirely—"

Her agitation was uncontrolled for a minute, and then she said, with feeling seemingly too strong to be kept in,

"If I were only sure of meeting her in heaven, I could be content to be without her till then!—"

"What is in the way, my dear madam?" said Mr. Carleton, with a gentle sympathy that touched the very spring he meant it should. Mrs. Rossitur waited a minute, but it was only till tears would let her speak, and then said like a child,—

"Oh, it is all darkness!—"

"Except this," said he, gently and clearly, "that Jesus Christ is a sun and a shield; and those that put themselves at his feet are safe from all fear, and they who go to him for light shall complain of darkness no more."

"But I do not know how—"

"Ask him and he will tell you."

"But I am unworthy even to look up towards him," said Mrs. Rossitur, struggling, it seemed, between doubts and wishes.

"He knows that, and yet he has bid you come to him. He knows that,—and knowing it, he has taken your responsibility and paid your debt, and offers you now a clean discharge, if you will take it at his hand;—and for the other part of this unworthiness, that blood cannot do away, blood has brought the remedy—'Shall we who are evil give good things to our children, and shall not our Father which is in heaven give his Holy Spirit to them that ask him?'"

"But must I do nothing?" said Mrs. Rossitur, when she had remained quiet with her face in her hands for a minute or two after he had done speaking.

"Nothing but be willing—be willing to have Christ in all his offices, as your Teacher, your King, and your Redeemer—give yourself to him, dear Mrs. Rossitur, and he will take care of the rest."

"I am willing!" she exclaimed. Fresh tears came, and came freely. Mr. Carleton said no more, till hearing some noise of opening and shutting doors above stairs Mrs. Rossitur hurriedly left the room, and Fleda came in by the other entrance.

"May I take you a little out of the way, Mr. Carleton?" she said when they had passed through the Deepwater settlement.—"I have a message to carry to Mrs. Elster—a poor woman out here beyond the lake. It is not a disagreeable place."

"And what if it were?"

"I should not perhaps have asked you to go with me," said Fleda a little doubtfully.

"You may take me where you will, Elfie," he said gently. "I hope to do as much by you some day."

Fleda looked up at the piece of elegance beside her, and thought what a change must have come over him if *he* would visit poor places. He was silent and grave however, and so was she, till they arrived at the house they were going to.

Certainly it was not a disagreeable place. Barby's much less strong minded sister had at least a good share of her practical nicety. The little board path to the door was clean and white still, with possibly a trifle less brilliant effect. The room and its old inhabitants were very comfortable and tidy; the patchwork counterpane as gay as ever. Mrs. Elster was alone, keeping company with a snug little wood fire, which was near as much needed in that early spring weather as it had been during the winter.

Mr. Carleton had come back from his abstraction, and stood taking half unconscious note of these things, while Fleda was delivering her message to the old woman. Mrs. Elster listened to her implicitly with every now and then an acquiescing nod or ejaculation, but so soon as Fleda had said her say she burst out, with a voice that had never known the mufflings of delicacy and was now pitched entirely beyond its owner's ken. Looking hard at Mr. Carleton,

"Fleda!—Is *this* the gentleman that's to be your—*husband?*"

The last word elevated and brought out with emphatic distinctness of utterance.

If the demand had been whether the gentleman in question was a follower of Mahomet, it would hardly have been more impossible for Fleda to give an affirmative answer; but Mr. Carleton laughed and bringing his face a little nearer the old crone, answered,

"So she has promised, ma'am."

It was curious to see the lines of the old woman's face relax as she looked at him.

"He's—worthy of you!—as far as looks goes," she said in the same key as before, apostrophizing Fleda who had drawn back, but not stirring her eyes from Mr. Carleton all the time. And then she added to him with a little satisfied nod, and in a very decided tone of information,

"She will make you a good wife!"

"Because she has made a good friend?" said Mr. Carleton quietly. "Will you let me be a friend too?"

He had turned the old lady's thoughts into a golden channel, whence, as she was an American, they had no immediate issue in words; and Fleda and Mr. Carleton left the house without anything more.

Fleda felt nervous. But Mr. Carleton's first words were as coolly and as gravely spoken as if they had just come out from a philosophical lecture; and with an immediate spring of relief she enjoyed every step of the way and every word of the conversation which was kept up with great life, till they reached Mrs. Plumfield's door.

No one was in the sitting-room. Fleda left Mr. Carleton there and passed gently into the inner apartment, the door of which was standing ajar.

But her heart absolutely leaped into her mouth, for Dr. Quackenboss and Mr. Olmney were there on either side of her aunt's bed. Fleda came forward and shook hands.

"This is quite a meeting of friends," said the doctor blandly, yet with a perceptible shading of the whilome broad sunshine of his face. — "Your — a — aunt, my dear Miss Ringgan, — is in a most extraordinary state of mind!"

Fleda was glad to hide her face against her aunt's and asked her how she did.

"Dr. Quackenboss thinks it extraordinary, Fleda," said the old lady with her usual cheerful sedateness, — "that one who has trusted God and had constant experience of his goodness and faithfulness for forty years should not doubt him at the end of it."

"You have no doubt—of any kind, Mrs. Plumfield?" said the clergyman.

"Not the shadow of a doubt!" was the hearty, steady reply.

"You mistake, my dear madam," said Dr. Quackenboss,—"pardon me—it is not that—I would be understood to say, merely, that I do not comprehend how such—a—such security—can be attained respecting what seems so—a—elevated—and difficult to know."

"Only by believing," said Mrs. Plumfield with a very calm smile. "'He that believeth on him shall not be ashamed;'—'shall *not* be ashamed!'" she repeated slowly.

Dr. Quackenboss looked at Fleda, who kept her eyes fixed upon her aunt.

"But it seems to me—I beg pardon—perhaps I am arrogant—" he said with a little bow,—"but it appears to me almost—in a manner—almost presumptuous, not to be a little doubtful in such a matter until the time comes. Am I—do you disapprove of me, Mr. Olmney?"

Mr. Olmney silently referred him for his answer to the person he had first addressed, who had closed her eyes while he was speaking.

"Sir," she said, opening them,—"it can't be presumption to obey God, and he tells me to rejoice. And I do—I do!—'Let all those that love thee rejoice in thee and be glad in thee!'—But mind!" she added energetically, fixing her strong grey eye upon him—"he does not tell *you* to rejoice—do not think it—not while you stand aloof from his terms of peace. Take God at his word, and be happy;—but if not, you have nothing to do with the song that I sing!"

The doctor stared at her till she had done speaking, and then slunk out of her range of vision behind the curtains of the bed-post. Not silenced however.

"But—a—Mr. Olmney," said he hesitating—"don't you think that there is in general—a—a becoming modesty, in—a—in people that have done wrong, as we all have,—putting off being sure until they are so? It seems so to me!"

"Come here, Dr. Quackenboss," said aunt Miriam.

She waited till he came to her side, and then taking his hand and looking at him very kindly, she said,

"Sir, forty years ago I found in the Bible, as you say, that I was a sinner, and that drove me to look for something else. I found then God's promise that if I would give my dependence entirely to the substitute he had provided for me and yield my heart to his service, he would for Christ's sake hold me quit of all my debts and be my father, and make me his child. And, sir, I did it. I abhor every other dependence—the things you count good in me I reckon but filthy rags. At the same time, I know that ever since that day, forty years ago, I have lived in his service and tried to live to his glory. And now, sir, shall I disbelieve his promise? do you think he would be pleased if I did?"

The doctor's mouth was stopped, for once. He drew back as soon as he could and said not another word.

Before anybody had broken the silence Seth came in; and after shaking hands with Fleda, startled her by asking whether that was not Mr. Carleton in the other room.

"Yes," Fleda said,—"he came to see aunt Miriam."

"Ain't you well enough to see him, mother?"

"Quite—and very happy," said she.

Seth immediately went back and invited him in. Fleda dared not look up while the introductions were passing,—of "the Rev. Mr. Olmney," and of "Dr. Quackenboss,"—the former of whom Mr.

Carleton took cordially by the hand, while Dr. Quackenboss conceiving that his hand must be as acceptable, made his salutation with an indescribable air at once of attempted gracefulness and ingratiation. Fleda saw the whole in the advancing line of the doctor's person, a vision of which crossed her downcast eye. She drew back then, for Mr. Carleton came where she was standing to take her aunt's hand; Seth had absolutely stayed his way before to make the said introductions.

Mrs. Plumfield was little changed by years or disease since he had seen her. There was somewhat more of a look of bodily weakness than there used to be; but the dignified, strong-minded expression of the face was even heightened; eye and brow were more pure and unclouded in their steadfastness. She looked very earnestly at her visiter and then with evident pleasure from the manner of his look and greeting. Fleda watched her eye softening with a gratified expression and fixed upon him as he was gently talking to her.

Mr. Olmney presently came round to take leave, promising to see her another time, and passing Fleda with a frank grave pressure of the hand which gave her some pain. He and Seth left the room. Fleda was hardly conscious that Dr. Quackenboss was still standing at the foot of the bed making the utmost use of his powers of observation. He could use little else, for Mr. Carleton and Mrs. Plumfield after a few words on each side, had as it were by common consent come to a pause. The doctor, when a sufficient time had made him fully sensible of this, walked up to Fleda, who wished heartily at the moment that she could have presented the reverse end of the magnet to him. Perhaps however it was that very thing which by a perverse sort of attraction drew him towards her.

"I suppose—a—we may conclude," said he with a somewhat saturnine expression of mischief,—that Miss Ringgan contemplates forsaking the agricultural line before a great while."

"I have not given up my old habits, sir," said Fleda, a good deal vexed.

"No—I suppose not—but Queechy air is not so well suited for them—other skies will prove more genial," he said; she could not help thinking, pleased at her displeasure.

"What is the fault of Queechy air, sir?" said Mr. Carleton, approaching them.

"Sir!" said the doctor, exceedingly taken aback, though the words had been spoken in the quietest manner possible,—'it—a—it has no fault, sir,—that I am particularly aware of—it is perfectly salubrious. Mrs. Plumfield, I will bid you good-day;—I—a—I *hope* you will get well again!"

"I hope not, sir!" said aunt Miriam, in the same clear hearty tones which had answered him before.

The doctor took his departure and made capital of his interview with Mr. Carleton; who he affirmed he could tell by what he had seen of him was a very deciduous character, and not always conciliating in his manners.

Fleda waited with a little anxiety for what was to follow the doctor's leave-taking.

It was with a very softened eye that aunt Miriam looked at the two who were left, clasping Fleda's hand again; and it was with a very softened voice that she next spoke.

"Do you remember our last meeting, sir?"

"I remember it well," he said.

"Fleda tells me you are a changed man since that time?"

He answered only by a slight and grave bow.

"Mr. Carleton," said the old lady,—"I am a dying woman—and this child is the dearest thing in the world to me after my own,—and hardly after him.—Will you pardon me—will you bear with me, if that I may die in peace, I say, sir, what else it would not become me to say?—and it is for her sake."

"Speak to me freely as you would to her," he said with a look that gave her full permission.

Fleda had drawn close and hid her face in her aunt's neck. Aunt Miriam's hand moved fondly over her cheek and brow for a minute or two in silence; her eye resting there too.

"Mr. Carleton, this child is to belong to you—how will you guide her?"

"By the gentlest paths," he said with a smile.

A whispered remonstrance from Fleda to her aunt had no effect.

"Will her best interests be safe in your hands?"

"How shall I resolve you of that, Mrs. Plumfield?" he said gravely.

"Will you help her to mind her mother's prayer and keep herself unspotted from the world?"

"As I trust she will help me."

A rogue may answer questions, but an eye that has never known the shadow of double-dealing makes no doubtful discoveries of itself. Mrs. Plumfield read it and gave it her very thorough respect.

"Mr. Carleton—pardon me, sir,—I do not doubt you—but I remember hearing long ago that you were rich and great in the world—it is dangerous for a Christian to be so—Can she keep in your grandeur the simplicity of heart and life she has had at Queechy?"

"May I remind you of your own words, my dear madam? By the blessing of God all things are possible. These things you speak of are not in themselves evil; if the mind be set on somewhat else, they are little beside a larger storehouse of material to work with—an increased stewardship to account for."

"She has been taking care of others all her life," said aunt Miriam tenderly;—"it is time she was taken care of; and these feet are very unfit for rough paths; but I would rather she should go on struggling as she has done with difficulties and live and die in poverty, than that the lustre of her heavenly inheritance should be tarnished even a little.—I would, my darling!—"

"But the alternative is not, so," said Mr. Carleton with gentle grace, touching Fleda's hand who he saw was a good deal disturbed. "Do not make her afraid of me, Mrs. Plumfield."

"I do not believe I need," said aunt Miriam, "and I am sure I could not,—but sir, you will forgive me?"

"No madam—that is not possible."

"One cannot stand where I do," said the old lady, "without learning a little the comparative value of things; and I seek my child's good,—that is my excuse. I could not be satisfied to take her testimony—"

"Take mine, madam," said Mr. Carleton. "I have learned the comparative value of things too; and I will guard her highest interests as carefully as I will every other—as earnestly as you can desire."

"I thank you, sir," said the old lady gratefully. "I am sure of it. I shall leave her in good hands. I wanted this assurance. And if ever there was a tender plant that was not fitted to grow on the rough side of the world—I think this is one," said she, kissing earnestly the face that yet Fleda did not dare to lift up.

Mr. Carleton did not say what he thought. He presently took kind leave of the old lady and went into the next room, where Fleda soon rejoined him and they set off homewards.

Fleda was quietly crying all the way down the hill. At the foot of the hill Mr. Carleton resolutely slackened his pace.

"I have one consolation," he said, "my dear Elfie—you will have the less to leave for me."

She put her hand with a quick motion upon his, and roused her self.

"She is a beautiful rebuke to unbelief. But she is hardly to be mourned for, Elfie."

"Oh I was not crying for aunt Miriam," said Fleda.

"For what then?" he said gently.

"Myself."

"That needs explanation," he said in the same tone. "Let me have it, Elfie."

"O—I was thinking of several things," said Fleda, not exactly wishing to give the explanation.

"Too vague," said Mr. Carleton smiling. "Trust me with a little more of your mind, Elfie."

Fleda glanced up at him, half smiling, and yet with filling eyes, and then as usual, yielded to the winning power of the look that met her.

"I was thinking," she said, keeping her head carefully down,—"of some of the things you and aunt Miriam were saying just now,—and—how good for nothing I am."

"In what respect?" said Mr. Carleton with praiseworthy gravity.

Fleda hesitated, and he pressed the matter no further; but more unwilling to displease him than herself she presently went on, with some difficulty; wording what she had to say with as much care as she could.

"I was thinking—how gratitude—or not gratitude alone—but how one can be full of the desire to please another,—a fellow-creature,—and find it constantly easy to do or bear anything for that purpose; and how slowly and coldly duty has to move alone in the direction where it should be the swiftest and warmest."

She knew he would take her words as simply as she said them; she was not disappointed. He was silent a minute and then said gravely,—

"Is this a late discovery, Elfie?"

"No—only I was realizing it strongly just now."

"It is a complaint we may all make. The remedy is, not to love less what we know, but to know better that of which we are in ignorance. We will be helps and not hindrances to each other, Elfie."

"You have said that before," said Fleda still keeping her head down.

"What?"

"About my being a help to you!"

"It will not be the first time," said he smiling,—"nor the second. Your little hand first held up a glass to gather the scattered rays of truth that could not warm me into a centre where they must burn."

"Very innocently," said Fleda with a little unsteady feeling of voice.

"Very innocently," said Mr. Carleton smiling. "A veritable lens could hardly have been more unconscious of its work or more pure of design."

"I do not think that was quite so either, Mr. Carleton," said Fleda.

"It was so, my dear Elfie, and your present speech is nothing against it. This power of example is always unconsciously wielded; the medium ceases to be clear so soon as it is made anything but a medium. The bits of truth you aimed at me wittingly would have been nothing if they had not come through that medium."

"Then apparently one's prime efforts ought to be directed to oneself."

"One's first efforts, certainly. Your silent example was the first thing that moved me."

"Silent example!" said Fleda catching her breath a little. "Mine ought to be very good, for I can never do good in any other way."

"You used to talk pretty freely to me."

"It wasn't my fault, I am certain," said Fleda half laughing. "Besides, I was sure of my ground. But in general I never can speak to people about what will do them any good."

"Yet whatever be the power of silent example there are often times when a word is of incalculable importance."

"I know it," said Fleda earnestly,—"I have felt it very often, and grieved that I could not say it, even at the very moment when I knew it was wanting."

"Is that right, Elfie?"

"No," said Fleda, with quick watering eyes,—"It is not right at all;— but it is constitutional with me. I never can talk to other people of what concerns my own thoughts and feelings."

"But this concerns other people's thoughts and feelings."

"Yes, but there is an implied revelation of my own."

"Do you expect to include me in the denomination of 'other people'?"

"I don't know," said Fleda laughing.

"Do you wish it?"

Fleda looked down and up, and coloured, and said she didn't know.

"I will teach you," said he smiling.

The rest of the day by both was given to Hugh.

CHAPTER LI.

O what is life but a sum of love,
　And death but to lose it all?
Weeds be for those that are left behind,
　And not for those that fall!

Milnes.

"Here's something come, Fleda," said Barby walking into the sick room one morning a few days afterwards,—"a great bag of something—more than you can eat up in a fortnight—it's for Hugh."

"It's extraordinary that anybody should send *me* a great bag of anything eatable," said Hugh.

"Where did it come from?" said Fleda.

"Philetus fetched it—he found it down to Mr. Sampion's when he went with the sheep-skins."

"How do you know it's for me?" said Hugh.

"'Cause it's written on, as plain as a pikestaff. I guess it's a mistake though."

"Why?" said Fleda; "and what is it?"

"O I don't much think 'twas meant for him," said Barby. "It's oysters."

"Oysters!"

"Yes—come out and look at 'em—you never see such fine fellows. I've heerd say," said Barby abstractedly as Fleda followed her out and she displayed to view some magnificent Ostraceans,—"I've

387

heerd say that an English shilling was worth two American ones, but I never understood it rightly till now."

To all intents and purposes those were English oysters, and worth twice as much as any others Fleda secretly confessed.

That evening, up in the sick room, — it was quite evening, and all the others of the family were taking rest or keeping Mr. Rossitur company down stairs, — Fleda was carefully roasting some of the same oysters for Hugh's supper. She had spread out a glowing bed of coals on the hearth, and there lay four or five of the big bivalves, snapping and sputtering in approbation of their quarters in a most comfortable manner; and Fleda standing before the fire tended them with a double kind of pleasure. From one friend, and for another, those were most odorous oysters. Hugh sat watching them and her, the same in happy simplicity that he had been at eleven years old.

"How pleasant those oysters smell," said he. "Fleda, they remind me so of the time when you and I used to roast oysters in Mrs. Renney's room for lunch — do you recollect? — and sometimes in the evening when everybody was gone out, you know; and what an airing we used to have to give the dining-room afterwards. How we used to enjoy them, Fleda — you and I all alone."

"Yes," said Fleda in a tone of doubtful enjoyment. She was shielding her face with a paper and making self-sacrificing efforts to persuade a large oyster-shell to stand so on the coals as to keep the juice.

"Don't!" said Hugh; — "I would rather the oysters should burn than you. Mr. Carleton wouldn't thank me for letting you do so."

"Never mind!" said Fleda arranging the oysters to her satisfaction, — "he isn't here to see. Now Hugh, my dear — these are ready as soon as I am."

"I am ready," said Hugh. "How long it is since we had a roast oyster, Fleda!"

"They look good, don't they?"

A little stand was brought up between them with the bread and butter and the cups; and Fleda opened oysters and prepared tea for Hugh, with her nicest, gentlest, busiest of hands; making every bit to be twice as sweet, for her sympathizing eyes and loving smile and pleasant word commenting. She shared the meal with him, but her own part was as slender as his and much less thought of. His enjoyment was what she enjoyed, though it was with a sad twinge of alloy which changed her face whenever it was where he could not see it; when turned upon him it was only bright and affectionate, and sometimes a little too tender; but Fleda was too good a nurse to let that often appear.

"Mr. Carleton did not bargain for your opening his oysters, Fleda. How kind it was of him to send them."

"Yes."

"How long will he be gone, Fleda?"

"I don't know—he didn't say. I don't believe many days."

Hugh was silent a little while she was putting away the stand and the oyster-shells. Then she came and sat down by him.

"You have burnt yourself over those things," said he sorrowfully;— "you -shouldn't have done it. It is not right."

"Dear Hugh," said Fleda lightly, laying her head on his shoulder,— "I like to burn myself for you."

"That's just the way you have been doing all your life."

"Hush!" she said softly.

"It is true,—for me and for everybody else. It is time you were taken better care of, dear Fleda."

"Don't, dear Hugh!"

"I am right though," said he. "You are pale and worn now with waiting upon me and thinking of me. It is time you were gone. But I think it is well I am going too, for what should I do in the world without you, Fleda?"

Fleda was crying now, intensely though quietly; but Hugh went on with feeling as calm as it was deep.

"What should I have done all these years?—or any of us? How you have tired yourself for everybody—in the garden and in the kitchen and with Earl Douglass—how we could let you I don't know, but I believe we could not help it."

Fleda put her hand upon his mouth. But he took it away and went on—

"How often I have seen you sleeping all the evening on the sofa with a pale face, tired out—Dear Fleda," said he kissing her cheek, "I am glad there's to be an end put to it. And all the day you went about with such a bright face that it made mother and me happy to look at you; and I knew then, many a time, it was for our sakes—

"Why do you cry so, Fleda? I like to think of it, and to talk of it, now that I know you won't do so any more. I knew the whole truth, and it went to the bottom of my heart; but I could do nothing but love you—I did that!—Don't cry so, Fleda!—you ought not.—You have been the sunshine of the house. My spirit never was so strong as yours; I should have been borne to the ground, I know, in all these years, if it had not been for you; and mother—you have been her life."

"You have been tired too," Fleda whispered.

"Yes at the saw-mill. And then you would come up there through the sun to look at me, and your smile would make me forget

390

everything sorrowful for the rest of the day—except that I couldn't help you."

"Oh you did—you did—you helped me always, Hugh."

"Not much. I couldn't help you when you were sewing for me and father till your fingers and eyes were aching, and you never would own that you were anything but 'a little' tired—it made my heart ache. Oh I knew it all, dear Fleda.—I am very, very glad that you will have somebody to take care of you now that will not let you burn your fingers for him or anybody else. It makes me happy!"

"You make me very unhappy, dear Hugh."

"I don't mean it," said Hugh tenderly. "I don't believe there is anybody else in the world that I could be so satisfied to leave you with."

Fleda made no answer to that. She sat up and tried to recover herself.

"I hope he will come back in time," said Hugh, settling himself back in the easy-chair with a weary look, and closing his eyes.

"In time for what?"

"To see me again."

"My dear Hugh!—he will to be sure, I hope."

"He must make haste," said Hugh. "But I want to see him again very much, Fleda."

"For anything in particular?"

"No—only because I love him. I want to see him once more."

Hugh slumbered; and Fleda by his side wept tears of mixed feeling till she was tired.

Hugh was right. But nobody else knew it, and his brother was not sent for.

It was about a week after this, when one night a horse and wagon came up to the back of the house from the road, the gentleman who had been driving leading the horse. It was late, long past Mr. Skillcorn's usual hour of retiring, but some errand of business had kept him abroad and he stood there looking on. The stars gave light enough.

"Can you fasten my horse where he may stand a little while, sir? without taking him out?"

"I guess I can," replied Philetus, with reasonable confidence, —"if there's a rope's end some place—"

And forthwith he went back into the house to seek it. The gentleman patiently holding his horse meanwhile, till he came out.

"How is Mr. Hugh to-night?"

"Well—he ain't just so smart, they say," responded Philetus, insinuating the rope's end as awkwardly as possible among the horse's head-gear, —"I believe he's dying."

Instead of going round now to the front of the house, Mr. Carleton knocked gently at the kitchen door and asked the question anew of Barby.

"He's—Come in, sir, if you please," she said, opening wide the door for him to enter, —"I'll tell 'em you're here."

"Do not disturb any one for me," said he.

"I won't disturb 'em!" said Barby, in a tone a little though unconsciously significant.

Mr. Carleton neglected the chair she had placed for him, and remained standing by the mantelpiece, thinking of the scenes of his early introduction to that kitchen. It wore the same look it had done then; under Barby's rule it was precisely the same thing it had been under Cynthia's.—The passing years seemed a dream, and the passing generations of men a vanity, before the old house more abiding than they. He stood thinking of the people he had seen gathered by that fireplace and the little household fairy whose childish ministrations had given such a beauty to the scene, —when a very light step crossed the painted floor and she was there again before him. She did not speak a word; she stood still a moment trying for words, and then put her hand upon Mr. Carleton's arm and gently drew him out of the room with her.

The family were all gathered in the room to which she brought him. Mr. Rossitur, as soon as he saw Mr. Carleton come in, shrunk back where he could be a little shielded by the bed-post. Marion's face was hid on the foot of the bed. Mrs. Rossitur did not move. Leaving Mr. Carleton on the near side of the bed Fleda went round to the place she seemed to have occupied before, at Hugh's right hand; and they were all still, for he was in a little doze, lying with his eyes closed, and the face as gently and placidly sweet as it had been in his boyhood. Perhaps Mr. Rossitur looked at it; but no other did just then, except Mr. Carleton. His eye rested nowhere else. The breathing of an infant could not be more gentle; the face of an angel not more peacefully at rest. "So he giveth his beloved sleep," — thought the gentleman, as he gazed on the brow from which all care, if care there had ever been, seemed to have taken flight.

Not yet—not quite yet; for Hugh suddenly opened his eyes and without seeing anybody else, said,

"Father—"

Mr. Rossitur left the bed-post and came close to where Fleda was standing, and leaning forward, touched his son's head, but did not speak.

"Father—" said Hugh, in a voice so gentle that it seemed as if strength must be failing,—"what will you do when you come to lie here?"

Mr. Rossitur put his hands to his face.

"Father—I must speak now if I never did before—once I must speak to you,—what will you do when you come to lie where I do?—what will you trust to?"

The person addressed was as motionless as a statue. Hugh did not move his eyes from him.

"Father, I will be a living warning and example to you, for I know that I shall live in your memory—you shall remember what I say to you—that Jesus Christ is a dear friend to those that trust in him, and if he is not yours it will be because you will not let him. You shall remember my testimony, that he can make death sweeter than life—in his presence is fulness of joy—at his right hand there are pleasures for evermore. He is better,—he is more to me,—even than you all, and he will be to you a better friend than the poor child you are losing, though you do not know it now. It is he that has made my life in this world happy—only he—and I have nothing to look to but him in the world I am going to. But what will you do in the hour of death, as I am, if he isn't your friend, father?"

Mr. Rossitur's frame swayed, like a tree that one sees shaken by a distant wind, but he said nothing.

"Will you remember me happily, father, if you come to die without having done as I begged you? Will you think of me in heaven and not try to come there too? Father, will you be a Christian?—will you not?—for my sake—for *little Hugh's* sake, as you used to call him?—Father?—"

Mr. Rossitur knelt down and hid his face in the coverings; but he did not utter a word.

Hugh's eye dwelt on him for a moment with unspeakable expression, and his lip trembled. He said no more; he closed his eyes; and for a little time there was nothing to be heard but the sobs which could not be restrained, from all but the two gentlemen. It probably oppressed Hugh, for after a while he said with a weary sigh and without opening his eyes,

"I wish somebody would sing."

Nobody answered at first.

"Sing what, dear Hugh?" said Fleda, putting aside her tears and leaning her face towards him.

"Something that speaks of my want," said Hugh.

"What do you want, dear Hugh?"

"Only Jesus Christ," he said with a half smile.

But they were silent as death. Fleda's face was in her hands and her utmost efforts after self-control wrought nothing but tears. The stillness had lasted a little while, when very softly and sweetly the notes of a hymn floated to their ears, and though they floated on and filled the room, the voice was so nicely modulated that its waves of sweetness broke gently upon the nearest ear.

"Jesus, the sinner's friend, to Thee,
Lost and undone, for aid I flee;
Weary of earth, myself, and sin,
Open thine arms and take me in.

"Pity and save my sin-sick soul, —
'Tis thou alone canst make me whole;
Dark, till in me thine image shine,
And lost I am, till thou art mine.

"At length I own it cannot be,
That I should fit myself for thee,
Here now to thee I all resign, —
Thine is the work, and only thine.

"What shall I say thy grace to move? —
Lord, I am sin, but thou art love!
I give up every plea beside, —
Lord, I am lost, — but thou hast died!"

They were still again after the voice had ceased; almost perfectly still; though tears might be pouring, as indeed they were from every eye, there was no break to the silence, other than a half-caught sob now and then from a kneeling figure whose head was in Marion's lap.

"Who was that?" said Hugh, when the singer had been silent a minute.

Nobody answered immediately; and then Mr. Carleton bending over him, said,

"Don't you know me, dear Hugh?"

"Is it Mr. Carleton?"

Hugh looked pleased, and clasped both of his hands upon Guy's which he laid upon his breast. For a second he closed his eyes and was silent.

"Was it you sang?"

"Yes."

"You never sang for me before," he remarked.

He was silent again.

"Are you going to take Fleda away?"

"By and by," said Mr. Carleton gently.

"Will you take good care of her?"

Mr. Carleton hesitated, and then said, so low that it could reach but one other person's ear,

"What hand and life can."

"I know it," said Hugh. "I am very glad you will have her. You will not let her tire herself any more."

Whatever became of Fleda's tears she had driven them away and leaning forward she touched her cheek to his, saying with a clearness and sweetness of voice that only intensity of feeling could have given her at the moment,

"I am not tired, dear Hugh."

Hugh clasped one arm round her neck and kissed her—again and again, seeming unable to say anything to her in any other way; still keeping his hold of Mr. Carleton's hand.

"I give all my part of her to you," he said at length. "Mr. Carleton, I shall see both of you in heaven?"

"I hope so," was the answer, in those very calm and clear tones that have a singular effect in quieting emotion, while they indicate anything but the want of it.

"I am the best off of you all," Hugh said.

He lay still for awhile with shut eyes. Fleda had withdrawn herself from his arms and stood at his side, with a bowed head, but perfectly quiet. He still held Mr. Carleton's hand, as something he did not want to part with.

"Fleda," said he, "who is that crying?—Mother—come here."

Mr. Carleton gave place to her. Hugh pulled her down to him till her face lay upon his, and folded both his arms around her.

"Mother," he said softly, "will you meet me in heaven?—say yes."

"How can I, dear Hugh?"

"You can, dear mother," said he kissing her with exceeding tenderness of expression,—"my Saviour will be yours and take you there. Say you will give yourself to Christ—dear mother!—sweet mother! promise me I shall see you again!—"

Mrs. Rossitur's weeping it was difficult to hear. But Hugh hardly shedding a tear still kissed her, repeating, "Promise me, dear mother—promise me that you will;"—till Mrs. Rossitur in an agony sobbed out the word he wanted,—and Hugh hid his face then in her neck.

Mr. Carleton left the room and went down stairs. He found the sitting-room desolate, untenanted and cold for hours; and he went again into the kitchen. Barby was there for some time, and then she left him alone.

He had passed a long while in thinking and walking up and down, and he was standing musing by the fire, when Fleda again came in. She came in silently, to his side, and putting her arm within his laid her face upon it with a simplicity of trust and reliance that went to his heart; and she wept there for a long hour. They hardly changed their position in all that time; and her tears flowed silently though incessantly, the only tokens of sympathy on his part being such a gentle caressing smoothing of her hair or putting it from her brow as he had used when she was a child. The bearing of her hand and head upon his arm in time shewed her increasingly weary. Nothing shewed him so.

"Elfie—my dear Elfie," he said at last very tenderly, in the same way that he would have spoken nine years before—"Hugh gave his part of you to me—I must take care of it."

Fleda tried to rouse herself immediately.

"This is poor entertainment for you, Mr. Carleton," she said, raising her head and wiping away the tears from her face.

"You are mistaken," he said gently. "You never gave me such pleasure but twice before, Elfie."

Fleda's head went down again instantly, and this time there was something almost caressing in the motion.

"Next to the happiness of having friends on earth," he said soothingly, "is the happiness of having friends in heaven. Don't weep any more to-night, my dear Elfie."

"He told me to thank you—" said Fleda. But stopping short and clasping with convulsive energy the arm she held, she shed more violent tears than she had done that night before. The most gentle soothing, the most tender reproof, availed at last to quiet her; and she stood clinging to his arm still and looking down into the fire.

"I did not think it would be so soon," she said.

"It was not soon to him, Elfie."

"He told me to thank you for singing. How little while it seems since we were children together—how little while since before that—when I was a little child here—how different!"

"No, the very same," said he, touching his lips to her forehead,— "you are the very same child you were then; but it is time you were my child, for I see you would make yourself ill. No—" said he softly taking the hand Fleda raised to her face,—"no more tonight—tell me how early I may see you in the morning—for, Elfie, I must leave you after breakfast."

Fleda looked up inquiringly.

"My mother has brought news that determines me to return to England immediately."

"To England!"

"I have been too long from home—I am wanted there."

Fleda looked down again and did her best not to shew what she felt.

"I do not know how to leave you—and now—but I must. There are disturbances among the people, and my own are infected. I *must* be there without delay."

"Political disturbances?" said Fleda.

"Somewhat of that nature—but partly local. How early may I come to you?"

"But you are not going away tonight? It is very late."

"That is nothing—my horse is here."

Fleda would have begged in vain, if Barby had not come in and added her word, to the effect that it would be a mess of work to look for lodgings at that time of night, and that she had made the west room ready for Mr. Carleton. She rejected with great sincerity any claim to the thanks with which Fleda as well as Mr. Carleton repaid her; "there wa'n't no trouble about it," she said. Mr. Carleton however found his room prepared for him with all the care that Barby's utmost ideas of refinement and exactness could suggest.

It was still very early the next morning; when he left it and came into the sitting-room, but he was not the first there. The firelight glimmered on the silver and china of the breakfast table, all set; everything was in absolute order, from the fire to the two cups and saucers which were alone on the board. A still silent figure was standing by one of the windows looking out. Not crying; but that Mr. Carleton knew from the unmistakable lines of the face was only because tears were waiting another time; quiet now, it would not be by and by. He came and stood at the window with her.

"Do you know," he said, after a little, "that Mr. Rossitur purposes to leave Queechy?"

"Does he?" said Fleda rather starting, but she added not another word, simply because she felt she could not safely.

"He has accepted, I believe, a consulship at Jamaica."

"Jamaica!" said Fleda. "I have heard him speak of the West Indies—I am not surprised—I know it was likely he would not stay here."

How tightly her fingers that were free grasped the edge of the window-frame. Mr. Carleton saw it and softly removed them into his own keeping.

"He may go before I can be here again. But I shall leave my mother to take care of you, Elfie."

"Thank you," said Fleda faintly. "You are very kind—"

"Kind to myself," he said smiling. "I am only taking care of my own. I need not say that you will see me again as early as my duty can make it possible;—but I may be detained, and your friends may be gone—Elfie—give me the right to send if I cannot come for you. Let me leave my wife in my mother's care."

Fleda looked down, and coloured, and hesitated; but the expression in her face was not that of doubt.

"Am I asking too much?" he said gently.

"No sir," said Fleda,—"and—but—"

"What is in the way?"

401

But it seemed impossible for Fleda to tell him.

"May I not know?" he said, gently putting away the hair from Fleda's face, which looked distressed. "Is it only your feeling?"

"No sir," said Fleda,—"at least—not the feeling you think it is—but—I could not do it without giving great pain."

Mr. Carleton was silent.

"Not to anybody you know, Mr. Carleton," said Fleda, suddenly fearing a wrong interpretation of her words,—"I don't mean that—I mean somebody else—the person—the only person you could apply to—" she said, covering her face in utter confusion.

"Do I understand you?" said he smiling. "Has this gentleman any reason to dislike the sight of me?"

"No sir," said Fleda,—"but he thinks he has."

"That only I meant," said he. "You are quite right, my dear Elfie; I of all men ought to understand that."

The subject was dropped, and in a few minutes his gentle skill had well nigh made Fleda forget what they had been talking about. Himself and his wishes seemed to be put quite out of his own view, and out of hers as far as possible; except that the very fact made Fleda recognize with unspeakable gratitude and admiration the kindness and grace that were always exerted for her pleasure. If her good-will could have been put into the cups of coffee she poured out for him, he might have gone in the strength of them all the way to England. There was strength of another kind to be gained from her face of quiet sorrow and quiet self-command which were her very childhood's own.

"You will see me at the earliest possible moment," he said when at last taking leave.—"I hope to be free in a short time; but it may not be. Elfie—if I should be detained longer than I hope—if I should not

402

be able to return in a reasonable time, will you let my mother bring you out?—if I cannot come to you will you come to me?"

Fleda coloured a good deal, and said, scarce intelligibly, that she hoped he would be able to come. He did not press the matter. He parted from her and was leaving the room. Fleda suddenly sprang after him, before he had reached the door, and laid her hand on his arm.

"I did not answer your question, Mr. Carleton," she said with cheeks that were dyed now,—"I will do whatever you please—whatever you think best."

His thanks were most gratefully though silently spoken, and he went away.

CHAPTER LII.

Daughter, they seem to say,
  Peace to thy heart!
We too, yes, daughter,
  Have been as thou art.
Hope-lifted, doubt-depressed,
  Seeing in part, —
Tried, troubled, tempted, —
  Sustained, — as thou art.

Unknown.

Mr. Rossitur was disposed for no further delay now in leaving Queechy. The office at Jamaica, which Mr. Carleton and Dr. Gregory had secured for him, was immediately accepted; and every arrangement pressed to hasten his going. On every account he was impatient to be out of America, and especially since his son's death. Marion was of his mind. Mrs. Rossitur had more of a home feeling, even for the place where home had not been to her as happy as it might.

They were sad weeks of bustle and weariness that followed Hugh's death; less sad perhaps for the weariness and the bustle. There was little time for musing, no time for lingering regrets. If thought and feeling played their Eolian measures on Fleda's harpstrings, they were listened to only by snatches, and she rarely sat down and cried to them.

A very kind note had been received from Mrs. Carleton.

April gave place to May. One afternoon Fleda had taken an hour or two to go and look at some of the old places on the farm, that she loved and that were not too far to reach. A last look she guessed it might be, for it was weeks since she had had a spare afternoon, and another she might not he able to find. It was a doubtful pleasure she sought too, but she must have it.

She visited the long meadow and the height that stretched along it, and even went so far as the extremity of the valley, at the foot of the twenty-acre lot, and then stood still to gather up the ends of memory. There she had gone chestnutting with Mr. Ringgan— thither she had guided Mr. Carleton and her cousin Rossitur that day when they were going after wood-cock—there she had directed and overseen Earl Douglass's huge crop of corn. How many pieces of her life were connected with it. She stood for a little while looking at the old chestnut trees, looking and thinking, and turned away soberly with the recollection, "The world passeth away,—but the word of our God shall stand forever." And though there was one thought that was a continual well of happiness in the depth of Fleda's heart, her mind passed it now, and echoed with great joy the countersign of Abraham's privilege,—"Thou art my portion, O Lord!"—And in that assurance every past and every hoped-for good was sweet with added sweetness. She walked home without thinking much of the long meadow.

It was a chill spring afternoon and Fleda was in her old trim, the black cloak, the white shawl over it, and the hood of grey silk. And in that trim she walked into the sitting-room.

A lady was there, in a travelling dress, a stranger. Fleda's eye took in her outline and feature one moment with a kind of bewilderment, the next with perfect intelligence. If the lady had been in any doubt, Fleda's cheeks alone would have announced her identity. But she came forward without hesitation after the first moment, pulling off her hood, and stood before her visiter, blushing in a way that perhaps Mrs. Carleton looked at as a novelty in her world. Fleda did not know how she looked at it, but she had nevertheless an instinctive feeling, even at the moment, that the lady wondered how her son should have fancied particularly anything that went about under such a hood.

Whatever Mrs. Carleton thought, her son's fancies she knew were unmanageable; and she had far too much good breeding to let her thoughts be known; unless to one of those curious spirit thermometers that can tell a variation of temperature through every sort of medium. There might have been the slightest want of forwardness to do it, but she embraced Fleda with great cordiality.

"This is for the old time—not for the new, dear Fleda," she said. "Do you remember me?"

"Perfectly!—very well," said Fleda, giving Mrs. Carleton for a moment a glimpse of her eyes.—"I do not easily forget."

"Your look promises me an advantage from that, which I do not deserve, but which I may as well use as another. I want all I can have, Fleda."

There was a half look at the speaker that seemed to deny the truth of that, but Fleda did not otherwise answer. She begged her visiter to sit down, and throwing off the white shawl and black cloak, took tongs in hand and began to mend the fire. Mrs. Carleton sat considering a moment the figure of the fire-maker, not much regardful of the skill she was bringing to bear upon the sticks of wood.

Fleda turned from the fire to remove her visitor's bonnet and wrappings, but the former was all Mrs. Carleton would give her; she threw off shawl and tippet on the nearest chair.

It was the same Mrs. Carleton of old,—Fleda saw while this was doing,—unaltered almost entirely. The fine figure and bearing were the same; time had made no difference; even the face had paid little tribute to the years that had passed by it; and the hair held its own without a change. Bodily and mentally she was the same. Apparently she was thinking the like of Fleda.

"I remember you very well," she said with kindly accent when Fleda sat down by her. "I have never forgotten you. A dear little creature you were. I always knew that."

Fleda hoped privately the lady would see no occasion to change her mind; but for the present she was bankrupt in words.

"I was in the same room this morning at Montepoole where we used to dine, and it brought back the whole thing to me—the time when you were sick there with us. I could think of nothing else. But I don't think I was your favourite, Fleda."

Such a rush of blood again answered her as moved Mrs. Carleton in common kindness to speak of common things. She entered into a long story of her journey—of her passage from England—of the steamer that brought her—of her stay in New York;—all which Fleda heard very indifferently well. She was more distinctly conscious of the handsome travelling dress which seemed all the while to look as its wearer had done, with some want of affinity upon the little grey hood which lay on the chair in the corner. Still she listened and responded as became her, though for the most part with eyes that did not venture from home. The little hood itself could never have kept its place with less presumption, nor with less flutter of self-distrust.

Mrs. Carleton came at last to a general account of the circumstances that had determined Guy to return home so suddenly, where she was more interesting. She hoped he would not be detained, but it was impossible to tell. It was just as it might happen.

"Are you acquainted with the commission I have been charged with?" she said, when her narrations had at last lapsed into silence and Fleda's eyes had returned to the ground.

"I suppose so, ma'am," said Fleda with a little smile.

"It is a very pleasant charge," said Mrs. Carleton softly kissing her cheek. Something in the face itself must have called forth that kiss, for this time there were no requisitions of politeness.

"Do you recognize my commission, Fleda?"

Fleda did not answer. Mrs. Carleton sat a few minutes thoughtfully drawing back the curls from her forehead, Mr. Carleton's very gesture, but not by any means with his fingers; and musing perhaps on the possibility of a hood's having very little to do with what it covered.

"Do you know," she said, "I have felt as if I were nearer to Guy since I have seen you."

The quick smile and colour that answered this, both very bright, wrought in Mrs Carleton an instant recollection that her son was very apt to be right in his judgments and that probably the present case might prove him so. The hand which had played with Fleda's hair was put round her waist, very affectionately, and Mrs. Carleton drew near her.

"I am sure we shall love each other, Fleda," she said.

It was said like Fleda, not like Mrs. Carleton, and answered as simply. Fleda had gained her place. Her head was in Mrs. Carleton's neck, and welcomed there.

"At least I am sure I shall love you," said the lady kissing her, — "and I don't despair on my own account, — for somebody else's sake."

"No—" said Fleda, — but she was not fluent to-day. She sat up and repeated, "I have not forgotten old times either, Mrs. Carleton."

"I don't want to think of the old time—I want to think of the new," — she seemed to have a great fancy for stroking back those curls of hair; — "I want to tell you how happy I am, dear Fleda."

Fleda did not say whether she was happy or unhappy, and her look might have been taken for dubious. She kept her eyes on the ground, while Mrs. Carleton drew the hair off from her flushing cheeks, and considered the face laid bare to her view; and thought it was a fair face—a very presentable face—delicate and lovely—a face that she would have no reason to be ashamed of, even by her son's side. Her speech was not precisely to that effect.

"You know now why I have come upon you at such a time. I need not ask pardon?—I felt that I should be hardly discharging my commission if I did not see you till you arrived in New York. My wishes I could have made to wait, but not my trust. So I came."

"I am very glad you did!"

She could fain have persuaded the lady to disregard circumstances and stay with her, at least till the next day, but Mrs. Carleton was unpersuadable. She would return immediately to Montepoole.

"And how long shall you be here now?" she said.

"A few days—it will not be more than a week."

"Do you know how soon Mr. Rossitur intends to sail for Jamaica?"

"As soon as possible—he will make his stay in New York very short—not more than a fortnight perhaps,—as short as he can."

"And then, my dear Fleda, I am to have the charge of you—for a little while—am I not?"

Fleda hesitated and began to say, "Thank you," but it was finished with a burst of very hearty tears.

Mrs. Carleton knew immediately the tender spot she had touched. She put her arms about Fleda and caressed her as gently as her own mother might have done.

"Forgive me, dear Fleda!—I forgot that so much that is sad to you must come before what is so much pleasure to me.—Look up and tell me that you forgive me."

Fleda soon looked up, but she looked very sorrowful, and said nothing. Mrs. Carleton watched her face for a little while, really pained.

"Have you heard from Guy since he went away?" she whispered.

"No, ma'am."

"I have."

And therewith she put into Fleda's hand a letter,—not Mrs. Carleton's letter, as Fleda's first thought was. It had her own name and the seal was unbroken. But it moved Mrs. Carleton's wonder to see Fleda cry again, and longer than before. She did not understand it. She tried soothing, but she ventured no attempt at consoling, for she did not know what was the matter.

"You will let me go now, I know," she said smilingly, when Fleda was again recovered and standing before the fire with a face *not* so sorrowful, Mrs. Carleton saw. "But I must say something—I shall not hurt you again."

"Oh no, you did not hurt me at all—it was not what you said."

"You will come to me, dear Fleda? I feel that I want you very much."

"Thank you—but there is my uncle Orrin, Mrs. Carleton,—Dr. Gregory."

"Dr. Gregory? He is just on the eve of sailing for Europe—I thought you knew it."

"On the *eve?*—so soon?"

"Very soon, he told me. Dear Fleda—shall I remind you of my commission, and who gave it to me?"

Fleda hesitated still; at least she stood looking into the fire and did not answer.

"You do not own his authority yet," Mrs. Carleton went on, — "but I am sure his wishes do not weigh for nothing with you, and I can plead them."

Probably it was a source of some gratification to Mrs. Carleton to see those deep spots on Fleda's cheeks. They were a silent tribute to an invisible presence that flattered the lady's affection, — or her pride.

"What do you say, dear Fleda — to him and to me?" she said smiling and kissing her.

"I will come, Mrs. Carleton."

The lady was quite satisfied and departed on the instant, having got, she said, all she wanted; and Fleda — cried till her eyes were sore.

The days were few that remained to them in their old home; not more than a week, as Fleda had said. It was the first week in May.

The evening before they were to leave Queechy, Fleda and Mrs. Rossitur went together to pay their farewell visit to Hugh's grave. It was some distance off. They walked there arm in arm without a word by the way.

The little country grave-yard lay alone on a hill-side, a good way from any house, and out of sight even of any but a very distant one. A sober and quiet place, no tokens of busy life immediately near, the fields around it being used for pasturing sheep, except an instance or two of winter grain now nearing its maturity. A by-road not much travelled led to the grave-yard, and led off from it over the broken country, following the ups and downs of the ground to a long distance away, without a moving thing upon it in sight near or far. No sound of stirring and active humanity. Nothing to touch the perfect repose. But every lesson of the place could be heard more distinctly amid that silence of all other voices. Except indeed nature's voice; that was not silent; and neither did it jar with the other. The very light of the evening fell more tenderly upon the old grey stones and the thick grass in that place.

Fleda and Mrs. Rossitur went softly to one spot where the grass was not grown and where the bright white marble caught the eye and spoke of grief fresh too. Oh that that were grey and moss-grown like the others! The mother placed herself where the staring black letters of Hugh's name could not remind her so harshly that it no more belonged to the living; and sitting down on the ground hid her face; to struggle through the parting agony once more with added bitterness.

Fleda stood awhile sharing it, for with her too it was the last time, in all likelihood. If she had been alone, her grief might have witnessed itself bitterly and uncontrolled; but the selfish relief was foregone, for the sake of another, that it might be in her power by and by to minister to a heart yet sorer and weaker than hers. The tears that fell so quietly and so fast upon the foot of Hugh's grave were all the deeper-drawn and richer-fraught.

Awhile she stood there; and then passed round to a group a little way off, that had as dear and strong claims upon her love and memory. These were not fresh, not very; oblivion had not come there yet; only Time's softening hand. Was it softening? — for Fleda's head was bent down further here, and tears rained faster. It was hard to leave these! The cherished names that from early years had lived in her child's heart, — from this their last earthly abiding-place she was to part company. Her mother's and her father's graves were there, side by side; and never had Fleda's heart so clung to the old grey stones, never had the faded lettering seemed so dear, — of the dear names and of the words of faith and hope that were their dying or living testimony. And next to them was her grandfather's resting-place; and with that sunshiny green mound came a throng of strangely tender and sweet associations, more even than with the other two. His gentle, venerable, dignified figure rose before her, and her heart yearned towards it. In imagination Fleda pressed again to her breast the withered hand that had led her childhood so kindly; and overcome here for a little she kneeled down upon the sod and bent her head till the long grass almost touched it, in an agony of human sorrow. Could she leave them? — and for ever in this world? and be content to see no more these dear memorials till others like them should be raised for herself, far away?—But then stole in consolations not human, nor of man's devising,—the words that were written upon her mother's tombstone,—

"Them that sleep in Jesus will God bring with him."—It was like the march of angel's feet over the turf. And her mother had been a meek child of faith, and her father and grandfather, though strong men, had bowed like little children to the same rule.—Fleda's head bent lower yet, and she wept, even aloud, but it was one half in pure thankfulness and a joy that the world knows nothing of. Doubtless they and she were one; doubtless though the grass now covered their graves, the heavenly bond in which they were held would bring them together again in light, to a new and more beautiful life that should know no severing. Asleep in Jesus;—and even as he had risen so should they,—they and others that she loved,—all whom she loved best. She could leave their graves; and with an unspeakable look of thanks to Him who had brought life and immortality to light, she did; but not till she had there once again remembered her mother's prayer, and her aunt Miriam's words, and prayed that rather anything might happen to her than that prosperity and the world's favour should draw her from the simplicity and humility of a life above the world. Rather than not meet them in joy at the last,— oh let her want what she most wished for in this world.

If riches have their poisonous snares, Fleda carried away from this place a strong antidote. With a spirit strangely simple, pure, and calm she went back to her aunt.

Poor Mrs. Rossitur was not quieted, but at Fleda's touch and voice, gentle and loving as the spirit of love and gentleness could make them, she tried to rouse herself; lifted up her weary head and clasped her arms about her niece. The manner of it went to Fleda's heart, for there was in it both a looking to her for support and a clinging to her as another dear thing she was about to lose. Fleda could not speak for the heart-ache.

"It is harder to leave this place than all the rest," Mrs. Rossitur murmured, after some little time had passed on.

"He is not here," said Fleda's soothing voice. It set her aunt to crying again.

"No—I know it—" she said.

"We shall see him again. Think of that."

"You will," said Mrs. Rossitur very sadly.

"And so will you, dear aunt Lucy,—*dear* aunt Lucy—you promised him?"

"Yes—" sobbed Mrs. Rossitur,—"I promised him—but I am such a poor creature—"

"So poor that Jesus cannot save you?—or will not?—No, dear aunt Lucy—you do not think that;—only trust him—you do trust him now, do you not?"

A fresh gush of tears came with the answer, but it was in the affirmative; and after a few minutes Mrs. Rossitur grew more quiet.

"I wish something were done to this," she said, looking at the fresh earth beside her;—"if we could have planted something—"

"I have thought of it a thousand times," said Fleda sighing;—I would have done it long ago if I could have got here;—but it doesn't matter, aunt Lucy,—I wish I could have done it."

"You?" said Mrs. Rossitur;—"my poor child! you have been wearing yourself out working for me,—I never was worth anything!"—she said, hiding her face again.

"When you have been the dearest and best mother to me? Now that is not right, aunt Lucy—look up and kiss me."

The pleading sweet tone of voice was not to be resisted. Mrs. Rossitur looked up and kissed her earnestly enough but with unabated self reproach.

"I don't deserve to kiss you, for I have let you try yourself beyond your strength.—How you look!—Oh how you look!—"

"Never mind how I look," said Fleda bringing her face so close that her aunt could not see it. "You helped me all you could, aunt Lucy—don't talk so—and I shall look well enough by and by. I am not so very tired."

"You always were so!" exclaimed Mrs. Rossitur clapping her in her arms again;—"and now I am going to lose you too—My dear Fleda!—that gives me more pleasure than anything else in the world!—"

But it was a pleasure well cried over.

"We shall all meet again, I hope,—I will hope,—" said Mrs. Rossitur meekly when Fleda had risen from her arms;

"Dear aunty!—but before that—in England—you will come to see me—Uncle Rolf will bring you."

Even then Fleda could not say even that without the blood mounting to her face. Mrs. Rossitur shook her head and sighed; but smiled a little too, as if that delightful chink of possibility let some light in.

"I shouldn't like to see Mr. Carleton now," she said, "for I could not look him in the face; and I am afraid he wouldn't want to look in mine, he would be so angry with me."

The sun was sinking low on that fair May afternoon and they had two miles to walk to get home. Slowly and lingeringly they moved away.

The talk with her aunt had shaken Fleda's calmness and she could have cried now with all her heart; but she constrained herself. They stopped a moment at the fence to look the last before turning their backs upon the place. They lingered, and still Mrs. Rossitur did not move, and Fleda could not take away her eyes.

It was that prettiest time of nature which while it shows indeed the shade side of everything, makes it the occasion of a fair contrast The grave-stones cast long shadows over the ground, foretokens of night where another night was resting already; the longest stretched away from the head of Hugh's grave. But the rays of the setting sun softly touching the grass and the face of the white tombstone seemed to say, "Thy brother shall rise again." Light upon the grave! The promise kissing the record of death!—It was impossible to look in calmness. Fleda bowed her head upon the paling and cried with a straitened heart, for grief and gratitude together.

Mrs. Rossitur had not moved when Fleda looked up again. The sun was yet lower; the sunbeams, more slant, touched not only that bright white stone—they passed on beyond, and carried the promise to those other grey ones, a little further off; that she had left—yes, for the last time; and Fleda's thoughts went forward swiftly to the time of the promise.—"*Then* shall be brought to pass the saying which is written, Death is swallowed up in victory. O death, where is thy sting? O grave, where is thy victory? The sting of death is sin, and the strength of sin is the law. But thanks be to God, which giveth us the victory through our Lord Jesus Christ."—And then as she looked, the sunbeams might have been a choir of angels in light singing, ever so softly, "Glory to God in the highest, and on earth peace, good will towards men."

With a full heart Fleda clasped her aunt's arm, and they went gently down the lane without saying one word to each other, till they had left the graveyard far behind them and were in the high road again.

Fleda internally thanked Mr. Carleton for what he had said to her on a former occasion, for the thought of his words had given her courage, or strength, to go beyond her usual reserve in speaking to her aunt; and she thought her words had done good.

CHAPTER LIII.

Use your pleasure: If your love do not persuade you to
come, let not my letter.

Merchant of Venice.

On the way home Mrs. Rossitur and Fleda went a trifle out of their
road to say good-bye to Mrs. Douglass's family. Fleda had seen her
aunt Miriam in the morning, and bid her a conditional farewell; for,
as after Mrs. Rossitur's sailing she would be with Mrs. Carleton, she
judged it little likely that she should see Queechy again.

They had time for but a minute at Mrs. Douglass's. Mrs. Rossitur had
shaken hands and was leaving the house when Mrs. Douglass pulled
Fleda back.

"Be you going to the West Indies too, Fleda?"

"No, Mrs. Douglass."

"Then why don't you stay here?"

"I want to be with my aunt while I can," said Fleda.

"And then do you calculate to stop in New York?"

"For awhile," said Fleda colouring.

"O go 'long!" said Mrs. Douglass, "I know all about it. Now do you
s'pose you're agoing to be any happier among all those great folks
than you would be if you staid among little folks?" she added tartly;
while Catherine looked with a kind of incredulous admiration at the
future lady of Carleton.

"I don't suppose that greatness has anything to do with happiness,
Mrs. Douglass," said Fleda gently.

So gently,—and so calmly sweet the face was that said it that Mrs. Douglass's mood was overcome.

"Well you ain't agoing to forget Queechy?" she said, shaking Fleda's hand with a hearty grasp.

"Never—never!"

"I'll tell you what I think," said Mrs. Douglass, the tears in her eyes answering those in Fleda's.—"It'll be a happy house that gets you into it, wherever 'tis! I only wish it wa'n't out o' Queechy."

Fleda thought on the whole as she walked home that she did not wish any such thing. Queechy seemed dismantled, and she thought she would rather go to a new place now that she had taken such a leave of every thing here.

Two things remained however to be taken leave of; the house and Barby. Happily Fleda had little time for the former. It was a busy evening, and the morning would be more busy; she contrived that all the family should go to rest before her, meaning then to have one quiet look at the old rooms by herself; a leave-taking that no other eyes should interfere with. She sat down before the kitchen fire-place, but she had hardly realized that she was alone when one of the many doors opened and Barby's tall figure walked in.

"Here you be," she half whispered. "I knowed there wouldn't be a minute's peace to-morrow; so I thought I'd bid you good-bye to-night."

Fleda gave her a smile and a hand, but did not speak. Barby drew up a chair beside her, and they sat silent for some time, while quiet tears from the eyes of each said a great many things.

"Well, I hope you'll be as happy as you deserve to be,"—were Barby's first words, in a voice very altered from its accustomed firm and spirited accent.

"Make some better wish for me than that, dear Barby."

"I wouldn't want any better for myself," said Barby determinately.

"I would for you," said Fleda.

She thought of Mr. Carleton's words again, and went on in spite of herself.

"It is a mistake, Barby. The best of us do not deserve anything good; and if we have the sight of a friend's face, or the very sweet air we breathe, it is because Christ has bought it for us. Don't let us forget that, and forget him."

"I do, always," said Barby crying,—"forget everything. Fleda, I wish you'd pray for me when you are far away, for I ain't as good as you be."

"Dear Barby," said Fleda, touching her shoulder affectionately, "I haven't waited to be far away to do that."

Barby sobbed for a few minutes with the strength of a strong nature that rarely gave way in that manner; and then dashed her tears right and left, not at all as if she were ashamed of them, but with a resolution not to be overcome.

"There won't be nothing good left in Queechy, when you're gone, you and Mis' Plumfield—without I go and look at the place where Hugh lies—"

"Dear Barby," said Fleda with softening eyes, "won't you be something good yourself?"

Barby put up her hand to shield her face. Fleda was silent for she saw that strong feeling was at work.

"I wish I could," Barby broke forth at last, "if it was only for your sake."

"Dear Barby," said Fleda, "you can do this for me—you can go to church and hear what Mr. Olmney says. I should go away happier if I thought you would, and if I thought you would follow what he says; for dear Barby there is a time coming when you will wish you were a Christian more than you do now; and not for my sake."

"I believe there is, Fleda."

"Then will you?—won't you give me so much pleasure?"

"I'd do a'most anything to do you a pleasure."

"Then do it, Barby."

"Well, I'll go," said Barby. "But now just think of that, Fleda, how you might have stayed in Queechy all your days and done what you liked with everybody. I'm glad you ain't, though; I guess you'll be better off."

Fleda was silent upon that.

"I'd like amazingly to see how you'll be fixed," said Barby after a trifle of ruminating. "If 'twa'n't for my old mother I'd be 'most a mind to pull up sticks and go after you."

"I wish you could, Barby; only I am afraid you would not like it so well there as here."

"Maybe I wouldn't. I s'pect them English folks has ways of their own, from what I've heerd tell; they set up dreadful, don't they?"

"Not all of them," said Fleda.

"No, I don't believe but what I could get along with Mr. Carleton well enough—I never see any one that knowed how to behave himself better."

Fleda gave her a smiling acknowledgment of this compliment.

"He's plenty of money, ha'n't he?"

"I believe so."

"You'll be sot up like a princess, and never have anything to do no more."

"O no," said Fleda laughing, —"I expect to have a great deal to do; if I don't find it, I shall make it."

"I guess it'll be pleasant work," said Barby. "Well, I don't care! you've done work enough since you've lived here that wa'n't pleasant, to play for the rest of your days; and I'm glad on't. I guess he don't hurt himself. You wouldn't stand it much longer to do as you have been doing lately."

"That couldn't be helped," said Fleda; "but that I may stand it to-morrow I am afraid we must go to bed, Barby."

Barby bade her good-night and left her. But Fleda's musing mood was gone. She had no longer the desire to call back the reminiscences of the old walls. All that page of her life, she felt, was turned over; and after a few minutes' quiet survey of the familiar things, without the power of moralizing over them as she could have done half an hour before, she left them—for the next day had no eyes but for business.

It was a trying week or two before Mr. Rossitur and his family were fairly on shipboard. Fleda as usual, and more than usual,—with the eagerness of affection that felt its opportunities numbered and would gladly have concentrated the services of years into days,— wrought, watched, and toiled, at what expense to her own flesh and blood Mrs. Rossitur never knew, and the others were too busy to guess. But Mrs. Carleton saw the signs of it, and was heartily rejoiced when they were fairly gone and Fleda was committed to her hands.

For days, almost for weeks, after her aunt was gone Fleda could do little but rest and sleep; so great was the weariness of mind and body, and the exhaustion of the animal spirits, which had been kept upon a strain to hide her feelings and support those of others. To the very last moment affection's sweet work had been done; the eye, the voice, the smile, to say nothing of the hands, had been tasked and kept in play to put away recollections, to cheer hopes, to soften the present, to lighten the future; and hardest of all, to do the whole by her own living example. As soon as the last look and wave of the hand were exchanged and there was no longer anybody to lean upon her for strength and support, Fleda shewed how weak she was, and sank into a state of prostration as gentle and deep almost as an infant's.

As sweet and lovely as a child too, Mrs. Carleton declared her to be; sweet and lovely as *she* was when a child; and there was no going beyond that. As neither this lady nor Fleda had changed essentially since the days of their former acquaintanceship, it followed that there was still as little in common between them, except indeed now the strong ground of affection. Whatever concerned her son concerned Mrs. Carleton in almost equal degree; anything that he valued she valued; and to have a thorough appreciation of him was a sure title to her esteem. The consequence of all this was that Fleda was now the most precious thing in the world to her after himself; especially since her eyes, sharpened as well as opened by affection, could find in her nothing that she thought unworthy of him. In her personally, country and blood Mrs. Carleton might have wished changed; but her desire that her son should marry, the strongest wish she had known for years, had grown so despairing that her only feeling now on the subject was joy; she was not in the least inclined to quarrel with his choice. Fleda had from her the tenderest care, as well as the utmost delicacy that affection and good-breeding could teach. And Fleda needed both, for she was slow in going back to her old health and strength; and stripped on a sudden of all her old friends, on this turning-point of her life, her spirits were in that quiet mood that would have felt any jarring most keenly.

The weeks of her first languor and weariness were over, and she was beginning again to feel and look like herself. The weather was hot and the city disagreeable now, for it was the end of June; but they had pleasant rooms upon the Battery, and Fleda's windows looked out upon the waving tops of green trees and the bright waters of the bay. She used to lie gazing out at the coming and going vessels with a curious fantastic interest in them; they seemed oddly to belong to that piece of her life, and to be weaving the threads of her future fate as they flitted about in all directions before her. In a very quiet, placid mood, not as if she wished to touch one of the threads, she lay watching the bright sails that seemed to carry the shuttle of life to and fro; letting Mrs. Carleton arrange and dispose of everything and of her as she pleased.

She was on her couch as usual, looking out one fair morning, when Mrs. Carleton came in to kiss her and ask how she did. Fleda said better.

"Better! you always say 'better'," said Mrs. Carleton; "but I don't see that you get better very fast. And sober;—this cheek is too sober," she added, passing her hand fondly over it;—"I don't like to see it so."

"That is just the way I have been feeling, ma'am—unable to rouse myself. I should be ashamed of it, if I could help it."

"Mrs. Evelyn has been here begging that we would join her in a party to the Springs—Saratoga—how would you like that?"

"I should like anything that you would like, ma'am," said Fleda, with a thought how she would like to read Montepoole for Saratoga.

"The city is very hot and dusty just now."

"Very, and I am sorry to keep you in it, Mrs. Carleton."

"Keep me, love?" said Mrs. Carleton bending down her face to her again;—" it's a pleasure to be kept anywhere by you."

Fleda shut her eyes, for she could hardly bear a little word now.

"I don't like to keep *you* here—it is not myself I am thinking of. I fancy a change would do you good."

"You are very kind, ma'am."

"Very interested kindness," said Mrs. Carleton. "I want to see you looking a little better before Guy comes—I am afraid he will look grave at both of us." But as she paused and stroked Fleda's cheek it came into her mind to doubt the truth of the last assertion, and she ended off with, "I wish he would come!—"

So Fleda wished truly; for now, cut off as she was from her old associations, she longed for the presence of the one friend that was to take place of them all.

"I hope we shall hear soon that there is some prospect of his getting free," Mrs. Carleton went on. "He has been gone now,—how many weeks?—I am looking for a letter to-day. And there it is!—"

The maid at this moment entered with the steamer despatches. Mrs. Carleton pounced upon the one she knew and broke it open.

"Here it is!—and there is yours, Fleda."

With kind politeness she went off to read her own and left Fleda to study hers at her leisure. An hour after she came in again. Fleda's face was turned from her.

"Well what does he say?" she asked in a lively tone.

"I suppose the same he has said to you, ma'am," said Fleda.

"I don't suppose it indeed," said Mrs. Carleton laughing, "He has given me sundry charges, which if he has given you it is morally certain we shall never come to an understanding."

"I have received no charges." said Fleda.

"I am directed to be very careful to find out your exact wish in the matter and to let you follow no other. So what is it, my sweet Fleda?"

"I promised—" said Fleda colouring and turning her letter over. But there she stopped.

"Whom and what?" said Mrs. Carleton after she had waited a reasonable time.

"Mr. Carleton."

"What did you promise, my dear Fleda?"

"That—I would do as he said."

"But he wishes you to do as you please."

Fleda brought her eyes quick out of Mrs. Carleton's view, and was silent.

"What do you say, dear Fleda?" said the lady, taking her hand and bending over her.

"I am sure we shall be expected," said Fleda. "I will go."

"You are a darling girl!" said Mrs. Carleton kissing her again and again. "I will love you forever for that. And I am sure it will be the best thing for you—the sea will do you good—and ne vous en déplaise, our own home is pleasanter just now than this dusty town. I will write by this steamer and tell Guy we will be there by the next. He will have everything in readiness, I know, at all events; and in half an hour after you get there, my dear Fleda, you will be established in all your rights—as well as if it had been done six months before. Guy will know how to thank you. But after all, Fleda, you might do him this grace—considering how long he has been waiting upon you."

Something in Fleda's eyes induced Mrs. Carleton to say, laughing,

"What's the matter?"

"He never waited for me," said Fleda simply.

"Didn't he?—But my dear Fleda I—" said Mrs. Carleton in amused extremity,—"how long is it since you knew what he came out here for?"

"I don't know now, ma'am," said Fleda. But she became angelically rosy the next minute.

"He never told you?"

"No."—

"And you never asked him?"

"Why no, ma'am!"

"He will be well suited in a wife," said Mrs. Carleton laughing. "But he can have no objection to your knowing now, I suppose. He never told me but at the latest. You must know, Fleda, that it has been my wish for a great many years that Guy would marry—and I almost despaired, he was so difficult to please—his taste in everything is so fastidious; but I am glad of it now," she added, kissing Fleda's cheek. "Last spring—not this last, but a year ago—one evening at home I was talking to him on this subject; but he met everything I said lightly—you know his way—and I saw my words took no hold. I asked him at last in a kind of desperation if he supposed there was a woman in the world that could please him; and he laughed, and said if there was he was afraid she was not in that hemisphere. And a day or two after he told me he was going to America."

"Did he say for what?"

"No,—but I guessed as soon as I found he was prolonging his stay, and I was sure when he wrote me to come out to him. But I never knew till I landed, Fleda my dear, any more than that. The first question I asked him was who he was going to introduce to me."

The interval was short to the next steamer, but also the preparations were few. A day or two after the foregoing conversation, Constance Evelyn coming into Fleda's room found her busy with some light packing.

"My dear little creature!" she exclaimed ecstatically,—"are you going with us?"

"No," said Fleda.

"Where are you going then?"

"To England."

"England!—Has—I mean, is there any addition to my list of acquaintances in the city?"

"Not that I know of," said Fleda, going on with her work.

"And you are going to England!—Greenhouses will be a desolation to me!—"

"I hope not," said Fleda smiling;—"you will recover yourself, and your sense of sweetness, in time."

"It will have nothing to act upon!—And you are going to England!— I think it is very mean of you not to ask me to go too and be your bridesmaid."

"I don't expect to have such a thing," said Fleda.

"Not?—Horrid! I wouldn't be married so, Fleda. You don't know the world, little Queechy; the art *de vous faire valoir* I am afraid is unknown to you."

"So it may remain with my good will," said Fleda.

"Why?" said Constance.

"I have never felt the want of it," said Fleda simply.

"When are you going?" said Constance after a minute's pause.

"By the Europa."

"But this is a very sudden move!"

"Yes—very sudden."

"I should think you would want a little time to make preparations."

"That is all happily taken off my hands," said Fleda. "Mrs. Carleton has written to her sister in England to take care of it for me."

"I didn't know that Mrs. Carleton had a sister.—What's her name?"

"Lady Peterborough."

Constance was silent again.

"What are you going to do about mourning, Fleda? wear white, I suppose. As nobody there knows anything about you, you won't care."

"I do not care in the least," said Fleda calmly; "my feeling would quite as soon choose white as black. Mourning so often goes alone, that I should think grief might be excused for shunning its company."

"And as you have not put it on yet," said Constance, "you won't feel the change. And then in reality after all he was only a cousin."

Fleda's quiet mood, sober and tender as it was, could go to a certain length of endurance, but this asked too much. Dropping the things from her hands, she turned from the trunk beside which she was kneeling and hiding her face on a chair wept such tears as cousins never shed for each other. Constance was startled and distressed; and Fleda's quick sympathy knew that she must be, before she could see it.

"You needn't mind it at all, dear Constance," she said as soon as she could speak,—"it's no matter—I am in such a mood sometimes that I cannot bear anything. Don't think of it," she said kissing her.

Constance however could not for the remainder of her visit get back her wonted light mood, which indeed had been singularly wanting to her during the whole interview.

Mrs. Carleton counted the days to the steamer, and her spirits rose with each one. Fleda's spirits were quiet to the last degree, and passive, too passive, Mrs. Carleton thought. She did not know the course of the years that had gone, and could not understand how strangely Fleda seemed to herself now to stand alone, broken off from her old friends and her former life, on a little piece of time that was like an isthmus joining two continents. Fleda felt it all exceedingly; felt that she was changing from one sphere of life to another; never forgot the graves she had left at Queechy, and as little the thoughts and prayers that had sprung up beside them. She felt, with all Mrs. Carleton's kindness, that she was completely alone, with no one on her side the ocean to look to; and glad to be relieved from taking active part in anything she made her little Bible her companion for the greater part of the time.

"Are you going to carry that sober face all the way to Carleton?" said Mrs. Carleton one day pleasantly.

"I don't know, ma'am."

"What do you suppose Guy will think of it?"

But the thought of what he would think of it, and what he would say to it, and how fast he would brighten it, made Fleda burst into tears. Mrs. Carleton resolved to talk to her no more, but to get her home as fast as possible.

"I have one consolation," said Charlton Rossitur as he shook hands with her on board the steamer;—"I have received permission, from head-quarters, to come and see you in England; and to that I shall look forward constantly from this time."

CHAPTER LIV.

The full sum of me
Is sum of something; which to term in gross,
Is an unlesson'd girl, unschool'd, unpractis'd;
Happy in this, she is not yet so old
But she may learn; and happier than this,
She is not bred so dull but she can learn;
Happiest of all, is that her gentle spirit
Commits itself to yours to be directed,
As from her lord, her governor, her king.

Merchant of Venice.

They had a very speedy passage to the other side, and partly in consequence of that Mr. Carleton was *not* found waiting for them in Liverpool. Mrs. Carleton would not tarry there but hastened down at once to the country, thinking to be at home before the news of their arrival.

It was early morning of one fair day in July when they were at last drawing near the end of their journey. They would have reached it the evening before but for a storm which had constrained them to stop and wait over the night at a small town about eight miles off. For fear then of passing Guy on the road his mother sent a servant before, and making an extraordinary exertion was actually herself in the carriage by seven o'clock.

Nothing could be fairer than that early drive, if Fleda might have enjoyed it in peace. The sweet morning air was exceeding sweet, and the summer light fell upon a perfect luxuriance of green things. Out of the carriage Fleda's spirits were at home, but not within it; and it was sadly irksome to be obliged to hear and respond to Mrs. Carleton's talk, which was kept up, she knew, in the charitable intent to divert her. She was just in a state to listen to nature's talk; to the other she attended and replied with a patient longing to be left free that she might steady and quiet herself. Perhaps Mrs. Carleton's tact discovered this in the matter-of-course and uninterested manner of her rejoinders; for as they entered the park gates she became silent, and the long drive from them to the house was made without a word on either side.

For a length of way the road was through a forest of trees of noble growth, which in some places closed their arms overhead and in all sentinelled the path in stately array. The eye had no scope beyond the ranks of this magnificent body; Carleton park was celebrated for its trees; but magnificent though they were and dearly as Fleda loved every form of forest beauty, she felt oppressed. The eye forbidden to range, so was the mind, shut in to itself; and she only felt under the gloom and shadow of those great trees the shadow of the responsibilities and of the change that were coming upon her. But after a while the ranks began to be thinned and the ground to be broken; the little touches of beauty with which the sun had enlivened the woodland began to grow broader and cheerfuller; and then as the forest scattered away to the right and left, gay streams of light came through the glades and touched the surface of the rolling ground, where in the hollows, on the heights, on the sloping sides of the dingles, knots of trees of yet more luxuriant and picturesque growth, planted or left by the cultivator's hand long ago and trained by no hand but nature's, stood so as to distract a painter's eye; and just now, in the fresh gilding of the morning and with all the witchery of the long shadows upon the uneven ground certainly charmed Fleda's eye and mind both. Fancy was dancing again, albeit with one hand upon gravity's shoulder, and the dancing was a little nervous too. But she looked and caught her breath as she looked, while the road led along the very edge of a dingle, and then was lost in a kind of enchanted open woodland—it seemed so—and then passing through a thicket came out upon a broad sweep of green turf that wiled the eye by its smooth facility to the distant screen of oaks and beeches and firs on its far border. It was all new. Fleda's memory had retained only an indistinct vision of beauty, like the face of an angel in a cloud as painters have drawn it; now came out the beautiful features one after another, as if she had never seen them.

So far nature had seemed to stand alone. But now another hand appeared, not interfering with nature but adding to her. The road came upon a belt of the shrubbery where the old tenants of the soil were mingled with lighter and gayer companionship and in some instances gave it place; though in general the mingling was very graceful. There was never any crowding of effects; it seemed all nature still, only as if several climes had joined together to grace one. Then that was past; and over smooth undulating ground, bearing a lighter growth of foreign wood with here and there a stately elm or ash that disdained their rivalry, the carriage came under the brown walls and turrets of the house. Fleda's mood had changed again; and as the grave outlines rose above her, half remembered and all the more for that imposing, she trembled at the thought of what she had come there to do and to be. She felt very nervous and strange and out of place, and longed for the familiar free and voice that would bid her be at home. Mrs. Carleton, now, was not enough of a stand-by. With all that, Fleda descended from the carriage with her usual quiet demureness; no one that did not know her well would have seen in her any other token of emotion than a somewhat undue and wavering colour.

They were welcomed, at least one of them was, with every appearance of sincerity by the most respectable-looking personage who opened to them and whom Fleda remembered instantly. The array of servants in the hall would almost have startled her if she had not recollected the same thing on her first coming to Carleton. She stepped in with a curious sense of that first time, when she had come there a little child.

"Where is your master?' was Mrs. Carleton's immediate demand.

"Mr. Carleton set off this morning for Liverpool."

Mrs. Carleton gave a quick glance at Fleda, who kept her eyes at home.

"We did not meet him—we have not passed him—how long ago?" were her next rapid words.

"My master left Carleton as early as five o'clock—he gave orders to drive as fast as possible."

"Then he had gone through Hollonby an hour before we left it," said Mrs. Carleton looking again to her companion;—"but he will hear of us at Carstairs—we stopped there yesterday afternoon—he will be back again in a few hours I am sure. Then we have been expected?"

"Yes ma'am—my master gave orders that you should be expected."

"Is all well, Popham?"

"All is well, madam!"

"Is Lady Peterborough here?"

"His lordship and Lady Peterborough arrived the day before yesterday," was the succint reply.

Drawing Fleda's arm within hers and giving kind recognition to the rest who stood around, Mrs. Carleton led her to the stairs and mounted them, repeating in a whisper, "He will be here presently again." They went to Mrs. Carleton's dressing room, Fleda wondering in an interval fever whether "orders had been given" to expect her also; from the old butler's benign look at her as he said "All is well!" she could not help thinking it. If she maintained her outward quiet it was the merest external crust of seeming; there was nothing like quiet beneath it; and Mrs. Carleton's kiss and fond words of welcome were hardly composing.

Mrs. Carleton made her sit down, and with very gentle hands was busy arranging her hair, when the housekeeper came in; to pay her more particular respects and to offer her services. Fleda hardly ventured a glance to see whether *she* looked benign. She was a dignified elderly person, as stately and near as handsome as Mrs. Carleton herself.

"My dear Fleda," said the latter when she had finished the hair, — "I am going to see my sister — will you let Mrs. Fothergill help you in anything you want, and take you then to the library — you will find no one, and I will come to you there. Mrs. Fothergill, I recommend you to the particular care of this lady."

The recommendation was not needed, Fleda thought, or was very effectual; the housekeeper served her with most assiduous care, and in absolute silence. Fleda hurried the finishing of her toilet.

"Are the people quiet in the country?" she forced herself to say.

"Perfectly quiet, ma'am. It needed only that my master should be at home to make them so."

"How is that?"

"He has their love and their ear, ma'am, and so it is that he can just do his pleasure with them."

"How is it in the neighbouring country?"

"They're quiet, ma'am, I believe, — mostly — there's been some little disturbance in one place and another, and more fear of it, as well as I can make out, but it's well got over, as it appears. The noblemen and gentlemen in the country around were very glad, all of them I am told, of Mr. Carleton's return. Is there nothing more I can do for you, ma'am?"

The last question was put with an indefinable touch of kindliness which had not softened the respect of her first words. Fleda begged her to show the way to the library, which Mrs. Fothergill immediately did, remarking as she ushered her in that "those were Mr. Carleton's favourite rooms."

Fleda did not need to be told that; she put the remark and the benignity together, and drew a nervous inference. But Mrs.

Fothergill was gone and she was alone. Nobody was there, as Mrs. Carleton had said.

Fleda stood still in the middle of the floor, looking around her, in a bewildered effort to realize the past and the present; with all the mind in the world to cry, but there was too great a pressure of excitement and too much strangeness of feeling at work. Nothing before her in the dimly familiar place served at all to lessen this feeling, and recovering from her maze she went to one of the glazed doors, which stood open, and turned her back upon the room with its oppressive recollections. Her eye lighted upon nothing that was not quiet now. A secluded piece of smooth green, partially bordered with evergreens and set with light shrubbery of rare kinds, exquisitely kept; over against her a sweetbriar that seemed to have run wild, indicating, Fleda was sure, the entrance of the path to the rose garden, that her memory alone would hardly have helped her to find. All this in the bright early summer morning, and the sweet aromatic smell of firs and flowers coming with every breath. There were draughts of refreshment in the air. It composed her, and drinking it in delightedly Fleda stood with folded arms in the doorway, half forgetting herself and her position, and going in fancy from the firs and the roses over a very wide field of meditation indeed. So lost, that she started fearfully on suddenly becoming aware that a figure had come just beside her.

It was an elderly and most gentlemanly-looking man, as a glance made her know. Fleda was reassured and ashamed in a breath. The gentleman did not notice her confusion, however, otherwise than by a very pleasant and well-bred smile, and immediately entered into some light remarks on the morning, the place, and the improvements Mr. Carleton had made in the latter. Though he said the place was one of those which could bear very well to want improvement; but Carleton was always finding something to do which excited his admiration.

"Landscape gardening is one of the pleasantest of amusements," said Fleda.

"I have just knowledge enough in the matter to admire;—to originate any ideas is beyond me; I have to depend for them upon my gardener,—and my wife—and so I lose a pleasure, I suppose; but every man has his own particular hobby. Carleton, however, has more than his share—he has half a dozen, I think."

"Half a dozen hobbies!" said Fleda.

"Perhaps I should not call them hobbies, for he manages to ride them all skilfully; and a hobby-horse, I believe, always runs away with the man?"

Fleda could hardly return his smile. She thought people were possessed with an unhappy choice of subjects in talking to her that morning. But fancying that she had very ill kept up her part in the conversation and must have looked like a simpleton, she forced herself to break the silence which followed the last remark, and asked the same question she had asked Mrs. Fothergill,—if the country was quiet?

"Outwardly quiet," he said;—"O yes—there is no more difficulty—that is, none which cannot easily be handled. There was some danger a few months ago, but it is blown over; all was quiet on Carleton's estates so soon as he was at home, and that of course had great influence on the neighbourhood. No, there is nothing to be apprehended. He has the hearts of his people completely, and one who has their hearts can do what he pleases with their heads, you know. Well he deserves it—he has done a great deal for them."

Fleda was afraid to ask in what way,—but perhaps he read the question in her eyes.

"That's one of his hobbies—ameliorating the condition of the poorer classes on his estates. He has given himself to it for some years back; he has accomplished a great deal for them—a vast deal indeed! He has changed the face of things, mentally and morally, in several places, with his adult schools, and agricultural systems, and I know not what; but the most powerful means I think after all has been the weight of his personal influence, by which he can introduce and carry through any measure; neither ignorance nor prejudice nor obstinacy seem to make head against him. It requires a peculiar combination of qualities, I think,—very peculiar and rare,—to deal successfully with the mind of the masses."

"I should think so indeed," said Fleda.

"He has it—I don't comprehend it—and I have not studied his machinery enough to understand that; but I have seen the effects. Never should have thought he was the kind of man either—but there it is!—I don't comprehend him. There is only one fault to be found with him though."

"What is that?" said Fleda smiling.

"He has built a fine dissenting chapel down here towards Hollonby," he said gravely, looking her in the face,—"and what is yet worse, his uncle tells me, he goes there half the time himself!"

Fleda could not help laughing, nor colouring, at his manner.

"I thought it was always considered a meritorious action to build a church," she said.

"Indubitably.—But you see, this was a chapel."

The laugh and the colour both grew more unequivocal—Fleda could not help it.

"I beg your pardon, sir—I have not learned such nice distinctions— Perhaps a chapel was wanted just in that place."

"That is presumable. But *he* might be wanted somewhere else. However," said the gentleman with a good-humoured smile,—"his uncle forgives him; and if his mother cannot influence him,—I am afraid nobody else will. There is no help for it. And I should be very sorry to stand ill with him. I have given you the dark side of his character."

"What is the other side in the contrast?" said Fleda, wondering at herself for her daring.

"It is not for me to say," he answered with a slight shrug of the shoulders and an amused glance at her;—"I suppose it depends upon people's vision,—but if you will permit me, I will instance a bright spot that was shewn to me the other day, that I confess, when I look at it, dazzles my eyes a little."

Fleda only bowed; she dared not speak again.

"There was a poor fellow—the son of one of Mr. Carleton's old tenants down here at Enchapel,—who was under sentence of death, lying in prison at Carstairs. The father, I am told, is an excellent man and a good tenant; the son had been a miserable scapegrace, and now for some crime—I forget what—had at last been brought to justice. The evidence against him was perfect and the offence was not trifling—there was not the most remote chance of a pardon, but it seemed the poor wretch had been building up his dependence upon that hope and was resting on it; and consequently was altogether indisposed and unfit to give his attention to the subjects that his situation rendered proper for him.

"The gentleman who gave me this story was requested by a brother clergyman to go with him to visit the prisoner. They found him quite stupid—unmovable by all that could be urged, or rather perhaps the style of the address, as it was described to me, was fitted to confound and bewilder the man rather than enlighten him. In the midst of all this Mr. Carleton came in—he was just then on the wing for America, and he had heard of the poor creature's condition in a visit to his father. He came,—my informant said,—like a being of a different planet. He took the man's hand,—he was chained foot and wrist,—'My poor friend,' he said, 'I have been thinking of you here, shut out from the light of the sun, and I thought you might like to see the face of a friend';—with that singular charm of manner which he knows how to adapt to everybody and every occasion. The man was melted at once—at his feet, as it were;—he could do anything with him. Carleton began then, quietly, to set before him the links in the chain of evidence which had condemned him—one by one—in such a way as to prove to him, by degrees but irresistibly, that he had no hope in this world. The man was perfectly subdued—sat listening and looking into those powerful eyes that perhaps you know,—taking in all his words and completely in his hand. And then Carleton went on to bring before him the considerations that he thought should affect him in such a case, in a way that this gentleman said was indescribably effective and winning; till that hardened creature was broken down,—sobbing like a child,—actually sobbing!—"

Fleda did her best, but she was obliged to hide her face in her hands, let what would be thought of her.

"It was the finest exhibition of eloquence, this gentleman said, he had ever listened to.—For me it was an exhibition of another kind. I would have believed such an account of few men, but of all the men I know I would least have believed it of Guy Carleton a few years ago; even now I can hardly believe it. But it is a thing that would do honour to any man."—

Fleda felt that the tears were making their way between her fingers, but she could not help it; and she presently knew that her companion had gone and she was left alone again. Who was this gentleman? and how much did he know about her? More than that she was a stranger, Fleda was sure; and dreading his return, or that somebody else might come and find her with tokens of tears upon her face, she stepped out upon the greensward and made for the flaunting sweet-briar that seemed to beckon her to visit its relations.

The entrance of a green path was there, or a grassy glade, more or less wide, leading through a beautiful growth of firs and larches. No roses, nor any other ornamental shrubs; only the soft, well-kept footway through the woodland. Fleda went gently on and on, admiring, where the trees sometimes swept back, leaving an opening, and at other places stretched their graceful branches over her head. The perfect condition of everything to the eye, the rich coloured vegetation,—of varying colour above and below,—the absolute retirement, and the strong pleasant smell of the evergreens, had a kind of charmed effect upon senses and mind too. It was a fairyland sort of place. The presence of its master seemed everywhere; it was like him; and Fleda pressed on to see yet livelier marks of his character and fancy beyond. By degrees the wood began to thin on one side; then at once the glade opened into a bright little lawn rich with roses in full bloom. Fleda was stopped short at the sudden vision of loveliness. There was the least possible appearance of design; no dry beds were to be seen; the luxuriant clumps of Provence and white roses, with the varieties of the latter, seemed to have chosen their own places; only to have chosen them very happily. One hardly imagined that they had submitted to dictation, if it were not that Queen Flora never was known to make so effective a disposition of her forces without help. The screen of trees was very thin on the border of this opening, so thin that the light from beyond came through. On a slight rocky elevation which formed the further side of it sat an exquisite little Moorish temple, about which and the face of the rock below some Noisette and Multiflora climbers were vying with each other; and just at the entrance of the further path a white dog-rose had thrown itself over the way, covering the lower branches of the trees with its blossoms.

Fleda stood spell bound a good while, with a breath oppressed with pleasure. But what she had seen excited her to see more, and a dim recollection of the sea-view from somewhere in the walk drew her on. Roses met her now frequently. Now and then a climber, all alone, seemed to have sought protection in a tree by the path-side, and to have displayed itself thence in the very wantonness of security, hanging out its flowery wreaths, fearless of hand or knife. Clusters of Noisettes, or of French or Damask roses, where the ground was open enough, stood without a rival and needing no foil, other than the beautiful surrounding of dark evergreen foliage. But the distance was not long before she came out upon a wider opening and found what she was seeking—the sight of the sea. The glade, here, was upon the brow of high ground, and the wood disappearing entirely

442

for a space left the eye free to go over the lower tree-tops and the country beyond to the distant shore and sea-line. Roses were here too; the air was full of the sweetness of Damask and Bourbon varieties; and a few beautiful Banksias, happily placed, contrasted without interfering with them. It was very still;—it was very perfect;—the distant country was fresh-coloured with the yet early light which streamed between the trees and laid lines of enchantment upon the green turf; and the air came up from the sea-board and bore the breath of the roses to Fleda every now and then with a gentle puff of sweetness. Such light—she had seen none such light since she was a child. Was it the burst of mental sunshine that had made it so bright?—or was she going to be really a happy child again? No—no,—not that; and yet something very like it. So like it that she almost startled at herself. She went no further. She could not have borne, just then, to see any more; and feeling her heart too full she stood even there, with hands crossed upon her bosom, looking away from the roses to the distant sea-line.

That said something very different. That was very sobering; if she had needed sobering, which she did not. But it helped her to arrange the scattered thoughts which had been pressing confusedly upon her brain. "Look away from the roses" indeed she could not, for the same range of vision took in the sea and them,—and the same range of thought. These might stand for an emblem of the present; that, of the future,—grave, far-off, impenetrable;—and passing as it were the roses of time Fleda fixed upon that image of eternity; and weighing the one against the other, felt, never in her life more keenly, how wild it would be to forget in smelling the roses her preparations for that distant voyage that must be made from the shores where they grow. With one eye upon this brightest bits of earth before her, the other mentally was upon Hugh's grave. The roses could not be sweeter to any one; but in view of the launching away into that distant sea-line, in view of the issues on the other shore, in view of the welcome that might be had there,—the roses might fade and wither, but her happiness could not go with their breath. They were something to be loved, to be used, to be thankful for,—but not to live upon; something too that whispered of an increased burden of responsibility, and never more deeply than at that moment did Fleda remember her mother's prayer; never more simply recognized that happiness could not be made of these things. She might be as happy at Queechy as here. It depended on the sunlight of undying hopes, which indeed would give wonderful colour to the flowers that might be in her way;—on the possession of resources the spring of which would never dry;—on the peace which secures the continual feast of a merry heart. Fleda could take her new honours and advantages very meekly, and very soberly, with all her appreciation of them. The same work of life was to be done here as at Queechy. To fulfil the trust committed to her, larger here—to keep her hope for the future—undeceived by the sunshine of earth to plant her roses where they would bloom everlastingly.

The weight of these things bowed Fleda to the ground and made her bury her face in her hands. But there was one item of happiness from which her thoughts never even in imagination dissevered themselves, and round it they gathered now in their weakness. A strong mind and heart to uphold hers,—a strong hand for here to rest in,—that was a blessing; and Fleda would have cried heartily but that her feelings were too high wrought. They made her deaf to the light sound of footsteps coming over the grass,—till two hands gently touched hers and lifted her up, and then Fleda was at home. But surprised and startled she could hardly lift up her face. Mr. Carleton's greeting was as grave and gentle as if she had been a stray child.

"Do not fancy I am going to thank you for the grace you have shewn me," said he lightly. "I know you would never have done it if circumstances had not been hard pleaders in my cause. I will thank you presently when you have answered one or two questions for me."

"Questions?" said Fleda looking up. But she blushed the next instant at her own simplicity.

He was leading her back on the path she had come. No further however than to the first opening, where the climbing dog-rose hung over the way. There he turned aside crossing the little plot of greensward, and they ascended some steps cut in the rock to the pavilion Fleda had looked at from a distance.

It stood high enough to command the same sea-view. On that side it was entirely open, and of very light construction on the others. Several people were there; Fleda could hardly tell how many; and when Lord Peterborough was presented to her she did not find out that he was her morning's acquaintance. Her eye only took in besides that there were one or two ladies, and a clergyman in the dress of the Church of England; she could not distinguish. Yet she stood beside Mr. Carleton with all her usual quiet dignity, though her eye did not leave the ground and her words were in no higher key than was necessary, and though she could hardly bear the unchanged easy tone of his. The birds were in a perfect ecstasy all about them; the soft breeze came through the trees, gently waving the branches and stirring the spray wreaths of the roses, the very fluttering of summer's drapery; some roses looked in at the lattice, and those which could not be there sent in their congratulations on the breath of the wind, while the words were spoken that bound them together.

Mr. Carleton then dismissing his guests to the house, went with Fleda again the other way. He had felt the extreme trembling of the hand which he took, and would not go in till it was quieted. He led her back to the very rose-bush where he had found her, and in his own way, presently brought her spirit home from its trembling and made it rest; and then suffered her to stand a few minutes quite silent, looking out again over the fair rich spread of country that lay between them and the sea.

"Now tell me, Elfie," said he softly, drawing back with the same old caressing and tranquillizing touch the hair that hung over her brow, —"what you were thinking about when I found you here? —in the very luxury of seclusion—behind a rose-bush."

Fleda looked a quick look, smiled, and hesitated, and then said it was rather a confusion of thoughts.

"It will be a confusion no longer when you have disentangled them for me."

"I don't know—" said Fleda. And she was silent, but so was he, quietly waiting for her to go on.

"Perhaps you will wonder at me, Mr. Carleton," she said, hesitating and colouring.

"Perhaps," he said smiling;—"but if I do I will not keep you in ignorance, Elfie."

"I was almost bewildered, in the first place,—with beauty—and then—"

"Do you like the rose garden?"

"Like it!—I cannot speak of it!"

"I don't want you to speak of it," said he smiling at her. "What followed upon liking it, Elfie?"

"I was thinking," said Fleda, looking resolutely away from him,—"in the midst of all this,—that it is not these things which make people happy."

"There is no question of that," he replied. "I have realized it thoroughly for a few months past."

"No, but seriously, I mean," said Fleda pleadingly.

"And seriously you are quite right, dear Elfie. What then?"

"I was thinking," said Fieda, speaking with some difficulty, "of Hugh's grave,—and of the comparative value of things; and afraid, I believe,—especially—here—"

"Of making a wrong estimate?"

"Yes—and of not doing and being just what I ought."

Mr. Carleton was silent for a minute, considering the brow from which his fingers drew off the light screen.

"Will you trust me to watch over and tell you?"

Fleda did not trust her voice to tell him, but her eyes did it.

"As to the estimate—the remedy is to 'keep ourselves in the love of God;' and then these things are the gifts of our Father's hand and will never be put in competition with him. And they are never so sweet as when taken so."

"Oh I know that!"

"This is a danger I share with you. We will watch over each other."

Fleda was silent with filling eyes.

"We do not seek our happiness in these things," he said tenderly. "I never found it in them. For years, whatever others may have judged, I have felt myself a poor man; because I had not in the world a friend in whom I could have entire sympathy. And if I am rich now, it is not in any treasure that I look to enjoy in this world alone."

"Oh do not, Mr. Carleton!" exclaimed Fleda, bowing her head in distress, and giving his hand an earnest entreaty.

"What shall I not do?" said he half laughing and half gently, bringing her face near enough for his lips to try another kind of eloquence. "You shall not do this, Elfie, for any so light occasion.— Was this the whole burden of those grave thoughts?"

"Not quite—entirely—" she said stammering. "But grave thoughts are not always unhappy."

"Not always. I want to know what gave yours a tinge of that colour this morning."

"It was hardly that.—You know what Foster says about 'power to its very last particle being duty'—I believe it frightened me a little."

"If you feel that as strongly as I do, Elfie, it will act as a strong corrective to the danger of false estimates."

"I do feel it," said Fleda. "One of my fears was that I should not feel it enough."

"One of my cares will be that you do not act upon it too fiercely," said he smiling. "The power being limited so is the duty. But you shall have power enough, Elfie, and work enough. I have precisely what I have needed—my good sprite back again."

"With a slight difference."

"What difference?"

"She is to act under direction now."

"Not at all—only under safe control," he said laughing.

"I am very glad of the difference, Mr. Carleton," said Fleda, with a grave and grateful remembrance of it.

"If you think the sprite's old office is gone, you are mistaken," said he. "What were your other fears?—one was that you should not feel enough your responsibility, and the other that you might forget it."

"I don't know that there were any other particular fears," said Fleda;—"I had been thinking of all these things—"

"And what else?"

Her colour and her silence begged him not to ask. He said no more, and let her stand still again looking off through the roses, while her mind more quietly and lightly went over the same train of thoughts that had moved it before; gradually calmed; came back from being a stranger to being at home, at least in one presence; and ended, her action even before her look told him where, as her other hand unconsciously was joined to the one already on his arm. A mute expression of feeling the full import of which he read, even before her eye coming back from its musings was raised to him, perhaps unconsciously too, with all the mind in it; its timidity was not more apparent than its simplicity of clinging affection and dependence. Mr. Carleton's answer was in three words, but in the tone and manner that accompanied them there was a response to every part of her appeal; so perfect that Fleda was confused at her own frankness.

They began to move towards the house, but Fleda was in a maze again and could hardly realize anything. "His wife"!—was she that?—had so marvellous a change really been wrought in her?—the little asparagus cutter of Queechy transformed into the mistress of all this domain, and of the stately mansion of which they caught glimpses now and then, as they drew near it by another approach into which Mr. Carleton had diverged. And his wife!—that was the hardest to realize of all.

She was as far from realizing it when she got into the house. They entered now at once into the breakfast-room where the same party were gathered whom she had met once before that morning. Mr. Carleton the elder, and Lord Peterborough and Lady Peterborough, she had met without seeing. But Fleda could look at them now; and if her colour came and went as frankly as when she was a child, she could speak to them and meet their advances with the same free and sweet self-possession as then; the rare dignity of a little wood-flower, that is moved by a breath, but recovers as easily and instantly its quiet standing. There were one or two who looked a little curiously at first to see whether this new member of the family were worthy of her place and would fill it to satisfy them. Not Mr. Carleton; he never sought to ascertain the value of anything that belonged to him by a popular vote; and his own judgment always stood carelessly alone.

But Mrs. Carleton was less sure of her own ground or of others. For five minutes she noted Fleda's motions and words, her blushes and smiles, as she stood talking to one and another;—for five minutes, and then with a little smile at her sister Mrs. Carleton moved off to the breakfast-table, well pleased that Lady Peterborough was too engaged to answer her. Fleda had won them all. Mr. Carleton's intervening shield of grace and kindness was only needed here against the too much attention or attraction that might distress her. He was again, now they were in presence of others, exactly what he had been to her when she was a child, the same cool and efficient friend and protector. Nobody in the room shewed less thought of her *except* in action; a great many little things done for her pleasure or comfort, so quietly that nobody knew it but one person, and she hardly noticed it at the time. All could not have the same tact.

There was an uninterrupted easy flow of talk at the table, which Fleda heard just enough to join in where it was necessary; the rest of the time she sat in a kind of abstraction, dipping enormous strawberries one by one into white sugar, with a curious want of recognition between them and the ends of her fingers; it never occurred to her that they had picked baskets full.

"I have done something for which you will hardly thank me, Mr. Carleton," said Lord Peterborough. "I have driven this lady to tears within the first hour of her being in the house."

"If she will forgive you, I will, my lord," Mr. Carleton answered carelessly.

"I will confess myself though," continued his lordship looking at the face that was so intent over the strawberries. "I was under the impression when I first saw a figure in the window that it was Lady Peterborough. I own as soon as I found it was a stranger I had my suspicions—which did not lack confirmation in the course of the interview—I trust I am forgiven the means I used."

"It seems you had your curiosity too, my lord," said Mr. Carleton the uncle.

"Which ought in all justice to have lacked gratification," said Lady Peterborough. "I hope Fleda will not be too ready to forgive you."

"I expect forgiveness nevertheless," said he looking at Fleda. "Must I wait for it?"

"I am much obliged to you, sir."

And then she gave him a very frank smile and blush as she added, "I beg pardon—you know my tongue is American."

"I don't like that," said his lordship gravely.

"Out of the abundance of the heart the mouth speaketh," said the elder Carleton. "The heart being English, we may hope the tongue will become so too."

"I will not assure you of that, sir," Fleda said laughingly, though her cheeks showed the conversation was not carried on without effort. Oddly enough nobody saw it with any dissatisfaction.

"Of what, madam?" said Lord Peterborough.

"That I will not always keep a rag of the stars and stripes flying somewhere."

But that little speech had almost been too much for her equanimity.

"Like Queen Elizabeth who retained the crucifix when she gave up the profession of popery."

"Very unlike indeed!" said Fleda, endeavouring to understand what Mr. Carleton was saying to her about wood strawberries and hautbois.

"Will you allow that, Carleton?"

"What, my lord?"

"A rival banner to float alongside of St. George's?"

'"The flags are friendly, my lord."

"Hum—just now,—they may seem so.—Has your little standard-bearer anything of a rebellious disposition?"

"Not against any lawful authority, I hope," said Fleda.

"Then there is hope for you, Mr. Carleton, that you will be able to prevent the introduction of mischievous doctrines."

"For shame, Lord Peterborough!" said his wife,—"what atrocious suppositions you are making. I am blushing, I am sure, for your want of discernment."

"Why—yes—" said his lordship, looking at another face whose blushes were more unequivocal,—"it may seem so—there is no appearance of anything untoward, but she is a woman after all. I will try her. Mrs. Carleton, don't you think with my Lady Peterborough that in the present nineteenth century women ought to stand more on that independent footing from which lordly monopoly has excluded them?"

The first name Fleda thought belonged to another person, and her downcast eyelids prevented her seeing to whom it was addressed. It was no matter, for any answer was anticipated.

"The boast of independence is not engrossed by the boldest footing, my lord."

"She has never considered the subject," said Lady Peterborough.

"It is no matter," said his lordship. "I must respectfully beg an answer to my question."

The silence made Fleda look up.

"Don't you think that the rights of the weak ought to be on a perfect equality with those of the strong?"

"The rights of the weak *as such* — yes, my lord."

The gentlemen smiled; the ladies looked rather puzzled.

"I have no more to say, Mr. Carleton," said his lordship, "but that we must make an Englishwoman of her!"

"I am afraid she will never be a perfect cure," said Mr. Carleton smiling.

"I conceive it might require peculiar qualities in the physician, — but I do not despair. I was telling her of some of your doings this morning, and happy to see that they met with her entire disapproval."

Mr. Carleton did not even glance towards Fleda and made no answer, but carelessly gave the conversation another turn; for which she thanked him unspeakably.

There was no other interruption of any consequence to the well-bred flow of talk and kindliness of manner on the part of all the company, that put Fleda as much as possible at her ease. Still she did not realize anything, and yet she did realize it so strongly that her woman's heart could not rest till it bad eased itself in tears. The superbly appointed table at which she sat, — her own, though Mrs. Carleton this morning presided, — the like of which she had not seen since she was at Carleton before; the beautiful room with its arrangements, bringing back a troop of recollections of that old time; all the magnificence about her, instead of elevating sobered her spirits to the last degree. It pressed home upon her that feeling of responsibility, of the change that come over her; and though beneath it all very happy, Fleda hardly knew it, she longed so to be alone and to cry. One person's eyes, however little seemingly observant of her, read sufficiently well the unusual shaded air of her brow and her smile. But a sudden errand of business called him abroad immediately after breakfast.

The ladies seized the opportunity to carry Fleda up and introduce her to her dressing-room and take account of Lady Peterborough's commission, and ladies and ladies' maids soon formed a busy committee of dress and decorations. It did not enliven Fleda, it wearied her, though she forgave them the annoyance in gratitude for the pleasure they took in looking at her. Even the delight her eye had from the first minute she saw it, in the beautiful room, and her quick sense of the carefulness with which it had been arranged for her, added to the feeling with which she was oppressed; she was very passive in the hands of her friends.

In the midst of all this the housekeeper was called in and formally presented, and received by Fleda with a mixture of frankness and bashfulness that caused Mrs. Fothergill afterwards to pronounce her "a lady of a very sweet dignity indeed."

"She is just such a lady as you might know my master would have fancied," said Mr. Spenser.

"And what kind of a lady is that?" said Mrs. Fothergill.

But Mr. Spenser was too wise to enter into any particulars and merely informed Mrs. Fothergill that she would know in a few days.

"The first words Mrs. Carleton said when Mr. Carleton got home," said the old butler, — "she put both her hands on his arms and cried out, 'Guy, I am delighted with her!'"

"And what did *he* say?" said Mrs. Fothergill.

"He!" echoed Mr. Spenser in a tone of indignant intelligence, — "what should *he* say? — He didn't say anything; only asked where she was, I believe."

In the midst of silks, muslins and jewels Mr. Carleton found Fleda still on his return; looking pale and even sad, though nobody but himself through her gentle and grateful bearing would have discerned it. He took her out of the hands of the committee and carried her down to the little library, adjoining the great one, but never thrown open,—*his* room, as it was called, where more particularly art and taste had accumulated their wealth of attractions.

"I remember this very well," said Fleda. "This beautiful room!"

"It is as free to you as to me, Elfie; and I never gave the freedom of it to any one else."

"I will not abuse it," said Fleda.

"I hope not, my dear Elfie," said he smiling,—"for the room will want something to me now when you are not in it; and a gift is abused that is not made free use of."

A large and deep bay window in the room looked upon the same green lawn and fir wood with the windows of the library. Like those this casement stood open, and Mr. Carleton leading Fleda there remained quietly beside her for a moment, watching her face which his last words had a little moved from its outward composure. Then, gently and gravely as if she had been a child, putting his arm round her shoulders and drawing her to him he whispered,

"My dear Elfie,—you need not fear being misunderstood—"

Fleda started and looked up to see what he meant. But his face said it so plainly, in its perfect intelligence and sympathy with her, that her barrier of self-command and reserve was all broken down; and hiding her head in her hands upon his breast she let the pent-up burden upon her heart come forth in a flood of unrestrained tears. She could not help herself. And when she would fain have checked them after the first burst and bidden them, according to her habit to wait another time, it was out of her power; for the same kindness and tenderness that had set them a flowing, perhaps witting of her intent, effectually hindered its execution. He did not say a single word, but now and then a soft touch of his hand or of his lips upon her brow, in its expressive tenderness would unnerve all her resolution and oblige her to have no reserve that time at least in letting her secret thoughts and feelings be known, as far as tears could tell them. She wept, at first in spite of herself and afterwards in the very luxury of indulged feeling; till she was as quiet as a child, and the weight of oppression was all gone. Mr. Carleton did not move, nor speak, till she did.

"I never knew before how good you were, Mr. Carleton," said Fleda raising her head at length, as soon as she dared, but still held fast by that kind arm.

"What new light have you got on the subject?" said he, smiling.

"Why," said Fleda, trying as hard as ever did sunshine to scatter the remnants of a cloud, —it was a bright cloud too by this time, "I have always heard that men cannot endure the sight of a woman's tears."

"You shall give me a reward then. Elfie."

"What reward?" said Fleda.

"Promise me that you will shed them nowhere else."

"Nowhere else?—"

"But here—in my arms."

"I don't feel like crying any more now," said Fleda evasively;—at least." —for drops were falling rather fast again, —" not sorrowfully."

"Promise me, Elfie," said Mr. Carleton after a pause.

But Fleda hesitated still and looked dubious.

"Come!—" he said smiling,—"you know you promised a little while ago that you would have a particular regard to my wishes."

Fleda's cheeks answered that appeal with sufficient brightness, but she looked down and said demurely,

"I am sure one of your wishes is that I should not say anything rashly."

"Well?—"

"One cannot answer for such wilful things as tears."

"And for such wilful things as men?" said he smiling.

But Fleda was silent.

"Then I will alter the form of my demand. Promise me that no shadow of anything shall come over your spirit that you do not let me either share or remove."

There was no trifling in the tone,—full of gentleness as it was; there could be no evading its requisition. But the promise demanded was a grave one. Fleda was half afraid to make it. She looked up, in the very way he had seen her do when a child, to find a warrant for her words before she uttered them. But the full, clear, steadfast eye into which she looked for two seconds, authorized as well as required the promise; and hiding her face again on his breast Fleda gave it, amid a gush of tears every one of which was illumined with heart-sunshine.

THE END.

Lightning Source UK Ltd.
Milton Keynes UK
UKHW030634200922
409139UK00001B/36